The Parkwood Murders

Chris Chibnall is a BAFTA, Royal Television Society, Broadcasting Press Guild and Peabody Award-winning screenwriter, executive producer and playwright whose work has been seen, translated and remade all around the world. He is the recipient of the prestigious FIPA Prix D'Honneur, and honorary doctorates from Edge Hill University. His television work includes *Broadchurch* – remade as *Gracepoint* in the US and *Malaterra* in France – *The Great Train Robbery, Doctor Who, Torchwood* and *Life on Mars*, as well as the Netflix adaptation of Agatha Christie's *The Seven Dials Mystery*.

His debut novel, *Death at the White Hart*, was a *Sunday Times* bestseller, a Waterstones Thriller of the Month, and was shortlisted for the British Book Awards Crime and Thriller Book of the Year. It is being published in thirteen languages, and is in production for a major television adaptation.

The Parkwood Murders

CHRIS CHIBNALL

MICHAEL JOSEPH

PENGUIN MICHAEL JOSEPH

UK | USA | Canada | Ireland | Australia
India | New Zealand | South Africa

Penguin Books is part of the Penguin Random House group of companies whose addresses can be found at global.penguinrandomhouse.com

Penguin Random House UK,
One Embassy Gardens, 8 Viaduct Gardens, London SW11 7BW

penguin.co.uk

Penguin Random House UK

First published 2026
001

Set in 13.5/16pt Garamond MT Std
Typeset by Six Red Marbles UK, Thetford, Norfolk
Printed and bound in Great Britain by Clays Ltd, Elcograf S.p.A.

The authorized representative in the EEA is Penguin Random House Ireland, Morrison Chambers, 32 Nassau Street, Dublin D02 YH68

A CIP catalogue record for this book is available from the British Library

HARDBACK ISBN: 978–0–241–67575–5
TRADE PAPERBACK ISBN: 978–0–241–67576–2

Penguin Random House is committed to a sustainable future for our business, our readers and our planet. This book is made from Forest Stewardship Council® certified paper.

MIX
Paper
FSC
www.fsc.org
FSC® C018179

To Mum, Dad & Julie
With love and fond holiday memories

Thus let me live, unseen, unknown;
Thus unlamented let me die;
Steal from the world, and not a stone
Tell where I lie.

Alexander Pope, *The Quiet Life*

Dear Guest,

It's Time to Start Getting Excited!

Your upcoming stay at Parkwood Dorset is fast approaching!

We're delighted to enclose an information pack which will help you make the most of your time with us.

Included in the pack are:

- *An orientation map to help you find your way around the site. With an array of incredible facilities set over 250 acres to explore, we know it can seem a bit daunting to begin with!*
- *Information about your lodge. Set in idyllic woodland but with the comforts of home, we've included a guide to all the facilities you can expect.*
- *Booking information for cycle hire**. It's the best way to get around while you're with us.*
- *Calendar of all bookable sports activities**. What new activities will you and your family discover during your break?*
- *A brochure for our award-winning Jurassic Spa**. Let us pamper you while you're with us!*
- *Information on childcare facilities* and babysitting services**. Because Parkwood is a holiday for parents, too!*

Your lodge number is 77.

Your arrival date is 22 June 2026.

Your departure date is 26 June 2026.

Arrival (yay!) is from 3 p.m.

Check-out time on day of departure (we know, we don't want to think about you leaving us either!) is by 10 a.m.

Please bring a valid form of ID for all adults who will be staying with us, and present it to your welcome host at the security gatehouse on check-in.

If you have any questions prior to arrival, please take a look at our website: www.parkwood-dorset.co.uk where you'll find the answers to many of the most commonly asked questions. You can also book all extra items there.

We can't wait to welcome you to Parkwood Dorset!

Best wishes,
The Parkwood Team

* *Incurs additional cost*

1

Nobody knew what the stone meant, or how it had come to stand there. But it had been there longer than Parkwood, longer than all the surrounding villages, and if you believed some of the wilder ancient myths, which Mandy sometimes perused as she sat alone in the security lodge at night, maybe even longer than humans themselves.

Standing in front of it now, as the pines creaked and swayed in the night wind, Mandy could not deny its hypnotic majesty. She knew that some within Parkwood felt there was too much fuss made about what was just a big rock. But she had seen first-hand the chaos the stone was still capable of provoking.

She broke off her gaze and continued patrolling the deserted pathways. It was just past 4 a.m. The sun would begin to peer through the darkness within the hour. As the day wore on, these paths would become littered with helmeted kids on bikes being watched over by anxious parents. 'Can we all just *stay together*?' would be the phrase exploding out of stressed mums and dads as they attempted to corral multiple strong-willed siblings.

For now, the pathway was black and silent. Some four hundred guests were asleep in their lodges, scattered across Parkwood's grounds. Mandy had the place to herself.

At moments like this, she thought, the job of a night-time security guard wasn't so bad. True, she'd had to shut a banging door in the high-ropes section which Lee had *again* neglected to secure, but otherwise it was almost serene.

As she pulled out her security key card to access the Splashdome pool complex, Mandy instantly saw something was wrong.

Her foot had struck something. She bent down to see what it was.

A thick piece of wood. Lodged in the door, preventing it from fully closing.

Mandy kicked it away from the doorway, holding the door, unease igniting.

How long had the door been ajar like this?

Mandy entered, flicking on and raising her torch, scanning around instinctively.

The centre – consisting of changing rooms, a large swimming pool, seven slides of varying sizes and a free-flowing Chill Waters route which linked the inside of the pool to the open-air section – was in low-lit darkness, as was usual at this time of night.

Mandy carefully checked the female changing rooms first, then the men's, then the joint family section, her torchlight reaching into every corner. She listened for anything unusual, but the only sound she could hear was the machinery powering the complex.

But then . . . as she got closer to the doors separating the changing rooms from the inner sanctum of the pool itself, she heard the other sound.

As she exited the changing rooms, that sound became louder and clearer.

A lone trumpet fanfare was echoing through the deserted pool area.

The 'Last Post'.

On a loop.

Regular Parkwood guests would know what this fanfare signalled; the wave machine about to start.

Mandy had once read a thread on Mumsnet (when searching for advice which could help an older single mum cope with wayward toddlers) which questioned the tastefulness of using this particular piece of music to herald the activation of the waves, but management had remained unfussed when challenged, saying it was 'an iconic part of the Parkwood experience'.

It was not an iconic part of the Parkwood experience at 4 a.m.

The pool should be silent at 4 a.m.

Her heart was beating faster.

She kept her torch scanning all around. Was the person, or people, responsible still present?

She tried to talk her fear away. *Probably kids, Mand.* A bunch of them stealing in for a midnight swim. It'd happened before.

Except it was too quiet for that.

She moved forward, her stomach clenching involuntarily.

This place was creepy when empty. It needed people in it to make sense.

She realized with an extra jab of dread that she could now hear another sound.

The swoosh and crash of the wave machine, pushing out artificial waves in the main pool.

The wave machine should not be active.

Two wrong sounds. Two wrong things. Had someone left all the systems running overnight? Surely not.

She walked cautiously towards the noise, rounding the corner to see the pool in all its glory.

First thing she noticed: the wave machine in full flow, churning up water. Waves were violently hitting the sides of the pool.

And within the noise of the waves, there was another, repetitive, thudding.

Thud, then nothing. Thud, then nothing.

Almost in rhythm with the waves but not quite.

Mandy moved the torch beam slowly across the ground and up the walls. The pool area was surrounded by large palm trees which didn't get anywhere near its transparent high roof, and lots of plants attempting to give the complex the air of . . . Hawaii? The Caribbean? Mandy wasn't sure. Something other than what it was. It was pretty effective, disguising all the pipes and tubes and steel and concrete.

Was someone hiding among the plants? Was she being watched?

The fanfare reprised, nagging relentlessly at her, clashing with the rhythm of the waves.

She was standing near the edge of the pool now, the gentle slope suitable for toddlers and children, where the water lapped people's feet, imitating a shoreline.

Her torchlight fell across the water washing up on the 'shore'.

It was tinged with red.

Mandy flicked her torch up immediately – it shone back across the plants, illuminating no one, and then across the water, the span of the pool. As the torch beam moved across the more distant areas of water, she saw it.

The source of the thudding noise.

A body, face down in the water.

Fully clothed, being washed up and down by the waves. As they moved and subsided, the waves washed the body back against a side wall of the pool, causing the low thudding.

Mandy threw down her torch, discarded her jacket and ran straight into the pool.

As the pool got deeper, she began to swim, heading for the body which was being buffeted back and forth. She was fighting the water and the waves, desperately hoping she could get to it in time.

When she finally made it, it was clear she was far too late.

2

'You go, it's not that big a deal.'

Nicola Bridge looked at her husband, conflicted. They were both in the hallway, next to the front door. Nicola could feel the phone in her coat pocket silently, insistently, vibrating with message alerts flooding in.

'It's a *pretty* big deal,' she started to argue back.

'We both know you've got to go. I'll cover this and keep you up to date,' replied Mike in his calmest, most reasonable manner.

Nicola felt simultaneously grateful, impressed and patronized. And impressed at being patronized.

He's managing me. My fireman husband is deploying his professional skills on me, talking to me like my house is on fire and he's going to sort it out.

They both knew the language and tone to use when trying to get people to do what you wanted. She'd never noticed him use that training on her before. Was it that he'd never done it before or that he'd previously done it so well she hadn't realized? She had the grace to laugh at herself inwardly.

Take the win, Nicola. He's giving you a pass. Leave!

She couldn't quite let it go, though. 'Why aren't you more worried?'

'I'm very worried! But we've called everyone. He's eighteen. We know he was out with his mates, and he's probably stayed over, not been arsed to tell us. I'll deal with it. Go, woman!'

Mike smiled. Still sexy when he smiled. His Scouse accent poked through even more when he was raising his voice, even in half-jest instructions to her.

'We said we'd talk to him this morning; he agreed to be here,' said Nicola, pulling on a jacket, fully contradicting her stated intent to stay.

'And he's gone AWOL because he smells an ambush. When he comes back later, which I'm sure he will, I can either talk to him on my own, or wait till you're back. Your call.'

The phone in her pocket felt like it was bouncing now, tugging at her like a child pulling its parent towards a toy-shop. *Come onnnnn . . .*

'I've got this,' emphasized Mike.

They both understood the subtext beneath his words: *we've danced this dance before and I did not meet the moment. But look: new era, new Mike.*

The old Mike had messed up, and messed around, and the fallout from his affair had brought them all here, back to her childhood home for the proverbial fresh start. Nicola finally had a husband who understood the priorities of her job and seemed not to begrudge them. How long had she been yearning for this?

'Thank you,' she said and gave him a quick kiss goodbye.

She raised her phone to her mouth and headed out to the driveway.

'Ethan, hi, darling, it's Mum. Can you call or message to let us know you're OK? I realize your phone may be out of juice, but when you get this, let us know.' Nicola pressed send on the voice note as she saw Harry's car pull up on the road outside her house.

He's legally an adult. He just stayed out; he's doing it deliberately to worry us, because he and his dad have been arguing. That's why he hasn't told us where he is.

All this she told herself as she strode down the drive towards Harry's car. She knew what her subconscious was doing: giving herself permission to think about the case that had been called in, using the short walk to transition from personal to professional. It didn't fully lessen the small knot in her stomach.

As she opened the car door, she glanced back and thought she saw Mike looking out of the front window. When she looked again, the window was empty.

Nicola got into the car and slammed the passenger door shut. She was instantly hit by two smells: Harry's scent and fresh coffee. Both smelled fantastic.

'Morning. Coffee's there,' said Harry, nodding at the cup holder between driver and passenger seat. It had become a ritual: he now brought the coffee.

Nicola took a sip. Incredible.

'Please tell me where you get it from, *please*!' she begged after a second sip.

'Nope,' said Harry, with a twinkle in his eye. 'You're on fourteen guesses now.'

'There can't be any places left I haven't thought of,' said Nicola as she clipped in her seat belt.

She felt a flash of guilt: was she a terrible mother for being able to switch out of family life into bantering about coffee? *It's not a fault*, she told herself, *it's a skill*. They had a job to do.

DS Nicola Bridge looked to DC Harry Ward. 'Let's get moving.'

'Male body, late fifties/early sixties, found in the pool at the Parkwood resort around five a.m. this morning. He was fully clothed, pool was shut at the time. SOCO are already there and working.'

Harry briefed her while keeping his eyes on the narrow lane ahead. The Parkwood resort was a forty-minute drive northwards, upwards and away from the coast, through the Vale, from Nicola's house in Bredy.

'You ever been there?' asked Harry.

Nicola nodded. 'Not this one, but we had a few days at the one in North Yorkshire when Ethan was seven, I think.'

The seven-year-old boy she'd pushed on the swings was now staying out all night and not listening to her voice note. Now she was messaging multiple chat groups of parents and friends checking his whereabouts, as Harry drove.

'Was it any good?'

'Yeah, but it cleaned us out. We could've gone to Crete for the same money!'

She had messaged the friendly control room supervisor at county HQ to alert her if anything came up that might relate to her teen not coming home last night. She phrased it in as jocular a fashion as she could. She knew Mike would be ringing round the hospitals.

Oi, aren't you supposed to be leaving all of it to Mike?

She returned to the conversation with Harry. 'You ever been?'

'My dad was always against the place on principle. "Plastic holidays" he used to call it. "We're not going on no plastic holidays," he'd say. "Not when we got the real thing on our doorstep."'

In the distance, Parkwood loomed up out of the Vale ahead of them. Situated on an elevated area of land which afforded the site a raised profile, as if those heading there were making their way to a place of worship, an altar on which they could lay their hopes. From here, the main view was of the large sculpted expanse of pine forest.

'He had a point,' said Nicola.

The holiday village ahead of them had been pulled together from a combination of farmland and forest some forty years previously. There had been much debate over the resort being built in that location, but the developers won out, mainly on the argument of the boon it would bring to the local economy. And it was true that over the years it had employed a large number of Dorset residents from a wide catchment area. If the locals had never really become fond of it, they recognized the opportunities it provided. At full occupancy, Parkwood could house over four hundred guests – more than many villages in the locale combined. Parkwood was very much its own ecosystem.

As they drew closer, Nicola's mind was already running through the potential challenges a suspicious death there would present.

'You good at being on holiday?' asked Harry as he turned left at the roundabout built to facilitate traffic flow towards Parkwood.

Nicola feigned offence. 'I'm amazing at it.' She wondered if Mike would agree. Sometimes she had got itchy feet a few days in and her mind would drift back to work. 'What about you?'

'Yeah, happy place. So long as there's a few activities, swimming or watersports, that's what I love. Little bit of sunbed zombie, little bit of splashing about.'

Nicola thought that sounded like fun.

Up ahead on the road was a huge heavy-looking free-standing sign carved out of wood with the Parkwood logo and the company slogan THE GETAWAY YOU DESERVE. An arrow directed arriving guests to turn off the main road and down the service road towards the main entrance. Nicola noticed a separate, much smaller sign which illustrated the turnings for STAFF (next left after the main entrance) and then DELIVERIES (the final turning at the top of the road).

She was already logging details of routes, pathways and fencing as Harry drove them down the smaller approach road. It was as though a switch had been flicked, the aesthetic turning in an instant from natural West Dorset to Parkwood-organized nature. They were surrounded by tall evergreen conifers as the car worked its way along the winding narrower track. It was unnervingly identical to the Parkwood resort Nicola had stayed at previously. The trees blocked any sight of the holiday village beyond, like scenic security bars across the window of the resort. It was presumably supposed to confer a sense of nature and exclusivity, but for Nicola it simply added to her growing unease: the approach felt creepy and claustrophobic.

'On check-in days, these approach roads get gridlocked with people waiting to get in,' said Nicola.

'Always great to start a holiday with a traffic jam,' commented Harry. 'Arguments before check-in.'

'You know what they say,' said Nicola as she studied the view. 'You go on holiday to get away – but you can't get away from yourself.'

'Bleak,' grinned Harry.

Nicola was looking at the road and already wondering whether a killer had come and gone from Parkwood and what route they might have taken. Was this way in also the only way out?

They arrived at the wooden security gatehouse complex which functioned as Parkwood's reception: six cabins, all separated from the rest of the resort by electronic barriers. Each cabin had two windows, one on each side. The barriers were operated by controls from within the gatehouse.

Nicola checked around – CCTV cameras were perched on top of the cabins' roofs, and in a couple of nearby trees, pointing towards the security barriers, and the approach. Only one was pointed towards the park.

A female security guard in her fifties, looking anxious and drawn, slid open the window as they drove up and attempted a welcoming front. 'Hello, folks, I'm afraid we've got a temporary pause on admissions for new guests at the present moment, but if I could have your booking reference, surname and ID, we can contact you when –'

Harry scrambled to talk over the guard, awkward, 'Oh, no, we're not –'

Nicola talked over him more definitely, showing the guard her warrant card. 'DS Nicola Bridge. This is DC Harry Ward. I believe some of our team are already here.'

'Oh God, sorry,' said the security guard, mortified. 'I thought you were – They're down at the pool. Leave your car over there and follow the signs. Let me give you these for now so you don't get any bother.'

She dropped a couple of lanyards in through the window and Harry passed them over to Nicola. 'If you see Mandy, tell her Mabs was asking after her. She found him, I heard. What should we say to anybody if they ask? We've been told no one should leave, is that still right?'

Nicola could spot the desire for gossip in the woman's eyes. 'We'll get you updated instructions as soon as we know, but yes, stick to that for now. Thanks,' she said as the barrier raised in front of them and Harry drove towards the car park.

The barrier slammed shut behind them.

3

Never run in public; it will alarm the guests.

Lindsey Moorfield, general manager of Parkwood Dorset, slowed deliberately as she approached the small crowd that had begun to form outside the Splashdome complex, smoothed her hands over her scraped-back and ponytailed brown hair and pushed her shoulders back to make herself taller than her five-foot-seven frame. She attempted to regulate her breathing, fixed a firm professional smile into place and, deploying all the experience she had learned across twenty years of working in hospitality, did her best to project an air of authoritative calm that she was absolutely not feeling.

'Ladies and gentlemen, ladies and gents,' she called, 'if I can have your attention for one sec, please.'

The crowd pivoted its attention away from the two uniformed police officers standing guard over the entrance and turned to focus its attention on her. Dozens of eyes.

Lindsey resisted the sudden urge to gulp. *Breathe slowly, speak calmly.*

'I'm afraid the Splashdome complex will be closed this morning due to unforeseen circumstances. We'll update you about plans for reopening as soon as we have more information.'

The sound that emanated from the crowd was less than a roar but more than a groan: an instinctive expression of their immediate annoyance. Lindsey had to suppress her own flash of rage.

You want your kids to swim in a crime scene, do you? Have a little paddle in blood-infected water?

The call had come in during the middle of the night: the call every resort manager dreaded receiving. A death on-site. Except this was even worse: not only a death but seemingly a murder, she was told. A violent death that was now her responsibility.

The first responders had arrived before Lindsey, and the police had subsequently kept her and her staff out of the pool complex.

She noticed people in the crowd looking to each other for affirmation of their collective irritation; their day's plans had been disrupted before the day had even got going. Lindsey had experience of mob rage erupting and knew she could not allow it to happen here – especially after last night. There had to be decorum. There had to be calm. She would be judged, and would judge herself, on how this all played out.

A muscled bloke in a white vest at the front of the crowd was looking particularly aggrieved, as Lindsey detected the sound of three or four separate young children beginning to wail and cry in response to the situation being explained to them by their parents.

'Why?' he asked insistently, with what Lindsey guessed was a Nottingham accent. 'Why's it closed?'

'Unforeseen circumstances,' Lindsey repeated, nodding empathetically, hoping this would communicate 'I understand your frustration'.

'What sort of unforeseen circumstances?' insisted Nottingham.

'I'm not able to share that with you right now.'

'Is it chemicals? Cos we went to another one and they had chemicals leaking into the pool.'

Oh, it's far worse than chemicals, sir.

'It's not a chemical leak, no, but I'm afraid that's all the information I can give you at this time.'

'What'm I meant to do with the kids this morning? I promised them the pool.'

'The pool is unavailable,' restated Lindsey – *if I keep repeating it, maybe you'll understand* – before moving smoothly into offering upsides. 'We do have over a hundred other activities. If you pop into the booking office on the other side of the pathway, my colleagues will be able to help you find something.'

'We have to pay extra for those. The pool's included. We can't afford to pay extra.'

Lindsey could feel her smile getting tighter. 'We have over thirty activities which are available at no extra cost, including our children's woodland trail.'

'They don't like woodland. Or trails.'

Then you, sir, have come to the wrong bloody place.

'I'm sure our staff will be able to help you find something.'

'Not good enough,' huffed Nottingham and walked away.

Lindsey wound in her emotion even more tightly; she knew his type: the guest who was always wanting to have the last word even when, as here, the situation was unavoidable and reasonable alternatives were being offered. This was not an argument she could win.

She hated the resort – *her* resort – being dissed like this, however casually or thoughtlessly the insult was thrown. She took it personally; she couldn't help it. This was her world. The guests were visitors, temporary residents. She poured her heart and soul into Parkwood on a daily basis in order to deliver on the promise of the getaway they deserved. Everybody needed a holiday and Lindsey's job was to provide the best in class. An insult to the resort, or a section or an incident, felt like an insult to her. Her husband, Ian, told her to not let it affect her. 'You let everything get to you,' he had snapped at her recently. Maybe he was right. Or maybe this was why she was more successful than him. Because his standards were not exceptional.

Lindsey's standards *were* exceptional and today would be the greatest challenge she had ever faced.

She already had multiple managerial fires to put out – the ugly fallout from last night's Solstice Ceremony by the standing stone needed to be addressed. And Lindsey knew that a death on-site would stir up other things, too. Her mind was roiling, switching between thoughts of past, present and future as the crowd began to slowly disperse. She reminded herself to stay in the present; the operational challenges today would be momentous enough without looking too far ahead, or back.

She machine-gunned smiles at the guests as she chivvied them away towards the booking office. 'Thank you, my colleagues will be able to help, thank you!'

She could feel her facial muscles relax slightly as everyone moved away. This job required Lindsey to be a woman of many faces – not all of which she enjoyed.

She glanced back towards the entrance, which had been hastily roped off before her arrival this morning. She had instructed staff to find Parkwood signage informing guests of their inability to access this particular zone. She hated the sight of uniformed police officers guarding the entrance, the police presence an incongruous bump in what was supposed to be a frictionless resort experience. The outside world was not supposed to intrude once guests were inside Parkwood, and yet here it was: the most dissonant intrusion of all.

She gave the officers a tight smile and as she turned to go, she almost bumped into two figures whose approach she had not noticed. A tall lithe woman who Lindsey guessed was around her own age flashed a police warrant card and a professional smile at her.

'DS Nicola Bridge, are you the manager here?'

'Yes, Lindsey Moorfield, thank you for getting here so quickly,' said Lindsey, instantly code-switching once more, this time to a cooperative managerial professional eager to assist a police investigation. 'I think the rest of your team are inside.'

'We'll want to talk to you once we've had a chance to assess the scene. Where can we find you?'

'In my office, but if not, any member of staff can put out a call.'

'Thank you,' nodded the detective, stepping past the cordon and heading through the Splashdome entrance. The younger male detective – thirtyish, Lindsey guessed, gym-bunny body slotted into a fitted suit – gave Lindsey a neutral clipped smile and followed his partner.

Lindsey stood taut and still, momentarily finding herself unable to move.

Come on, Lindsey Moorfield, you've got this. Get to work.

Yesterday had run wildly out of control. She could not let the same happen today.

4

The first thing Nicola noticed was the heat. As she and Harry pulled on forensic suits, overshoes, gloves and masks from the doorway, the temperature in the Splashdome was already stifling.

Just as she was finishing pulling the suit on (and quietly enjoying seeing Harry struggle with his: the suits were one size fits all and not made for a bloke who worked on his muscles), her phone buzzed.

Ethan.

Almost. Two messages within seconds. The first from one of Ethan's mate's mums: Letting you know Ethan was here with us last night. He'd asked Ciaran not to tell me cos I'd tell you! Hope all well. And then, a message from Mike: He's back. Seems OK. Not chatty.

Relief flooded through her. Her prime concern had been extinguished. Her son was alive and fine. Thank God.

She would be having words with him later, though.

All geared up, she and Harry walked into the main pool area. As they entered, Nicola looked up and around at the stupendously high ceiling. Far above, glass panels let daylight in and intensified the heat. A crisscross of panelled tubing lined the far end of the building, where the vast network of slides intersected each other. Trees and plants had been added to the space to make this most artificial of constructs feel as if it were bursting with nature. Without holidaymakers the complex felt ominous and brutalist. The rumbling hum of distant machinery was the main sound disrupting the eerie silence.

To the edge of the pool was the inner cordon, marked out by red-and-white tape. A white SOCO tent had been erected, a wise move given the amount of foliage and moisture present (any of which could fall on to the body and contaminate the scene), as well as the transparency of the roof, which made it susceptible to observation.

As they walked towards the inner cordon, Harry was looking around.

'Thoughts?' she prompted.

'Open space, limited number of entrances and exits. Easy to be seen, either while you're in here, or coming in and out. Also, loads of nooks and crannies here and in the changing rooms; you couldn't be sure you weren't being watched, or somebody wasn't hiding. If I was planning to do something malicious, of all the places, not sure I'd choose here.'

They entered the inner cordon of the SOCO tent. Kneeling over the dead body, which was laid out on the floor, was Reeta Patel. Reeta was one of the people Nicola was always glad to see – an older sister or cool aunt, always straight-talking, always warm. Today, however, Reeta's manner spoke volumes about the challenge ahead of them.

'This is going to be a nightmare to forensicate. Heat, moisture and hundreds of people in here yesterday,' said Reeta. 'Duty pathologist is off sick and her assistant is some hundred and fifty miles away, so no current indication when they can get to it.'

Nicola looked at the body: a man in casual shirt and trousers, the shirt discoloured by blood stains. The report had estimated him to be in his late fifties or early sixties, but laid out like this he looked older.

'Any ID?' asked Nicola.

Reeta shook her head. 'All pockets empty. No phone, wallet, keys or anything that might identify him.' She carried on dispassionately. 'Found floating in the pool by a security guard. Two stab wounds in the back of the neck, and one in the front, so we might presume stabbed before being thrown in the pool, but TBD. Fully clothed, as you can see. He'd been in the water a little while when found, judging by the maceration and wrinkling of the skin on his hands.'

'Anything of note other than the stab wounds?' asked Harry.

'Superficially very little – no obvious bruising. But the hands showed signs of cadaveric spasms – tightly clenched. And from my limited expertise I'd say there were traces of foam at the nose and mouth – which would suggest he was struggling, possibly trying to resist submersion.'

'Being held under?' asked Harry.

Reeta shrugged. 'We're neither of us pathologists. Be great to have one, but apparently that's too much to ask right now.'

'So not natural causes or accidental death. Reasonable to assume he was killed,' said Nicola. These preliminary conversations were so simple, so direct, yet the conclusions would shape many lives in their aftermath.

'I'm afraid so,' said Reeta, softening slightly.

Fuck.

The scale of what this meant was unfolding in Nicola's brain at speed. How many hundreds of people were staying at Parkwood right now? Was one of them the killer? Her head swam with the numbers that would be involved, let alone the thought that anyone might leave at any moment, especially when the news of a murder began to filter out.

They were in a race against time and daunting numerical odds.

And they didn't even know who the victim was.

She stared at the body.

Who was this man?

And who could have wanted him dead?

5

The distant sound of a door slam penetrated down into the deep fug of Conor's sleep. He woke with a start.

He bolted up, adrenaline-fuelled, throwing back the duvet, ready to tackle whatever was coming at him. It took a second for him to realize he had gone reflexively into fight-or-flight mode.

For a moment he could not remember where he was. He was on his own and his surroundings were completely unfamiliar. The place smelled new. Curtains were drawn. He groped around for his phone. It was nowhere to be found.

'Daddeeeeeee!' A blur of blonde curls and energy flew up from the floor on to the bed and on top of him. Bella, his four-and-a-half-year-old daughter, had launched herself into the air, on the working understanding that he would be her soft landing.

'Oooof!' exclaimed Conor, as his daughter knocked the wind out of him and he slumped back down on to the pillows. 'Can you stop growing now, please! You're getting too strong!'

'I can't *stop* growing!' laughed Bella, tickled by the idea. 'I have to be an adult first. I'll stop when I'm as tall as Mummy.' She considered this. 'Maybe a teeny bit taller.' Conor could see the impossible idea of one day being taller than her mother was already giving Bella dreams of power beyond her current imagining. 'Is that allowed?' she asked Conor in all seriousness.

'Only if you're very well behaved,' said Conor.

'You weren't awake when you said you would be,' admonished Bella.

'True,' said Conor.

'And you went to sleep in the wrong room,' Bella went on.

'I didn't get last night right at all, did I? Silly Daddy,' said Conor.

'Silly Daddy!' giggled Bella.

You have no idea, thought Conor.

'I'm hungry,' Bella announced, in a tone that suggested this was the end of their exchange for now, which indeed it was as she bounced back down to the floor and straight out of the bedroom.

Conor had a respite of approximately fifteen seconds before his wife, Emma, stuck her head in.

'Thanks a lot!' she said and swooshed the curtains open, revealing the endless pine forest out of the window.

Conor shielded his eyes from the harsh summer sunlight. 'I didn't want to disturb you,' he said, looking away from the window. It was not entirely untrue.

'I woke up and thought you'd gone missing!'

'What time is it now?'

'Just after ten. Thanks for getting up and taking Bella swimming, while I had my promised lie-in.'

He'd had barely any sleep. 'Shit.'

'You dodged a bullet. Something's gone off – the pool's closed for the morning and there's police down there.'

That news sent a small zap around Conor's system. 'Really?'

Emma nodded. 'Anyway, we went on the swings and the roundabout and the thing that looks possibly like a caterpillar and just bounces around a bit. And I feel like I've been awake for two days.' Her tone changed. 'D'you think we should be complaining?'

Conor poked around what currently passed for his mind. 'About . . .'

'Yesterday evening. That ceremony and all those people.'

'Ohh . . .' The memories were trickling back. So much had happened since.

'Cos it's like it's the whole reason we come at this point – I mean, that plus Bella not being in school yet – but that was so out of order. It's not like it isn't costing us a fortune, and then that happens.' Emma paused for breath. 'Where were the staff, that's what I said. Why was it on you to deal with it? I think we should complain. We might get a refund at least.'

The Solstice Ceremony, that's right. The earlier part of yesterday evening. The reason they'd come. A peculiarly Parkwood Dorset ritual, which involved families all dressing up in wafty white outfits and proceeding to the standing stone on the edge of the Parkwood resort, where a ceremony led by a Parkwood staffer gave thanks to the sun. They'd taken Bella since she was a baby, and it had become a family tradition, harmless fun.

Except yesterday it wasn't. The masks among the group processing were more gruesome and the vibe was just off. When they arrived at the standing stone, the cause became apparent: some guests had infiltrated the procession deliberately to question its existence. There were arguments and a fight. Conor had been involved in both.

It had not been the most fraught part of his past twenty-four hours.

'By the way, did you put a wash on?' asked Emma, confused.

'Did I?' asked Conor, unable to remember for a second. Then it came to him and he tried not to let the emotions he was feeling spread to his face. 'Maybe, yeah. Probably. I mean, if you didn't, then I did.'

‘Did you shit yourself, babe?’ Emma grinned mockingly. It was one of the things he only discovered about his wife once they were a year into their marriage: her sense of humour and jibes often veered more towards the scatological than his.

‘I’d hate to let light in on magic,’ said Conor.

‘But you’re all right?’ The joshing had stopped and she looked genuinely concerned.

No. I am not all right. I am the very opposite of all right. I am fucked.

‘I’m always all right.’

That seemed to be enough for Emma. She smiled and said, ‘Gonna join for breakfast? We went to the shop instead of swimming. We have loads of unhealthy things.’

‘Great!’ said Conor and meant it. ‘Let me have a quick shower, wake myself up.’

‘Gotta wash the shit off!’ called Emma merrily as she left, and Conor winced.

He sat on the edge of the bed, rubbing his hands across his stubbled face.

He remembered what he had done last night, he knew where he had been and his soul was consumed with a tsunami of shame.

He could not tell Emma about any of it.

Not now, not ever.

6

The scale of the task ahead was overwhelming. The size of the Parkwood site, the amount of people in the immediate vicinity (let alone the fact they were all holidaying), the complexity of the crime scene, the absence of an ID . . . the list of challenges ahead was already running on a loop in Nicola Bridge's mind.

First things first.

It was a deceptively simple, almost childlike mantra, but one Nicola clung to at moments like this. There were times, especially at the beginning of major investigations, where simplicity and process were all you had.

Her problem here was: *which* first things should come first? Fast-track actions were a set of priorities laid down for every detective to cleave to in situations such as this. But even fast-track actions needed ordering and prioritizing. There were about twenty-seven first things in Nicola's assessment, and as she tried to order them in her mind, she felt like she was momentarily suffering from professional vertigo.

Stay in the room, Nicola.

The room in question was the Parkwood manager's office. Harry and Lindsey Moorfield, the manager, were looking at her, awaiting her lead. She needed to leave this room with a strategy in place and the resort manager firmly in line.

First, say the obvious bit out loud.

'We're treating this man's death as suspicious,' Nicola began.

She was sitting next to Harry on a sofa in the 'lounge' area of Lindsey Moorfield's office. Nicola noted that Lindsey had done all she could to make the office homely and welcoming while still Parkwood-branded. This informal seating area – a sofa and two comfortable chairs arranged round a low coffee table – was framed by a handful of pot plants. There were two other sections in the low-ceilinged, beige partition-walled office: a medium-sized dark-wood meeting table with six chairs crammed round it, and Lindsey's desk, flanked by filing cabinets. On top of one cabinet were pictures of (Nicola presumed) Lindsey's husband, and a big collage of staff members in uniform having great times together. On the opposite wall from Lindsey's desk (so in Lindsey's line of sight when she was sat working) was a board of letters, drawings and photos from happy customers. In the centre of the table sat a transparent Perspex award trophy from some hospitality organization whose name Nicola wasn't close enough to read. Nicola noted that Lindsey Moorfield liked to surround her self with affirmations of how good she was at her job.

'Meaning . . . he was killed. Here,' said Lindsey. Her professional tone clashed with the fear in her eyes.

'Yes,' replied Nicola. 'I'm not able to give you any further details at present.'

Lindsey nodded, remaining very still. After a moment she spoke. 'We have protocols for what happens when a guest dies on-site – inform the family, inform the police, summon a funeral director. I'll also need to inform head office,' said Lindsey.

Nicola nodded too. 'So long as you provide the names of anyone you inform, and until we make any public statement, which must come from us, not Parkwood, nothing must be shared further without my express permission. Is that clear?'

There was silence before Lindsey replied, 'Of course.'

Nicola noted how every time Lindsey spoke she had taken a beat, as if organizing her response, or checking the words she was about to say. Nicola hoped this exchange had established her authority and control in an environment where they would normally belong to Lindsey. It was vital to Nicola that Lindsey understood the subtext: *I'm in charge here now.*

'And what am I allowed to tell the guests?' asked Lindsey. It appeared she had got the message and would be cooperative.

'Only that there has been an incident, the pool is closed and will remain so for the foreseeable future.'

Nicola watched Lindsey exhale. A closed pool was clearly going to be a big deal for all concerned. 'What are your protocols for communicating emergency information to guests?' asked Nicola.

'We can put it on the TV screen of every lodge. I'd also normally distribute hard copies of a letter to the guests from me, and have housekeeping leave them in every lodge.' She paused. 'There's going to be a lot of gossip.'

'Let us deal with that,' said Nicola. 'Your job is to keep the resort running as close to normal as possible. It's key we don't set off a panic.'

Lindsey looked at Nicola with some incredulity. Nicola expected her to say *of course this is going to set off a panic!* But instead she saw Lindsey recalibrate, push her emotional response away in favour of being more practical. 'I'll increase security patrols. Will you be providing additional officers?'

Nicola shook her head. 'A heavy police presence could provoke even more alarm. If you're happy to increase your staff coverage in the first instance, then we can keep checking in on what feels right.'

There was a shard of truth in that statement, but it was also a little disingenuous. Nicola was all too conscious of the state of her own police force, which seemed to be deteriorating by the day. She knew that the absence of a duty pathologist was likely to only be the beginning of her struggles; she was certain a battle for resources and staff lay ahead. It would be better on all fronts if she could utilize Parkwood's own personnel to provide a reassuring presence.

She watched Lindsey note the action in her book. Good, thought Nicola, the power base in the room was moving in her favour. Lindsey was taking instructions.

Nicola pressed on. Her priority was to identify the dead man: she hoped Parkwood's systems would help. 'Has anyone to your knowledge come forward to report a member of their party missing?'

Lindsey shook her head. 'Nothing's been reported to me, but I'll check with department heads, including our cleaning supervisors – they often hear things first.'

Nicola asked, 'What about solo guests? Do you have a list of guests who are staying on their own?' It was possible that might explain why no one had yet sounded any alarm.

'I'll check,' Lindsey said. 'It's quite rare. We're not really a place where people come alone.' She handed across a thick pile of A4 paper. 'This is a list of all guests currently staying – names, ages, home addresses, car registrations and which lodges they're in.'

Nicola took the documents. 'Any staff who've not reported in today?'

'There's always a couple, but I'll get it confirmed.' She made another note. Lindsey's to-do list was growing at an exponentially fast rate, thought Nicola, much like her own.

'As well as guests, we'll need a full list of staff,' said Nicola, 'highlighting everyone on duty yesterday, as well as those who were on-site overnight, and a list of staff who have access to the pool complex for work. We'll also need details of any contractors who have passes for the resort. Plus information on how and where staff enter and exit the site, whether these times are monitored and logged, plus all details of any surveillance relating to that.'

Nicola noticed Lindsey starting to look like a punch-drunk boxer as she wrote everything down. *Oh, that's nothing*, Nicola thought. *Wait until you hear this.*

'We'll want to interview every guest on an appointment basis, starting as soon as possible. We'll need to requisition spaces for this. We'll come back to you with a detailed plan shortly.'

Even Harry glanced at Nicola on hearing that one. She could see that even he had not countenanced the variables already at play. Everyone staying here was not only a potential suspect but a potential witness, whether they realized it or not. They would all have to be spoken to, in order to confirm where they had been, whether they had seen anything, or knew anyone who might have. These were the building blocks of any thorough investigation.

'*Every* guest?' repeated Lindsey.

Nicola nodded. 'I'm going to need you to suspend all shuttle buses from the main site to the car parks, in order to discourage anyone from leaving. If any guests do attempt to leave, you must let us know immediately.'

'The shuttle service? I'm not sure we're allowed to do that,' said Lindsey.

'A man has been killed,' replied Nicola. 'I need you to assist in every way you can. Suspending services will help.'

The minor emotional manipulation was deliberate. Some of these requests relied on goodwill and consent rather than any legal force. Nicola knew she did not have any real power to keep people here, so if she was to successfully investigate this case, she would need to deploy every possible ounce of guile and persuasion (not to mention gentle coercion), starting immediately. It was obvious they were going to have an alarmingly brief window of opportunity to question people before guests started losing patience.

She could already see this was not going to be a normal investigation. It would demand an entirely different pace and shape.

Nicola pushed on to her next demand. 'How quickly can you convene a meeting of all staff currently on-site?'

She watched Lindsey's mouth opening and closing before the reply came. '*All* staff would mean every activity is suspended. We have children in crèches and classes and sports clubs scheduled – we can't stop all of that! Their parents might be occupied, at lunch or at the spa – and there's all the spa appointments,' Lindsey pushed back. 'If you really don't want to start a panic, I'd suggest you brief the key facility and department heads, and they can pass information down, and schedule time later today or tomorrow for their staff members to speak with your officers.'

'OK, good,' said Nicola. 'Now. Is there CCTV around the pool complex, either inside or out?'

Lindsey shook her head. 'There's only minimal CCTV inside all Parkwood resorts, as a matter of policy.'

Nicola could sense Harry's pen halt and hover above his notebook.

Shit.

'Why's that?' queried Nicola.

'The company founders were a Scottish couple, very pro-nature, libertarian, anti-surveillance. They wanted the

Parkwood experience to be as close to being in nature as possible. So we have the minimum necessary for insurance purposes. We have cameras at the security lodges, entrances and exits, and on the approach roads, and monitoring car parks. But all activities and sports are unmonitored. The founders always said there are no cameras if you go for a walk in the forest and the company's policy is to honour that connection between our guests and nature.'

An immediate setback. Company policy had just given Nicola and her team a major headache.

'OK,' said Nicola, keeping her tone neutral. Never let anyone see your concern. 'Last thing for now,' she said. 'Is there somewhere on-site we can use as an incident room? It needs to be private and secure.'

Lindsey thought for a moment. 'We have two lodges not in service. I could let you have access to one of those.'

'Perfect,' said Nicola.

It was all looking very far from perfect.

7

His ankle was killing him.

Lee Parker, Parkwood high-ropes instructor, a veteran staff member at thirty-four, moved along the high-ropes course, the morning sun on his face and arms, pain throbbing through his ankle.

This view, from this vantage point, at this time of day was what he had imagined when, at his first Parkwood interview twelve years ago, he had described the role as his destiny. That twenty-two-year-old was now more jaded, more tanned, more built and, well, more blond, thanks to all those days in the West Dorset air and a friendly hairdresser.

At this point, he normally felt like the king of all he surveyed. Today, other thoughts were preoccupying him.

Lee was always first here, out alone among the trees before guests rose and the majority of staff arrived. His routine was to check the equipment for the day – ropes, harnesses, helmets (various sizes thereof), buckets of carabiners – and then check the routes. Run every junction, check all the clips and the rungs on the trees, monitor the smoothness of the upper rope tracks, testing everything for tensile strength, movement and safety.

Strictly speaking, Lee was not supposed to do this alone, in case he got into difficulty, but he was not one for rules and he was definitely not a bloke who ever got into difficulty. He was too good for that.

On each course, Lee would use this solo time to test

himself against his own personal best, each morning: could he take a second off yesterday's time while also running the routine security testing that needed to be done? Lee was not cavalier – he knew safety was paramount and nothing would be unchecked on his watch – but after twelve years he needed more to combat the boredom: new thrills, new achievements, a sense he was still winning.

He always needed to win.

Lee had read it was best to get out into nature within an hour of waking up, and over the years he had perfected his routine so that he was out on the course, in the air, within fifty-five minutes of his alarm going off – no matter who was in bed beside him.

On arrival this morning, he realized he had not properly closed things down the night before. He had been distracted by other things. Other people. People who were still concerning him now as he took another step, leaned into his vulnerable ankle, slipped and missed his footing.

For a second he thought he was going to do the unprecedented and come off the ropes completely. He thought he was about to be left dangling, his newly injured ankle throbbing with pain. But as the shock at his own vulnerability flooded his nervous system, he managed to right himself.

His ankle was screaming.

That guy had got him good, the fucker.

Grimacing, he carried on with the checks. Got back down in a slow and poor time, cursing himself.

Once back in the base office he dug out some painkillers. The course was due to open soon, and he still hadn't had breakfast.

He also needed to urgently speak to a number of people today.

First, the new girl at bike hire, obviously, after their moment together. Literally behind the bike sheds. She had been eager, and he had seen no reason to decline, but now he was experiencing buyer's remorse. (Not that he had paid. He would never need to pay.) He had thought she'd be cool about it, and she was, beforehand. After, and since, less so. Why she thought this might be the start of something, was beyond him. Her feelings were not on him. If she'd been here any longer, maybe his reputation would've come before him. (And she definitely came before him, he grinned to himself, as he set his little coffee machine going.)

As he sipped on the too-hot coffee, he saw there were grazes on the back of his other leg too –

'Lee!'

The yell made him jump, and he spilled coffee down his bare legs – it scalded and stained him and he felt a flash of rage as he looked up at the person who'd called his name, ready to unleash a torrent of swearing

Lindsey. All he needed.

'I need you to do more numbers today. We'll shorten slots, in order to create more.'

Lee balked at the imposition. 'No, that's not gonna work.'

Lindsey was in no mood to hear any protests. 'Guests will be aware it's a tighter turnaround. We have an issue at the Splashdome. It'll be out of service today. We have a number of guests who'll need something else to do. We'll direct them here, and to archery and the football pitches in the first instance. I need you to do this for me.'

'What sort of issue?' he asked, sipping ostentatiously on the remains of his coffee in an attempt to appear casual.

'Staff meet at the conference room in my block, twelve thirty, where we'll give further details. I'd like you there.'

'Sure,' he said magnanimously.

He watched her go as he sipped. He was thinking of the Splashdome, and his ankle, and his now scalded leg, and bending her over her office desk, and what she might know about last night. And then Barney, the young and overexcitable assistant whose first season this was, came skipping in, a look of gleeful horror on his face.

'Did you hear?' asked Barney.

'Hear what?' said Lee.

'Body in the pool, man. Body in the fucking pool!'

He looked at Lee expectantly for signs of a mind having just been blown.

Lee blew on his coffee.

'Jeez,' he said. 'Is that right?'

8

The aroma of paint and cleaning product was the first thing to hit Nicola as she stepped inside Parkwood Dorset Lodge 227.

Within, the property was pristine, recently redecorated, waiting to be occupied by a fresh group of holidaymakers. It was about to have a different purpose entirely.

Harry had gone ahead of her and already shifted furniture around, bringing in the outside table to make the space more work-practical and less domestic. As she entered, Nicola paused to watch Harry for a moment. He was Blu-tacking site maps and guest lists over a photorealistic mural of a lake which took up an entire wall of the lodge. The way he had developed over the year or so since they first met never ceased to impress Nicola. Both as a detective and as a human being, Harry Ward was a great find.

He turned to notice her, smiled and then fired questions as if they were still mid-conversation.

'What do you want us to do about letting people in – day visitors, deliveries, staff coming in and out? They're holding people now at the gate. I said I'd let them know.'

Hello again to you too, thought Nicola, before responding, 'Hold deliveries for today, unless essential or time-critical. Anyone that comes in needs to be logged, names and ID. They should also suspend all day-visitor passes for the time being.'

She could not be certain any of those decisions were

correct, but she had learned long ago that the speed of a decision was sometimes just as important as it being right. A decision could always be changed. Dithering could be catastrophic.

'So basically we want the resort locked down, nobody in or out, as fast as possible.'

'Without freaking out the guests,' confirmed Nicola.

'O-K,' said Harry, his emphasis on the second syllable the verbal equivalent of a raised eyebrow, before asking the key question. 'What resources are we gonna get?'

Ah. Yes. About that.

Before following Harry to the lodge, she had returned to the car to call her DI who had sounded spectacularly uninterested – a mode he seemed to specialize in. The call had been to seek guidance and assurance, but she had received precious little of either.

'Manage the scene and don't worry about bothering me with the details. I'm sure you've got it all covered, Nic,' he said. He sounded like he was driving. If she knew where he was, then she would've sped there and rammed his car for still calling her 'Nic' despite her having told him in pretty much every encounter that she hated the shortening. 'Don't like Nic-names, eh? Got it!' laughed her boss, elbowing her in the side as they left an office about six months ago, shortly after he'd taken up the post. But nevertheless he persisted with it. Nicola had begun to wonder: was he that much of a wanker that he was doing it deliberately? She could no longer confidently rule that out.

Nicola had returned to Dorset, and the newly formed Three Counties Police, on the promise of a well-resourced team, newly built headquarters and a modern regional force focused on the future of policing. Every promise had been betrayed. This new regional force – formed from the ashes of previously malfunctioning county forces – was teetering on bankruptcy as soon it came into existence. The chief constable had resigned in disgrace only months after being appointed and the HQ building was now three and a half years behind schedule with no sign of completion. Nicola's initial frustration had since given way to cold fury. The work environment kept deteriorating, resources kept getting scarcer and the turnover of senior officers was farcical. This structural incompetence only increased the pressure on officers like her and Harry to deliver for the people they were meant to be serving.

'Mel's imminent and I'm in negotiations with the DI for more,' she told Harry.

'In negotiations?' queried Harry.

'We're not gonna get the number we need,' she admitted.

Harry nodded.

She liked that. No fuss. He had expected it. He was getting on with the job. Gold star, DC Ward.

'How many d'you expect?' he asked.

'Ten, total.'

'Ten, plus us?'

'No, ten, including me, you and Mel. Six uniform, one junior DC,' said Nicola.

Harry's equilibrium broke as he looked at her. 'Seriously?'

Nicola nodded. They both knew it was nowhere near enough to cover triaging all the guests and staff, identifying witnesses and taking statements.

She tried bravado. 'Lucky it's us, right? We're worth ten of anyone else.'

Keep telling yourself that, Nic!

Harry looked genuinely worried. 'How are we going to do it?'

The front door blew open. Standing there, buckling beneath two large crates of computer equipment, was an out-of-breath DC Mel Hardiman, his bald head and grey face beaded with sweat. A decade older than Nicola, Mel was an officer rarely seen in the wild. He surveyed his two colleagues with weary annoyance, as if he had woken up expecting the worst today and events had confirmed not only this suspicion but his entire worldview.

'I'm not happy about this,' Mel announced.

Nicola had never felt quite so happy to see him.

The trio gathered in front of Harry's map of the resort.

'That Blu-tack will mark the walls. We won't get our deposit back,' said Mel.

Harry, inured to Mel's comments, launched in. 'Quick orientation: Parkwood is just over two hundred and thirty acres in total, there are a hundred and fifty-seven lodges. Normally operates around ninety-three per cent occupancy. Body found in the Splashdome here. Lodges are grouped into named areas, like districts. Closest set of lodges to the pool are the Cerne lodges – fifty-two lodges in total. Three other groups of lodges – Dolmen, Maiden and Abbas – spread across the site, all at a distance from each other.'

He pointed out other areas on the map. 'Key sites of interest: historic standing stone dating back millennia here, restaurants here, here and here. Indoor sports centre, here, sports courts at the rear. Sports bar there, leisure bar there, retail village here, kids' facility – crèche and activities for young children. Leisure lake for boating activities and the like. High ropes there. Woodland trail goes through the forest here, which is also where most of the other outdoorsy activities take place. Oh, and –' he pointed to the edge – 'this is the spa.'

'Don't get me started on spas,' said Mel disapprovingly. 'Few oils, little speaker with woo-woo music, and an under-trained worker pressing bits of your back. All that and they charge you best part of a hundred quid. Pure profit. Absolute rip-off.'

'I don't mind a massage,' said Harry.

'Yes, well, you wouldn't.' Mel sniffed, looking his colleague up and down in a manner which suggested Harry's response only confirmed everything Mel had ever suspected about him.

'It's Tuesday –' started Harry.

'No flies on you, Westlife,' interrupted Mel unhelpfully.

Harry bowled on. 'This guest cohort arrived yesterday, Monday.' He glanced at Mel, daring him to add a sarcastic comment. 'They're all booked to be here until Friday morning. That gives us three days maximum with them before they depart and the weekend guests arrive.'

Harry had zeroed in on one of the bigger questions nagging at Nicola: how to keep everyone at Parkwood long enough. It was essential they spoke to every guest – not just for their own evidence but also to identify other witnesses who may not otherwise come forward. Suspending shuttle services and implying guests had to stay would only work for so long.

First things first.

'We have to move as fast as possible, which means working on aspects simultaneously rather than sequentially,' said Nicola. 'Mel, your priority is victim ID. If DNA and fingerprints yield nothing, this is your next port of call.' She handed him the sheaf of documents Lindsey had provided. 'Guest records for those currently staying. Reeta should have photos of the victim now, start by checking appearance against the photo IDs guests provide on check-in. If he's staying here, he'll be in that pile. We've also got current staff records on the way, although the manager doesn't think anyone is missing.'

Nicola turned to Harry. 'While he's doing that, I need you to devise a system whereby we get to speak to every guest ASAP. That way, we can start to build an immediate picture of every person's whereabouts last night and this morning. It should also offer any early flags on people without alibis.'

She looked at the map they were all standing in front of. 'I'd suggest we divide up interviewees by accommodation district: you take one, I'll take another, uniform can take the remaining two. Initial interviews can be ten minutes maximum, six per hour, better if you can. Confirm no one in their party is missing, find out where everyone was between ten p.m. last night and six a.m. this morning, if they were near the Splashdome complex, alibis and whether they witnessed anything unusual since arrival. Contact with as many people as possible as quickly as possible should help us minimize any sense of alarm on-site. Mel, you'll be responsible for getting the results of those interviews immediately on to the system here. Break them down into those who can be triaged and ruled out, potentially significant witnesses, people of interest and possible suspects. Obviously those latter categories will only become truly live when we have more intel on the victim. Those we don't rule out, we re-interview.'

'For a moment there I thought you were going to have me talking to the great unwashed,' said Mel in a tone approaching relief.

'I wouldn't put you through that indignity,' smiled Nicola. 'For now, interviews can be conducted in family or accommodation groups – be alert to dominant personalities overly influencing what's being said. We aim to have a sense of where everyone was in order that we can plot it up on a map and start cross-referencing and checking. Obviously all of this is subject to amendment as we go – it's going to be a live and fast-moving situation – but that's how we start.'

She stopped talking. Mel and Harry were both staring at her. 'What?'

'When have you had time to come up with that strategy?' asked Harry.

Nicola brushed away the compliment. 'Just thinking on my feet.'

'Plenty of room for errors going at that speed,' said Mel.

'Just like life, Mel.' Nicola knew she could rely on Mel to highlight pitfalls and bring doubt. She'd learned never to let his concerns infect her or Harry, or paralyse the investigation. His Eeyore nature was part of what made him good at his job. And to be fair, the plan was undoubtedly imperfect, the scale of the challenge dizzying.

'Now please get to work on the victim's ID.'

9

A loud yawn escaped Alice Smith's mouth as she placed her triple-shot mocha and large can of White Monster on the bench opposite her locker. She hurriedly placed a hand over her mouth – she hated people seeing inside her gob – and turned to see if anyone had noticed.

Leah, her supervisor, was standing in the doorway to the changing room. Always there when Alice didn't want her to be.

'Out clubbing, was it?' Leah's tone was always matey with an edge of superiority. Alice always felt Leah was patronizing her, as if they were from different generations. Even though Leah was only seven years older than Alice, she behaved like she had twenty-six years on her subordinate.

'I wish,' said Alice, pulling out her cleaner's uniform. 'Babysitting here.'

'Dunno where you get your energy from,' said Leah with a hint of envy. 'Wish I was still a teenager.'

Alice hated being called a teenager. She had lived enough lifetimes to not feel anything like a typical nineteen-year-old. Alice knew it wasn't the years, it was what they had contained. And Alice's years had been densely packed, often with events she would never have chosen, or wished on anyone else.

Alice could not wait to be twenty. Nine weeks to go. Then Leah could stop slipping the word 'teenager' into every exchange they had. Alice also hoped Leah would stop coming and standing nearby as Alice got changed. Leah often commented, 'I wish I had your figure. All tightly packed and in proportion, aren't you?' while looking Alice up and down. It made Alice feel like Leah's possession and was a reminder that people had talked about Alice's body as if it was up for grabs ever since she had hit puberty. She looked forward to the day it stopped.

Alice only saw a small, slim, brown-eyed girl with long dark hair who craved less attention than she attracted and just wanted to get her cleaning job done.

'Natalie and Philippe called in sick today,' said Leah. 'Gonna need you to cover four more lodges.'

Four more lodges meant nearly double the work in the same amount of time. Alice knew there would be no extra pay.

'Sure,' she said simply. *Do the job, don't make trouble, take the money, they don't just pay you for the work, they pay you to do as you're told.* The words of her mum echoed in her ears most days.

'It's a day for the quick vics, darling,' added Leah. Quick vics – quick victories in Leahspeak – was code for: a fast shiny surface clean, rather than going any deeper. Make people *feel* like they'd been cleaned. Shine the taps, plump the pillows, tuck the duvet sides in, switch the towels, spray a bit more cleaning fluid around so it all smelled clean when the guests arrived back. And draw a smiley face on the in-lodge chalkboard with a THANKS AND HAVE A GREAT DAY FROM YOUR HOUSEKEEPING TEAM!

Alice said, 'I just need to be clear by one, so I can have my break and then start at the market by two.'

Leah nodded sympathetically. 'I don't think you'll manage a break, will you? Not with four more lodges. I have said you're taking on too much.'

Alice knew that Leah liked to look upon Alice as her protégée. She often offered advice, most of it useless or downright bad and wrong. Alice felt that Leah would like to control Alice a bit more. Alice didn't know why this was, what signals she had given or why Leah had attached herself to her in this way.

Alice just shrugged and said, 'Need the money, don't I?'

They'd had this conversation before. She wasn't going to let a supervisor in housekeeping, with a partisan position, tell her what to do or not do.

Alice depended on Parkwood. On the morning shift as housekeeper, on the afternoon shift on the checkout in the market, and in the evenings doing babysitting work. It wasn't unusual for her to be on-site for fourteen hours, and some days it could easily stretch to sixteen hours in a row. Alice wasn't sure it was legal, but she wasn't going to check or kick up a fuss because she didn't want to disrupt a pattern that suited her for now.

'What time did you even leave last night?' asked Leah, watching as Alice tied back her hair.

Alice felt herself instantly become more alert. 'I don't know. Late.'

A thought struck Leah. 'Oh, by the way, the pool's closed this morning. We're not being told why yet. Got a meeting later. If any guests ask, just say the latest info will go up on their TV.'

Alice stayed very still, looking at herself in the mirror, seeing Leah behind her.

'Any idea why it's closed?'

Leah shrugged. 'They don't tell us. Probably someone threw up or shat in the pool again, and they've gotta decontaminate it. I heard a few of the fitness lot were going in there last night for a party. Wouldn't put it past one of them to have chundered all down the rapids. Shit, look at the time. Come on, chop-chop.'

Alice watched Leah bustle out. She thought about the pool being closed. In the short term that would mean more people still in their lodges when she wanted to clean them. In the longer term, well, she'd have to wait and see.

She drained the mocha and chugged the White Monster, before heading out to collect her equipment basket. The caffeine would kick in and she would be anonymous in the lodges. People did not see cleaners. She could put her earbuds in, clean and block out the world.

She would need to. There was a lot to block out.

10

As she marched towards the emergency staff meeting, Nicola began to realize with a sense of embarrassment that she had no idea where she was going.

Parkwood Dorset reminded her enough of her previous Parkwood experience that she had just assumed she'd be able to find her way. But once she'd taken only a couple of turns, she realized the layout was entirely different. She cursed the fact she'd not brought a map with her. She'd been thinking about too many other things.

Schoolgirl error, Nic!

The voice of her DI echoed in her brain. She increased the pace of her stride, hoping she'd be able to get her bearings soon. All around she saw families enjoying their break. She circled the boating lake and watched the zip wire whizz overhead. She couldn't help but smile as she dodged the parade of bikes, crossing from one side of the path to the other. And she caught herself slowing by a large playground to watch a family playing with their young daughter in a sandpit. She was suddenly caught out by the aching memory of Ethan in his younger years, laughing in playgrounds like this. Every child here felt like a reminder of him. She checked her phone. No updates from Mike. He was most likely trying not to bother her.

She spotted a map on a noticeboard and, checking it, discovered she had managed to walk in precisely the wrong direction. She would need to run.

*

As Nicola arrived in the conference room, trying to disguise her breathlessness from fast striding across the site, heads turned to look at her. She walked to the front, simultaneously assessing the gathered group while trying to ignore the faces now swivelling towards her.

She thought there must be about fifty supervisors in total perched on folding metal chairs, their chatty gossip descending to a low mutter as Nicola neared the front of the room. She noted all the differing uniforms: housekeeping, kitchens, catering, front of house, administrative/clerical, activities and sports. No doubt there were cliques and hierarchies here, like any workplace. Might any of those have led to a death in the pool complex?

Lindsey came running in, looking even more harried than Nicola felt. Lindsey nodded stiffly, turned to the group, and clapped her hands unnecessarily like a headmistress.

'Thank you, everyone, I appreciate you gathering so rapidly. As some of you may know, there has been a serious incident overnight which will affect all operations and the guest experience over the next few days. We will all need to pull together to overcome the challenges of the coming hours and days and I appreciate all your support in advance. This is Detective Sergeant Nicola Bridge who would like to say a few words.'

Lindsey looked at Nicola with a professional smile, and Nicola stepped forward. She hated addressing large crowds but over her career had forced herself to learn how to do it.

Deep breaths, go slow, direct eye contact, commanding and confident.

'Thank you, Lindsey. Some of you may be aware that early this morning the body of a man was found in the pool of the Splashdome complex –'

The muttering and quiet wave of shock that rippled across the room prevented Nicola from carrying on immediately.

Some people gasped, others swore under their breaths, others looked at their colleagues knowingly, and at least three mouthed 'told you' or some variation, to the person sitting next to them.

'Shhh, shhh, shhh,' intervened Lindsey sharply, 'Listen, please,' and the wave of low noise subsided.

'We are treating the death as suspicious,' Nicola continued, 'and we will be carrying out investigations here over the coming hours and days. We will be interviewing all guests, as well as setting times to speak to all members of staff – er, yes?'

There was a hand up in the middle of the room.

This isn't a Q&A, mate!

A young, short bloke in football-like kit, with an inappropriately enthusiastic tone. 'When you say "suspicious death", are you saying someone's been murdered?'

That word electrified the room into silence. Heads swivelled back to Nicola.

'We're keeping an open mind until we have the post-mortem, but we can't currently rule out the possibility.'

'Was that a yes or no?' persisted FootballKit.

'It was an "it's possible",' said Nicola.

Another low hum of muttering. Another hand. *Fuck sake.* FootballKit had started a wave. Nicola nodded at the woman in a cleaning uniform with her hand up.

'Was he staff or a guest?'

The heads and eyes flicked back to Nicola again, as if they were watching a game of tennis. She knew what they wanted to know was: *is it one of us or one of them?*

'We don't yet have a confirmed identity and I would ask everyone here not to speculate. When we can release any information, we will.'

Now a voice came without a raised hand. 'What do we say to guests?'

'Management will be issuing a letter to everyone. Please don't engage in discussion or speculation, other than to acknowledge what's happened. If they have questions, point them in our direction.'

An older, thin-faced man in a gardener's uniform stood up. This was becoming a free for all: the opposite of what Nicola had intended.

'Is this connected to what happened at the Solstice Ceremony last night?'

There was a murmur of consternation which swiftly evolved into full-blown concern.

Nicola turned to Lindsey, quizzically.

Lindsey blanched. 'I can give you a full briefing about that.'

I would've preferred you already had.

Nicola turned back to the crowd and said, 'We're still getting up to full speed with the details on that.'

A woman's voice from the middle of the crowd. 'Who's keeping *us* safe, then?'

The room was on high alert. Nicola reached deep for her reserves of calm authority. 'We're increasing security patrols and deploying additional police officers. We have nothing to suggest there's any immediate threat to anyone else.'

Now one of the cleaning supervisors. 'Yeah, but presumably there was nothing yesterday to suggest this man would be killed!'

Mumbling, muttering, agreement.

Lindsey stepped forward to control her staff. 'Thank you, Leah. As DS Bridge said, our job is not to speculate, our job – *your* job, right now – is to ensure guests continue to receive an exceptional Parkwood holiday experience. I'd ask you all to remember that the vast majority of our guests book way in advance, save both money and holiday allowances to be here.

So we owe it to them to continue to provide our services at the highest level. We can and must take their minds off all of this. You all do incredible work, please focus on that and overdeliver. Your behaviour will influence how our guests respond.' She was halted by another hand. 'Yes. Margot.'

A woman in her forties with a seen-it-all-before expression asked, 'Are we getting paid for coming to this meeting? Cos we get docked for every fifteen-minute segment we're found not to be working, and this will have taken, I dunno, maybe thirty or forty-five minutes, by the time we get back.'

Murmurs of assent. The meeting seemed to have turned from a police briefing to a union meeting.

Lindsey looked disappointed. 'Yes, you'll be paid, Margot.' She looked to Nicola. 'Anything else, Detective Sergeant?'

'If anyone has anything they wish to share, please do come and speak to me now. That's all.'

At that, the chairs scraped along the floor, like class had ended. Lindsey called out to ask if everyone could please restack the chairs before leaving, and all the workers began to disperse. A couple of Margot's colleagues buzzed around her, laughing.

As Nicola suspected, nobody hung back or came forward to talk to her. Nobody wanted to stand out, nobody wanted to make eye contact with her, and clearly nobody wanted their co-workers to see them going up to the police. Even as an adult, even in 2026, nobody wants to be seen as a snitch.

Somebody here must know something, thought Nicola. Had she just looked out upon the dead man's killer?

For now, she parked that question and turned back to Lindsey.

'Tell me about the Solstice Ceremony.'

11

'The whole ceremony thing was my predecessor's idea,' explained Lindsey as she drove Nicola on an electric buggy back towards the Splashdome complex where Reeta would be waiting. Nicola detected a whiff of disapproval in Lindsey's tone.

'The site sits on ancient ley lines if you believe in all that. There was a degree of resistance to the resort being built, partly because it included this single standing stone, so the founders pledged to preserve that area, and it was decided to make a feature of it in the middle of the woods. My predecessor brought in a ceremony around the summer solstice, set around the stone, in which guests could participate. For an extra charge,' she added pointedly.

'What does the ceremony involve?'

'A procession across the site and then the laying of tributes at the stone, as the sun begins to set. It was conceived to maximize occupancy in the weeks prior to the schools breaking up, and it was very effective. We have multiple repeat bookers who we know come just for that. People dress up in all sorts of outfits, and there's a parade down the paths.'

'You don't sound convinced,' said Nicola.

Lindsey stared ahead, her face set. 'I argued against it but I was overruled. Commercializing ancient traditions to bring in extra revenue . . . we can do better than that. Problem is, now we've created a new tradition and a market, so I'd be derelict in my duty if I stopped it. Equally I have sympathy with those who're angry about us profiting from what they see as sacred spaces and ancient rituals. There are all these different opinions concerning what happened on that site in the past and what the stone represents. If you ask me, people project whatever they want to believe on to it. I mean, some even believe human sacrifice took place there.'

Lindsey paused. 'Obviously we don't mention anything about human sacrifice in our brochure,' she added.

'What happened at the ceremony yesterday?'

'I wasn't there, but my understanding is we had a party of guests who had decided to come dressed in full pagan garb and skull masks with a view to disrupting the ceremony. I think it was four or five people. One of my jobs today was to find out which lodge they're staying in. Anyway, apparently they blockaded the stone, barricading the way for the end of the procession and refusing to allow all the children to lay the tributes. And their costumes were very scary. I have some sympathy, but stopping five-year-olds from laying flowers near an ancient stone seems a little churlish.

'Anyway, there was some sort of fight, which involved people on both sides, maybe even a member of staff – I'm waiting on a full report. A few punches were thrown, people were pulled apart, lots of crying children and bad feeling.' Lindsey looked frustrated. 'This is what I mean – if it were down to me, I'd stop it, but I know I'd get complaints.'

'You're literally caught between a rock and a hard place.' Nicola regretted the flippancy immediately as Lindsey looked at her, uncomprehending. She wasn't bantering with Harry now, she reminded herself, and continued hastily. 'Let me have the names of the guests who were involved as soon as you know. We'll raise it when interviewing.'

Lindsey nodded as she brought the buggy to a halt and

Nicola got out. 'Please keep me up to date with everything,' she said stiffly and accelerated away.

As Nicola walked towards the external cordon she considered what Lindsey had just told her. Had tensions remained after the ceremony and escalated later that night? And even if that were the case, how would it have ended with a body in the pool?

Nicola found Reeta in the area at the rear of the pool complex, itself cordoned off from public view. As Nicola walked over, Reeta was wiping her sweating brow in between taking gulps of cold water from her bottle.

'Could you have made it any trickier for us?' she asked Nicola.

'I had it arranged entirely to test you,' replied Nicola.

'Might as well have done,' said Reeta. 'Here's what we're dealing with right now: one, dilution and loss of trace evidence. Blood, fibres, DNA, fingerprints, bodily fluids are all quickly dispersed or destroyed by water. That's before we get to chemical interference: chlorine and other chemicals in the pool can degrade DNA and might alter any toxicology results.'

'OK,' said Nicola evenly.

'My other concern is that we're working in a high-traffic environment. That whole area naturally involves hundreds of guests and staff, which means huge contamination issues. Basically, there are many legitimate reasons why people's DNA or fingerprints or clothing fibres could be present in that space, making it hard to isolate anything that categorically links to the killer.'

Nicola exhaled.

'Exactly,' said Reeta. 'We'll get the water chemically tested;

my team are just recovering all the filters and skimmers from the pool in case they've trapped anything of significance. I'm gonna talk to all my 'ologist mates via the NCA about deaths in water, see if there's anything I'm missing. Can you ask Mel to source company cleaning records, so we have timings, history, all that?' She wiped more sweat away before looking back up at Nicola. 'We've got so much to get through here. It's not going to be quick, no matter how much you might want it to be.'

That final sentence was the exact opposite of what Nicola had hoped to hear. She was by nature an optimist, but with every passing moment, the challenge here at Parkwood felt like it was becoming insurmountable.

12

Alice had worked at double speed, cleaning the lodges she had been assigned, including the extras.

Of all the days for anyone to call in sick.

She did all the tricks she'd been schooled on, especially since Leah had all but told her to skimp. She ran from room to room. She blasted Doechii in her earbuds, the bass pounding her on. By the time she'd done all her assigned lodges, she was sweating buckets. Still smiling at the guests, still avoiding questions (another reason for the earbuds).

Leah had also done the rounds after the staff meeting, dropping in on all her staff to tell them: something has happened, sounds pretty bad, don't talk to anyone about it.

Fine by Alice.

Work done, she made her way across the site at a clip, not wanting anyone to spot she was running. Luckily, she knew the best route for shortcuts. Even more luckily, she didn't see anybody she knew.

This lodge was on the edge of the site, close to the perimeter. It sat apart from the other clusters of lodges, a more recent addition to the site carried out by the previous management in an attempt to maximize revenue from every corner of the land available. It stood alone and almost hidden from view by a bank of trees.

Alice let herself in to the lodge, knocking and calling out, 'Hello? Housekeeping!'

No voice, no response. Good. Not even Lee. She half expected him to be in here.

She had already prepared her reply if there was an unexpected guest, or someone within the lodge going, 'We've already been done!' *Really sorry! I'll go and talk to my supervisor! Sorry for the disturbance!*

But there was no reply, no presence, no sound of any movement.

Alice slid in and gently pulled the door closed behind her. She paused, listening.

Emboldened, she checked in all the rooms to be sure. All empty of occupants.

She had decided to put on sanitary gloves so she could check in drawers and wardrobes. Better safe than sorry.

Lounge first, then bathroom.

Into the bedroom. Bed unmade but slept on.

Alice stared at it for a minute, thinking. Hypnotized by it.

Back to the job in hand.

Checked under the bed. Maybe under the sofa. Under the sink even!

Anything?

It was then she heard the click of a key in the lock.

Shit.

A key turning, then turning back in confusion. The door handle lowering – the door opening.

It's fine, don't sweat it, style it out. Styling it out is what you do these days.

A figure walked in – a figure Alice recognized.

Lindsey. Oh shit.

'Hi!' said Alice.

'Oh, Alice!' said Lindsey.

Lindsey had given Alice her chance at Parkwood. Lindsey

was the reason Alice loved working at Parkwood. For Alice, Lindsey *was* Parkwood. It was no exaggeration to say that Lindsey was the mother Alice no longer had.

Alice had cleaned Lindsey's office once a week for most of this year. It had cemented a bond between the two, at least that's how Alice felt. Lindsey was lovely. She had been kind. She had even confided in Alice some mornings when she'd got in there early, or been there late, while Alice was working or doing extra shifts. She had asked Alice about her life, her ambitions – and listened, too. Alice asked questions back – she knew this year had been difficult for Lindsey at home and occasionally at work. Recently she had even added Alice to a mentorship scheme at Parkwood and suggested she might be able to be Alice's mentor if she had time.

'What are you doing here?' Lindsey asked.

'Just finishing up,' said Alice. 'Supervisor said it needed doing.' She held her breath. Would Lindsey challenge her on it?

'Right,' said Lindsey, looking around. A check of the watch. 'I don't know why they sent you in here. It's late to be finishing up. Cleaning shifts should be done by now.'

'Sorry, it's cos there's a couple off sick,' added Alice.

'Yes, no, of course,' said Lindsey supportively. 'Thanks for all you're doing. Sorry, it's a very hard day all round.'

'Must be difficult for you,' said Alice sympathetically.

Lindsey looked startled. 'Yes.' She looked as if she suddenly felt seen. 'It is. Thank you for saying that, Alice.' She took a beat and then said warmly, 'You know, we should follow up on the mentorship programme. I was thinking recently that my office has never been better cleaned since you started doing it. Thank you.'

Lindsey smiled a full-beam smile, and Alice smiled one

back. That was nice of Lindsey; she didn't have to say that. Alice felt validated. She never got any praise from Leah, not about the quality of her work anyway.

'Right, well, I won't disturb you while you're mid-clean,' said Lindsey. Then she added, 'Who asked you to do it?'

'Leah,' said Alice, and regretted it instantly.

'Oh, right,' said Lindsey, as if that explained everything.

She wandered around, looking in doorways, either checking Alice's work or something else. Then her phone buzzed, and she checked it and grimaced.

'I'll leave you to it,' Lindsey said distractedly, walking to the door.

'Let me know if there's anything else I can do,' Alice called after her.

Lindsey hovered in the doorway, as if she might have a list of requests. Then she seemed to think better of saying anything. A formal smile. 'I will.'

And she was gone.

Leaving Alice wondering exactly why Lindsey had just chosen to drop in on this particular lodge. Was it a random spot-check or something more?

13

Dear Guests,

Following an incident at the Splashdome, we regret to inform you that the facility will be closed today and tomorrow. The closure is due to circumstances beyond Parkwood's control.

We are very sorry for any inconvenience this may cause to your stay. We are doing all we can to reopen the facility as soon as is feasible.

We would like to take this opportunity to remind you of all the other great facilities which remain in place, including bike hire, high ropes, zip lining, archery, football classes, cycle hire and our award-winning spa facilities.

We have also had to temporarily suspend the shuttle bus service between the main drop-off point by Cycle Hire and the guest car parks.

We will, of course, let you know as soon as these situations have been rectified. If you have any questions in the meantime, please go to the Information Office where one of my colleagues will be pleased to assist you.

I will update you with further information as soon as any becomes available.

In addition, each lodge is now being allocated a time to speak with police officers about recent events. This is for your safety and welfare, and it is important that you give them your full cooperation and support. You may also see additional security officers and police officers during this time in the resort.

We trust this will not adversely affect your break and hope you are enjoying your stay with us at Parkwood.

With best wishes,
Lindsey Moorfield
Resort Manager

14

A long way from the Parkwood site, an old battered computer made a soft trilling sound.

The computer's owner walked slowly over from the task that had been occupying them, to check the source of the unexpected noise.

A news alert for 'Parkwood Dorset'.

It had been a long time since they had set up that alert; so long they'd almost forgotten having done it.

Almost but not quite.

15

Time was quickly becoming Nicola Bridge's enemy.

She had spent much of her early detective career on tedious surveillance ops, observing the movements of known criminals, the seconds dragging like weeks. And yet today, when she needed every moment, time felt like it was continually being stolen from her. There were so many elements needed to get this investigation up and running, each of which already felt in some way compromised.

Then this is the challenge, she told herself. *You love a challenge, you're good at them, so here's the mother of all challenges. Crack on!*

She had to issue a statement to the media, presenting the facts in a clear manner while downplaying any sensationalism. On some cases media coverage was invaluable – the more the better. Here, it would be a complicating factor. Nicola did not want the media to lay siege to the Parkwood site and inhibit the investigation. The more that could be achieved before the media became too interested, the happier she would be.

So she sat on the back patio of the incident-room lodge, as Harry and Mel worked away inside, phrasing the initial statement economically and innocuously. 'Officers from Three Counties Police are currently investigating the death of a man whose body was found on-site at the Parkwood Dorset resort earlier this morning.' It was the minimum required, to be issued as text rather than video. She did not want to reveal more, especially given she had not yet spoken to next of kin.

She checked her watch and stepped back inside. 'How are we doing on victim ID, Mel?'

Mel looked up from multiple piles of paperwork as if he could not believe she had disturbed him. '*We* are working through. *We* will tell you when *we* have something to report, but it's going to take a hell of a lot longer if *we* keep being interrupted!'

Nicola reminded herself not to rise to Mel's admonishment. Parkwood's bespoke IT systems had been infuriatingly unable to export digital records in a format that other computers could read or convert. Nicola recognized an organization not unlike her own: superficially functioning but compromised underneath. So Mel was having to work the analogue way: comparing Reeta's photos of the victim with paper records of guest ID photos. Mel looked up again, already realizing he'd been too sharp and trying to minimize it by making another point.

'And if you must know, they've given us double the amount of records you asked for.'

'What?'

'They've included all the guests who were here for the weekend but checked out on Monday. All jumbled in together with the current guests. So I have over a thousand to go through and weed out. Plus, the weekend guests included a golf club outing of more than a hundred men around the same age and profile as our victim.'

Great. They needed to catch a break and instead things had become doubly difficult for Mel. While she trusted him to get the right result, she had less faith in his ability to move at lightning speed. She knew what his answer would be if she tried to broach an increase in pace: 'If you want it done less well, you're welcome to ask someone else.'

Harry was looking out of the window. 'Looks like the cavalry is here.'

Nicola walked over to see a small ragtag-looking group of officers, the reinforcements she'd requested, walking towards the lodge. They did not, Nicola had to admit, have the look of a particularly dynamic cavalry, but beggars (as her DI had reminded her) could not be choosers.

'Are you done outside? Can I brief them there?' asked Harry. Nicola had initially hesitated in assigning him the job of briefing the new arrivals, but he had worked out the rotas, drawn up the areas and laid out an interview structure for them all to follow. He was growing in stature all the time. She would let him run it.

'All yours,' said Nicola, looking at the time. She had a window of thirty minutes before the first interview. 'I'll be back shortly.'

She strode to the front door, ignoring Mel and Harry's quizzical looks. There was something else she needed to do.

She did not know the lie of the land.

That's why she had got lost on her way to the staff meeting earlier. She needed to get her bearings, to understand the layout of Parkwood. It was no use locking herself away in their operational base; Nicola needed to physically traverse the territory.

It's how she operated in Liverpool, where over two decades she had walked (or run) most streets within the city's radius. And on her first major case having returned to Dorset, she understood the village of Fleetcombe from growing up in the area.

Parkwood was different – a constructed village, hermetically sealed, a fabricated reality. Worse: this Parkwood site was a half-echo of the one she had spent a week in previously. Some bits were identical, some were entirely different. Having only been at Parkwood Dorset for a few hours the two locations kept merging unhelpfully in her mind.

Nicola exited the lodge to find three bikes had already been delivered. Lindsey ran an efficient operation, she thought. As the new group of officers trudged past her into the lodge, she nodded and instructed them to report to DC Ward. She grabbed a bike, and holding the map to the handlebars, she set a time limit and began to pedal hard.

She started by heading to the Splashdome complex and circumnavigating it, checking for emergency exits, the flow of people even when it was closed, noting which other facilities and lodges were closest. From there, she worked outwards across the site, rigorously and quickly. She was glad to be out in the air, looking around as she rode the pathways and identified a stopping point for each different area of the resort. She stood, feet down on the ground, still on her bike, in front of each 'neighbourhood' of lodges, scanning 360 degrees, seeing where the pathways snaked off, the sightline and visibilities, the signs. She made a note of distances, and noted the time it took to cycle between different facilities.

She arrived at the last point of interest on the map within twenty minutes. She was breathless from her fast site profiling, her mind buzzing with the to-do list ahead, as she cycled down a pathway which led deeper into the forest and a small clearing. She slowed up and came to rest in front of the standing stone.

Sound dropped away in this clearing, as if it were separate from the rest of the site. The birdsong felt more distant, as if living creatures were giving this area a wide berth. There was less breeze here, but that did not translate into calm. Instead, the stillness felt eerie and unsettling.

She looked around with the feeling she was being watched. There was no one in sight. She laid the bike down on the pine-needle-strewn floor. All she could hear was her footsteps on the carpet of needles as she approached the stone and stood directly in front of it.

The stone itself was about eight feet tall, five feet wide, three feet deep, misshapen and undeniably old. Its texture was mottled, mossy in places, its lumpy grey-brown surface worn away by millennia. Standing there, Nicola felt as if she were somehow confronting it, her presence demanding an answer to a question she had not yet formulated.

All around the base of the stone were laid a warped smorgasbord of contradictory offerings: children's drawings (some cute, some weird or gruesome), posies of wild flowers, as well as a few things which looked to Nicola like they had been made by children in craft classes here at Parkwood – painted stones, straw dolls. Scattered around were small stone cairns seemingly constructed from stones found nearby, as well as a couple of pyramid-like stick arrangements about six inches high.

In addition, at the base of the stone, lay a carefully arranged dead raven whose black feathers were splayed out. Nicola knelt down and leaned in to it. She could not work out whether it was real or a replica, perhaps even a piece of taxidermy. Either way, it was weird. She took out her phone, stepped back and took pictures of the stone and its surroundings.

As she took a photo of the raven, she could see on the camera image something behind it, some sort of dark fabric behind the bird's claws, almost tucked under the bottom of the stone. Her detective's instincts kicked in. She reached in her pocket for a pen, and also an evidence bag – just in case.

She carefully teased out the fabric, latching the pen on to a corner of it, and slowly retrieved the item: a long thin piece of sheer black fabric which revealed itself to be . . . a woman's thong.

Nicola held it up on the end of her pen, momentarily thrown, and then wondering what to do with it. *Quick decisions, Nicola.* She deposited it into the evidence bag and sealed it.

She looked back at the stone as she got to her feet. How had that item got there, under the raven? What had happened here, either during or after the Solstice Ceremony? Was any of it connected to the body in the pool?

As she turned to pick up the bike, she thought she heard a noise beyond the clearing, only just audible.

She began wheeling the bike back the way she'd come, up the pathway and back into the open. She listened again. Yes, there it was.

It was coming from the grass somewhere nearby. She walked a few steps towards it, trying to not only locate it but identify it. A high-pitched whizzing-buzzing. Like a fan going? Not a big fan, a tiny portable fan. Insistent.

It reminded Nicola of the sound of the Hot Wheels toy racing cars Ethan had adored and collected as a child. The sounds they made as they whizzed round the track she and Mike had bought him (sorry, she meant Father Christmas had bought him, obviously) was etched into her memory.

Oh, that sweet little boy. Please can I have him back?!

Distracted, she nearly stepped on it.

A drone lying in the grass. Still active but winding down. Like a wounded bird with a broken wing. Grounded, trying to get airborne once more.

Nicola knelt and picked up the drone. Its noises were slowing as it was losing power. She had a rudimentary knowledge of drones and knew enough to be able to power it down.

She looked around for its operator but the area seemed deserted – had it come from within Parkwood and got lost – a child's toy? Or had it flown in from outside? She examined it more closely: it had a GoPro camera attached. Was that active now? Was it taking pictures or filming? Was it transmitting now? She placed it face down in the grass and as she did –

'That's mine, thanks.'

A large man in his sixties was lumbering round the bend in the path. He pocketed his phone as he advanced, looking at her accusingly. 'Leave it there.'

He walked past Nicola and knelt by the drone, picking it up, checking it.

'I don't think drones are allowed here,' said Nicola.

He looked up at her, cradling the drone. 'And who are you?'

Interesting tone, she thought. She flashed her warrant card. 'DS Nicola Bridge, Three Counties Police.'

The man stared up at her, weighing her up. He did not move, as if waiting for her to say more. 'Haven't you got more important things to be doing right now?'

Nicola was not going to take that bait. 'Are you a guest here, sir?'

'Keith Hammersley. Lodge 50.' He seemed to wait, as if expecting a specific response.

Nicola nodded at the drone. 'Please don't use that again in here, especially not while there's an investigation ongoing.'

Keith Hammersley gave a sort of nod-shrug, which Nicola interpreted as 'we'll see'.

Then he asked, 'What happened at the pool?'

Nicola resisted the urge to ask him why he wanted to

know. Instead she said, 'We'll release any further information about the incident as and when appropriate. You should have a time allocated to speak with one of my team today.'

Keith Hammersley from Lodge 50 picked up his drone in disgust and walked past her.

Nicola watched him go. She was going to be late for her own interviews, but she quickly wrote down his name and lodge number, a litany of questions exploding in her mind.

Why had he been flying a drone when they were prohibited? Was it something to do with the standing stone? Had he been looking for something? Or, most unsettling of all, had he been watching her?

16

Harry Ward shuffled the sheaf of printouts with names, addresses and lodge numbers into a neat pile, opened his notebook, clicked his pen and prepared to get started.

He was in a small white-walled room just off the sports courts, which appeared to be the first-aider's office, a fact given away by the curtained-off section with a bed at one end. The room smelled vaguely of antiseptic and Harry felt like he was interviewing people in a GP's surgery. He did not mind that there was grunt work ahead. He already knew, from his short time working with Nicola, that the grunt work was often where cases were solved. The added complication here was the lack of time and the mountain of work. Harry knew he had to work rigorously and at speed. He decided he would treat this as a fun challenge.

Go.

He kicked off and moved fast, keeping to a quick clip, shepherding people in and out. He worked hard to keep to time or do better than the plan, even getting through some groups in five minutes. He did not even take a break for a coffee or to go to the toilet. He was *focused.*

A couple of hours in, he was regretting this approach.

His head was starting to spin. He had seen all modern society parade through: friend groups, family groups, pensioner groups, stag groups, hen groups (not connected), archery groups, even pool slide enthusiasts (very bummed out by the closure of the pool). But as time wore on, the families began to look the same, the married couples felt interchangeable, the bewildered small children wandered around and tugged at their parents' clothes, asking what are we *doing* and this was the worst holiday and please, Mum, stop talking to the man.

Most people were friendly and cooperative. The majority had seen nothing, or were asleep, and had clear alibis. Some were keener to ask questions than to answer them and were disappointed when Harry wouldn't go into further detail. A select few people looked terrified or didn't want to know anything about the incident, as if the nature of it would infect their lives. 'Just ask what you need to and let's be out of here,' said one small sniffling white-haired woman, as her husband clasped her hand tightly. ('It's a long story,' the husband had gently said to Harry and clapped him on the shoulder as they departed.)

Conor and Emma Slater were from Lodge 141. Harry had assessed the couple as they set up their four-year-old daughter Bella at the colouring-in table. Emma was an interesting mix: tall and lithe, long sandy hair, funky clothes, giving off a vibe of sand between her toes, but also an air of professional middle-class certainty. Conor with his sharply cut dark hair, carefully unshaven face, toned physique, crisp shirt, shorts and shoes had piercing blue eyes and a wary expression. He was, to Harry's observation, more tightly wound than his wife. And he was doing all the talking.

'We took Bella for an early tea at the Italian restaurant in the Food Square about five, we were out by six thirty. Back to the lodge to prepare for the Solstice Parade thing.'

'We've come this week for the past few years,' added Emma. 'Bella loves the parade.'

'But obviously that got ruined,' said Conor, clearly still angry. 'I don't know what motivates people like that, wanting to spoil it, telling us we should be ashamed of ourselves. Fine whatever you believe, but they scared the kids and spoiled the parade.'

'There was a bit of a scuffle,' admitted Emma, looking to Conor.

Conor took over. 'I was fuming. Ended up almost wrestling one bloke, who was banging on, saying we wouldn't be parading if we knew the human sacrifice that had gone on here . . . There was a lot of shouting, nobody was stepping in and . . . and I just lost it. It's supposed to be a holiday, right?' He saw Harry's expression and added hastily. 'Nothing terrible, just had him on the ground, shut him up, till security came. He was yelling all sorts of stuff saying he'd come for me.'

Emma interrupted. 'Parkwood security could've done a lot better. I've put our experience in an email.'

'D'you know the names or lodge numbers of the people who were protesting?' asked Harry. Both Emma and Conor shook their heads. 'What happened after that?'

'They got removed,' said Conor. 'Everyone finished the parade, a bit half-heartedly. We came back to the lodge, bath-story-bedtime. Babysitter came at eight thirty. Em and I went out for a drinks at the cocktail speakeasy place they have. We were there till closing, then we came back, so the babysitter left at . . . what was that, eleven thirty, twelve?' He checked his phone. 'Alice, that's the babysitter's name.'

Harry wrote down the name and looked up. 'And then you went to bed?'

'Yes,' said Conor, and Harry watched Emma turn to him quizzically. 'I mean, not exactly. Em went to bed. I did some tidying, washing-up, getting things ready for the morning.

That's my routine, our routine. Em needs more sleep than me. She's the worker. I only ever sleep four hours, five maximum.'

Harry was unsure whether, had Emma not been there, Conor would have made the correction. 'You went to bed after tidying then?'

Conor thought for a second. 'Uh, yeah!' He nodded for a while.

Emma looked at her husband. 'Or did you go for a run?' She turned to Harry. 'He often goes for a run before bed.'

Harry turned his gaze to Conor, who was meeting Emma's gaze. There was a moment's silence.

'Did I? I *did.* Yes. That's right,' said Conor, placing his hand on Emma's arm.

'What time was that?' asked Harry.

Conor considered. 'Not sure, some time after midnight.'

'And how long did you run for?'

'Forty-five minutes, an hour? Running helps me sleep.'

'Where did you run?'

'On the paths,' said Conor evasively. 'I had a light thing on my head,' he added, as if this was helpful clarification.

'Did you see anyone?'

'A few, yeah. Not to say hello to. I had my earphones in.'

'You got back to the lodge when?'

'One or one thirty. Maybe later. Not sure,' said Conor.

Conor was not sure about a few things once Emma had gone to bed last night, thought Harry. He nodded at the smartwatch on Conor's wrist. 'Would your device tell you the exact timings?'

Conor looked at Harry, then his wrist, as if he'd never seen it before. 'Oh. No. It . . . The system went all glitchy this morning, wouldn't sync and it was corrupted, and I had to do a whole reset, which erased all the data, so it's only recorded today.'

Emma was staring at her husband as Harry asked Conor, 'Did your run take you past the Splashdome?'

Conor thought for a moment. 'Probably, it'd be on the route.'

'And did you notice anyone hanging around or any disturbance – anything like that?'

'No,' said Conor.

'You didn't stop anywhere or go anywhere else on your run?'

Conor shook his head and Harry turned to Emma.

'You were asleep when he came in?'

Emma nodded. Both had gone quiet in the latter part of this conversation, Harry noted.

'Daddy, I've finished it,' said Bella from the corner, holding up a page of her book to Conor who paid no attention.

'Oh, Bels, that's beautiful,' said Emma, walking over. 'Such neat work, and all within the lines. I love your choice of colours on this bit.'

Harry said to Conor, 'But your fitness data is probably saved to the cloud or on your account, right? Not just the device. Would you check it and let me know about the route and timings?'

Conor stood and took the card that Harry was holding out. 'Definitely. Anything else?'

Harry said, 'That'll do for now.'

He watched as Conor hurried the rest of his family out, unable to achieve it fast enough. As they left, Harry noted that Conor's smile had become tight and uneasy.

17

Where were you last night?

Who were you with?

What did you do?

Did you go anywhere else?

Were you anywhere near the Splashdome?

Nicola would be saying these questions in her sleep tonight, she'd gone through them that many times. People entered, sat, had their name and lodge checked, answered questions as Nicola evaluated each word, alibis were offered, explored and queried, instincts were checked. Thanks very much, you've been very helpful, we'll be in touch if we need more, send the next people in, hi, I'm DS Nicola Bridge . . .

After each interview she checked her phone for messages from either Mel or Mike. Updates on Ethan, an ID for the victim. Her phone remained stubbornly silent. As the clock ticked along, the whispering voice in her head – the voice which always accompanied Nicola even in her most strident or confident moments, but especially when pressure kicked in – the Voice of Doubt.

Who says the killer is still here? Who says they didn't just come in from outside and then sneak off after the murder? You don't even know if they're a guest or a member of staff. You don't know anything.

You don't know anything.

The fear that haunted any investigation. The doubt, the quiet nagging terror of Not Knowing, of having Got It Wrong From The Start. When people talked about the pressures of police work, of being a detective, they usually meant the running around, or facing down criminals. The pressure for Nicola always came with the doubt: I am doing my best, but what if my best isn't good enough? What if I'm just completely on the wrong track?

She had not often been on the wrong track. But she could not say she had always been right. This was the point: the Voice of Doubt wanted her to feel shame for those one or two occasions where things had not gone well. Not the ninety-eight times out of a hundred where she had deployed her team brilliantly or come up with a deduction or process that unlocked a case and sent criminals down. Success was supposed to be a given. Doubt was always waiting, poised and ready, to infect like a virus, to tell her she was not good enough. She had to resist it.

So shut up, Voice of Doubt. I can do without you today, thanks very much.

She had just finished interviewing a group of women in their twenties from Lodge 97, mates on a week away, led by extrovert Karina, proud they'd been up all night drinking in Parkwood bars and then their lodge, and that Karina had pulled a bloke whose name they claimed not to remember but who had stayed most of the night. Nicola wondered if any of the male guests would confess to being Karina's companion in any of the other interviews.

As that group left, Nicola checked her watch. Checked outside. No one there. She referred back to her list. Her first no-show: Lodge 77, Valerie Doyle from Darlington. One of the rare guests here on her own.

Why are you a no-show, Val? You do realize that makes you look suspicious?

If Val wouldn't come to her, she would go to Val.

Just as she finished making the note, her phone rang, startling her.

It was Mel. 'You'd better get back here. I've got an ID.'

Nicola pedalled back to the lodge as fast as she could, while still trying to project an air of controlled calm. She just about managed to avoid mowing down a number of young families on the Parkwood pathways. Outside the lodge, she threw the bike down without locking it, mentally daring someone to try to nick it.

Inside, Harry was already there and Mel was uncharacteristically pacing. He looked even more agitated than normal.

'Finally!' said Mel.

'You only called me seven minutes ago!' said Nicola.

'He wouldn't tell me until you got here,' said Harry.

'What have you got, Mel?' asked Nicola.

'The photo matches to a guest by the name of Neil Summers, who's one of the guests staying alone.' He laid out the papers on the lodge's dining table. 'These are the photos taken of the victim this morning. This is the ID photo from Neil Summers' guest record.'

Nicola and Harry leaned in at the same time, brushing into each other and recoiling, like they'd both been hit by an electric charge.

'No, sorry, you go,' said Harry hastily.

Nicola examined both sets of images. The visual match was almost identical: facial structure and features, hair colour and length, all matched.

'Agreed,' said Nicola. She didn't understand why Mel was looking so unhappy. 'What's the problem?'

'I ran his details. There is no UK citizen called Neil Summers with that date of birth. His address on the guest record is false, a non-existent street, town and postcode. There's also no vehicle registration listed, so Lord knows how he got in here.'

'That doesn't make sense,' said Harry.

'Oh, thank you so much for stating the obvious, Westlife,' said Mel. 'And here's the cherry on the cake: his lodge number is incorrect. He's listed as 217. But he's not 217 because a whole other booking is in 217. I know because I just went to 217. I met a very nice couple, Sandra and Alan, here for their ruby wedding anniversary, who've already given a full account to one of our constables and who've never seen or heard of a Neil Summers.'

Questions were going off like fireworks in Nicola Bridge's mind. There was only one place to start in search of answers.

'We need to talk to Lindsey Moorfield.'

18

Lindsey Moorfield was wearing her best corporate smile as she looked directly into the camera pinhole above her computer screen to give the impression of greater direct eye contact. She had long ago analysed and perfected her Zoom performance.

On the other end were two people she had never met before. Thierry, tanned, serious and clean shaven, who had introduced himself as head of legal, and Maria, head of comms, fifties, elegantly dressed all in black, flawless skin. They were calling from the expensively minimalist London-based offices of Parkwood's ultimate owners, a venture capital company called Atraska.

They had insisted on this call, even though it was the last thing Lindsey needed. She had been running around the site all day ensuring operations continued, and she still had a long list of time-critical tasks set by the police to attend to, along with a list of calls and messages from multiple people demanding to speak to her. She did not have time to run Thierry and Maria through the events of the day so far, but that was what they had demanded, so she had complied. They listened, nodded, and when Lindsey had completed her rundown, Maria asked, 'Have you talked to the media at all?'

'No,' said Lindsey. 'I've been told not to by the police. They've issued the statement I shared with you on email.'

Maria nodded. 'Good, that's the correct approach. If any

reporters turn up, or queries come in, do not admit them to the site or answer any calls, just refer all enquiries to me.'

'Are there further operational protocols, other than those I've just described, that I should be putting in place?' asked Lindsey. She had assumed Parkwood's head of operations would be on this call. His absence only deepened her concern.

There was a beat then Thierry replied, 'We will check in with Operations, but it sounds like you're doing a good job. The only thing I would add is, please resist any temptation to discuss compensation with guests at this stage. As things stand, this is not our responsibility or financial burden to shoulder.'

As Thierry was speaking it dawned on Lindsey that the reason nobody from Operations had joined the call was because if they absented themselves from the call, they would have clean hands in any subsequent corporate inquest. If anything went wrong, it could be blamed firmly on her.

As that thought occurred to her, there was a knock at the door and it opened before she could respond. Lindsey looked past the screen, irritably. She had placed the Do Not Disturb sign on her handle to indicate exactly that.

She saw who it was: the two detectives. She mimed to them that she was in a meeting. It had no impact.

'This can't wait,' said the female detective.

Lindsey had always been a Parkwood loyalist. For her, Parkwood was an experience; not a brand or a franchise, something so much more beautiful than those words suggested.

Lindsey had bought in fully to the vision of the Parkwood founders from the moment she joined some fourteen years ago. Their passion for 'nature-based family holiday experiences' was infectious, and she had assimilated their beliefs, values and approach. She had devoted her working life to ensuring that Parkwood Dorset was best in class. She would visit rivals and other Parkwoods and note down everything. Then when she returned to *her* Parkwood (yes, she did think of it as hers), she would put all her notes into practice – adding the things she'd been impressed by elsewhere and ensuring that the faults of other Parkwoods were not replicated here in Dorset.

It had been a joyous decade of work for her. Her diligence had got her noticed and she had ascended to the giddy heights of assistant manager and then, finally, manager.

Then, two and a half years ago, the founders cashed in and sold up.

Lindsey had felt an irrational feeling of betrayal. Her loyalty to the ideal was for life. She was surprised that theirs was not.

She was warned by a friend when the sale to Atraska was going through. 'They flip businesses like other people flip houses.'

Lindsey could not believe this would be the case. Parkwood was special. Her friend had looked at her with pity. 'Linz, you must never care more for your work than those above you. Companies will never love you back. Don't be a client falling for a sex worker.'

Lindsey had suggested she call Maria and Thierry back on Zoom once the police had finished. Instead, and much to her disquiet, they insisted they would keep the call active and be ready as soon as she returned to the screen. It felt like a power move. Lindsey shut off the camera and microphone her end and moved round to the sofa area of the office, but could not shake the feeling that Marie and Thierry were still in the room.

The detective sergeant called Nicola began. 'We have a positive ID for the man who was found in the pool. He's in your guest records as a Neil Summers, but we don't believe that's his real name. There is false and missing information on the guest profile, including an incorrect lodge number.'

Lindsey bristled. 'That's not possible.'

'Here's the guest record.' The younger detective laid the printout on the table. Lindsey could see unusual gaps in sections of guest information. Then her eyes drifted up to the photograph and in an instant her body was flooded with feelings of confusion, anger and fear.

Time suddenly seemed to slow down. She was aware both detectives were studying her. She needed a moment to think.

'Let me look into this as a matter of urgency and get back to you.'

She knew that would not fly. The DS was staring at her beadily. 'Do you know this man, Lindsey?'

Lindsey's head was spinning. What should she say? What should she do?

Nicola persisted. 'Does he work here?'

Lindsey shook her head.

She heard the tone of the detective's voice toughen.

'I'd like you to take a look at another photograph of the victim.' Lindsey noted a glance from the woman to the man. 'This image was taken post-mortem. I'm afraid it's rather distressing but I'd be grateful if you'd look to confirm whether you can identify the man in question.'

The young detective placed the photograph on the table. Lindsey could sense the other detective's gaze on her.

She did not want to look.

Lindsey looked.

She felt like she was about to vomit.

'Do you recognize that person, Lindsey?'

Lindsey stared at the photo, hypnotized. She knew evasion or omission would not work a second time. The pressure of the gazes on her, the physical reactions flooding her body, left her no choice.

She nodded.

'His name is Darren Winters,' she said.

Nicola asked, 'Are you certain of that?'

Maria and Thierry were still waiting. She wanted to run out of the office screaming.

'How do you know Mr Winters?' asked Nicola.

For a moment Lindsey said nothing.

Then she said, 'He used to be the manager here. He used to be my boss.'

19

Nicola had sensed it immediately. The shift in Lindsey Moorfield, her reluctance to give a straight answer.

Now she peppered a reeling Lindsey with questions. She sensed she had limited time. Lindsey looked dazed and upset. Was it shock, or something else?

'When did he leave his job, Lindsey?'

'Four years ago.'

'Do you have an address for him?'

'It's in Eagleforth; we'll have it on file.'

'Next of kin?'

'I don't know. Grandchildren. His son died. But … daughter-in-law, I think.'

'How many people here would know him?'

'A handful, not lots. We've had a lot of turnover since he left.'

'We'll need a list,' said Nicola.

'Why is he on the system as a guest?' asked Harry. 'Is he staying here?'

Lindsey looked out of her depth now. 'I don't know why he's on there.' She glanced over at her desk. 'I should get back to the call –'

Nicola ignored the ploy. 'When did you last see Mr Winters, Lindsey? Did you know he was here?'

'CAN YOU JUST STOP?! JUST *STOP*!' Lindsey exploded at Nicola.

There was silence. Lindsey was breathing heavily. Nicola said nothing.

'You've just told me he's dead! I can't – you can't just barrage me with questions like that! It's not fair!'

Nicola kept her gaze on Lindsey but didn't respond. Was this outburst genuine or a distraction tactic? She watched Lindsey take a breath and compose herself.

'I'll answer everything you want, I'll get you all the information you need, but . . .' She nodded at the computer. 'I have to finish that call –'

'Would you like me to talk to them?' Nicola offered.

'No,' snapped Lindsey. 'This is my resort. They need to be reassured I'm in control of everything. Which I am. Now please. I need to look into everything you're asking me. I don't have all those answers. And I just need to . . .' She trailed off. 'I need to process.'

She looked like she was on the verge of tears. Nicola calculated. 'We can come back in half an hour,' she suggested.

Lindsey looked incredulous, as if Nicola were devoid of all empathy. Then nodded, worn down.

'We want to find whoever did this and stop them doing anything else,' said Nicola pointedly, as she and Harry stood up.

They left Lindsey retaking her seat to continue her call. Nicola resisted lingering at the door to listen in.

What did Lindsey know? What wasn't she telling them?

20

Lindsey did not really take in anything Maria or Thierry said after she rejoined the video call.

She felt as if she was having an out-of-body experience. She wrote down whatever instructions or advice they continued to give her. She glossed over the conversation she had just had with the two detectives by informing Maria and Thierry that the police had needed urgent information on how the pool complex was run.

As the call ended, Lindsey felt certain of only one thing. She was on her own. With it all.

She sat in her chair for a long time afterwards, staring into space.

She thought about whether there was anyone she could call. She did not want to tell Ian. Her husband would only have more questions which she was in no state to answer. If she could have chosen anyone, it would have been her mum. She could tell her mum anything. But her mum had been dead for the best part of six years now.

So she sat and thought. She knew the police would soon know more about Darren Winters. There would be a lot to deal with. She would have to think carefully about what she would say.

She told herself not to fall into a deep well of emotion. She could not afford to be that indulgent right now. Many people were depending on her.

All the same, if she had been able to call her mum, she would have said one thing:

Help me.

21
Before

She took a long walk alone to regain her equilibrium. Wandering through the depths of the pine forest, she slowly sucked in and expelled lungfuls of air, enjoying its purity.

She had been thrown by how much she was enjoying the resort. She had initially been suspicious of Parkwood, despite its convenience and its self-billing as a carefully curated rural idyll. She had been pleasantly surprised to find that the place delivered what it promised online: a bucolic woodland getaway, majoring on outdoor life. Exactly what was required.

She had never been good at being on holiday; she had been told that throughout her life, by friends and boyfriends. She had always pleaded a lack of experience – she had never been taught.

And now here she was on holiday with the person who had never taught her.

Well, you know, *reasons*.

Her mum's suggestion to take this break together had actually been manna from heaven. For once, she had been there when needed, with perfect timing.

Ironically.

First of all, the thought of not being shut away within four walls, restricted, trapped, and fearful. It was nothing short of a liberation. She was an outdoors person at heart. Like so many, she was craving it.

Second of all, well . . .

She'd had to come out and walk, to escape. She knew now: a holiday isn't just the setting, is it? A holiday is also about who you're with.

How was it possible, with everything that was going on, for her mother to be so lacking in sensitivity or empathy for her daughter's situation? Seemingly the only thing her mother could talk about was the upset caused to *her* by her daughter's inability to deliver a grandchild. Why, after all these years, was this woman still unable to understand the impact of her words and actions?

The sense of shame. It pervaded her body.

She was drowning in it.

She did not need to be told she was a failure. She knew it. She felt it, viscerally. She saw it in Tim's eyes too.

She had spent the majority of her life being submerged by the feelings and opinions of others. It caused her palpitations in the night, when she woke in the small pristine bedroom with the trees crowding round the windows, branches audibly brushing the edge of the roof. Even here, everything was pressing in on her.

No more.

Soon nothing would be the same. There would be no going back. It was not something you could retrieve or unarrange. It would all be final. That was the whole point.

It was the first time in her life where she had a secret so absolute that literally no one else could know. She had heard that every person who was told a secret, even if sworn to secrecy, would always tell one other person. So she had made sure she had told no one about this. Even though she had felt the temptation: to write a letter or a note, to leave a confession that could be found later. But that would undermine everything.

It must be absolute.

What was she worrying about anyway? No one cared about her. No one thought about what she needed.

Well, maybe one person. But that was entirely transactional.

She emerged into the clearing which housed the standing stone. No one else was around. She walked up to it and laid her hands on it for a few minutes, leaning in, putting her whole body's energy into it until she felt stupid.

Then she sat beneath it, her back pressed up against the lumpy texture, in silence, for half an hour, thinking about what was ahead.

She felt strangely calm. She would go through with it; she was certain. It was the only option, the only thing that was keeping her going.

The reason she had come here.

22

Alice had already managed to pass the high-ropes area of Parkwood a number of times today without bumping into Lee Parker. This time, however, as she moved, head down, through the same area, she saw him notice her, immediately stop what he was doing and jog-run over to intercept her.

'Hey!' She watched him look round to check nobody else was observing. He seemed tense. Normal Lee was difficult enough. Lee under pressure was a man they all knew to avoid.

'Been looking for you. Nasty day.'

His tone was matey, but Alice and Lee were not mates. When she'd started work at Parkwood she had once let slip that she had been brought here for a day when she was younger, with a distant aunt who had taken pity on her. (Alice's parents could never afford to bring her somewhere like Parkwood.) Lee had been one of the instructors who had first taken her on the high ropes. He had joked how that made him feel old (Alice felt that Lee did not want to consider himself as anywhere near old) but he was glad he'd popped her cherry. Since then if he needed or wanted something he would remember that little factual nugget and bring it out into the light to emphasize their connection. Alice suspected Lee did not do that with just her. She'd once heard someone describe him as 'transactional' and she thought she understood what that meant.

'Quick one, sure we're both busy,' he said. 'If anyone asks, can you say you gave me a lift home last night? Cos my car had a puncture.'

Alice processed the request. 'Um . . .'

'Trust me. It'll make things simpler. Don't worry about anything you saw, or how it'll reflect on anyone. That stuff happens all the time – has done for ever.'

He was asking her to lie. 'I don't know,' she said.

'Honestly, people won't even care. There's bigger stuff going on.'

Alice knew she had to be careful. She did not feel she could predict Lee's behaviour. She did not know the full extent of what he had done the night before. As she considered her options, she judged that it would be best to agree now and figure it out later. It would mean she could get away from him swiftly.

So she responded with a simple 'OK.' Non-committal, non-judgemental. Could she go now?

Lee nodded, and squeezed her shoulder. 'Good girl.'

She looked him in the eye. 'Any idea who it is? Or what happened?'

He evaded her gaze, again checking if they were being watched. 'Not a clue.' Then he clapped his hands together, which made her jump slightly. 'Right, back to it.'

He ran back to where he'd been working previously.

Alice thought she had said the right thing.

For now.

23

'You realize we look like we're doing some kind of extreme walking,' said Harry.

It was true, thought Nicola. She and Harry were not-running. The sight of two police officers running through the site could set off panic. They couldn't even jog. So they had to walk purposefully, back from Lindsey's office to the incident-room lodge. Nicola tried not to laugh as she thought how daft they must look. She told herself to keep a straight face. As bad as running would look, a detective having a fit of the giggles would look much worse.

They were both struck by a key realization at exactly the same moment.

'We left our bikes back at Lindsey's office, didn't we?' said Harry.

'Yeah,' said Nicola. 'We did.' The day, now inexplicably edging into evening, had been a whirl and her mental bandwidth was clearly fully occupied with all the information they now had to impart to Mel. 'And we're supposed to be the brains of this investigation.'

'Speak for yourself,' said Harry, and now they were both trying not to laugh, still doing weird fast walking. Nicola was grateful for even the tiniest shard of levity. At times like these Harry was the exact partner she needed.

As they strode back towards their lodge, they passed near the front security gate. Nicola glanced over. A woman in her twenties, with cropped dark hair, was leaning on the security gate in a way that did not instantly endear her to Nicola. She was holding a phone and waiting to be dealt with.

'DS Bridge, can I help you?' asked Nicola as they got to the gate.

'Imogen Swift, I'm a local reporter. Can you confirm that a man has been killed here overnight?'

Nicola felt her instinctive reaction to this woman had been right. This was not going to be helpful.

'I'm going to have to ask you to move back from the gate, please, and return to the main road.'

'You didn't answer my question.'

'Where did you say you were from?'

'I'm a locally based reporter. I supply stories to a number of outlets,' said Imogen.

'Then you'll have seen the media statement we put out.'

'I'm looking for more detail.'

'That's all the detail we'll be supplying for now.'

'Is the victim local? Was it a violent death?'

Nicola stepped in close to Imogen Swift and spoke calmly. 'You are taking up time we do not have. Move away from the gate and off-site now, and let us carry out our investigations. You'll be kept informed when we have something to say.'

Nicola turned on her heel and walked away. Harry remained for a second longer and Imogen caught his eye.

'What about you, cutie? Anything for me?'

Nicola stopped in her tracks and turned back, infuriated by hearing this woman flirt with Harry.

'Away from the gate, please,' smiled Harry and strode to catch up with Nicola.

Nicola nodded to Harry, glad he hadn't fallen for the easy compliment.

When she looked back, Imogen had gone.

As they re-entered the living space of Lodge 227, they saw it had been transformed. Mel had already begun to process the information gathered from today's interviews and transferred it to the walls of the lodge, which were now crammed with large graphic breakdowns of the Parkwood sites. Each wall had a different named section, on which were all the lodges and facilities. Next to each lodge, Mel had begun to put the names, ages and ID photos of the people who were staying there. He had also begun to colour-code each lodge by placing small dot stickers next to their profile, according to whether or not they could be ruled out. Mel had turned the living space of Lodge 277 into a diagrammatic representation of Parkwood Dorset.

'Whoa,' said Nicola appreciatively as they walked in.

'Incredible work, Mel,' said Harry.

'Uniform just dropped off their interview notes. Seemingly, they've not done a terrible job,' said Mel, not even looking up from his computer, once again demonstrating that compliments were wasted on him. 'Oh, and they've gone for the night, other than the two who'll be patrolling for visibility. I said that was fine.'

'Oh, did you?' said Nicola. She resisted the temptation to say: *maybe check with me first, next time!*

'So are you going to tell me about the victim's ID or shall I keep on with the task you've interrupted me from?' asked Mel.

'Neil Summers is actually Darren Winters,' Nicola began. 'Lindsey Moorfield's predecessor in the job as manager of Parkwood Dorset.'

'Which puts her in the frame, right?' asked Harry.

'Her and everyone else associated with this site, until we determine otherwise,' said Nicola, before machine-gunning out instructions. 'Now we've confirmed the victim's identity, we need to begin a "last seen alive" inquiry, nail down the last point he was seen and by whom. Prioritize talking to any staff who knew Winters or worked with him.'

She looked at the clock, realizing it would be too late to start questioning the majority of the staff this evening; it would have to be their priority in the morning. She felt the day vanishing from under her. 'We need to secure Winters' property, clothing and digital devices – Harry, assigning responsibility to you.'

Harry nodded. 'Copy that.'

'Mel, fast-track actions on Winters himself: background checks, lifestyle, associates, recent activity. Seemingly, no relatives here, but please confirm. Next of kin may be a daughter-in-law in Australia; Lindsey is providing details. Set up a video call for me as soon as possible, time difference allowing.'

Nicola took a second to mentally run through all the information they had gathered since their arrival less than twelve hours ago. 'He had nothing on him when found, not even a phone, and SOCO haven't located anything in the pool complex. Could he have been killed for something he had on him? Did the killer take stuff from the body? And a reminder we do not yet have sight of the murder weapon.'

Harry asked, 'How did he get into Parkwood? How did he get on to the system under an assumed name? Did he do it himself or did he have help? And if so, who? Doesn't that point to Lindsey herself?'

Nicola nodded. 'We also need to debrief on all the intel gathered today. Not least the guest in Lodge 50, who had a drone.'

'I'll add Conor Slater, 141. Not convinced on his alibi,' added Harry.

Nicola felt the need to collapse on to the sofa, as she processed this blizzard of information. There was a momentary silence within the lodge. She noticed Harry had also slumped on to a chair, staring into space.

She realized Mel was looking at them both. 'Have you two eaten?' he asked.

Nicola and Harry looked at each other blankly.

'Not since this morning, now you mention it,' said Harry.

Nicola looked at the clock. It was unaccountably half past seven. How was that possible? Mel was right. She could not think straight for much longer without sustenance.

'Not like you to be worried about our well-being, Mel,' Harry said.

'I'm not. It would just be helpful if you could both not be here until I've completed processing today's information. Perhaps you can go and eat food somewhere else while I do that.'

Harry looked to Nicola. 'I could eat,' he said. 'Then go on to Winters' address.'

'If we're quick,' Nicola replied. 'Mel, shall we get you something –'

'No,' said Mel. 'I've ordered. They're delivering to me here.'

'Oh!' said Nicola brightly. 'We could do the same, then.'

Mel looked up, horrified. 'I want you to go out. So I can work. You've already disturbed my rhythm.'

Mel's head dipped back down to focus on the screen and Nicola could not resist one more question. It was a game she and Harry sometimes played to make Mel's head bob up and down from his screen. 'What time are you planning to be here until?'

She saw Mel's face rise once more in exasperation, and she knew Harry was also suppressing a grin. 'I'm staying,' said Mel.

'What?'

'There's a bed, isn't there? I'm not wasting time travelling. I thought this was urgent.'

'No, it is,' said Nicola, impressed.

'Do you think you could go out immediately?' demanded Mel. It felt more of an order than a question now.

'Sure,' said Nicola and headed to the door, followed by Harry who threw a 'good luck' behind him as they stepped out the front door. Nicola was just pulling it closed when she heard Mel muttering to himself, 'It's not *luck*!'

As they walked towards the nearest food outlet, Harry said, 'I'm thinking it's not a bad shout from Mel about staying. We're probably gonna be here till gone midnight, maybe later. An hour's drive home, sleep badly, hour's drive back first thing, doesn't seem the best use of time.'

'You're going to stay as well?' asked Nicola.

'I've got everything I need in the car: spare clothes, toiletries, the lot,' bragged Harry. 'It was you who told me to always be on standby.'

It was true, she had. Right now, however, Nicola was torn. She should be going home tonight, to see her son Ethan and make sure he was OK. But her urgent duty was here. She couldn't expect Harry and Mel to make this sacrifice and not demand it of herself. That's what leadership was. And in a case this time-sensitive, where the hours were evaporating before her eyes, extra hours on-site would be invaluable.

It was as if Harry could sense her divided loyalties. 'Wouldn't expect you to do it, though, Skip. You've got family obligations.'

That settled it. She could do without being patronized by Harry. 'There's three bedrooms, right?'

*

'You're going to *stay*?' said Mike on the phone.

He had just described his conversation with Ethan as 'bumpy but not disastrous' when she told him her intent.

'Yeah,' she said breezily. No biggie, Mike. 'Would you be able to grab me a few things, shove them in the bag by the front door and drive them over?'

She spent so much of her time trying to achieve a work-life balance and then a new case came along and ruined everything. This was the past source of conflict for her and Mike, which had resulted in his relationship with another woman and a near catastrophic break in their marriage. It was the reason they had relocated to Dorset. She did not need him to remind her of all the promises she had made as part of that move. Not at this moment. She knew she was pushing it.

There was a pause, and then, 'All right.'

Nicola and Harry grabbed a table in the corner of the Italian restaurant: terracotta tiles and nearly realistic plastic plants. The plants reflected so much at Parkwood, thought Nicola: ersatz, designed to feel like the real thing, but not the real thing itself. The whole site was an unnerving impression of reality. It was not alive, not spontaneous; it was planned and charged for.

She remembered discussing it with Mike on their car journey home from the North Yorkshire Parkwood, as seven-year-old Ethan slept in the back. Mike had said, 'It's just Butlin's for the middle classes,' as if that were an end of it. She had defended it then, grateful for its convenience and sheen of quality. Today, though, she saw Mike's point. It felt forced, false and a little creepy.

The restaurant was only half full, despite the site being at almost full occupancy. 'Quiet tonight,' she commented to the girl (pale, gaunt, no more than nineteen) taking their order.

'Everyone's freaked out,' said the girl matter-of-factly. 'Staying in, in case it's a serial killer. You ready to order?'

They ordered: salad with extra chicken for Harry, pizza for Nicola.

'I don't think we've ever eaten together at an actual table,' said Harry.

Nicola realized he was probably right: in cars, at desks, sitting waiting for someone or for something to happen. But not at a table. 'Well, cheers.'

They chinked soft drinks. She felt for a brief flash like they were on a date, which they absolutely were not.

Almost as soon as the glasses chinked Nicola realized there was a group of people hovering, moving closer in to the table where she and Harry were sitting.

'You're the police, right?' Before Nicola could respond, the woman asking the question had followed up with: 'What aren't you telling us?'

There was a murmur of assent from the group round the woman which emboldened her as spokesperson. 'Should we be worried? Should we even be staying here right now? Are any of us safe?'

Here we go.

Nicola angled her chair and utilized her most reassuring tone. 'There's nothing to suggest anyone else here is at risk. If that changes, we'll let you know immediately.'

'They won't give us refunds if we leave,' said a man at the back accusingly, as if this was Nicola's fault. 'I checked. And we won't be able to claim on insurance either.'

'We've saved all bloody year for this,' said another man who Nicola guessed might be the first man's brother.

'I can imagine,' said Nicola sympathetically, before the first woman chimed back in.

'Why's there not more police? I'd think the place would be swarming with your lot, but I haven't seen anyone in uniform. As a deterrent, like.' She seemed to have another thought and began to look confused, tripping over her own thinking. 'I mean, I know it's a bit late for a deterrent for whoever got killed, but for the rest of us, like, how do we know it's not gonna happen again tonight?'

'We have uniform, plain clothes and forensic officers currently operating on-site,' said Nicola.

The waitress deposited their food with no comment about either the food or the crowd that had gathered. Nicola moved her chair back round to face the table, in order to demarcate that the conversation was over, but a twenty-year-old woman with a thick Devon accent butted in: 'Have you interviewed the staff? Cos me and my mum are thinking: it's probably one of the staff. Got to be, hasn't it?'

'Not *necessarily*, Jade,' cautioned a woman who Nicola presumed to be Jade's mother.

Nicola could sense people at other tables going quiet, and the occupants starting to turn and look over. It felt like all the eyes in the room were turning to them. As she glanced around, she saw that three of the chefs and two of the serving staff (including their own waitress) were watching from the open kitchen pass.

'We're asking every single person to account for their movements. It's a very fast-moving investigation.'

'Doesn't look that fast-moving at the moment,' said a chippy bloke with a Bristol accent, nodding at Nicola's pizza. 'Three courses, is it? And wine too! I s'pose us taxpayers are on the hook for that.'

Before Nicola could respond, the man's wife slapped his arm. 'Right! Go and stand outside, Brian,' she snapped, as if to a toddler. 'They're not even drinking wine; anyone can see that. Go on! Out!'

Nicola watched as Brian, amazingly and rather sheepishly, got up and headed to the exit. 'I'm sorry,' said his wife to the group. 'He never used to be like this. It's since we got high-speed fibre; he just spends hours on YouTube.'

'Bloody hell, love,' said another woman. 'I wish *my* husband would put himself on the naughty step like that every time I tell him to shut up!'

The whole group laughed then, and Brian's wife clasped the arm of the other woman, while fanning herself, laughing. But then five men who looked to be in their thirties stood up from the next table and squared up to Nicola and Harry's table.

'We've decided we'll be patrolling tonight,' said the leader. He was thickset, with neck tattoos. 'Keep people safe.'

Nicola pushed her chair back fast and stood eye to eye with the man. He took a step back involuntarily – just the effect Nicola had intended. Her height always came in handy at moments like these.

'I'm afraid you won't, sir. There are to be no unauthorized patrols around this site.'

'And how you gonna stop us?' asked the second of the men.

'I'll arrest you,' said Nicola succinctly. *Duh.*

It seemed to take the man by surprise. 'Can you do that?'

'Of course I can do that. I'm police.'

'Arrest us for walking?!'

'I can arrest you for obstructing an investigation, which is what you'll be doing. And I'll recommend you get a lifetime ban from all Parkwood resorts.' Nicola felt both these statements were a stretch, but she had had enough and wanted to eat her pizza. 'You do not need to, and must not, take matters into your own hands.'

The ringleader wasn't shying away. 'Well, if something else happens tonight, the blood's on your hands,' he said.

'I beg your pardon, sir?' Nicola said, stepping forward. As she did, she saw the ringleader's mate behind him wince and lay a hand on his arm. 'Come on, man, let's go and have another pint.'

The men left, leaving the first group of complainers still watching. The woman who'd kicked it off looked awkwardly at Nicola as if she regretted her earlier tone. 'We're all a bit on edge, aren't we?' she said apologetically and walked away.

No, thought Nicola, watching her go. You're just keen to air your grievances, or form a mob, without thinking. This was the mood these days. It did not augur well. Nicola found it unnerving.

The whole incident only proved how much they needed to get a grip on this case before the mood at Parkwood soured further. She suddenly felt guilty for even having taken twenty minutes out of their evening to come and eat.

Harry had been gesturing for the waitress to come over and as she arrived, he said, 'I think we're gonna take these back to the lodge. Could you box them up?'

The girl looked panicked. 'I can ask,' she said, as if it was the most revolutionary question she'd ever heard.

As the girl departed to find takeaway boxes, Harry turned to Nicola and said in a low whisper, 'Is it bad to say how much I fucking hate the British public?'

Nicola burst out laughing, despite herself. People at other tables looked back round, and she stifled her laugh.

Harry looked back at her, beaming, enjoying having made her laugh.

24

'How was dinner?' asked Mel as they came back into the lodge clasping takeaway boxes.

'Opinionated,' said Nicola, checking her messages. The pathologist, claiming to have driven 'like a lunatic' to examine the body, was available for a Zoom call at 9 p.m. to give preliminary findings. Harry was placing their takeaway boxes on the side, when they both glanced at what Mel was eating while sat at his computer.

Chips and rice on a white plate.

Mel caught their eye. He paused with his fork midway to his mouth. 'What?'

'Nothing,' said Nicola quickly, as Harry said, 'No, nothing,' almost simultaneously.

'No, go on!' said Mel defiantly, sensing there was something he was being picked up on.

Nicola knew she and Harry were thinking the same thing. They had joked that Mel only ate carbohydrates that were as pale as his own complexion.

'No vegetables?' asked Harry.

Mel looked down at his plate, uncomprehending. He stabbed at a chip and held it up.

'A potato is a vegetable, Westlife.'

'All right, no protein, then?' asked Harry.

'It fills me up. That's what food's supposed to do, isn't it? It's fuel.'

'Not just fuel,' said Harry. 'You need nutrients, vitamins, minerals –'

'Yes, thank you, Dr Brian Cox,' said Mel huffily.

'He's an astrophysicist,' said Harry.

'And you're not the food police.'

'Just tell me that's not how you eat every day,' persisted Harry, and Nicola could see Mel becoming a little more prickly.

Leave it now, Harry.

'Obviously, when I cook at home, I have different things,' said Mel.

Nicola felt herself being drawn in. They knew nothing of Mel's home life. 'Sorry, Mel, I don't even think I know if you're married or single,' she said.

He looked at her. 'No, you don't, do you?' He speared a quartet of chips, and bit them off the edge of the fork, without adding anything else. He seemed, as ever, comfortable (if not pleased) with the awkward silence that followed. Nicola had come to think, over the past year, that Mel lived for these moments when others might feel awkward, and part of his joy in life was creating opportunities for them to occur. 'I didn't realize we were doing personal information now we're out of the office. Isn't that an HR breach these days? How's your new girlfriend, Westlife?' he added from beneath a mouthful of white rice.

Nicola's head spun like an owl who had just been alerted to the presence of a mouse.

'Fine, thank you,' said Harry, suddenly fascinated by a particular piece of paper. 'Early days.'

Was he blushing? He was! Harry was blushing! He also couldn't look at her.

'And what's her name?' pursued Mel.

‘Audra,’ muttered Harry.

‘Audrey?’ said Mel loudly, leaning forward for clarification. ‘That’s very old-fashioned.’

‘*Audra*,’ Harry hissed back.

Mel’s face grimaced, as if he refused to countenance the reply. ‘There’s a lot of names these days.’

‘I like it,’ said Nicola, looking at Harry. ‘Where’d you meet?’ she followed up, as casually as she could.

Harry winced like he’d pulled a muscle.

Oh God, am I causing him physical pain by asking that?

‘On an app,’ said Harry, nodding.

‘Oh. Yes. Course,’ said Nicola sympathetically.

‘Dear Lord,’ said Mel, chasing the last grains of rice around his plate with a teaspoon, as he looked at Nicola. ‘It’s a different world now, isn’t it?’

Nicola took exception to Mel lumping her in with him. *I’m closer to Harry’s age than to yours*, she thought indignantly. Then: *Aren’t I? I must be.*

Her phone was buzzing. She fumbled for it.

‘Still, I wish you the best, Westlife, I really do,’ Mel was saying. ‘Or should I say, I wish your lady the best!’

‘I’m off to Winters’ home address in Eagleforth,’ said Harry.

Nicola held up her phone. ‘That’s Mike with my stuff.’ She made for the door, hearing Harry saying to Mel, ‘We’re all staying now.’

Mel sounded disappointed, bordering on offended. ‘I was looking forward to having the place to myself!’

25

The door on the wardrobe in Lodge 141 was slammed open. The clothes within were grabbed from the rail and thrown down on to the bed, still on their hangers.

A suitcase was shoved on to the bed, next to the clothes, and flipped open, before the assailant returned to the wardrobe to grab a second tranche of clothes.

'Do we really think this is the best idea?' asked Emma, attempting to process Conor's decision-making.

'Yep,' said Conor as he slipped clothes off hangers, folded them up with little regard for future creases, and piled them into the open suitcase.

'I don't want to go. We never get this much time together normally,' said Emma.

Conor was emphatic. 'The whole trip has got a shadow over it now.'

'Not for us. Not so much that we need to *leave.*' There was a pause as an atom of doubt made its way speedily through Emma's mind. She stopped Conor from folding up another shirt, placing her hand on her husband's arm. 'Is there anything you need to tell me?'

'Of course not,' Conor snapped back. He took a breath. 'We only have a precious few days to relax and switch off – and instead we get this. Police interviews – I mean, did you see the way he looked at us? Also, it's not half the place it could be without being able to use the pool.'

'I think you're being a little paranoid,' said Emma

gently. 'Bella's having a great time. We still have loads of stuff booked. She's out in the fresh air playing all day, exhausted in the evenings and sleeping brilliantly. As am I, for once!'

Thankfully, thought Conor.

'And we'll still get time together, all three of us. That's the reason we came. Right?'

Conor was having none of it. 'I'm too tightly wound now,' he protested.

'I'll get you a deep-tissue massage at the spa!' said Emma. 'And then after that massage, I'll give you my own special massage treatment. With the emphasis on *treat*.'

Emma was moving in on him, but Conor shook her off.

'Come on, Em. I've decided and I'd like your support.'

'You can't just ask for support like I'm obliged or not allowed to have an opinion. Also, if we skedaddle out of here, how's that gonna look to the police?'

Conor folded his arms defiantly. 'They can't keep us here by force. It's not a prison. We're not legally obliged to stay. Anyway, we've already talked to them. What else do they need? Look, if we get away now, we might be able to book a long weekend break somewhere else. Maybe another Parkwood even. There's one in Gloucestershire, I think. It wouldn't take us so long to get there. If I drive, you can check availability. Bella can sleep in the car.'

'Don't be daft! Take a breath and stay here,' insisted Emma. 'It's getting late.'

'I'm telling you, we're going!'

Conor did not know how to be any more definite. Emma had to understand. He had to make her, but his mind was so jumbled that he felt unable to present a clear case which might prove helpful to his cause right now.

They needed to leave, before someone asked him more questions he did not have good answers for.

He reached past Emma to grab another handful of clothes.

26

Nicola met Mike at the lodge. He handed her a bag with clothes over the barrier pole. His car was parked the other side.

'They won't let me in,' he said.

'That's my fault,' said Nicola. 'No exceptions. Not even husbands.'

'Everything all right?'

Nicola shook her head and said, quietly, 'Body in the pool.'

Mike's eyebrows raised. 'Oh, *fuck*.'

'Yeah.'

She had to give him something, for him to understand the seriousness, and the demands. He had driven all the way out here after all.

'So, Ethan?'

'Came in, went to his room, didn't see him, then hour or two later, didn't see him really, he made food, AirPods in, then a bit later I heard the door slam and he was out and he's been out ever since. No note, no nothing. So that's gone well.'

Nicola winced. 'I'm sorry I'm not there.'

Mike smiled. 'You're not missing anything. I'll let you know if anything changes.' He looked ahead into the resort and asked, 'So where are you staying?'

'In one of the lodges.'

'What, all of you?!'

'They're big enough for all of us. You've been in them. It's three bedrooms.'

'Who's all of us?'

Nicola sensed, for a second, something in his tone.

Oh. This is new.

'Me, Mel . . . and Harry.'

She was slightly ashamed that she enjoyed the power of the moment. She had understood for a while that Mike thought Harry was just a little bit too pretty to be her work partner. And he had occasionally remarked on how 'you and he seem to have good . . . chemistry' with a tone that suggested chemistry was on a par with chlamydia.

'All in the same lodge?' asked Mike.

'All in the same lodge.'

'Right,' said Mike tersely. 'Any idea when you'll be back?'

'Too early to say,' replied Nicola.

'OK,' said Mike in a tone which indicated he did not really think it was OK. 'Let me know if there's anything else you need.'

He leaned over the pole to offer a kiss. She leaned in and he pulled her to him. A lingering kiss. She wouldn't say it was a power move or a message, but somehow it had an edge of that. It felt like a statement of ownership.

'I'll call you tomorrow,' she said.

They parted and walked away in opposite directions.

As Nicola began to head back towards the lodges, not sure how she felt about that gesture of Mike's, she saw a car pulling out of the car park. As it came near, she stood in the middle of the road, flagging it down. The car slowed, seemingly reluctantly. Nicola gestured to it to stop and for the driver to wind down the window. He complied.

'Hi,' said Nicola. 'DS Bridge. Can I ask what you're doing?'

The man in the driver's seat looked like he was in his forties. He smiled at Nicola. 'We've decided we'd like to leave.

Because of everything.' He gestured to a daughter in the back. 'We're worried for her, you know?' His tone appealed to Nicola's empathy, talking to her as an equal.

Nicola gave no ground. 'We're asking all guests to remain on-site until we've finished the initial phase of our investigation.'

The woman in the passenger seat – most likely the driver's partner – quietly muttered, 'Told you . . .' in a sing-song voice while looking out of the windscreen.

'What's your name, sir?' Nicola asked the driver.

'Conor Slater.'

'Which lodge are you in?'

'141,' said the passenger and then pointed to herself. 'Emma Slater – Conor's wife.' She pointed to the child in the back. 'And that's Bella. Say hi to the nice detective, Bella.'

'Hello,' murmured Bella sleepily, waving at Nicola.

Nicola saw Conor give Emma an irritated glare – *let me do the talking, please!* He turned back to Nicola. 'You're saying we can't leave: is that an edict – or a request?'

Edict. Get you.

'It's a request, from the police, sir.'

Conor smiled at her. 'But it's not legally binding?'

Don't smile at me when you're disobeying my request.

'Do you have an urgent reason for leaving now?'

'Bella, you know . . . we're worried, you understand.'

I understand you have the air of a panicked man.

'The lodges are secure. Parkwood have put extra security staff on patrol and my officers are also on-site. We have no reason to suspect anyone's at risk.'

'We did give all our details to your colleague earlier today,' said Conor. 'Is that not enough?'

'We're in the process of analysing and cross-referencing

all today's interviews. That may take us a moment as you'll understand. Until then, the request to remain on-site remains in place.'

He was keeping the engine still idling. Was that defiance?

'What would be the consequences if we did leave, Detective Sergeant?' asked Conor.

'That would make you the first party to leave in the wake of this incident. That would draw attention to you, and mark you out compared to those who've stayed, and so you – both – would become persons of interest to the inquiry. We would focus more attention on you, in order to rule you out. Your leaving would also increase pressure on our resources, which would be especially unhelpful.'

'Whereas if we stayed?' asked Emma from across the other seat.

'None of that would apply,' responded Nicola. 'And you would not have diverted any police resources.'

Nicola watched Emma look to Conor with a raised eyebrow.

Conor sighed. 'This whole thing is really confronting.'

'You are, as you've said, legally free to leave; I'm just asking for your cooperation and patience for a bit longer.'

Nicola stood back to allow the occupants of the car time to think. She watched Conor staring ahead at the security lodge and the barrier currently blocking the car's exit. She looked on as he tapped the steering wheel absently, weighing up his decision.

She noticed Emma's eyes widen in a subliminal signal. *I don't agree with him.*

After what seemed like an age, Conor looked back up at her. 'Fine. You win. We'll stay.'

'I'll let you turn the car around.' Nicola was magnanimous in victory.

She stood back from the road and watched Conor wind the window up and manoeuvre the car round and back into the car park. As he drove past, Nicola could see him and Emma having heated words.

Nicola stood where she was, observing the car as it slid back into the parking space it had vacated a few minutes earlier. She noted down the car's licence number. She watched Conor and Emma get out of the car and take their luggage and Bella back in the direction of Lodge 141.

Then she went to the security lodge and stressed again that nobody should be allowed to leave the site without her or Harry being made aware.

As she walked back to the lodge, and in spite of what she had implied, Nicola reflected that Conor Slater had just done a terrific job of pulling the spotlight of the investigation round on to himself.

27

It was many years since Harry had had any reason to go to Eagleforth.

His memory was of a sleepy village, so he was surprised to find a bustling community even at this time of the evening. The pub and carvery's large car park was full, the petrol station and convenience store had a continuous throughput of cars and the main street's cafes, coffee shops and takeaways were doing steady business. This, Harry thought, must be the Parkwood proximity effect.

The housing stock too had changed. One side of Eagleforth comprised terraced streets of workers' cottages, which had presumably served what had once been the old country estate, along with a handful of more grand Edwardian houses. On the other side of the main road sat a large new-build estate constructed within the past twenty years to accommodate Parkwood employees.

Winters' house was located at the outer edge of the older section, where the terraces were replaced by more spaced-out old-school bungalows. Harry parked outside a corner bungalow. A small fenced-in garden surrounded the house on both sides, the low fencing curving to mirror the road. It had an entrance arch and a small wooden gate with peeling white paintwork framed with honeysuckle.

As Harry opened the gate, it creaked and stuck. After a couple of shoves, he managed to get it to give, and he walked through.

Then he heard it.

A dog was howling.

The sound was coming from inside the house: not angry or aggressive but mournful, sad.

Harry walked up the path, getting closer to the dog's howl. He tried the front door carefully. Locked. Harry looked up to see if there were any windows open. Nothing.

He walked through a side gate and round the side of the house past the bins. At the back of the house there was a small relatively bare garden – a lawn and a few plants. Harry pushed his face against the back window – the kitchen. He could hear the dog more clearly now and as he peered through, he could see all the way to the front door, and the dog sitting by it, its head thrown back as it howled disconsolately.

Harry stood back and looked at the house.

A small top window to the side of the kitchen was half open. At a guess Harry thought it was the downstairs loo. He got on tiptoes, reached in through the gap and further down to unlatch the larger main window below it.

It was big enough to climb through.

Harry landed unceremoniously on top of the lid-down loo and proceeded from there into the kitchen. As he opened the door from the cloakroom into the kitchen, he heard the clatter of claws and some very yappy barking and growling.

The dog was approaching fast and loud and had some sharp teeth, despite it being small to medium-sized – Harry thought it could easily take a chunk out of his leg.

Harry had been waiting for this moment for many, many months.

He reached inside his pocket, pulled out a small baggy, and scattered a handful of treats in front of him. The dog froze, confused. It looked up at Harry, cocking its head, and then launched itself on to the scattered offering. It took about three seconds for the dog to hoover them up, after which it turned back to Harry, unsure.

For once, Harry had Mel to thank. Mel had been telling him about an old colleague who carried dog treats with him every day on the job, in case he had to deal with a recalcitrant dog. Harry thought that sounded stupid, until he thought about it more and realized it might be genius.

Right now, it was indeed genius. The dog's expression seemed to say *Do we know each other? Cos I don't think so, but you have treats.*

'Sit,' said Harry optimistically.

The dog sat, neatly.

Harry's eyebrow shot up in delight. 'Oh! Good dog!' He threw down some more for good measure.

He was never going to give Mel the satisfaction of telling him what had happened here. He would be unbearable.

Harry took the opportunity to look around. He started with the kitchen, which he noted was minimal, tidy. He opened the cupboards – a small number of plates, bowls, glasses and mugs. Same with the cutlery drawer. The house of someone who lived alone. Harry wondered how long Darren Winters had lived here.

He headed into the back bedroom. As he pushed the door open, he saw it.

The room had been trashed.

Drawers all over the floor, their contents tipped out. Wardrobe doors open, contents scattered across the floor.

Harry knew better than to touch anything. He put in a call immediately to Nicola, who told him to ring Reeta and get her and her team out there. All the while, as Harry paced the hall, the dog followed him back and forth, looking up at him for guidance, or possibly treats.

Before he rang Reeta, Harry took a look into the front room. The same was true of this room. It had been upended. Chairs turned upside down, cupboards ransacked.

And yet the kitchen had been left. No sign of any disturbance when he came in. Why?

Had Darren Winters' killer been here, either before or after the murder?

And why had the dog not barked or attacked whoever had done this?

Harry sat on the floor in the hall and waited for Reeta and her team to arrive.

The dog came to sit at his feet.

Harry scrumpled its ear and tried not to think too much about this cute, friendly dog now being an orphan.

28

The Zoom summarizing the pathologist's initial report was short and not particularly sweet.

Darren Winters had been killed by three stab wounds. The blade was most likely a kitchen knife with an eight-inch blade. He went into the water when he was still alive, and it's likely his head was held under to ensure he was dead. Reeta's analysis of signs of a struggle was correct. Given the number of complicating factors, time of death could only be reliably limited by the closing time of the pool and the discovery of the body.

The call was over within seven minutes.

Nicola knew the next call would not be as short. It would be difficult and painful for the next of kin. But she hoped it might finally bring them some answers about Darren Winters.

'I'm sorry to have to tell you this, and most of all I'm sorry it can't be in person,' said Nicola.

The face of the woman on her laptop screen did not move, and for a second Nicola thought that the connection between this small lodge in Dorset and the woman's house in Melbourne had gone down.

After a moment, Donna – mid-forties, sharp-featured, tanned, blonde-haired – looked away from the screen, seemingly trying to process what she'd just been told.

'Fuck,' she exhaled quietly, before looking back down

the camera lens at Nicola half a world away. 'How did it happen?'

'We're still establishing the exact circumstances, but we believe he was killed.'

Nicola noticed Donna recoil slightly, her neck jerking back in. But then something more unexpected.

Another silence, during which Donna nodded to herself. A couple of times. Small nods of acceptance.

'Right.'

That was the only word, but even thousands of miles away over a dodgy internet connection, Nicola wanted to excavate the thoughts behind it. Before she could, Donna spoke again.

'I'm surprised I'm still down as his next of kin. I hadn't heard from him in a few years.' If Nicola had been expecting an emotional outpouring, Donna was not providing it. 'How did it happen?'

Her curiosity seemed factual, thought Nicola.

'I'm afraid he was stabbed. It's unclear what the motive was. I know this must be a shock, but would you mind if I asked you a few initial questions? So we can get a picture of him.'

Donna shrugged, resigned. 'Sure, but . . . look, I don't know how much I can tell you.' She checked her watch. 'I guess I can give you a few minutes before the kids start kicking off.'

'How old are your kids?' asked Nicola, using them to segue into information-gathering. She was looking down at the scant data she had been provided.

'Ten and eight,' replied Donna. 'Ely and Fleur.'

'And, forgive me, their father –'

'Mark,' completed Donna.

'Mark was Darren's son. Correct?'

Donna nodded. 'Yeah.'

'And Mark died when?'

'In 2019,' said Donna. 'We'd been here in Melbourne just under two years. Darren came over and stayed for, like, two weeks when Mark died. And obviously I knew he was going through as much as I was, but it just didn't work. It's not like we'd ever been the same people. Mark wasn't like his dad. And without Mark there, to mediate or whatever, or even just to provide a reason for why we were in the same room . . . it was pretty disastrous, at an already disastrous time.

'I'm not sure we ever got over that. When he went back, that was the last I saw of him. I would send pictures of the kids twice a year, birthdays and Christmas, but I didn't get replies. It's not like he was present in their lives. If I want to give him the benefit of the doubt, maybe it was too painful, maybe they reminded him of Mark. I dunno. I could never figure it out.'

She paused, reconsidering. 'Who am I kidding? I don't have to give him the benefit of the doubt. He was cold. He was self-interested. He offered nothing, unless it gave him an advantage.'

It wasn't hard to detect the anger in Donna's voice. She wasn't mourning Darren Winters, even two minutes after learning of his death. It felt to Nicola as if Donna was telling her that the moral balance of the universe might have been righted a little.

She kept to establishing the facts. 'D'you mind telling me how Mark died?'

Donna nodded. 'Car accident. Out driving on a remote road, off to a sales appointment for work, took a corner, car went off the edge, down a ravine.' She took a breath, shaking her head. 'Fucking idiot,' she said, not without affection.

Nicola was noting all this down in her notepad at the side of her laptop. 'And his dad was married at that time?'

Donna shook her head. 'Divorced. Way before I met Mark.' She paused. 'I think she got out pretty quick when she saw the guy she'd got herself. She divorced Darren when Mark was two, I think. He was brought up by his mum. She died maybe ten years ago.' She took a breath. 'Lot of death.'

As Donna spoke, Nicola felt a presence beside her, just out of the range of the camera so that Donna would have been unaware. Mel was standing there, like he wanted to tell her something. She gave him a glance: not now!

But Mel stayed there. It was like he was vibrating.

She threw him a second glance: go away! She used her hand out of the sight of the camera to wave him away. But instead of going, Mel shoved a piece of paper on the table in front of her laptop. He nodded at it meaningfully, silently.

God's sake. He looks like a toddler bursting for the loo.

Donna was looking straight down the camera at Nicola now. 'So I can't sit here and tell you I'm a hundred per cent surprised. Not after all that business with the woman at Parkwood.'

Nicola felt a jolt go through her system.

At her side, Mel flapped his arms up and down in frustration at Nicola as if to say: *see!*

'The woman,' said Nicola neutrally, wondering how she could get out of this call.

'I mean, do you guys even know to this day what the fuck went on there?' asked Donna.

What am I meant to say?

She settled on, 'Right,' and looked sympathetic as Mel pointed at the paper – open the paper, read what's on the paper. She tried to, without looking distracted. But the piece of paper was dense with text.

'Listen, if that's all, can we leave it for now? I appreciate you letting me know. But I'm supposed to be meeting someone and I'm already way behind.'

'Of course,' said Nicola. 'I may need to get back to you with other questions. I'm sorry to be the bringer of bad news.'

Donna nodded, and then shrugged once more. 'Like I say . . . Anyway, thanks.' She raised a hand and logged off.

As soon as the call had ended, Nicola spun towards Mel. '*What* is the matter with you?!'

Mel was looking fit to burst and his tone was as insistent as Nicola had ever known.

'You have to read that. *Right now*.'

29

The preceding hour had been an unusual and uncomfortable situation for Mel Hardiman; he did not have as much information as he would like.

Mel sometimes reflected that he had chosen an occupation which occasionally put him in a place he didn't relish: under-informed. So he had always treated it as a point of principle that anything he said, any information or thesis he provided, had its basis in fact and could be backed up with hard data and documentation.

He realized that's what made him irritating to others, including colleagues who were more relaxed about speculation and hypothesizing. That was not for Mel. Mel felt facts were out there; they just needed to be caught in his butterfly net.

His greatest asset in this was his computer. Mel regarded his computer, his portal to the universe of information, as his trusty sidekick. Mel regarded his laptop as he believed American cops regarded their handguns: essential to doing the job properly. Facts were Mel's weapon.

So it was startling to Mel that as the day had worn on, and fact-gathering happened at pace all around him, he had found himself feeling discomfited and anxious. At least, more discomfited and anxious than usual.

At first he thought it was the environment: the smell of fresh paint and new furniture was unnerving him. It was at odds with the waft of history Mel rather enjoyed in their supposedly temporary office in an old bank on Bredy High Street, let alone the old and pleasantly musty house Mel lived in just outside of the town. This, coupled with the fact that the first day of this investigation had whizzed by so fast, with tasks, questions and set-up demands being blasted at him, meant that he had not had time to think for himself.

Gradually, across the afternoon and into the evening, as people stopped barging in and out of the lodge and he was able to take a breath, he realized it was something else entirely that was disturbing him: the half-sense of an incomplete fact.

Something nagging him about Parkwood. Something from the distant past. Had there been some kind of incident here? But he didn't know what it was, or how it had resolved. It clearly had not been major enough to lodge in the repository of his brain.

So, as he ate and then digested the meal that Westlife and his boss had seemed unreasonably amused by, he finally got to be fully informed.

And rather worried.

'So, 2021, everything's weird, don't know if you remember,' said Mel to Nicola and Harry, just returned from transporting Winters' dog to the local rescue centre, as they stood behind him at his laptop.

In the screen he saw Nicola glance at Harry, thinking Mel couldn't see her, and say, 'Yes, I'm aware of the global pandemic.'

'Hospitality had been opened and closed and opened again. There were some restrictions, but this was the sort of place you could be outdoors, in your designated bubble of six. Meanwhile, Wessex Police – before our some would say ill-fated merger into Three Counties – is in what could politely be called something of a state. There's the whole mad business of what we should be policing, we're fining gatherings, losing public support, we've been through two chief constables in three years, morale is poor and I'm not sure we were attracting the best of the best.'

He stopped and assessed his own words. 'I may be a partisan narrator. I'd been exiled to the far east.'

'What, China?' asked Harry, incredulously.

'No!' said Mel. 'Bournemouth. Far east of the *county*. They had me doing all the fag-end stuff nobody else wanted.'

'But *here* . . .' said Nicola, and Mel realized she was nudging him back on to what happened at Parkwood. His own story of that time would have to wait.

'Yes, right, well, I had a vague memory but I had to check up on it. There was a report of a woman going missing. Name of Sarah Welland, here with her family. She just vanished overnight. Went to bed in a lodge one night, gone the next morning. The family believed she'd been killed. But there was no body. She's still registered as a missing person. What's unclear is how well it was investigated. The family said the police were disinterested, and treated it as a missing persons case rather than a suspicious death.'

'Tricky without a body,' said Harry.

'Quite,' said Mel. 'And it reads to me as if there was also a sense that the people running this place then wanted it played down and sort of washed their hands of it, too. Like they didn't want to be tarnished with it. So it wasn't picked up by the press or anything like that.'

'There were a lot of other things going on at that time,' said Harry.

‘Have there been any developments since then?’ asked Nicola.

‘That’s what I looked up while you were on that call,’ said Mel, ‘and the answer is no. No body ever surfaced. There’s been at least one internal review of actions taken by us, prompted by the family, but no admission that mistakes were made. And no sightings of the woman. She vanished into thin air.’

He watched Nicola rub her eyes, which he read as a sign of exhaustion and mental overload.

‘Fuck,’ she said eloquently.

‘That’s what I thought,’ said Mel.

‘Why has nobody mentioned this to us?’ asked Harry.

‘I’m not generally a fan of this phrase but, *to be fair*,’ said Mel, utilizing a phrase he normally mocked, ‘it has been a very short amount of time since we arrived, and there has been a large amount going on.’

‘Lindsey Moorfield must know,’ said Nicola and checked her watch. ‘Fuck, I was supposed to go back and talk to her.’

Mel wasn’t sure he’d ever seen his DS look quite this frazzled, as if the evening had entirely got away from her and this new piece of information had tipped her over the edge. He watched her just about manage to say, ‘We need all the files, Mel. Fast.’

‘I’ve requested them, of course. As for how fast we get them, not down to me. I’ve made it clear how urgent it is. Now –’ he took a breath, ready to share one last nugget of information – ‘when I say it was five years ago, it was five years ago . . . *yesterday*. Summer solstice.’

30

How was it possible for her head to be both pounding *and* spinning?

Nicola headed through the dark to Lindsey's office with little hope. When she got there, she found the door locked. She called Lindsey but it went to voicemail. She tried again. It was late, Nicola grudgingly conceded to herself. All the same, she had hoped Lindsey would have answered.

She cycled back, almost numb from the amount of facts she was trying to assimilate.

Information overload.

She stood back in the living space of Lodge 227, trying to get her bearings. She felt unsteady on her feet. All around her were Mel's updated wall records: the coloured dots, the annotations. Reeta was attempting to corral a team to get to Winters' house in Eagleforth, but that now looked like it wouldn't be until the morning.

The walls of the lodge would start swirling in a minute, she thought, if she didn't stop. Mel's final revelation of the day had pushed her to the edge. She needed rest. Her brain needed respite. The information would remain the same in the morning and she would hopefully be able to process it more rigorously then. If she slept.

'I have to go to bed,' she told the others.

She grabbed her bag and looked over at Mel, still at the kitchen counter with his ad hoc computer set-up and piles of paper spread around him.

'Don't you stay up too late either,' she counselled.

Mel didn't take his eyes off his computer screen. 'This isn't late,' he muttered.

'I'm gonna head off, too,' said Harry, picking up his own bag.

'Can't skimp on that skincare regime, Westlife,' said Mel, his skeletal features harshly illuminated by the blue-white of the computer screen. 'Oh, by the way,' he added, 'I bagsied the bunk room.'

Nicola and Harry both stared at him.

'Why?' asked Nicola.

Mel looked up from the screen as if she'd asked him the most ridiculous question. 'I like bunk beds.' His eyes drifted back to his work. 'Not often I get the opportunity these days.'

And with that the matter was seemingly settled.

Harry opened the door to the bedroom corridor and gestured to Nicola that she should head down the corridor first.

Chivalry, thought Nicola. She liked it. Then wondered, should she like it? Should he do it? Was that old-fashioned? Was it inappropriate for him to do that for a colleague, like holding a door open?

Her brain had started musing on the pros and cons of modern chivalry. It was definitely time to sleep.

'You OK?' asked Harry, with a level of concern she had not noticed from him before, as they headed towards the bedrooms.

'Yeah, why? Don't I seem OK?' she responded.

'You looked like you'd been kicked in the stomach when Mel told us about the woman disappearing,' said Harry.

Ah. So much for projecting a veneer of calm, strong leadership.

'Hard drive's full, and I'm trying to figure out what that might mean, using a brain that is insisting I go to sleep immediately.'

'Same,' said Harry. 'Reboot needed, right?'

'Right,' said Nicola. 'Any preference on rooms?' she asked as she arrived by a door. Harry stopped by the one next to it.

'I mean, I *really* wanted the bunks,' smiled Harry.

Nicola smiled back. 'You can always go in with Mel.'

'I'd rather eat my own arm,' said Harry. 'So I'll settle for an actual adult's bed.'

'The police service appreciates your sacrifice.'

'A commendation will be fine.'

'George Cross at the least,' agreed Nicola.

They were both grinning and nodding in close proximity in the narrow corridor.

There was a lull as they stood looking at each other.

'Start at seven, then,' said Nicola, her final command of the day.

Harry nodded. 'Copy that. Sleep well.'

'You too.'

They both entered their rooms and closed the doors.

Nicola lay in the fresh crisp white sheets, staring at the ceiling.

Through the walls she could hear Harry on the phone, presumably to his new girlfriend. Audra.

She heard him laugh. She couldn't make out words, but the muffled sounds had the air of flirtation.

She tried not to listen.

It's a private conversation.

I can't help if these rooms aren't soundproofed!

She tried to focus on other things, on the many questions arising, on the missing murder weapon, on a woman called

Sarah Welland, on Lindsey Moorfield and Conor Slater, and on the new Everest of work to do tomorrow. *Just give me a break*, her subconscious wailed. *Let me be and we'll go again in the morning, promise.*

Her mind strayed on to Ethan with a pang. She should message him. She hadn't all day, since Mike had told her he was safe. She picked up her phone.

You OK? Thinking of you! Xxx

She pressed send and awaited a reply. Then told herself it would be foolish to expect one any time in the next day or two.

She wondered *why* Ethan had not turned up for their conversation at home that morning. He had been dismissive, incommunicative lately. Was that just teenagerdom? Or something more specific? She was trying hard with Mike, and Mike was trying hard for all of them – they must deserve some credit for that, at least!

Harry's laugh came through the walls – and then she heard him shushing. She thought she could just make out him saying, 'My boss is in the room next door!'

Is that what he said? Could've been something else.

There was a silence and Nicola strained to hear. She was tempted to kneel up in bed and listen to the wall to get a clearer sense of his words. She looked at the glass of water next to her on the bedside table. She thought of people listening to walls via glasses. Did that even work?

Harry was saying something again. It seemed to be, 'No, she's all right, really.'

All right, really?

What the fuck did 'really' mean?!

The cheek of it!

I'm a GREAT boss!

Aren't I?!

This is what you get for listening to other people's conversations, she told herself. 'Eavesdroppers never hear good of themselves,' her grandmother used to say.

She checked her phone for a reply from Ethan.

Nothing.

She could hear Harry still talking.

Shut the fuck up now, Harry – none of us need to hear your cooing.

The problem was, she rather liked the sound of his voice. Even through a bedroom wall.

She put the phone face down and covered her ears with another pillow, clasping it to the sides of her head.

Her mind was flooded with the case. It had been less than eighteen hours since she had arrived here. Now she was wondering about Darren Winters, the whereabouts of the murder weapon, the amount of statements she had taken today, Lindsey Moorfield's reaction to seeing Darren Winters' photo, Conor Slater attempting to leave, the no-show of Valerie Doyle . . . a cascade of faces, times and places.

Make the cascade stop.

She wondered about meditating. She kept meaning to try it properly but could never stop the thoughts flooding in – work, home, the past, the future. Apparently, that was OK, but she had eventually felt it was just another thing to fail at and so she had sacked it off.

Maybe she'd try it tomorrow.

She heard Harry say 'night-night' and then something else she couldn't make out.

Was it 'love you too'?

Is he in love?

The room next door was silent.

Go to sleep now, Nicola. Shut down.

She thought about the body in the pool, the list of staff they had to speak to in the morning. She thought about Harry's report on the trashed house in Eagleforth.

She thought of the encounter in the restaurant, those idiotic men, and tried not to think of the possibility that somebody else would be killed tonight. Would she have blood on her hands like they said?

What could she do to prevent it? Get up, walk this huge site? She had sorted the extra patrols. She had stopped the wannabe vigilantes. Her going out there would not make a difference, she told herself.

Sometimes she wished she could lose her overdeveloped sense of responsibility. As a detective and as a parent. Did she have to bear every burden?

Other times, she knew it was what made her good.

She turned the light off and lay on her back in the dark.

She wondered if Harry was asleep.

She knew she would not sleep.

She wondered if the headboard of her bed was against the opposite side of the wall from Harry's headboard. If their heads were the width of a wall apart, on their respective pillows.

She lay there, thinking about him.

Later, she slept.

31

In Lodge 141, as Conor unpacked all he had earlier packed, Emma rounded on him.

'What the *hell* was all that about?!' she demanded.

He focused on the clothes hangers. 'Don't want to talk about it.'

'That was completely humiliating. What is your problem? You've been antsy since we arrived, even before last night.'

'I haven't.'

'Con, this is supposed to be a relaxing break, and you have been on edge the whole time. I don't understand why.' Emma's tone softened a little. 'Help me out a bit.'

Conor wondered if this was the moment. He could make himself vulnerable; he could open up to his wife. She was a good listener. It was one of the many things Conor had found attractive about Emma when they first met.

Except Conor knew the facts. He knew if he told his wife what she thought she wanted to know, things might never be the same again.

His wife, not unreasonably, thought she knew everything about him. But Conor knew all the things which Emma did not. The deep, dark things which Conor felt sure would destroy their marriage and all else beyond it.

So he shrugged and the shrug made her despair and leave the room.

Conor felt both ashamed and relieved. He picked up his phone, opened up Instagram and checked his DMs.

He was not surprised to see a new message from one particular number. The message read:

what did you say to the police

Conor looked at the message for a long time before shutting off his phone and trying to sleep.

He knew he was unlikely to sleep at all.

32

Lee Parker ventured quietly back into the high-ropes area. He knew the territory well and so refrained from using torchlight. Tonight was not the night to draw attention.

He had kept his nerve and waited deliberately until the site was asleep and – he hoped – the police had retired for the day, before he set about clearing things out of the container to the side of the high-ropes facility.

The container was his kingdom. Lee held the only key and he had always relied on the fact that nobody else ever needed, or thought, to look inside. But now this secret storage in plain sight was a ticking time bomb.

He used the large black equipment bags. If seen, even at this time of night, nobody would necessarily think anything of him moving about the park with them.

He had a lot of stuff to redistribute, but he also had to be careful.

He was in luck – he managed to get to his car without even seeing anyone.

He thought that the talk of enhanced security patrols was perhaps mostly bravado. A bit of flannel designed to keep the punters quiet.

Lee shoved both huge bags into the boot. He started the car.

There was no one checking on the rear staff gate this time of night. The biggest relief. He had worried that there might have been someone stationed there.

He drove out of the park without quite realizing he was holding his breath.

Lee's conscience did not often trouble him. He had to admit today was different.

He drove steadily and uncharacteristically just under the speed limit all the way home.

33

The phone was buzzing. What the *fuck*? What time was it?

3.52 a.m.

Nicola fumbled at the phone. She did not recognize the number. Suspected spam. She declined. She had not put her Do Not Disturb on. She had been woken after around three hours' sleep. Please God, let her get back to –

Here it was again. Same number, not one she recognized, but . . .

She was awake, so she answered it. If it was a person, she would give them hell.

She'd learned the trick from Ethan of not saying anything when she answered potential junk calls as this was the way to detect whether it was a spam or robocall. The recorded participant at the other end would just start talking anyway. And if it was a cold call offering her a new mobile deal or solar panels she'd hear the call centre in the background and hang up, with or without simply saying, 'No, thank you!'

A young male voice on the other end. 'Hello?' Then silence. 'Skip?'

What?

Nicola spoke curtly. 'DS Bridge, yes?'

There was a warmth to the voice on the other end. 'Skip, it's Mac.'

Nicola instantly put a face to the voice – the young uniformed officer who she first met guarding a macabre crime scene on the A35.

On those intermittent occasions when their paths had crossed since, he had always reserved a wide smile for her and raised his eyes in disbelief and said, 'What about that case, Skip? That was a weird one, eh? Good job we had you on it.' She felt like he would go on saying it for the rest of their careers. She rather liked it.

'Mac, hi. What is it?' Her tone was warmer now, but she also wanted to communicate that she was *somewhat* occupied! He really should've known that.

'Bit of a delicate one, Skip, cos I know you're super, super busy. But the sarge said I should let you know directly, given the situation.'

'What situation's that, Mac?' He was never one to get to the point the quickest.

'We've got your boy here.'

Shit.

She sat up. 'You've got my what?!'

'Yeah, your boy Ethan.'

Oh my God.

'Is he all right? What happened?'

'Yeah, no, he's fine. Truth be told, we're holding him in custody.'

Noooooo.

'You're shitting me.'

'No. That's why we thought it best to tip you the nod. As a courtesy, like. In case you wanted to pop on over.'

She kept her voice cool, despite her insides suddenly feeling like a kettle about to boil over.

'Why is he in custody, Mac?'

'Got himself arrested, didn't he? For possession with intent to supply.'

What.
The.
Actual.
Fuck.

34

'Ketamine?!'

'And weed,' replied Alan, the big bearded custody sergeant who always looked like he'd been squashed into his uniform.

Nicola buried her head in her hands as she leaned on the custody desk.

'I am going to kill him,' she said.

'Now then, I don't want to be seeing two of the same family behind bars on the same night,' said Alan.

'How long can we throw him away for?' asked Nicola. 'Could you pin a few other charges on him too? What other loose ends need clearing up?'

Alan laughed. Thank God it was him on duty, thought Nicola.

'I think I'd be the same if it was my lad. Who'd be a parent, eh?' he said kindly.

'Isn't this supposed to be the other way round?' asked Nicola. 'Aren't you supposed to be arguing for him to be sent to Dartmoor and I plead for understanding?'

'We'll let him off with a caution.'

'What an idiot,' said Nicola.

'Teenagers,' said Alan. 'I did far worse when I was his age.'

'Did you?' asked Nicola, leaning in. 'Tell me everything.'

'All my youthful indiscretions shall remain lost in the mists of time,' grinned Alan.

Nicola checked her watch. 'All right then, if it's a no to the electric chair, I'd best take him home.'

Alan chuckled. 'I reckon the chair'd be an easier go-round than what you're about to unleash on him.'

'And you would be right,' smiled Nicola.

'How's everything at Parkwood?'

'Complex.' She did not want to go into any detail or have anything leaking. She liked Alan, but you never knew who was happy to ring up a journalist. She had learned that the hard way.

'I bet,' said Alan. 'This is the last thing you need in the middle of the night.'

'Yup,' agreed Nicola ruefully. 'Right, get the little ratbag out of there.'

'Oi,' said Alan. 'He might be a little ratbag, but he's your little ratbag.'

'Don't remind me.'

'You're an idiot,' said Nicola, as she drove back down a dark country lane.

'Thanks,' said Ethan again.

'A *fucking idiot*,' stressed Nicola, in case the nuance of the message had got lost between the driver's and passenger seat.

'Got it, Mum.'

'What were you *thinking*?' said Nicola.

Ethan shrugged and looked ahead silently.

Nicola looked from the windscreen to the profile of her son.

'Was that a shrug? Don't fucking shrug at me! And put that fucking hoodie down!' She slapped him round the head, a bit harder than she'd intended, but she was trying to keep her eyes on the road.

'Ow!' said Ethan, recoiling. 'Police brutality!'

'Wait till your dad hears about this.'

Ethan looked concerned. 'We don't have to tell him as well, do we?'

Nicola was astonished. 'Oh! Now you're worried.' She adopted a whiny voice: '*Oh, Mummy, please don't tell Daddy.*'

'I actually hate you,' said Ethan sincerely.

'Feeling's mutual right now, kiddo.'

'Why didn't you just leave me in there then? I'm an adult. I can look after myself.'

That does it!

Nicola slammed on the brakes in fury – throwing both her and Ethan against their seat belts.

The car juddered to a standstill, with Ethan staring at Nicola. There was a new expression on his face – he'd never seen her behave like this.

'Out,' said Nicola.

'What?'

'Get out.'

He looked at her incredulously. 'Why?'

'I don't want you in the car. I come and get you, and you're not in the *least* apologetic. Get out. Go on! You're such an adult. I'm not telling you again.'

Ethan slowly opened the door. It was pitch black outside. Deserted narrow country lane. No street lights, hedgerows and unseeable fields either side.

He got out. 'Where even are we?'

Nicola flicked off her seat belt, opened her door and got out, standing in the doorway, leaning on the roof of the car, looking over at him.

'About seven miles from home. Start walking.'

'What?!'

'You're an adult, aren't you? What's the problem?'

'My phone doesn't have any charge.'

'Why's that my problem?'

'You're not gonna make me walk all the way home!'

'Yes, I am.'

'I won't know the way!'

'There are signs.'

'I can't see them in the dark! And I don't have any light.'

Nicola shrugged.

Ethan looked at her, uncertain. 'You don't mean it. It's not safe!'

Nicola stared at him for a second and got back in the car. Inside, she leaned over and pulled the other door shut.

She started the car and drove off, leaving her eighteen-year-old son alone in the dark, watching his figure grow smaller in her rear-view mirror.

35

Somewhere about a mile after marooning her only son in the middle of the Dorset night, Nicola's fury began to subside and her parental worry began to kick back in.

She slammed the brakes once more and did a clumsy, many-points U-turn, cursing the size of the car.

Just to keep him worried, she turned off the headlights, so he wouldn't feel the relief of her returning, until she was really close. She did not want to make this easy for him.

She knew it was petulant. She felt she was allowed a tiny moment of that right now. For a few seconds only.

She saw a lone figure trudging along the road.

He was walking in the wrong direction for home. So much for being a trainee adult. He had a long way to go. In all senses.

Yeah, but he's allowed to have a long way to go. He's a child, navigating a scary adult world. It's not like you *didn't make mistakes.*

Nicola shushed her own inner voice. They didn't need to get into her mistakes.

She cruised the car slowly and quietly in, and, as she got closer, flicked the headlights on, shining them on to his back. He had turned, shielding his eyes from the glare. Nicola brought the car up alongside him.

He had kept walking, not looking at her.

She wondered who might reopen the conversation. When he didn't, she decided to be the more mature of them.

'Would you like a lift?'

'Not if you're gonna be a dick about it.'

I would never have used that language with my parents, Nicola thought, not for the first time. She still wouldn't use that language with her parents, however much she sometimes wanted to.

Ethan was no less defiant. 'I knew you wouldn't just leave me.'

'That's interesting, cos I did. I got a mile down the road. And by the way, you're walking in the wrong direction, smart arse.'

Ethan stopped and looked into the night as if he was weighing up his options, then sullenly got in the car.

The door slammed. The seat belt clicked. The eighteen-year-old flipped his hoodie back up and slumped. Arms folded.

Nicola drove.

Try again.

'Where did you get the stuff from?'

'No, don't do that!'

'Oh, we're doing it.'

'You're police. I can't tell police. I'd be a grass.'

'I'm your mother, and if you don't tell me, you'll be homeless tonight!'

Ethan huffed. Silent. Then: 'I got it off Nani. He said he knew a guy. It's not like I had loads.'

'And you use it, do you?'

'Sometimes.'

'God's sake, Ethan!' She was so exasperated by him.

'Everyone does it!'

'You're not everyone!' Nicola felt like she was standing outside herself, hearing herself lay out the parental tropes the way her father had once tediously done to her. She didn't like it at all.

'That's the problem!' snapped Ethan. 'I'm trying to be! I want to be. D'you know how hard it's been? This is what everyone does, and if I want to be mates with everyone, I do this too.'

'There's other ways –'

'There's not! This is the best way!'

'If these are the sorts of things your friends do, they're not worth having –'

'Everyone does it, Mum. Everyone. Not just a couple. There's nothing else to do here! We all live in the middle of fucking nowhere so we might as well get blasted out of our heads. You took me out of a city and brought me here, so don't blame me! You got what you wanted and I have to live with it!'

There was silence.

He was lashing out, she knew.

She also knew he was not wrong.

He's your boy. Listen to what he's saying. Acknowledge it.

'I understand you're angry with me,' said Nicola.

'You don't understand anything,' came the response.

'I'm trying to. I'm listening to you. You're angry we're here; you're angry you have to do stuff like this to fit in.'

'Oh my God, no! That's not it!'

'OK, fine, what is it then?'

Ethan looked out of the side window for a moment, then snapped his hooded gaze back to her.

'Why the fuck did you take him back?'

What?

Nicola felt like the wind had been sucked from her lungs.

Ethan continued. 'I'm angry because he humiliated you and you took him back, and he's not worth being taken back, and you want us all to pretend that it never happened and everything can be put right, when it can't, because one day he'll do it all over again and we all know it.'

Holy shit.

Say something, Nicola.

Ethan said, 'You wonder why I want to block out the world? We were fine in Liverpool. I was happy. Then he fucked it up, and now you've double fucked it up. And I'm the one in this fucking bomb site, which you two are trying to mend but that's just gonna explode again one day. *That's* what I don't have to think about when I'm taking something. Why the hell you'd want to . . . *humiliate* yourself again, Mum.'

She struggled to know what to say. All she had was admonishment.

'Ethan, I would *never* have talked to my parents this way.'

'Yeah, well, maybe they didn't fuck up this royally.'

Ohhhh, you have no idea and may that always be so.

She wanted to say, I did it for you. I did it for us. I did it to not give up on this unit, this family.

They did not speak again all the way home.

Nicola's mind was cartwheeling. And returning to the same question.

Is he right?

36

'What are you doing here?!'

She and Ethan had just arrived in the kitchen when Mike blearily shuffled in from upstairs in T-shirt and trunks.

'I got called away,' said Nicola. 'Because of this one.'

'Called away?' Mike's tone was ominous as he looked over to Ethan.

'Leave it, Dad,' warned Ethan, his head inside the fridge as he drank milk from the plastic bottle. Nicola noticed how young and tired he looked. 'I'm going to bed,' he said, and shuffled past Mike.

'Hold on,' said Mike as Ethan pushed past him. Mike tried to grab his son's arm but Ethan shook him off. Mike called after him, 'What's been going on?'

Nicola could hear Ethan trudging upstairs as Mike turned to her. 'Is anyone gonna tell me?'

'He got arrested,' said Nicola, leaning against the kitchen counter.

'You're joking. What for?'

'Ket and weed.'

Nicola watched Mike's face go through about three different expressions within as many seconds. It ended with him saying, 'I'm gonna fucking kill him.'

'Join the queue,' said Nicola. 'He's lucky they called me. If it had been anyone else, they would've thrown the book at him. As it is, he'll get off with a caution.'

'What a twat.'

Nicola nodded. 'I'll let you deal with the school tomorrow.'

'Thanks.'

Mike leaned against the counter. 'Jesus. What are we doing wrong?'

Nicola looked up at her husband, studying him. She had loved him for many years. He was kind and funny and loving. He was, despite Ethan's current contentions, a good father. He was practical and useful. He did not expect unreasonable things. He was, in his work, often heroic.

There aren't many like him.

Her friends in Liverpool – God, how she missed them right now – had always told her that. *Where did you find him? Has he got any mates? Can we clone him?* Nicola's response was always, 'Hands off, he's mine.' She'd been known to do a version of the old ska song 'Hands Off She's Mine' at karaoke, amending the pronoun. She would sing it in the faces of her mates, as they all fell about laughing.

They had worked so hard to put things back together since his betrayal. They had uprooted, they had counselled (they were still counselling), they had reset, they had wailed and keened and confessed and scheduled and fucked and laughed and kissed and held. They had, as the phrase went, done the work.

She was exhausted. Her mind was full of Parkwood, forensics, interviews, maps in their ridiculous incident room and all the while the sand running through the hourglass before all the current guests left on Friday morning.

'I'll talk to him,' said Mike. 'I'll deal with it. You shouldn't have to worry about this. I'm sorry they called you. Though I'm glad they did if it gives him leeway.'

There he goes. Taking it on the chin, being active, making things happen. Creating action. Delivering. Showing up.

Mike kept showing up.

Nicola said, 'Thanks.'

'You sure you're safe to drive back?' said Mike.

'I'll be fine,' she said.

''K,' said Mike. 'Go. I'll keep you up to date. Thanks for stepping out of work.'

She wanted to stay but she knew she would rue it in the morning. She kissed him on the lips. He pulled her to him. The kiss lingered. She liked it but she wanted to cry.

They separated. She headed for the door.

'Nic,' called Mike.

She turned.

'Love you,' he smiled and gave her the wink she remembered from the fireman she met in Liverpool nearly two decades ago when the world was young.

'Love you too,' she said.

37

At 5.52 a.m. Nicola crept back into the lodge at Parkwood.

As she entered, she was confused by the waft of coffee. As she rounded the corner from entrance area into the living space, she was further surprised to see Harry, up and dressed.

'Oh!' he said. 'We thought you were still asleep. Did we disturb you? Coffee?' He pointed to a mug on the side, with steam rising off the top.

Nicola suddenly felt aware of how dishevelled she must look, in contrast to Harry, who somehow managed to look chiselled, stylish and spritely before 6 a.m.

She saw him take a second look at her. 'Wait, are you just coming in? Have you been out already?'

'Morning,' came another voice. Mel was at his computer station, right where she'd left him last night.

'I had to go out,' said Nicola. As she got closer to Harry, she thought, *God, he even smells good first thing*. Scent and coffee, this time in a kitchen. 'Have either of you even been to bed?'

'I was awake at five. Had a quick run to clear my head. There's a few things I wanted to check before the world wakes up,' said Harry.

'I had a perfectly serviceable four hours,' said Mel, about as cheery as Nicola had ever seen him.

'Which bunk did you choose?' asked Harry.

'Top, of course,' said Mel, as if that was the only option any sensible human would take.

'Valid,' said Harry.

'I'm going to take a shower,' said Nicola, groggily hoping that steaming water would be her temporary saviour.

The cascade of water renewed her. She stood beneath it, staring straight ahead, her mind wandering through the events of the night. The moment she realized what she was doing, she pointed her mind back in the direction of the case.

She thought about all the lodges. She thought about the murder weapon. She thought about Keith Hammersley, the man with the drone, and Conor Slater, the man trying to leave. She thought about Lindsey Moorfield and what she knew about Darren Winters.

Many things were nagging at her from yesterday, but a tiny little thing, a hobgoblin of a thought was jumping up and down waving and calling 'over here!', tugging at her mind and demanding she pay attention. She had learned to notice these hobgoblins, as inconvenient as they were. But sometimes it was hard to make out what they were saying. What was this one telling her she had missed? Something in the speed of yesterday that she had omitted. Something in her own working where she hadn't gained the full picture.

As the water thundered down, she realized.

I stuck to the path.

She slammed the shower off, burst out of the cubicle, and dried and dressed as fast as she could. She grabbed a site map as she headed straight for the front door, ignoring Mel and Harry. She did not want to have to explain.

She grabbed the same bike as yesterday and started pedalling furiously.

Duh.

The route she had taken yesterday was safe, ordered and

logical – the layout of the site as designed by its original architects. A customer-friendly, bike-facing route. It had given her what she thought she wanted: a mental map of the Parkwood site, and a physical experience of being in it, understanding distances, the spatial and relational dynamics, how all the different aspects of Parkwood related to each other.

She had cycled the surface village: the village in most guests' minds. The village they had been sold and told – the shape of it, the purpose of it, the relational form of it.

But there was more to Parkwood than that. That map was not the map of the staff's journeys around the site: the shortcuts and back routes and staff entrances.

But even that wasn't the map a killer would be working to.

It wasn't even the true physical shape of the site. She had not been anywhere near the perimeter – there were so many more areas unmarked, unhighlighted. More to be found.

If I'm a killer, I don't automatically stick to the paths. That would be madness. More likely to meet people, more likely to be seen from the lodges.

Parkwood guests were staying in a rural retreat where they didn't notice the true nature. It was a backdrop. Setting, not circumstance. People experienced their holidays set against nature, not truly within it. She had to be careful her investigation didn't fall into the same trap. There was uncharted territory she should be exploring.

Get off the paths, dumbo. Get into the wild. Walk the actual perimeter. Then you'll have a truer picture.

Leaving the bike on the ground, Nicola slid awkwardly down a steep slope behind one of the lodges, hoping nobody saw her graceless descent.

She was looking for the edge – the perimeter fence which

marked the boundary between Parkwood and the outside world. The grass down here was rougher, less cared for and manicured. There was evidence of molehills, which Nicola realized she had not spotted anywhere else on-site. Did even the moles obey the route maps? She began to wonder how the Parkwood grounds team managed it.

She picked her way through a wilder patch of tall brown and green ferns, moving towards a man-made barrier she could just about spot behind the ferns.

There it was: the edge of Parkwood.

She stopped and listened. The sounds of holidaymakers within Parkwood were distant, only just audible. The only other sound was the trees brushing against each other in the breeze. For a moment she felt they were whispering about her.

Nicola estimated the fence was some ten feet high, and held up by tall, thick (and now rusting) metal poles which had been forced into the ground at intervals of around fifteen feet all along the perimeter. She often estimated distance by using the useful six-foot height of her husband, imagining him lying down. The gap between the vertical poles looked about two and a half Mikes.

The fence itself was split into two components. The six feet or so coming up from the ground (one Mike) was densely packed crisscross wire – like chicken wire, Nicola thought, only tighter and more effective. She plucked at it: strong, thick and taut. The top section of around four feet (66% of a Mike) consisted of eight lines of gnarly barbed wire set at an angle of sixty degrees pointing out and up into the air, making it very challenging, if not impossible, to scale from the other side.

No mean feat from this side either.

On the other side of the fence Nicola could see that the trees instantly became more varied, with a preponderance of ancient-looking silver birch trees. The fence, snaking away to her left and right as far as the eye could see, cut through the land as a definite statement: the dividing line where the silver birch forest had been felled and replaced with more on-brand trees: low maintenance coniferous pines. On Nicola's side: curated, uniform Parkwood calm. On the other: nature ran free and unfettered.

As always with fences, the question was: was it there to keep the outside world out, or the inside world in?

Standing there, Nicola felt it was the latter. Parkwood was sold as a holiday experience in nature where nature was strictly controlled. A frictionless experience with the edges taken off the rural experience for city or suburban dwellers. Parkwood was the countryside without the dirty, smelly, bumpy or dangerous bits. Inside that perimeter fence, risk was mitigated – every tricky activity within it would come with its own health and safety certificate.

Nicola marked an X on the map – suddenly a small girl with a pirate map – then turned to her right and strode on through the overgrown ferns, cleaving to the fence at her side. She needed to walk the perimeter, fast. She had mapped the inner architecture. What lay at the edges?

As she walked, she looked back and up. The main part of the Parkwood site sat on raised land, like a sprawling castle estate on a very small hill. The edges of the site tailed off on to the slope which led down to the fence. Nicola presumed that the foundations and inner workings of the resort's systems sat within the raised aspect. She took a second to laugh at herself: what foundations and inner workings? Since when were you an architect or an expert in holiday resorts? But then she also remembered her own brilliance – *yes, brilliance, thanks very much* – when taking out a particularly nasty drugs boss in Liverpool about twelve years ago.

She had – by guile, charm and sheer painstaking detailed graft – managed to get hold of and analyse the architect's blueprints and drawings for the remodelling of his house. It was a user's guide to all the bespoke facilities he had had built in, digging down deeper to add extra basement levels to the property (much to the fury of his neighbours in a particularly upmarket corner of Crosby). Nicola had started to nag at it, when she noticed the drawing had accounted for two huge steam rooms on the same basement floor. It had bothered her that anyone would need two steam rooms, but while the men on the team dismissed her Spidey-sense and speculated that maybe it had been mislabelled and that perhaps one of the rooms was a sauna rather than steam, or an ice bath or something suitably fitness-y ('He's a drug boss, not a footballer!' she'd retorted), Nicola had figured out that neither room had any technical specifications which would enable steam or water to be piped in. She was proven right when they raided the house: the two steam rooms were, in fact, a weapons room and a punishment cell.

Did the steam fog up your brains, lads?

Always look at the structures, always look at the maps.

After fifteen minutes of walking the perimeter, however, her confidence began to ebb. The walk offered little of note. She worried she was wasting her own precious time, with so much pressing, back at the lodge.

And then she saw it. A few feet away.

She instantly quickened her step to check whether her eyes were deceiving her.

There was a breach in the fence.

You couldn't see it unless you were close – the arrangement of the ferns disguised it.

The fence had been cut open.

Seemingly from the other side.

Nicola pulled it back – it yielded and opened wider. She put her arm through. Easy. She pulled it open further. How far would it open? She gripped the cut section of the fence and forced it back. With a certain degree of effort, she could now slip her body through.

She pushed into the gap and out the other side of the fence. Outside Parkwood.

Having left the site, Nicola scanned around. Was there anything here? Markers or clues to the gap in the fence? Anything remarkable about the area where it came out? It didn't seem so. For now, at least to her, this area of forest felt anonymous.

Having looked around, Nicola tried the return journey: going in through the breach from outside the perimeter.

If anything, it was much easier.

As if it had been done before now.

Nicola snuck back into Parkwood and closed up the breach in the fence behind her as best she could. Then she ran up the hill towards the nearest pathway, and located her bike.

Nicola pedalled hard, setting a direct course back to Lodge 227, her mind buzzing. There was another way in, or out, of Parkwood. Unmonitored.

One thought kept bouncing around her mind. Who had been through that gap in the fence before her?

Had they been too quick to assume that the killer was someone from the Parkwood site or had remained there? Did the killer know about this gap? Had they used it? Every time she felt they were approaching solid ground in this investigation, something shifted.

She was thinking so many things, and pedalling so hard and so fast, she almost missed it. But out of the corner of her eye she spotted it.

Nicola squeaked to a halt. *Those brakes really need oiling*, she thought, wincing.

She sat on the saddle, hands on handlebars, feet on the ground, bemused, looking ahead.

She pulled the map out of her top pocket and looked at the lodges that had been crossed off from her route yesterday. Every lodge had been accounted for.

She looked up again. This didn't make sense.

Immediately in front of her, on its own, a way past the cluster of lodges Nicola had crossed off was a lodge.

A lodge on its own.

A lodge not on the official Parkwood map.

A ghost lodge.

38

'There's a hole been cut in the perimeter fence . . . here,' said Nicola, drawing an X on the wall map in Lodge 227, as Harry and Mel stood either side of her. 'Big enough for a person, or people, to come through and access the site.'

'What were you doing down there?' asked Mel.

'Investigating in the field,' said Nicola. 'Or *a* field, at least. Tell you what else I found out: there's a lodge that's not marked on any of the maps we have. Just here. I had a walk around, tried to look in, but it was locked up.' She marked it on their map.

'You've been very busy this morning,' said Mel as if she'd just demonstrated witchcraft. Mel clearly struggled with the idea of being out and nosing around, when you could be near a computer, on a chair, looking at information.

'The benefits of being on foot. Never trust diagrams or maps. They're only what the person who drew them wanted you to know.'

'Makes me think about Darren Winters being on the guest system but with a fake lodge number. Could he've been in there?' asked Harry. 'And why would any lodge not be on the map?'

'All the right questions, Harry. I'll be asking Lindsey Moorfield,' said Nicola. She now turned to Mel. 'Did you get details of any day passes that were issued on Monday – people that came in for that day only?'

'No,' said Mel.

'Why not?' asked Nicola.

'They don't issue day passes on Monday; it's a changeover day. Previous guests leaving, new ones coming in. They have a policy of no day passes on changeover days.'

As Mel spoke, she poured herself some coffee. She sipped it and then looked at Harry.

'This is the coffee!'

Harry winced and nodded reluctantly. 'Yeah.'

'Wait. You *make* the coffee. It's not from a shop? You make the coffee every day? And you've been making me guess where it came from? And it's from you?!'

'I'm very good at coffee,' he said.

'But . . . how have you got it here?'

'I keep some in the car and an espresso pot.'

She had many questions – where did he get the beans or the coffee? Why had he been doing that every day? What was behind such a thoughtful gesture and why was he hiding it? – but she had enough questions arising from the case and had to focus on that. She slurped gratefully on the coffee and poured herself some more, before rooting around in the box of grocery essentials Parkwood staff had dropped round the night before for something breakfast-y.

As she did, Mel was talking to her without looking away from his screen, his thin fingers still tapping away as he spoke. 'Printouts on the table for you, more to come.'

Nicola glanced over to the table which had hitherto escaped her notice. It was stacked high with neatly organized documents. Mel's overnight work: his homework, responses to all the things she had asked of him yesterday, waiting for teacher. Mel had many idiosyncrasies – *so many* idiosyncrasies – but in this hybrid set-up, where he was required to be both office manager and a working detective constable, his brilliance with systems and administrative legwork made him an invaluable asset.

'I can talk you through what's what,' said Mel. 'But for starters we have the list of number plates for guests who are currently staying, as well as for staff cars. Westlife has started comparing the physical cars in the car park with the list, in case there's a car on-site that's unregistered.'

Nicola was impressed. 'When did you get time to do that?'

'Factored it into my run earlier.'

These two. Overdelivering, just when needed.

Mel carried on. 'I've checked all guest IDs for previous convictions – four in total, no major red flags, but we can go through them individually. I will say that trying to get any clear information out of Parkwood systems is driving me bananas. They either supply the wrong thing, half the thing, none of the thing or a thing in a format that's unreadable.'

'OK,' said Nicola. 'That's great, Mel. Priorities for today. We have a new schedule of staff interviews. Then we have our victim: Darren Winters. SOCO are at his address. If the killer was the one who got in there, was this after killing Winters? If so, which way did they leave the site? Or did they have an accomplice and is there more than one person involved? What were they looking for at the house, and did they find it? Mel, we need a full victim profile: background, all available intelligence. I've given you my notes from the call with his next of kin. Obviously we're still looking for belongings, especially his phone. No sign at the house, Harry says.' She ran her hand through her hair. So much to cover. 'We still don't have the murder weapon: a knife with an eight-inch blade. I've asked for a search team but they're caught up with a case in Devon.' She tried to disguise the contempt with which she held her boss's responses to her urgent requests.

As she said the words 'murder weapon' she watched Mel peel off to the kitchen area. He opened one of the kitchen drawers and said, 'On that, you do know you'll find a knife matching the description of the blade in every lodge.' He held up a knife.

'Oh shit,' said Nicola. *Of course.*

'And that's before we get to all the restaurants and bars. So what's that, two or three hundred knives answering that description within the perimeter here? And you'd think by now it would've been cleaned and wiped, if not discarded.' He seemed to notice Nicola's expression for once. 'Not to rain on anyone's parade. Just hard to know how to narrow down that search. Unless you want to test hundreds of knives. But that will take a lot of time and money.'

'OK,' said Nicola firmly. 'But we can't just not look for it. Once the staff interviews have been concluded, assign uniform to searching for the murder weapon. They can start by checking the big industrial bins round the back of all the facilities, as well as the public bins around the park.'

'They'll love that,' said Harry.

'It's character building,' said Mel.

'Motive. Who would want this man dead? Now, clearly, the disappearance of Sarah Welland may be a key lead. We'll get more information this morning. But also, keep an open mind till we know for certain there's a connection. Right now, we don't know what he was doing here; we don't know whether he was killed by someone he knew, or who knew him, or by a complete stranger. It's possible he could've just come across something going on in the pool and been killed because of it. We don't know how he got on-site or why he was here. Who knew him, who did he see, what was he doing, how did he go unnoticed?'

Her old boss used to say, 'Look under every rock.' The problem here was that there were a fuck of a lot of rocks. Where they put their resources next was key. She was getting stonewalled for more resources from her boss. His phone was going to voicemail and texts and emails were going unanswered. Whenever she thought about him and the infuriating lack of support, Nicola felt a surge of anger. With a bigger team, she could attack this with gusto. Instead, a successful outcome was reliant on her wiles, her ability to make do and mend. It wasn't fair. Why should this just be on her and her team?

Tough shit. It just is. Pull on your big-girl pants and get on with it.

'If you could both get on with things elsewhere, then I can keep working,' said Mel. 'I did actually get up early so I could avoid all *this* . . .' His sentence trailed off, but his pained expression remained.

'Human interaction?' asked Harry.

'If that's what you call it,' said Mel.

'Fine,' said Nicola. She downed her coffee, grabbed a banana and opened the front door to welcome the fresh air into the stale and, she now realized, male-dominated funk of the lodge. She looked back. Mel was working with his shoes off. She would have to lay down some rules about that.

For now, she had a much more important priority.

'I'm going to find Lindsey Moorfield,' she said.

39

Lindsey Moorfield looked like she had not slept.

No, wait, it wasn't *quite* that.

Lord knows Nicola could sympathize, given the night she'd had. She was fuelled by caffeine courtesy of Harry right now, but she knew it was going to take a monumental effort of will to get through the day. But Lindsey looked – not dishevelled, that wasn't the word – slightly less put together than yesterday. Nicola's Scouse colleagues would've called it the JFL – the Just Fucked Look – indicating someone who'd slept at someone else's last night. The look was the same, the context was not.

Nicola had an instinct: Lindsey had not gone home last night.

Nicola surveyed Lindsey's office with a beady eye. She noted a large bag shoved in the corner, just visible behind a big pot plant. Then she began to surreptitiously stick her hand down the side of the sofa on which she was currently sitting. She slid it down between the cushion and the side of the sofa. Aha! She found what she had been looking for. Instead of just cushion and base, her hand alighted on the cold metal and springs of a sofa bed mechanism.

Had Lindsey slept here last night? Did that mean she'd hidden from Nicola when she'd knocked at the office door late last night? Was Lindsey wearing the same clothes as yesterday? Difficult to tell when Parkwood had a uniform policy, even for its managers, but Nicola would guess that she was. And if she'd slept here last night, was there a chance she'd slept here on Monday night also?

She went straight in. 'Why didn't you tell us about Sarah Welland, Lindsey?'

Lindsey came strongly back at her. 'Are you kidding me? After everything that happened yesterday, everything I've had to contend with in the past twenty-four hours? I barely had chance to draw breath! I'm still in shock now. And you're accusing me of what, withholding information?' She was riled, and her tone was becoming more strident. 'Besides, why is it down to me to tell you about all that? You're the police, aren't you? You must have records – shouldn't you know? Weren't you around then?'

'I was up in Liverpool.' Nicola adopted a more emollient tone. 'I understand this has all been a shock. But we're all working at speed. And I need to know everything about Darren Winters. Including what happened with Sarah Welland.'

Lindsey nodded, as if she'd been expecting this to be her first conversation this morning. She had regained her composure. 'Darren was one of Parkwood's most experienced resort managers. He'd been with the company twenty years at least. He'd managed three different sites, increased profitability in each location. I first worked with him at the Gloucestershire resort, and he basically trained me up. I was working in guest relations, doing all the bookings and looking after complaints, and he spotted something in me, recommended me for an internal training and mentoring programme for potential managers. He taught me everything about how to do this job. Then when he was moved here, he asked me whether I wanted to join as deputy resort manager. So I was at his right hand for a long time.'

'How was he as a boss?' asked Nicola.

Lindsey took a moment to choose her words. 'Demanding. Focused on profit. A little cynical for my taste.'

'In what way?'

'Look, he gave me my chance. I don't want to speak ill of him. Especially not now. But he was tough, he was commercially minded, his decision-making was always about prioritizing margins, increasing profitability, ensuring the company got the maximum value out of staff. If he thought something would make money, he would demand it happened, whatever that meant. He was good at all that. He was less good on the people side.' She paused, before adding, 'He always made sure he got what he wanted. And that could be difficult.'

'What do you mean by that?'

'If people were upset, or didn't feel supported, or were burned out . . . He didn't have the largest amount of empathy for other people. He expected everyone to work as hard as he did, and he didn't want to hear complaints. He could be cold. But if you're in that job for that long, you get used to having your own way. I think that's why he appointed me, to do that side of things, to . . . clear up after him. He used to say to me, oh, you go on in and do the touchy-feely stuff.'

Lindsey stopped, looking like she felt she'd said too much. 'I just think after his wife died, his work became his life. And losing his son too.'

'Was he liked?' asked Nicola.

'He was respected,' responded Lindsey carefully. 'Until Sarah Welland's disappearance.'

Nicola let the silence sit, but Lindsey showed no inclination to continue without being nudged. 'Tell me what happened,' she said.

'Sarah Welland had come down here with her mum; they were having a break together. And, as far as I know, one morning she'd just gone. Like, disappeared, vanished. All her stuff was still in the lodge where she was staying, nothing superficially wrong, no disturbances or anything. Her mum didn't have any idea where she'd gone and . . .' Lindsey looked accusingly at Nicola. 'To be honest, the biggest problem at first was getting the police interested. Her mum was worried out of her mind but until it had been twenty-four hours, your lot weren't going to do anything.' Nicola couldn't fail to notice the accusatory tone of 'your lot'. 'It was almost three days before you all engaged with it and that's only because I went over to a station myself and had to drag someone over here. Her poor mum was going spare. She'd been out driving, looking for Sarah; she was losing her mind.

'And then, when you do turn up, it's one person and he's not overly interested. I know it was a strange time, when the world was half opening up after Covid, people were doing weird things, but the level of disinterest really shocked me. He was like, fine, we'll do what we can; call us if there's a body.'

'I'm sorry,' said Nicola. 'That's unacceptable. Her poor family.'

'Wessex Police never had the best reputation with us even before that,' said Lindsey.

'I'm aware,' said Nicola. 'It's one of the reasons they changed the name.'

'Not that everything was right on our side either. Head office sent three people down to manage it, and honestly, their main concern was keeping it out of the papers and off social media, playing it down; they said they didn't want it toxifying the brand. So while I was trying to chivvy your lot, they were trying to stifle talk about it.' She paused. 'I'm still ashamed about it actually. It wasn't right.'

'So how was Darren Winters involved?'

'Your colleagues, once they finally engaged with it, seemed sure he was connected. He'd been seen talking to her a number of times, he'd upgraded their lodge, comped her drinks and dinner. And he had no alibi. Also, there seemed to be no one else in the frame. The detective was so sure. And I could see what was happening; it was wearing Darren down. And then . . . look, it started spreading here. People started gossiping, offering tips, saying things to the police about him, which I don't even know if they were true; there was even one or two people saying, oh, here's where he buried her body, then there was talk of a satanic ritual by the stone. It just took on a life of its own. And the longer it went without her reappearing . . .

'I don't know how you stop that once it starts; it was like a storm gathering. And you could see him getting more tightly wound. He said to me: how do I prove a negative?'

'Do you think he had anything to do with her disappearance?'

Lindsey was quiet for a moment. 'Why would he do that? Why would he risk his job, his family . . . everything that he worked for? Your lot never proved anything. But it hung over him. Never quite went away. Then on the first anniversary of her disappearance, some journalist did a piece. The family obviously didn't want the trail to go quiet. And of course management said Darren wasn't allowed to talk to the press or anything, because they were wanting to sell the business.

'So then he wrote a post online protesting about his treatment, saying he refused to stay quiet any longer, how he'd been the victim of a whisper campaign . . . It was such a bad idea, I'd told him not to, but he felt the stigma had attached itself to his name cos he'd found some posts supposedly naming and shaming him as the person who killed her, and he was furious. And there was a point where he just sort of started spiralling and that became his main focus, rather than work.'

'Which must have impacted you,' said Nicola.

'Of course,' said Lindsey. 'I was having to deal with everything he was neglecting at work, but also I had to cover up his mistakes, which were getting more and more common. And it was having a detrimental effect on morale, on the quality of guest experience. And then the sale was beginning to gather momentum and someone came auditing everything and I remember them saying if Dorset was supposed to be a crown jewel in Parkwood's portfolio, why was it not being run like one? She and Darren clashed big time. He didn't always like being told what to do by a woman, and that was the beginning of the end for him and the company.

'I was caught in the middle. I owed him a lot, but I wasn't blind to who he was or what he'd become. It was unsustainable. It was horrible to witness, like a slow-motion car crash. I wanted to stop it happening but I couldn't. He was eased out. Period of leave for illness which became a redundancy. I covered for him, I managed up, and then they gave me his job when he was manoeuvred out.'

'Did you speak to him about that?'

'Not much. He thought I'd betrayed him. Fired off all sorts of emails saying all sorts of things. It got him a lifetime ban from all Parkwood sites.'

Nicola made a note of that, before returning to one of the key questions. 'And you still don't think he had anything to do with Sarah Welland's disappearance?'

Lindsey thought. 'I told you, I don't know,' she said.

Nicola instinctively felt that response wasn't genuine. She was sure Lindsey knew more than she was letting on. Could she be trusted? Was she really telling Nicola everything?

'When did you last see Darren Winters?' she asked.

Lindsey seemed to make a pretence of thinking. 'We met at his house in Eagleforth. He accused me of all sorts of things, said I wouldn't have stood a chance without him. It got quite personal and I left.' She exhaled. 'I shouldn't have gone.'

Nicola noted her evasion on the time frame of that meeting. 'When was that?' she persisted.

'This year? End of last year? I can check.'

'Please,' said Nicola. 'Lindsey, if he was banned from Parkwood, how did he come to be here as a guest and on the system?'

'I don't know,' said Lindsey. 'I feel like it was a final *fuck you*.'

'So you didn't know he was here?' asked Nicola.

'Why would I have?' It was not a denial. Was it a deliberate evasion?

Nicola brought out a map and pointed to the area she'd walked this morning. 'There's a locked lodge on the edge of the site set apart from most other properties.'

She saw Lindsey's look of alarm. 'Yes,' she said non-committally. 'It's not commonly in rotation.'

'I'd like my team to take a look in there,' said Nicola.

'Why?'

'Because we're conducting a murder investigation,' replied Nicola sharply. 'Darren Winters was on-site, under an assumed name and allocated a false lodge number. If he knew about a lodge that was not often occupied, might he have thought about using it?'

'It's possible,' said Lindsey. The frost level was rising.

‘I’ll have it opened for your team.’ She didn’t seem happy about it.

‘Where were you between ten p.m. Monday night and six a.m. Tuesday morning, Lindsey?’

Lindsey stared at Nicola. ‘Me?’

Nicola was interested by the sudden shift in Lindsey’s demeanour. There was a brittleness bordering on anger when confronted with a question she didn’t like.

Lindsey did not launch into her account immediately. She took a moment, carefully parcelling out her words. ‘I was here till just after nine –’

‘Is that usual?’ Nicola interjected deliberately. It was an old trick to throw an interviewee off any prepared or thought-out statement.

Lindsey gave Nicola something approaching a glare. It had worked. ‘No, I normally leave just after seven. But, as I told you, there was the incident at the Solstice Ceremony. I was dealing with the initial fallout from that. I eventually left just after nine. I was home around twenty past.’

‘Was anyone at home when you arrived?’

She noticed Lindsey’s expression tighten. ‘Mm-hmm. My husband.’

‘Did you go out subsequently, or were you in together for the evening?’

Lindsey seemed to stumble. ‘No, we – we . . . were in for the evening. We didn’t go out. We were there. Together.’

The whole of the sentence had tumbled downhill into an absolute lack of conviction.

Nicola made a note. She could feel Lindsey watching her. They both knew Lindsey had sounded unconvincing. That was enough for now. Nicola felt certain she would return to that question at a later point.

She moved on. 'So you and your husband were at home together all evening. And you remained there till the following morning. What time did you get in?'

'Seven a.m.,' said Lindsey. 'I was called by Mandy when she found the body and I told her to call the emergency services and I'd come in right away.'

'Thank you,' said Nicola, writing the time down in her notebook.

She felt Lindsey's gaze linger on her.

Nicola was certain that not everything Lindsey Moorfield had told her was the truth.

40

It was the situation Alice most disliked on her cleaning shift: when a guest remained in the lodges while she was working.

First of all, she felt like they were checking on the quality of her work, like having a supervisor present throughout. Even though most of them weren't, some of them actually were and it just put her on edge, like her work was suddenly a performance being judged, like they might hold up little paddles at the end with numbers marking her performance, like on *Strictly*.

Second of all, they were in the way. Sat on sofas, or kitchen stools, or making cups of tea. Invariably they'd say, 'Don't mind us!' or 'Pretend we're not here!' but it meant Alice had to vacuum under their feet, or plump cushions around them, or wait for them to finish using the toilet before she went in to clean it. (Her absolute worst thing.)

Third of all, she did not want to know about their lives. She had enough to think about with her own. Alice did not like gossip. She had been brought up to say little and work hard. She felt people should stay out of the lives of others and then the world would be a better place. The people she found trickiest were those who took too much of an interest in other people's business. She was absolutely not one of them.

Fourth of all, she might have to actually interact with them, and this was not something she relished. She felt too young and too inexperienced to do that properly. That's why she'd chosen cleaning (where you could just get on with things), supermarket checkout (where people wanted to hurry away by the time they realized you were actually there and not just a scanning robot) and babysitting (hours not having to talk to anyone, with a bit of luck).

She was going to have to interact with this guest and she really could do without it.

Alice was staring at an absence. The guest – a woman in her sixties or seventies, she couldn't be sure, who had introduced herself as Val and made Alice a very strong (too strong!) cup of tea which Alice had poured down the sink when Val wasn't looking – had come to join her.

'Everything all right, pet?' she'd asked in an accent Alice put as somewhere north-east-y.

Alice was looking into one of the kitchen drawers.

'You're missing a knife,' she said.

'Am I?' said Val, following Alice's eyes down into the drawer.

'Yeah. There should be a carving knife in here, but there isn't.'

The two women – separated by a couple of generations – looked at each other.

'Is it not in the dishwasher?' asked Val.

Alice shook her head.

'Or the sink?'

Alice shook her head again.

Val looked around the kitchen, and beyond into the living space. 'I don't think I'd've put it anywhere else,' said Val. 'You didn't see one anywhere while you were cleaning?'

'I didn't, no,' said Alice quietly.

'Maybe they didn't give us one at the start,' said Val.

'No,' said Alice.

There was definitely one here before you checked in, thought Alice. She had done the inventory of this lodge herself, and her supervisor had also done the standard pre-arrival double-check.

There was a pause as they both stared at the drawer again.

'Bloody hell, that's not good, is it?' said Val. 'What with all that's going on.'

Alice wondered if either of them were going to mention that and was glad it didn't have to be her.

'Has anyone else been in here maybe?' asked Alice.

It looked like Val was thinking, or having a thought, but then she just shook her head.

Alice said, 'Would you like me to get another knife brought up for you?'

She watched Val think further. 'Not yet. I'll have a look around when you're done, and if I don't find it by tomorrow, you can report it then. How about that?'

'OK,' said Alice hesitantly. 'Just if the supervisor comes to ask or check or –'

'Don't worry,' said Val. 'I won't land you in it.'

'Thank you,' said Alice.

Val patted Alice on the hand. 'I'll let you get on with it. I'm off out,' she said and squeezed a five-pound note under Alice's hand and walked out of the front door.

Alice looked at the five pounds.

Then she looked again at the space where the carving knife wasn't.

41

'Some people reckon you've got the best job around here.'

Harry had decided that a matey approach was the best way to talk to Lee Parker. He could see that this was not the opening gambit that Lee had expected. Harry had watched Lee swagger in and look Harry up and down, scanning disdainfully. This morning's job had been to begin the staff interviews, and Lee's attitude immediately set him apart from the others Harry had been talking to. Harry recognized the type of person Lee was immediately.

So he knew to let this man be the alpha dog he clearly thought he was.

'Oh yeah?' said Lee, non-committal.

'I was obsessed with high ropes as a kid – my favourite bit of any holiday. Except we hardly ever came to places like this – well, only once. So they were like a glamorous forbidden thing. I used to beg my mum to take us to Go Ape or whatever for the day. I had mates who would send pictures of them at a Parkwood or a Center Parcs.

'We don't use the C-word here,' said Lee.

'Is that right?' said Harry.

'It's like Butlin's and Pontins, you're either one or the other.'

'And you're a Parkwood loyalist all the way?'

Lee held a clenched fist up. 'Parkwood ultra, mate.' He continued to stare at Harry. 'How old are you?'

There we go, thought Harry. The challenge to authority,

to established order. The subtle undermine. 'Twenty-nine,' he said. 'Big three-oh approaching. All downhill from there. What about you?'

'Thirty-four,' said Lee.

'Mate, condolences,' said Harry. He watched Lee stiffen slightly, vanity pricked.

Harry had run with plenty of Lees. Half his friendship group for a start. Men who built their lives on charm and jokes and being in their twenties. Men who felt their boyish attractiveness was a quality that would sustain them until they died, and that therefore they could under-index in other areas such as knowledge, responsibility and thoughtfulness for others. He had been trending in that direction himself until the scales fell from his eyes. There was little future in being a Lee. Though Harry already felt that Lee himself did not see things this way.

'How long you been a detective?' asked Lee.

Now he's trying to get up in my grill, thought Harry. He was ready for it. He had noticed Lee limp as he entered. 'Hurt your leg?'

'Work injury,' said Lee, unfazed by the sudden change of topic. 'No biggie.'

Harry wrote it down ostentatiously, allowing the quiet as he marked it in his notebook, enjoying Lee watching. Lee shifted in his chair.

'There's a rumour going round it was Darren Winters in the pool,' said Lee. 'Is that true?'

Interesting, thought Harry. Naming Winters and seeing people's reaction was part of the second half of these interviews today. But Lee had pre-empted that.

'Did you know Darren Winters?'

'Course. Used to be the big boss here. Gave me my first break.'

'When did you last see him?'

Lee shrugged and looked away. 'Been a while.'

'Can you be more specific?'

Lee met Harry's gaze once more. 'Not right away, no. He'd been having a tough time, though, right? After everything that happened.'

Harry nodded. Lee's breezy reticence felt a little studied.

'Where were you between the hours of ten p.m. Monday night and six a.m. Tuesday morning?' Harry continued.

'I was here, finishing up, till late. Then found my car had a puncture. So I got a lift back home with one of the cleaners, Alice. Then I was probably in bed, doomscrolling, and/or kipping. I usually get up half six, go gym, then here for my shift.'

Harry wrote all this down, noting the specificity of the language in Lee's answer. The abstracts.

Probably. Usually. Lee hadn't replied with what he had done; he had spoken in generalities.

'Were you on your own, or was anyone with you?'

'Like I said, Alice gave me a lift. Then on my own, yeah. Unusually.' Lee grinned. The subtext was clear.

'You live alone?'

'Mostly, yeah.'

'When were you last in the Splashdome complex, Lee?'

Lee looked thrown. 'I'd have to think,' he said.

'OK,' said Harry, and waited.

'I meant, I'd have to think and get back to you,' said Lee, fiddling with the loose end of a plaster on one of his fingers.

'We don't have time for that, mate. Were you there Monday night?' Harry pushed, noting Lee was hedging his bets. Why was that?

'I have to be honest, the days here blend into one after a

while. You know, I set up the course, I check my bookings, people turn up, there's adults and kids, I take them through everything, I help out anyone who's worried or in trouble . . . But if you asked me, did this kid come on Sunday, Monday or Tuesday, I really wouldn't know.'

'I'm not asking you that,' smiled Harry. He was deploying what Nicola had recently called his assassin's smile. 'I'm asking were you in the Splashdome on Monday night?'

Lee looked back, as if he was re-evaluating Harry. Weighing him up.

'Yeah, I think it *was* Monday, maybe evening before close. Actually, maybe even after close.'

Harry paused his writing and looked up. 'You were in the pool area after it closed to customers on Monday night?'

Lee nodded. 'A few of us on the staff sometimes go into the pool after-hours, before home, let off a bit of steam. It's a perk. Obviously it's harder to do when the norms are in there because –'

Harry interrupted him. 'Sorry, did you say *norms*?'

'It's what we call the punters, the guests.'

Harry wrote it down. 'And so on Monday night, you were in the pool after it was closed to guests. And you were with some other people?'

'Right.'

'How many of you?'

'Hard to say.'

'Was this before or after you were finishing up at the high ropes?'

'Oh, er –'

'And this Alice, was she with you there?'

'No, no, no – that was just a lift. That was later.'

'I'm going to need the names of everyone who was there

with you. Then I'll speak to them to confirm what you're saying.'

'Fine,' said Lee.

Harry tore a piece of paper out of his notebook and handed it to Lee. 'Here you go. Names, jobs, everything.'

Lee didn't take it. 'No, wait. That was Sunday. Late Sunday. No, Monday, wasn't there.'

What the fuck?

Harry recapped. 'You weren't there Monday, but you were there Sunday.' Lee nodded, as if challenging Harry. 'And Alice gave you a lift home Sunday.'

'No, lift home was Monday. Definitely,' said Harry.

Harry held out the paper more insistently. 'Write down the names of the people you were with on Sunday, and we'll check with them. Also, Alice's surname, please.'

Lee slowly, reluctantly, took it. He started to write.

Harry watched. 'While you're doing that, is there anything you'd like to correct, or any other useful or relevant information you'd like to tell me about?'

'Don't think so,' said Lee without looking up.

This whole short interview had felt like a minor arm wrestle. As it came to an end, for now, Harry continued to look at Lee with just one word pinging around his mind.

Liar.

42

Mel Hardiman was mad as hell and not going to take it any more.

He stormed over (in Mel world this meant walking but being quite put out while doing it) to demand some answers from Parkwood's head of IT / security systems manager (she seemed to have two job titles) Esther Arthur. The person he found was not what he expected. In her late forties (Mel estimated, but really he was terrible at assigning ages to humans), garrulous, heavily tattooed, with a shock of cropped blue hair and a thick Dorset accent, she greeted Mel with a beefy 'All right, mate?' and a serious nod. She assured Mel that despite the 'shocking fucking business' she was 'happy to open up the doors. *Mi systema es su systema*'.

Mel wasn't sure there was such a word as 'systema', but he understood what Esther was getting at. Nevertheless, he pointed out that he'd been waiting to receive all the information he'd requested and it was, you know, pretty bloody urgent what with there having been a murder.

'Shit on a stick, what do you *mean* you haven't got it? I sent it all over late last night. You emailed the request. I emailed back. Didn't I? I did. I'm covering two jobs since redundancies – I know, who isn't these days, but the whole last forty-eight hours has put everything in a spin. Absolute *fucking* tragedy. Horror show. Who'd've thought. Jeezy peeps, man.'

Esther had her own office in the same block as Lindsey – two doors down. Where Lindsey's office was light and plants and pastel-coloured soft furnishings, Esther's had slatted charcoal blinds letting in diagonal shafts of light. Her furniture was harder edged, darker tones and the room was dotted with a handful of seemingly randomly placed action figures moulded into comical fighting action poses with each other.

'So which are you?' asked Mel. 'Security systems manager or head of IT?'

Esther shook her head in despair. 'Mate. It's a fudge. Big clumsy reorg when the new owners came in, and it's just never-fucking-ending, it's like a rolling reorg, the reorg that just won't die – fuck, bad choice of words, sorry. Before I was in charge of security, rotas, staffing, any issues that arose, but the job's expanded, or more like fucking *collapsed* into IT, because of the overlap, apparently. And if you can see overlap, or think it makes sense, then you're a better man than me. It's caused havoc – not just here, but at the other parks too. And if you complain or raise a valid point about how things could better, then there's an insidious little vibe you get back where it's like "you do realize how lucky you are to have a job and aren't we nice trusting you to do more and acquire new skills", but what you can do? Welcome to the enshittification, as my mother never said and never will, God rest her soul. We are twenty-first-century girls and we're living in their world. Right?'

Mel found he had a not unpleasant swirling sensation in his stomach having been designated a twenty-first-century girl. He wasn't sure he'd ever met anyone like Esther. 'But you can help me with the access system for the pool complex?' Mel refused to call it the Splashdome. This was not *Mad Max*.

'I can, for my sins,' said Esther. 'BUT. Big but – d'you like big buts and you cannot lie, Mel?' Mel looked confused as

Esther laughed. 'The new owners – I mean, I say new, but they've been in place for a good while now, haven't they? – brought in a whole new software system, all centralized, in fucking Cuckooclockandchocolateland, or Switzerland as some people call it, I presume so they can monitor everything that's going on remotely, and they rolled that out across all the parks simultaneously. That week was a fun month, I can fucking tell you. You could do case studies on how not to move software systems based on what we went through. They keep saying we're through the worst now. But we are not. We can't even export spreadsheets, man, let alone get two networks to talk to each other. And has anyone actually taken us through exactly how it works? No, they have not. Only been two years.'

Mel continued his quest for facts. 'So the system is run from head office, but you maintain local operations here?'

Esther nodded. 'In theory, yeah. I will say it does not live up to the billing they gave when installing it. And d'you wanna know what Kizu, my deputy – she's on maternity leave at the moment – found out on the grapevine? They said they had it specially designed but actually they got a system that was designed for another company but never used, possibly because *it didn't fucking work properly* so they got it for a knockdown price and had their geeks bang it into shape for Parkwood and then told us, oh, here's your bespoke thing we made from scratch. Now let me tell you, if you were genuinely building it for Parkwood, you wouldn't have it working the way it does. It's like that Irish joke about the driver who's lost and stops to ask a farmer for directions and the farmer says, "Well, I wouldn't start from here." That's what we've got.'

'It's not an unfamiliar scenario,' said Mel, which he felt was quite a sprawling conversational gambit.

'So what are you, tech or copper, or both?'

'I did a lot of coding in the nineties,' said Mel in a tone which he imagined people used in bars. He thought he might even let a truth bomb drop. 'I was a hacker for a while.'

Esther Arthur's face exploded with delight. 'No!'

'I was. When I got nabbed, they let me off on the proviso I went over to the dark side. The police, I mean. Not that we're the dark side, I shouldn't say that, especially not on a murder. This is very serious.' He tried swearing, like Esther. '*Fucking* serious.' He didn't think it sounded as good coming from his mouth and now he was full of regret at showing off and starting to get a headache. 'I just want to know how the staff pass keys work,' he said in a hurried attempt to get back on track. 'Your colleague reported that the door to the pool was propped open. But for someone to prop it open, it must have first already *been* opened.'

'Got you! Right.' Esther launched in. 'Each member of staff has their own card-style pass on a lanyard. Their keys are coded to their own personal ID and they're given access to the buildings and areas appropriate to their duties.'

Mel nodded, noting all this down. 'And does the system store a record of which key card accesses a given area at a given time?'

Esther looked serious. 'Course it does.' She jabbed at a button on her keyboard and the printer near to Mel whirred into life, churning out paper at speed. 'That's for you,' said Esther as she peered at the screen.

Mel collected the paper as it came out. There were three pages of close-set data, arranged into coded columns which would've meant nothing to most people.

'You need help to translate it?' Esther asked. 'It's just raw data, really.'

'No,' said Mel. 'Well, maybe. Just the headlines.'

Esther got up from her desk and came over to Mel. She leaned in over him and pointed to a particular section of the dataset. It was the closest he'd been to somebody he didn't know in about seventeen months and he noted his pulse rate quickening involuntarily. 'This is the period you're looking at. That entry is for pool closure at ten twenty-eight, that's ninety minutes after the pool has closed, and there's been a clean-down for the night. These two entries are most likely to be my security team, beginning of the night, ten forty-three, and then there should be another . . .'

Here she faltered and Mel looked up at her.

She carried on, still pointing at one dataset. 'Another at, um, five forty-seven when the body was found and we raised the alarm, but I can't see one . . .'

'Because the door was already propped open.' Mel pointed to two further entries. 'But there are two entries *after* the late-night security check, and before the time your guard discovered the body.'

Esther looked ashen. 'There are, aren't there? And there shouldn't be. Also, something's off here. Because the close-down the night before is a temp card but with Splashdome privileges.'

'A temp card being?'

'A security pass issued to someone who's lost their primary key. They have a time limit. Except this one doesn't seem to have had an expiry put on it.'

'Who was the card issued to? And who by?'

Esther was starting to look like a dictionary definition of the word 'uneasy'.

'It's not recorded. It's just saying the employee record

who the temp key was issued to is *also* temporary. Like a contractor. But we don't issue cards like that. None of it makes sense.'

Esther lowered her voice and got even closer to Mel. 'Not gonna lie to you, Mel, this looks a bit fucking sinister.'

43

Alice still had more lodges to clean. Then she had products to scan and payments to take at the checkout. Then she had babies to sit. That always cheered her up that phrase. *I've got babies to sit.*

And yet here she was. In a room, with a detective. Being asked questions.

She had never even imagined that at some point in her life she would be questioned by the police.

This was not her life. It couldn't be.

She glanced at her watch.

'You OK?' asked the detective who had introduced herself as Nicola. She reminded Alice a bit of Lindsey. They were around the same age, Alice imagined, and exuded a similar air of calm authority. This detective, like Lindsey, felt and behaved like she was in control. She spoke calmly, evenly and smiled at Alice. Again, just like Lindsey. It made Alice want to tell this Nicola everything she knew about what had been going on around Parkwood.

'Just worried about the work I've got to get through,' said Alice.

'Your boss has given us dispensation to talk to you; there's no issue about that. We're talking to all staff members this morning. I won't keep you long.'

'Yeah, but I still have to do the same amount of work, just in less time,' explained Alice.

'Ah. Right, got you,' said Detective Nicola. 'And you have, what –' she checked a list – 'three separate jobs here?'

Alice was impressed she knew all that. Well prepared. Another similarity to Lindsey. 'Yeah. Mornings I do lodge cleaning, afternoons I work the checkouts in the Marketplace shop, and in the evening I'm available for babysitting. I just go from one to the other.'

'Any breaks?' said the detective, and when Alice shook her head she added, 'I think they have to legally give you breaks during the day.'

'They treat it like three jobs,' explained Alice. 'I'm paid by different bits of the company; it's like each one is its own little company. And the guests pay me directly for babysitting – the company just does the booking and I pay them a fee for arranging it. So, as far as they've explained it to me, I'm not doing one long shift for a company, I'm doing three jobs for separate companies, which they say I'm choosing to do, and it's my responsibility to take breaks between the different jobs because the actual shifts in any of the jobs aren't long enough to qualify for paid breaks.'

'That's tricky,' said the detective.

'Yep. Way it is, though, isn't it?' Alice shrugged. 'I need the money, it's local and people are nice generally.'

'And where d'you live, Alice?'

'In Eagleforth. A lot of people who work here live there.' She watched the detective write it down.

'Can you tell me what you were doing on Monday night, between ten p.m. and six a.m. the next morning, please?'

'I was babysitting for a family in one of the lodges. They were a bit late back. I usually set eleven o'clock as my end point, also cos pretty much everywhere's shut by then anyway, but these guys didn't get back till midnight.'

'And this was Emma and Conor you babysat for? Lodge 141?'

She *really* was good. 'Yeah,' said Alice, impressed, adding cheekily, 'Don't know you need to ask me anything; you know more than I do!'

Detective Nicola didn't smile. 'And how were they when they got back?'

'They just said they'd lost track of time. And to be fair, they gave me an extra fifty quid, so not really a problem. Beautiful daughter, slept all the way through, no issue at all. Mind you, I was back in at seven the next morning.'

The detective was writing quickly now and Alice felt worried.

'I haven't said anything bad, have I? They were really nice. I don't want to get anyone in any trouble.'

'And you haven't.' The detective smiled. 'So you left Lodge 141 after twelve, and then what?'

'I went to my car in the staff car park. It's quite a way from 141.'

'And did you notice anything along the way?'

Alice went quiet and looked at the floor.

'Any detail, no matter how small, could be really helpful.'

Alice looked up again. 'I mean, I did see Conor, the husband, again, I think. He came out of the lodge when I was walking away and ran off somewhere.' She wondered if she should be telling Nicola this. 'I think maybe he saw me, so if you say anything to him, he'll know it was me.'

'Do you know where he was running to?'

Alice shook her head. 'Sorry.'

'Anything else I should know, Alice?'

Alice thought. She was already regretting mentioning Conor. All the same, she *did* have more information.

‘I noticed there’s a knife missing from Lodge 77.’ She saw Detective Nicola’s neck straighten. ‘The woman in there said I shouldn’t worry about it, but I reported it to Leah. My supervisor.’

‘Do you know the woman’s name in Lodge 77?’ asked the detective, with the sort of calm that felt to Alice very disciplined.

Alice nodded. ‘Val.’

The detective stared at Alice but it was clear her mind was somewhere else. After a couple of seconds she said, ‘Val *Doyle*?’

‘Not sure of the surname,’ said Alice apologetically. She watched the detective write something in her notebook and then look back up.

‘Is that everything?’ she asked Alice.

Alice’s head was spinning. There was so much going on. People had been doing odd things. She didn’t know that she could keep them all in her head, let alone tell someone else everything. Was that everything? Wait. What about Lee? Lee *asked* her to tell them! That must come under anything else, right?

‘I gave Lee Parker a lift back, cos his car had a puncture.’

‘Lee Parker,’ said the detective. ‘He works here too, right?’

Alice nodded. ‘High ropes.’ She was now going to use as few words as possible.

The detective nodded and wrote that down. Then she looked up and smiled. Her tone was brisk. Outside, Alice could see the next member of staff hovering.

‘Right, well, I really appreciate you sharing all that information with us, Alice. If we have any further questions, we’ll be back in touch soon. Now, don’t let me keep you from your work.’

*

As she walked away from her interview, Alice wondered whether she should have mentioned the knife, or whether saying about giving Lee a lift had been the right thing.

But she had done what Lee had asked of her.

44

The team gathered back at the lodge the moment the morning interview sessions were over.

The walls were blooming with even more information, noted Nicola, but Mel was characteristically downbeat. He muttered something about security data, which had clearly soured his mood if that were possible. Nicola had neither the time or inclination to get wrapped up in that right now – she trusted he would resolve it and report any conclusions. To break him out of his funk, she asked him to summarize interim observations on lunchtime of day two.

'Which one of the two cases we now appear to be investigating are we discussing?' he asked caustically.

'Darren Winters, please,' said Nicola.

'Very few key witnesses who saw anything that night,' Mel said, staring at the walls. 'Hardly surprising given the time it all happened. Which means a large number of people can be ruled out. We have a smaller set of people of interest, people without alibis, or whose comments in interview merit another conversation. They are asterisked – we can start with Keith Hammersley in Lodge 50, who you encountered with the drone. That would on its own be enough, but in his interview he gave very little away other than telling our constable to, and I quote, "fucking catch up".'

'Wow,' said Harry.

'Now I'd understand that if he were talking to you, Westlife,' said Mel, 'but the report said it came out of the blue.'

'He's on my list,' said Nicola. 'I also have to flag Lodge 77. Valerie Doyle. Didn't turn up for interview and one of the housekeeping staff told me this morning that there was a knife missing from her lodge. She's my next port of call for obvious reasons.'

Mel darted to his computer. 'I had something about her. Repeat booker, been coming for a number of years . . . Where is she? Ah, wait, I didn't complete the identity search. Got interrupted, you'll be amazed to hear . . .'

Mel went silent and started typing. Harry and Nicola exchanged glances and Harry took up the briefing baton.

'I would also now asterisk Lee Parker, the guy who runs the high ropes,' he said. 'Evasive. Been here long enough to know Darren Winters. I didn't trust him.'

'I don't think we can yet rule out Lindsey Moorfield,' added Nicola. 'Her account of that night needs interrogating further. Plus she looked rather shifty when I asked about gaining access to that locked lodge, which I'd like you to take a look at this afternoon, please, Mel.'

'Am I not busy enough here?' moaned Mel, still fixated on his screen.

'All hands to the pumps,' said Nicola. 'As manager, Lindsey has ultimate access: places, data records, equipment, knows the site inside out. On that alone, she has to be close to the top of our list.'

At that moment, Reeta burst in to the lodge. 'Sorry I'm late. I've got about four minutes. Two ongoing sites.' She stopped and wrinkled her nose. 'It smells of socks in here, and not in a good way.'

Nicola knew she should've said something to Mel. 'Anything new for us?' she asked Reeta, quickly moving the conversation on.

'The tiniest of tinies but it might be something. We've retrieved the backing paper from a waterproof plaster in the skimmers. It had a small trace of blood on it.'

'Couldn't that be from anyone on-site?' asked Harry.

Reeta shook her head. 'Skimmers were cleared at closing time the night before. What we found must have gone in the pool between closing and when we arrived. This is the only thing to have come up. Now whether the killer injured themselves and applied a plaster there, whether it's connected to the victim, we'll find out. But we may have something to test against.'

Harry realized something. 'Lee Parker had a plaster on his finger when I spoke to him,' he said.

'Thank you, Reeta,' said Nicola. 'Anything else?'

'Yup. From Darren Winters' home. Amid the debris, this.'

She held up an evidence bag with a glove inside it. 'Parkwood staff glove, singular.'

Harry looked to Nicola. 'Winters was managerial. Would he be likely to have had a pair?'

'It's possible,' said Nicola.

'Also possible it was dropped by whoever ransacked the house, no?' said Reeta. 'We can get it tested against Winters' DNA and find out whether there's a match.' She checked her watch. 'Right, that's your minutes up. Try not to find any more crime scenes, please, we're too busy.'

As she headed out of the door, Mel let out a squawk. 'Knew it!' The other two looked at him. 'Lodge 77. Valerie Doyle. New information suggests you should very much prioritize her.'

'Why's that?' asked Nicola.

'Valerie Doyle is the mother of Sarah Welland, the woman who went missing five years ago.'

45

Val Doyle had thought it was only a matter of time before there would be a knock at the door of Lodge 77, so she was unsurprised when it came. At least it had given her time to think and to consider what she would say.

She opened the door to the two detectives: the detective sergeant called Nicola and a young detective constable, Harry Ward. She invited them in and offered them tea, which they declined.

The detective called Nicola asked, 'Why didn't you turn up for your interview yesterday, Val?'

She fixed the detective with a stare. 'I don't have anything to say to you lot.'

'Why's that?'

'Are you kidding me?'

Val found her breath catching unexpectedly in her throat in reaction to a surge of rage. She tried to control it and said with quiet force, 'You didn't even recognize my name. After all that went on.'

Val could feel the anger and the pain building again, a familiar feeling. It was always there, on quiet simmer, she had come to realize. And then at moments like this it would suddenly flare to a fast boil. She was not in control of it.

The detective nodded and said, 'Neither myself nor DC Ward were stationed here in 2021. We're only just catching up with what happened. And I apologize for that. It sounds like things were not handled well.'

Val laughed bitterly. 'You could say that.'

This detective at least presented as sympathetic, but Val reminded herself that it may be a ploy: to get Val to trust her, to lower her guard. *Be careful, pet.*

'All right. Before we ask you our questions, would it be an imposition to ask you to tell us what happened then? So we start by hearing it all from you?'

Val stared at Nicola. Was this woman different?

She took a deep breath, ready once more to retell the story of the worst time of her life.

'We were coming out of lockdown, this was when there were tiers and bubbles – you could go outside but only meet at a distance of two metres. Places like this had reopened cos they were worried about the hospitality industry. It was Sarah – my daughter – it was her idea to come. She booked it all.'

'Tell me about her,' said Nicola.

'She was thirty-nine then. She'd be forty-four now. She'd worked in cosmetics ever since school, worked her way up through sales, big company. She really liked the job cos she got to travel, and for the past ten years she'd had secondments: Australia, Japan – she was crazy for Japan, went back twice – and even America. Loved a big American city, that girl. Always on the go, always looking to be somewhere else.

'I think that was why she'd found lockdown tricky – she'd never really found the right man and she'd been with this feller Tim for a few years but they'd never lived together and then they decided to bubble together or whatever they called it. They just jumped into it. And that hadn't been as easy as she'd thought. I mean, it wasn't easy for any of us, was it? Makes me shudder when I think about that time; we didn't have a clue what was going on, or how long it'd last, or whether we'd all bloody die. We don't really want to talk about it now either, do we? We've swept it under the carpet, like it never happened.

'So we had a week here. Sarah and me. I'm not gonna tell you we had a perfect relationship because we didn't. You're only as happy as your least happy child, that's what they say, isn't it? And she just . . . she never had the knack of being happy, not with herself. Anyway, about a month before we came away, she said she and Tim had been doing IVF for a few years and that it hadn't worked, and how humiliating it had been for her, and how ashamed and broken she felt. Why couldn't she meet a decent man, why couldn't she get pregnant, this deluge of stuff she'd never told me. And I was in shock.'

Val was very quiet for a moment, staring into her cup of tea, swirling it around as if it offered answers.

'And I wasn't sympathetic. I can admit that now. I think because I felt hurt that all this had been going on and she'd kept it from me for years. So I gave her short shrift: you never stick at anything, always on the move, it's hard for all of us. And I think . . .'

Val was surprised to realize that the next breath wasn't coming in the way she expected – she pulled at the air, trying to inhale. She knew it sounded like it bordered on a sob. She realized her eyes were moistening. Her body was once again doing things she didn't quite feel. She wanted to carry on.

'I was just wrong. I've often been wrong. We never quite clicked, her and me. I could never say the right thing, and she never . . . I thought we'd be off shopping and having lunches together by now. But it's . . . We were never friends.'

Another sip of water.

'And then she was like, well, maybe it's good I can't have kids, I'd be a terrible mother cos . . .' There was a silence. 'Cos look who I had to learn from.'

Val wiped her eyes. 'Anyway.' She took a deep, deliberate breath. 'But, all that aside, there was this weird thing while we were here.'

'What sort of weird thing?' nudged Nicola.

'I was sure she was meeting someone. She would sneak off without saying anything for hours. And when she came back she'd just say, oh, I went for a walk. I even tried to follow her one day and she bloody deliberately lost us! So I knew there was something. But she wouldn't admit it. I thought maybe that's why she wanted to come here, maybe that's why she had problems with Tim, because she had someone else she was having a thing with. I was like, oh, she's brought us here so she could have a bit of afternoon delight, the cheeky cow. It's like I was her cover.'

'But she denied it?' asked Nicola.

'She did. I didn't believe her. But the police say they spoke to everyone who was here and there was no connection. I dunno . . . I have my theories but it's no use telling you.'

'Why not?'

'Cos you're on their side,' said Val.

'Whose side?'

'The police,' replied Val. She watched Nicola's brow furrow. 'There was a stag do going on here, and it turns out the stag was a copper, some of the other lads as well. And I know Sarah had a little bit to do with them because, you know, she was pretty and friendly, and people – well, I say people, but I mean men, obviously – took that as flirty when it wasn't . . .'

Val felt herself drifting off. She looked at the two detectives listening intently. After all this time she had the opportunity to talk and she was just so tired. So empty.

'I've always wondered . . . was she meeting one of them? Was evidence destroyed or things not followed up in order to protect your own, those young lads on the stag do, young police. Not like it'd be the first time, would it?'

'You think Sarah could've been meeting one of the policemen?'

Val shrugged. 'I have no idea. I mean, they were younger than her, but . . .' She sighed. Was it bad to admit this? 'Thing is . . . she always caused this sort of chaos, Sarah. As a kid, she'd just go walkabout without telling us. And then a few hours later, she'd turn up, blissfully unaware of everyone's worry. Saying, "what you making such a fuss about?" Like she just . . . she only ever existed in her world. And I suppose I thought for a while that that was maybe it when she didn't come back here.' A long pause. 'And then it wasn't.'

Val looked up. 'It's just the uncertainty. The never knowing. And feeling . . . you could've done something. Should've done something. We just came for a little break, like people do all the time, and then everything fell apart, and it's like I've been stuck in this . . . I dunno how to describe it . . . like I'm going round and round the same roundabout, desperate to get off, in a nightmare. And nobody's ever said, this is the way. Nobody's ever helped.'

The old feelings were surfacing. The powerlessness that infected her whole body like a virus. She had to tamp it down. 'Can I have a coffee? Do you two want one?'

They took a break. Val made three instant coffees and opened the patio door, letting air in. She stepped outside on to the back patio, where the barbecue sat, caffeine and oxygen hitting her system at the same moment. She felt the eyes of the police on her the whole time.

When they sat back down, the woman called Nicola spoke.

'Val, the man who was found dead in the pool yesterday morning was Darren Winters.'

Val could feel the proximity and intensity of the two detectives' gazes on her. This was a test; they were checking how she would react.

She was quiet and then nodded slowly. 'Right,' she said.

'We know you must have known him. When did you first meet him?' asked Nicola.

Val took the deepest of breaths.

'In 2021. He was the manager then. He was the face of the place. He'd call us his favourite ladies. And actually, he had us moved from one lodge, which had a dodgy shower, into another, and it was a bit of an upgrade, so we were very grateful and he'd ask if everything was all right any time he saw us. He definitely took a shine to Sarah. Everyone did.'

'Do you think he could've been the person Sarah was meeting?'

Val was silent for a while, as if wrestling with her conscience.

'I don't know, love. That's the conclusion they came to, but they could never prove it, could they?'

'Val, would you mind talking us through where you were on Monday evening, say from six p.m., until first thing Tuesday morning?'

Val took a moment to compose herself. 'Well. I had dinner at the Italian, then went for a drink in the sports complex with my book. I got talking to some people there who asked me to join them for bowling to make up numbers. Another drink after, then back here, maybe ten thirty. On my own till the following morning. I was first in the gym, six thirty or so. Don't sleep much,' she added pointedly.

There was a silence. The detectives were very still, looking at her.

'No,' said Nicola.

'I'm sorry?' said Val, startled. 'How d'you mean "no"?'

'We've talked to a lot of people, taken a lot of statements, and we have a very good officer, DC Hardiman, who is excellent at cross-referencing. And before we came here, he gave us details from other people's statements who named you.'

Val felt her face reddening. 'What d'you mean named me? Who named me?'

Harry checked his notebook before replying. 'The people you met in the Sports Arena. Occupants of lodges 167 and 202.' He closed his notebook and looked at her. 'They remembered your name, and said you were there, till closing, talking to a man quite animatedly. And that he bought you a drink, that you were huddled together in the corner. And that you left together, after closing time.'

A thousand thoughts flooded Val's mind. All she said was, 'Right.'

There was silence, before the young detective asked, 'Who was the man?'

Val looked down. *Fuckety fuck.*

'Darren Winters,' she said.

46

'I didn't know he'd be here. He was the last person I expected to see.'

'How did you get talking to him, Val?' Nicola asked.

She knew for certain that Val Doyle had already lied once in her account of what had happened in the Sports Arena bar on Monday night, and as she watched her carefully, she had no doubt Val was capable of lying again.

'He saw me. He looked like he'd aged twenty years. It was such a shock. I didn't even know he was allowed here. I thought there was something about him being banned. I'm sure they told us that at some point. And then he saw me and came over. And I could barely speak. But the first thing he said was: I'll go if you don't feel comfortable with me being here. And I was like, just please stay away. Which he did. But then later, after a stiff drink, I felt really strongly that I had to talk to him. So I went over.'

'What did you talk about?'

Nicola watched Val thinking – or was it organizing her story?

'It wasn't the conversation I thought I'd have, I'll tell you that. I've thought about it a lot over the years. I mean, all these years, and all those thoughts, and . . . she's still . . . we still don't know where she is, if she's alive or dead, and if something did happen, where's her . . . where's her body?'

Nicola could see how difficult those last words were for Val.

'We talked about what it was like back then. For me. For him. First of all, he swore it wasn't him. That he'd had nothing to do with her disappearance, that he hardly knew her. He said the police had victimized him. He said it had destroyed his life, too, that he'd lost everything. He wanted to know who did it; he still wondered if she was buried here. He said he wanted to prove his own innocence, because nobody else would now.'

'Did you believe him?'

Val looked surprised at the question, and then it seemed as if exhaustion overwhelmed her. 'I don't know who to believe any more. He's not gonna confess to me, is he? I mean, he seemed as broken as I am. But then he'd want to come across like that, wouldn't he? That could be an act. Very easily.' She looked sad. 'Problem is, when something like this happens, there's never any truth any more. You never trust anyone ever again.'

'So you drank with him until close?'

'Yes.' Val looked straight at Nicola. 'Look, I didn't mention it when you asked because . . . well, lots of things. I thought you should've known who we were. And I was ashamed. To think I'd been drinking with him.'

Nicola nodded neutrally. She wasn't sure she believed Val, but it tracked. Val's problem now was she was, by her own admission, an unreliable witness.

'What happened after closing time?'

Val looked out of the window. 'He asked if I'd go to his lodge the next evening. He said I was the only person he could talk to about this and maybe we could figure it out together.'

'When did you leave him?'

'Bit before midnight. We'd just been standing chatting; it was still warm. Like I say, I was a few drinks down and I was in shock that we'd even talked. But he was the one who called it a night. He said he had someone else to see.'

Nicola felt Harry lean forward. 'Did he say who that was?' she asked. 'Or where they were meeting?'

Val shook her head. 'I didn't ask.' She looked hesitant. 'I mean, he seemed lonely. It seemed like he was talking about a woman, that he had a woman to see, but that might just be me getting the signs wrong.'

'Did you go straight back after leaving him?'

Val shook her head. 'I went and sat on a bench by the boating lake. I needed to process it all. I must've been there an hour or two. I don't think I got back till gone two.'

'Did you see anyone else in that time?'

Val shook her head again. 'It was pretty out there, just the moonlight and the water. All still and calm. Except in my head.'

Nicola felt Harry shift on his chair, which she had learned indicated he was keen to ask the next question. She left the space for him.

'Val, I'm sorry for all you've been through. I'm sorry the initial investigation failed you and your family, and that you don't have any answers about Sarah. Do you mind me asking, given how traumatic your experiences have been, why come here again?'

Nicola watched Val's cheeks puff out as if with toxic air she needed to expel. She exhaled slowly and painfully.

'I've come every year,' was her response. 'Same week. Sometimes I tell myself it's to do your – the police's – job. Maybe I'll see something that they missed, or there'll be people, or something, or . . .'

She looked up to the ceiling and her breathing had become heavy. Nicola realized Val was trying to disguise a sob. Val looked back down and across at Nicola and Harry. Her eyes were red and damp. She breathed out through the O-shaped hole her mouth was now making.

And when she spoke it was so plaintive. So simple.

'Maybe Sarah would be here. Maybe she would have come back.'

Nicola nodded.

'Stupid,' said Val, scolding herself and her absent daughter. 'I know. Totally daft. But . . . until they find a . . . there's still a chance.' Her expression became more of a plea. 'Don't you think?'

There was quiet for a moment.

Nicola said calmly, 'Val, I have to ask the next question. Did you have anything to do with Darren Winters' death?'

Val eventually said, 'How would that get me answers?'

Nicola said, 'Maybe you got them during that chat.'

'No,' said Val simply.

'We know a cleaner reported a knife missing from this lodge,' said Nicola.

Val looked alarmed. 'Yeah, she mentioned that this morning. But I can't say I remember seeing it since I've been here.'

'Did you use it or touch it?' asked Nicola.

'I haven't cooked anything. Haven't been here long enough. Ate out Monday.' She stared at them. 'You can't think – You don't think I used that knife . . .'

There was silence in the lodge.

'I mean, I didn't,' she said.

She looked defiantly at them both.

Nicola thought that was the end of the conversation.

But Val had one more thing to share.

'By the lake, on Monday night,' she started. 'D'you want to know what I really thought, sitting there? I thought, maybe, if I see him again, Winters, if I go and meet him, with a bit of luck, I go there and he kills me, too. Then that'll prove it. And it'll all be out in the open. I thought that would be OK. That might make it all worthwhile.'

Nicola and Harry walked away from Val Doyle's lodge in silence, heading to their next task.

'Do you believe her?' asked Harry.

'Which bit?'

'Any of it.'

Nicola was battling with now having two investigations to weigh up. Were they separate or connected? She had only just begun to get her head around the death of Darren Winters, and now this. 'I can't imagine what she's gone through. It gives her motive. She seemingly had opportunity.'

'We only have her account of the conversation with Darren Winters,' said Harry. 'We don't know it went that way. Easy to imagine they're here, she's had a few drinks, they strike up a conversation, she's disguising her animosity, and with all that pent-up emotion, anger – five years' worth – she kills him. Revenge for her daughter.'

'It's possible, maybe even plausible,' acknowledged Nicola. 'Except how would she get in the pool? Unless they went straight there? That when she's telling us she was sitting alone at the lake, she was with him in the pool complex.'

'The door was found propped open. Maybe they saw that, maybe Winters had arranged for it,' suggested Harry. 'If they were getting on well, he was trying to impress her, or make things right, or just do a cool thing after-hours. She could have had the knife from her lodge . . .'

'What, she goes out to the bar with it? Doesn't add up,' said Nicola.

'Unless she had time to go back to her lodge, get it, meet him at the pool.'

Nicola pondered. Had Val stabbed Darren Winters in retaliation for her daughter's disappearance? What would a mother do for their child? Even now, after being disturbed in the middle of the night to get her son out of a police station, Nicola would still throw herself on top of a ticking bomb to protect that boy. That was the paradox of parenthood. When you were a child you had no idea of it; when you became a parent it became blindingly clear.

Was that what Val had done? Finally struck back on her daughter's behalf, after years of pain from not knowing what happened? As a mother, Nicola could understand that.

Her phone buzzed suddenly and she checked it. 'For God's sake,' said Nicola, stopping in her tracks.

'What is it?' asked Harry.

'From Mel,' said Nicola. 'On Keith Hammersley.'

'What about him?'

'He was the lead detective on Sarah Welland's disappearance, back in 2021.'

Nicola's mind was recalibrating, fast. Was everything that had happened here in the past forty-eight hours connected to the events of 2021?

47

He was sitting very close to the screen when he heard the knock.

Freda was out, doing all the things that Freda did. Keith instead was peering closely at images, slowing them down, speeding them up. He had been doing this for many hours now, today and yesterday. When he was not out with the drone, he was back in here reviewing what the drone had picked up.

Most of it was innocuous: landscape, people going about their holidays. He'd picked up a couple of fights and a near drowning on the boating lake. A few arguments were apparent. He was surprised people weren't more aware they were being filmed. The drone wasn't silent. Mind you, it could fly high, and then zoom in the camera far below. It was amazing what Keith had seen. Surely people knew nowadays there was no such thing as privacy. He had once unwittingly captured a young couple having sex in a bush.

He had been violently sick yesterday, as the news of a suspicious death spread around the site. He had been wound up as he watched the police operate. He was unimpressed by his interactions with them. He did not believe he was delusional. There was something he was looking for and it was crucial he concentrated.

And today he had something that would show them.

The knock at the door could not have come soon enough.

*

'You should've told us you were ex-job,' said Nicola, as they entered Lodge 50.

'Thought you were detectives,' said Keith.

Nicola bit her tongue. Sarah Welland's disappearance was a sidewinder to her investigation. Was one connected to the other or were they entirely separate? What was Keith doing here? Did Val Doyle know he was here? If Keith was the original detective, on a case that had been tainted both by the lack of a result and allegations of either corruption or incompetence, what did that mean in relation to Darren Winters?

'What exactly are you doing here?' asked Nicola.

'What d'you *think* I'm doing?' snapped Keith, as he opened the door to one of the bedrooms.

Nicola and Harry peered in. On the bed were four storage containers full of documents. On the walls and doors of the wardrobe were pinned maps, diagrams, lists of names, lodges and even a photo of the Parkwood site from 2021.

For a moment Nicola was speechless. Then she walked in and began to open one of the crates. 'You kept all the original case files?'

'Just copies,' said Keith defensively. 'I took duplicate files with me on a USB stick when I left. Printed all this out myself. Like to have it with me.'

'You know you're not allowed to do that,' said Nicola. 'I should report you.'

'How many times have you been back here?' asked Harry.

'Couple of times a year.'

'Seriously?'

'Across different seasons, to see if the ground changes or anything's been disturbed. I still think her body's here somewhere. There's no other explanation. And then, the week of the anniversary, I always make sure I'm here. This is the first time I've come with the wife. She'd worked out something was going on, thought I was having an affair. Which in some ways . . .'

'You've come here every year on the anniversary?' echoed Nicola.

Keith nodded. 'I always think maybe this year there'll be someone who was around then, or whose memory gets jogged, or . . . I compare all the guest lists, see who's back, talk to returning people if I can . . .'

'And Parkwood know about this?' asked Nicola.

'The manager, Lindsey, she worked here at the time. I think she feels some obligation or desire to have it finally concluded, too.' Nicola watched him fiddle with some of the files. 'I come back in case I see something different. The case was my failing, right?'

'You can't think like that,' said Nicola.

'Easy to say if you've never had one of these cases,' replied Keith. 'The one you don't solve, the one you can't shake, the one you feel is staring you right in the face. We all get at least one in a career. You're lucky if you've not had yours yet. But trust me, it'll come.'

Who says I've not had mine, thought Nicola, as she focused her attention on the contents of the boxes. She pulled out a crisp white T-shirt, seemingly unworn, and held it up.

'That belonged to the lads on the stag do.'

Nicola stared: on the front of it were printed in bold black letters: WHAT HAPPENS AT PARKWOOD STAYS AT PARKWOOD!

'Jesus,' said Nicola.

'Didn't age well,' agreed Keith. 'It wasn't one of them,' he added.

'I wouldn't mind looking at their profiles –'

'I'm telling you, it wasn't. It's all documented. There's no trail there.'

'All the same,' said Nicola.

'No, not all the same,' said Keith tetchily. 'I know what they said, that we're just looking after our own. That bunch were not my own. They were from Kent, absolute louts. I had, and have, no reason to protect them. If there was even the smallest speck of evidence which suggested any link to the case, I would have been on it. I looked. There was nothing.'

'OK,' said Nicola. She noted how riled the suggestion had made Keith. Was that defensive posture designed to repel interest, or had he genuinely exhausted that particular investigative avenue?

'Do you think Darren Winters' death is connected to Sarah's disappearance?' asked Nicola.

Keith looked out of the window and pondered this. 'It took me all of yesterday to get my breath back. I don't see how it can't be.'

Nicola decided to take a collegiate approach. 'We had a huge investigation in front of us, before we even thought about Sarah Welland. What should we be looking at in these files?'

Keith considered. 'The day she went missing, they'd had a big night before and her mum was suffering the next morning. Sarah's up first, seemingly leaves a note saying she's going for a morning run. People see her on the route. But . . . she doesn't come back. Phone, purse, ID, everything still at the lodge. And last sighting is by the boating lake, near the high ropes, by a guest.'

Lee Parker's territory, thought Nicola.

'In the run-up to coming here, she takes out three thousand pounds from her account. Clears it out completely.

Classic two hundred and fifty quid a day over a couple of weeks, various cashpoints, all cash. We've got all the footage from the machines; she's not being threatened by anyone or under duress while she's doing it.'

'Unless she was being blackmailed,' said Nicola.

'Or doing a bunk,' added Harry.

'Then how come we never found that money?' asked Keith. 'We have the numbers of the banknotes. And if she was doing a bunk, why did we never catch her at any airports or UK departure ports?

'Have a look at her notebook. She had a little to-do journal thing, work stuff, shopping, reminders, everything about her life; she was quite analogue rather than techy. Her mum said she had a bit of a penchant for nice stationery ever since she was in Japan.'

'The point being?' asked Nicola, trying to hurry him along. She felt they were being pulled off course.

Keith looked almost hurt. 'A lot of the stuff in that notebook, it's pretty banal, but there's an entry where she writes down *£3k*. And there's other bits and pieces on that page that don't really connect. But it's like, I dunno, it feels like the doodle of someone who's on the phone or meeting someone and making a note . . . but it's in the middle of things like party invite lists or restaurant bookings, friends stuff, lists of work products she's supposed to pick up . . . That's the one that drives me mad. One of the last few entries. Part of me thinks it was just nothing, that all her scribblings are just that, the random thoughts of a girl.' Nicola bristled. Sarah Welland was a woman, not a girl. 'But what do I know?'

That was the question, thought Nicola, as she stared at Keith: what *did* he know?

'Why was Darren Winters the main suspect?'

Keith counted off the reasons on his fingers. 'No alibi, couldn't account for his movements at the time of her disappearance, couldn't prove he was at home, possible he could've been here. There was landscaping work going on across a wide part of the site at that time; he would've known where to dispose of a body. And it was like he'd sought her out, to be nice, to give her a better lodge. There were stories he kept bumping into her. It was like he was grooming her. And then when we interviewed him, his story was never straight. He looked panicked. He told lies. Now you could say they were white lies, he was anxious, but he just had the air of it. The sniff test. His manner, his behaviour. But also, nobody else was even close. There was nothing to suggest it was anyone but him.'

'Do you still think you were right?' asked Harry.

Nicola looked at Keith. How strong was *his* Voice of Doubt?

'Nobody came up with a theory that beat it. I'm not saying we were perfect. We were late, we didn't give anything enough credence, we were three steps behind before we started, but I did everything I could. I'm still trying to do everything I can. So have a look and tell me what you think happened, genius,' said Keith defiantly.

'We still have to talk about what you were doing on Monday night,' said Nicola.

Keith looked furious. 'Oh, come *on*, woman. Look around. I'd have to be a lunatic to want to kill the only man who might know what happened to Sarah.' Nicola noted how Keith and Val spoke about Winters in the same way. Could they somehow be in cahoots? 'Him dying does none of us any favours at all.'

He led them out of the bedroom. 'Now sit down in here. This is why I came to you.'

He gestured to them to sit on the sofa and flicked the television on. He had uncoupled the GoPro camera from his drone and hooked it up to the TV. He had already started playing the footage, so Nicola and Harry did as they were told.

The screen showed the drone launching from outside Keith's lodge earlier this morning. From there it rose into the sky and took what seemed like a tour of Parkwood. A lot of the time it was low to the ground, tilting down. When it came near people, it rose further up, but always looking at the ground.

Harry asked, 'What are you looking for?'

'Anything. Sarah Welland's body.'

Nicola's attention flicked from the screen to Keith himself. Keith was transfixed as the footage played on.

'Whenever I've come here, I stay in this same lodge, have the drone take the same routes, at least once, slowly all around everywhere. And compared it to Google Earth pictures from before she was killed. See if anything has changed, or moved, or got disturbed. Any tiny little clues.'

'You really think she was killed and buried here?' asked Harry.

'Here or nearby. Only explanation. So I let the drone go out past the fence into the woodland. Look, don't get me wrong, this is needle-in-haystack stuff. I know that. But what else can we do, after all these years? I'm retired. I've got time. And in the absence of anyone else doing anything, here we are. Now. Here we go. Somewhere round here.'

They all leaned in to the screen. The drone was flying through the tops of pine trees.

'I have to take the drone high here, because of all the

high ropes. I do it early before anyone's awake and the site becomes active, obviously. See here, just coming up, I was piloting through here in order to get to the ground on the other side, but I'm enjoying the beauty of the sunrise, then I could swear I see a flash coming off one of the trees. There. Did you see it? Here you go – you can see me move around. I've just seen it. And again, another flash.'

The image pivoted round and slowed as the drone turned to focus on something.

'And I'm like, where the hell was that coming from?' narrated Keith. 'And I thought, well, that's interesting. Those rungs.'

The image was moving in on one of the trees in particular. It had rungs built into the thick pine trunk, and the drone hovered at the top of the rungs.

'Then this . . .' said Keith as the drone closed in on a tree whose trunk spanned out into a couple of thick branches.

The drone was hovering, getting closer . . .

And now they could begin to see it.

Stuck into the bark of the tree was a knife.

A large kitchen knife embedded into a branch of the majestic pine, glinting in the early-morning sun.

48

Alice was hurrying towards the staff entrance of the supermarket when she saw Conor Slater pacing up and down by the door.

She saw him a split second before he saw her and it gave her no time to think about avoiding him. She didn't know why her instinct was to avoid him. Something about the look on his face. She could tell he wanted something. Alice had learned from a young age to spot when people were about to ask for something, especially something Alice might be reluctant to do or give them. It was a very specific type of expression, unique to every person, but Alice somehow had a sixth sense for it.

'Hey!' called Conor, and smiled, as if delighted to see her. This was very much what Lee had done, thought Alice with the shock of clarity.

'I don't think you should be back here,' said Alice.

'Oh, really?' said Conor and looked around, faking surprise. 'I'm really glad I bumped into you, though. I just wanted to say thank you for the babysitting the other night. Umm, this is awkward, well, it doesn't have to be awkward, but we feel awful, Emma, my wife, and myself, me, both of us thought the other was going to, or *had*, in fact, tipped you for babysitting, but then when you were gone we were talking and realized that neither of us had done it and you'd been so great and we'd been later than we said, and so anyway I thought I'd better come and find you and give you the tip that we should have given you. If that's all right, if you don't mind.' With this, he held out a note.

Alice noticed it was red. She didn't ever get red-note tips, well, except from this man. Blue or brown, sometimes the mauve-y one on a good day. But this was red. And red was fifty pounds.

Conor stiffened his arm and sort of bounced his hand towards her, as if to say, *take it then, quick, or it might go.*

'You've already tipped me with one of those,' said Alice.

'No, I know, we know, but you were so great and presumably the company takes a cut and . . . I don't know how it works, but really we'd like to!' He proffered the note again, and his expression was pained, almost a plea. He looked around as if to check no one was watching.

Why did people want to keep giving her money? Not that she didn't need it, but she didn't want it right now, not for the reasons people were giving her money today.

Even before today, Alice had noticed that people behaved very strangely when they were on holiday. They behaved in ways that would be weird in their normal lives. Alice did not know why. Alice had never been on holiday. She had never had anyone to go with, and she had not been taken as a child. She had seen them, of course, in adverts, on people's socials, in films and TV. A holiday seemed to her to be the most glamorous idea possible. A week (or, unimaginably, *two* weeks!) with no work (*no work!*) and all you had to do was, well, nothing. Alice was unsure whether she would find them enjoyable. She liked being busy. If she had nothing to do, how would the days go?

That's why she understood people who came to Parkwood. People at Parkwood were *busy* from the start to finish of the day. They had booked all their activities and knew how their days were going to go way in advance. And then when there was nothing scheduled, they could go on the bikes they had rented, or walk on the set paths, or go in the Splashdome. A Parkwood holiday made sense to Alice. You didn't have to get on a plane (she did not want to get on a plane; she had done that once and it made no sense. Plus, airports, man!) and you were busy. And if you didn't like it, or you got bored, you could go home, no bother. Although Alice noticed people did not tend to go home from Parkwood. A couple of times when she'd been cleaning in one part of a lodge, she had heard tense conversations from couples in another part of the lodge where someone would be saying, 'Well, we've paid for it now, so you might as well try and enjoy it!' or 'We've got all these things booked – we can't just up and leave!'

Alice had noticed that holidays were not relaxing for some people. She had heard quite a lot of people say that. Sometimes she heard people moan about being 'all crammed into these pokey lodges', although Alice did not consider them pokey, she thought they were spacious and well equipped. People would also yell about not being able to 'bear living on top of each other like this!', and that they wanted to go home, but they never seemed to end up going home early. Quite often things seemed to be resolved with pizza. Pizzas, or the promise of pizzas, seemed to settle a lot of things.

Alice often thought she would like a holiday at Parkwood. It would be her type of break. But the problem was that she would want to help out: if things hadn't been cleaned well or quickly enough, or if there was a big queue of tutting people at the supermarket checkout. She would feel bad if she didn't help out. Her problem was she knew too much of what went on behind the scenes. But then that was cool, too. She knew the workings. She was important and valued here. And that had not always been the case in her life. She had found happiness here and long may it continue.

She was staring at Conor and the fifty-pound note.

'I think that's a lot,' said Alice, not taking it. She knew it wasn't just a tip. It was too big for a tip. People never just gave you something for nothing or because they were being nice.

This situation did not feel like a reward, as Conor was saying. It felt like a request. Lindsey had, early on in Alice's Parkwood career, said, 'Be very careful about taking money off guests. They are allowed to tip, but be sure you know what it's for or what they want.' That advice, given long ago, felt made for this moment.

'Honestly, you deserve it,' said Conor. 'Please, we'd be so happy if you took it.'

He was very keen for her to have it. If she didn't take it, it would feel awkward, the guest would feel rejected and then maybe he'd give bad feedback on the form or to her supervisor and she might lose the babysitting work. And she loved sitting the babies – it was easy and she could pretend she lived in the lodges and just watched Netflix. She got paid for watching Netflix.

'Thank you,' said Alice, and she took the note and put it in her pocket. She felt herself blushing hard. She wished she were able to rely on her ability not to blush. She never liked the feeling.

They stood there for what seemed to Alice like for ever but was probably about half a second.

'I should get in and start my –' She nodded towards the supermarket.

'Yes! Sorry! Didn't mean to hold you up!' said Conor,

smiling and waving her past him, as if gesturing to an invisible red carpet.

As she began to move, he said, 'Oh –'

Alice stopped. Looked at him.

He was looking thoughtful and moved the thoughtful gaze to her eyeline. 'Did you . . . ? What did you . . . ? Have you had to . . . give a statement to the police, about this terrible thing?'

Here it is.

'We all have,' said Alice.

'Yeah, God, just awful,' said Conor. 'And you would've told them where you were. And where we were. And when we came back. What time, all that.'

'Mm-hmm,' said Alice, nodding.

'Great, good, great,' said Conor, turning away as if heading to go.

Then he turned back.

'Did we . . . did I . . . did you . . . did we see each other afterwards?'

Yes.

'Um.'

'Cos I had to run back, I'd left something, my phone, I think. Proper panic. I was just wandering around like a loon trying to think where it was, but it was very late and everything was closed –'

'Right. Yeah, maybe.'

'Only I wouldn't want you to think – I dunno, I just – Also Em, my wife, she didn't know about that, and did you tell the police I was . . . that I'd lost my –'

Alice shook her head. 'No.'

'OK, great.' Conor seemed to almost laugh and sigh at the same time. Alice sensed relief. 'That's great cos – yes, thank you.' He held up his phone. 'It's about Em as much as anyone that I – I found it, though, you'll be glad to know. In the lodge, of course. What's the last place you had it, right?'

Alice smiled politely and nodded.

'Anyway,' said Conor, who was backing away towards the exit, 'really sorry for delaying you.' He raised a hand. 'Have a great day!'

And he was gone.

Alice stood there for a moment. At least that was cleared up. He had given her the fifty pounds because she knew something that he did not want going any further.

She wondered if it was dangerous to know this many things about this many people. She had not deliberately gathered all this information; it just seemed to stick to her. Maybe it was being here for so many hours a day. Maybe it was doing the three different jobs in different areas of Parkwood. She was beginning to realize that being everywhere meant being around when people ended up doing things they didn't want other people to know about.

She looked at the fifty-pound note and found worrying thoughts trickling into her mind.

She put it away and went to start her shift.

Keeping busy was good.

49

Harry Ward (2026 version) viewed himself as a can-do sort of guy.

It was one of the aspects he was proud of himself for changing.

In his life and career before the police, he was not that. He let other people take the slack and the strain. He had been an absolute 6.5 out of 10 effort guy. Low-level effective. His colleagues at his previous jobs labelled him BMG: Bare Minimum Guy.

Harry had been BMG for the first half of his twenties. Outside work, he didn't really give a shit, turned up places late but had enough charm to dazzle people when he got there. A party never really started until Harry arrived. 'Now it's on!' would be the cry of his best mates once Harry appeared.

When life changed catastrophically in his mid-twenties, so did his attitude. He did what people had been suggesting for a number of years: he took a long hard look at himself. And he wasn't thrilled by what he saw.

He did not welcome the events that had shaped those two years of his life between twenty-four and twenty-six. He had shed several layers of skin, several versions of himself. He had been forced to look into his core. And he wasn't impressed. He had understood life all wrong. He had been shown that life was both fragile and precious. Gradually, he had rebuilt his life and his self.

And now things were different.

When there was a task to be volunteered for, 2026 Harry Ward (*DC Harry Ward, thank you very much*) would volunteer first, even if it caused him physical or mental (or even emotional) discomfort. If there was something that caused other people to pause, Harry saw that as a sign to step forward. Because he had once been the person who paused.

He was glad his current colleagues had never met that version of Harry Ward. He didn't want to be that person any more, and he didn't want to get into that time. His colleagues would think less of him. He thought less of himself. Now he was fine to shuttle under the moniker of 'Westlife' – good-looking and keen. It was so much better, so much more than he was before. It gave him somewhere fresh to start from, and somewhere to go.

Sometimes, though, this version of Harry Ward would feel that perhaps he had taken the 'stepping forward' a fraction too far.

This was one of those moments.

He wished his brother were here to witness it. To see all the hard-won changes that had occurred. And to see him in this get-up.

He looked down. He was strapped into a harness and he had a rope line in his hand with a carabiner on the end.

He looked up: there was a crisscross network of rope lines above him, going high up into the trees above.

There had been much discussion among Harry, Nicola and Reeta. Could they allow Parkwood staff to work their way along the high ropes to retrieve what looked like, from the zoomed-in photo they had pored over, a potential murder weapon? Even if they were careful, and gloved, it allowed for cross-contamination.

Reeta had also made clear her feelings: 'There is no way in hell you are getting me up there. I've got kids, and sense.'

Other members of her team looked at their shoes when Nicola asked if anybody else fancied it. Mel said, 'Not on your nelly,' which was not a phrase Harry had heard before and he wondered if it was an actual phrase that other humans used or just something Mel said. He would check with Nicola because he was discovering there were quite a few Mel-only phrases.

Nicola said she'd do it. Reeta had asked incredulously, 'Do you *want* to do it?' and Nicola had replied, 'Of course I don't *want* to do it, but it needs doing and it needs doing fast!'

At which point Harry Ward, Westlife himself, had stepped forward and said, 'I'll do it if you like.'

'Yes – you *love* high ropes!' said Nicola with relief.

'Our hero!' Reeta had beamed.

'You sure?' Nicola had asked him, clearly desperate for him not to recant.

'You said it, I love the high ropes!' said Harry lightly. He had learned, since he had stepped into being the best possible version of himself, that making people positive *you* were positive was part of the package.

So here he was, trussed up like a turkey, with an uncomfortable harness digging into his groin.

The staff member who was the most qualified to take him up through the trees was currently a key person of interest in their murder investigation. Lee would not be leading Harry to find the murder weapon which Lee may or may not have put in the trees. A nineteen-year-old called Annie would be doing that instead.

Lee Parker was being kept, along with other staff members, further away for now. He had expressed his bewilderment and frustration – he would be the best person to be sent up there. Reeta had calmly and authoritatively disabused him of this belief.

There was also a disappointed group of guests who had booked into the high ropes for the end of the day. On being told it was closed, they lurked, curious, rubbernecking at what was going on.

The other person present, smoothing guests' feathers, and also keeping a beady eye on what was happening, was Lindsey. She had given her permission but had wanted to be there 'in case of any incidents'.

As well as the high-ropes kit, Harry was equipped with forensic gloves and an evidence tube. He smiled and nodded at his colleagues. He did not mention that he had ever so slightly exaggerated his high-ropes experience.

He'd been on high ropes three times. The second time was because he'd bottled out halfway across the first time, and his dad had said, 'If you don't give it another go, you never will.'

His dad had been right, to be fair. That was why he went on a third time. He had enjoyed it no more. And, since becoming a fully fledged adult, he had become ever more certain that big heights were just not really his thing.

He had decided against sharing this. And so here he was for a fourth time, projecting confidence. *Happy, Dad?*

It did all come flooding back to him. Clip the carabiners on and off, look ahead not down, keep a steady pace and keep your balance.

Keep your balance.

The whole of life in a high-ropes methodology.

Don't look down, don't let your mind wander or start getting philosophical.

Annie was striding off to the course, keen to get there. She would lead and assist Harry through. 'I've never hunted for a murder weapon before,' she had said to Harry excitedly.

'Well, that's good,' said Harry.

'Nobody's saying it's categorically a murder weapon,' Nicola had interjected. 'This is just exploratory, to see what's up there.'

'OK,' said Annie, looking at Nicola as if she was a pompous and thick great-aunt. Then she smiled at Harry. 'Ready, Hazza?'

Why was everyone starting to call him Hazza?

They went straight for the Black Route. There were four in total: Bronze, Silver, Gold and Black. Black was the most difficult, normally only reserved for the people who had completed the first three and wanted a tougher challenge. The price of entry was having successfully done the other three. This did not apply to Harry. He was going straight to the top. He wouldn't have minded the practice.

The Black Route was higher and there were more obstacles. They had to make their way across wobbly rope paths, wooden stepways with large gaps between and big drops below. Stepping from one to the other required Harry to use the fullest extent of his stride, and all his upper-body strength holding on to the single rope keeping him attached to the safety line above.

'You OK?' asked Annie, glancing back at him.

'All good,' said Harry tightly.

Annie seemed to skip through the Black Route, the sign of someone who'd been up here many times, and possibly been tutored in all the pitfalls and tricks of the route. It reminded Harry that, much like playing video games, things are easy once you know how to do them. Once you've figured it out, it seems idiotically simple and you can't believe you were once unable to do it. Maybe he'd feel like that about the Black Route after this.

They got to a staging point of a thick tree, and Harry hugged the trunk gratefully as he edged round it on to a platform. It looked out over the final upward line running diagonally up to high in the trees.

Harry looked down, seeking out Reeta and Nicola looking up from below.

That was a mistake.

They were a long way away, staring up.

The world wobbled beneath him. He felt himself swaying. He lost his bearings.

'You good, Hazza?'

Annie's voice broke through his spinning world. He looked back up and over at her.

'Yep,' he lied.

'Did you look down?' asked Annie, her eyes dancing with laughter.

'Maybe.'

'Yeah, wouldn't do that.'

'Nope,' said Harry.

'One more, then you're at the base platform for the steps. Up there is the place you're looking for.'

Harry nodded.

They ascended the rising diagonal line. This was the toughest incline of all on the Black Route, and Harry felt it both physically and mentally. He did not really want to keep going higher. He wanted to go down.

He gave himself an inner mental pep talk: *Harry, the definition of bravery is not doing something you find easy, but attempting something you find difficult or don't want to do.* He then thought that actually right at this moment he wasn't interested in pep talks or the abstract theories of bravery. He just wanted to be on the ground.

He kept looking up. Kept climbing. He thought of his dad. His dad who encouraged him to do the course one more time but never went on it himself. Bloody hypocrite.

It was not the greatest of his dad's contradictions or issues.

'Last step, Hazza,' Annie's encouragement came floating on the air and he realized he was there. He took the step and landed on the platform.

'Congrats,' smiled Annie. 'This is as high as any punters ever go.'

Ahead of them was the start of a zip line. Harry could see the direction it took, going through the trees and out across the boating lake and into the woods on the other side of the lake. It was the fastest way down and off the high ropes, and he was really looking forward to it.

Unfortunately, Harry now had to go even further up.

Annie nodded at the small metal rungs built into the thick pine trunk. 'And up there is the highest place on the whole site. Maintenance access for the top of all the ropes and zip line. We call it the stairway to heaven.'

Harry looked at the first rung, and then straight up. It seemed to him right now that the tree went into the sky, beyond sight. A vertical pole waiting to be ascended. Up there, he would be fifty feet off the ground, possibly more. He hadn't wanted to know.

There were branches running off the main pole. On one of them, supposedly, was lodged a knife which was still glinting at the people standing down below.

'I can go,' said Annie.

Harry shook his head. 'Thanks. I've got it.'

I have not got it. Not in the least.

They could have got a cherry picker. Why hadn't he said yes to a cherry picker? Why had he put himself in the middle of this? It would have taken longer to source and cost money, and been a bit of a logistical headache, but it had been offered.

But no, you had to be heroic. You had to volunteer. You've got what you wanted now. Enjoying it?

Very much not enjoying it. Very much bricking it.

Annie shrugged. 'I'll be waiting here. You get the Infinity Stone, we zip-line down to a heroes' welcome. Cool?'

Harry knew that his absolute lack of certainty was plastered across his face. 'OK.'

'Up you go then,' chivvied Annie. 'Slow and steady, though.'

Harry began to ascend.

It's just like climbing a ladder.

One hand after another. One foot after another.

Slow and steady. Don't look down. Keep looking up.

He could feel the sway of the tree. It made his stomach flip.

He paused, holding on for a second.

He wanted to hug the pine, to wrap his arms round it, to stay there.

He could not hug it; he would not get his arms round it. If he did hug it, that would mean taking his hands off the rungs above. And the rungs were the only thing keeping him on the tree rather than sliding down it or falling off it.

Every rung was a step closer.

Harry could see the branch above him. The rungs stopped just alongside it. The highest place in Parkwood.

Who the fuck put it up here? Who would even have the ability to do that?

Had to be someone fit and strong. Had to be young, too. Didn't they?

Unless it was more than one person. Or someone disposed of the weapon as a favour for the actual killer.

Stop speculating, keep concentrating on the work. Thinking is for later.

DC Harry Ward reached his staging post.

There it was.

A large kitchen knife was jammed into the point where the branch met the trunk of the tree.

As if the tree had been stabbed in a similar fashion to Darren Winters.

It was going to require a little bit of effort to extract it.

For a second an image ran through Harry's mind. He would pull the knife from where it was lodged in the tree – like King Arthur retrieving the sword from the stone.

And he would loosen it from its lodging and in so doing he would shift his balance and his foot would slip from the rung –

And he would fall backwards through the air, holding the knife victoriously aloft, tumbling down, down, down –

Finally hitting the forest floor of pine needles, air being smacked out of him, and, knowing his luck, his arm convulsing so awkwardly that the knife landed in his chest.

What a way to go. Awful.

Mustn't do that, noted Harry to himself.

He held steady on the rung. He pulled the evidence bag from the small rucksack he had on his back. He took off the gloves he had on for climbing. Underneath were forensic gloves – two pairs, Reeta had suggested. One to prevent contamination from the high-ropes gloves themselves.

Harry got close to the knife. The blade was at eye level. The tip was buried in the tree, though it didn't go in far.

There was what looked like dried blood on one section of the knife.

Harry held the end of the handle as lightly as he could. He wanted to wipe as little evidence from it as possible. But he had very little leeway. The only way to get it out was to grasp the handle and work it out.

He grabbed it and moved it around in a circle.

It loosened.

Harry's left foot slipped off the rung.

Just fractionally, a slip caused by his movement –

His adrenaline spiked, as did his heart rate – for a second he thought he was about to fulfil his own hallucinatory image and fall to his death.

But he regained his footing, planting both feet on the rung, holding the rungs above with both hands, steadying himself.

A worried call drifted up.

'All right, Hazza?' Annie was somewhere down there. He did not want to look at her.

Harry took a deep breath. *Do not fall.*

'Yep,' he yelled back. Minimum of words, minimum of effort. No ability to chat.

Back to work.

He went back to attempting to ease the knife out of the bark.

It began to give –

And then, smoothly, it came away in Harry's hand.

Done it.

He pulled the evidence tube from his pocket. Deposited the knife into the tube, then screwed the top on. Back into his pocket.

Now he had to climb back down. With a knife in a tube in a rucksack on his back.

He began to slowly descend.

One rung at a time.

*

On the platform below, Annie high-fived him and expressed her previously unsaid doubts that he'd be able to do it. Harry wasn't sure how he felt about being patronized by a nineteen-year-old.

But now it was time for the fun bit.

DC Harry Ward zip-lined high over the boating lake at Parkwood Dorset, while making a substantial effort to repress his deeply felt desire to yell 'wooohoooo!' as he whooshed through the air high above the water.

But he felt, in the circumstances, it would be unseemly.

At the other end, he saw the impressed faces of his colleagues. He handed over the evidence tube. Reeta and Nicola crowded round to see what was in it. Reeta's analysis was swift.

'Right size of blade, blood markings – we'll get it tested, but it matches the weapon we're looking for.' She looked at Harry. 'Nice work, Westlife.'

Great, now Reeta was calling him Westlife too.

Nicola patted him heartily on the back. 'Good job, you OK?'

Harry nodded, and heard Reeta begin to discuss with Nicola the cordoning-off of this area and the logistics and realities of what SOCO could and couldn't do in an area open to the elements, let alone that high up. After the two women were out of sight, Harry collapsed to his knees and decided to sit down on the very welcoming ground.

He stayed there for a while.

He might think twice before volunteering next time.

50

'Who do you want to start with?' asked Harry when they were back in the lodge. 'Smart place to hide something if you're worried about the ground level being searched. Whoever put it there had that knowledge and thought it would be not just out of sight but out of reach. We would never have found it if it weren't for Keith's drone.'

'You think it points us to Lee Parker,' said Nicola.

'He knows the route; he has access. I mean, not just access – he can get up there without being daunted. I'm not sure he's accounted for his movements properly yet. He has to be top candidate because how many other people even know about that section?'

Nicola thought about this. 'It's hardly a secret – you can see the rungs clearly in daylight if you know where to look. Or if you've been on the high ropes and had them pointed out to you.'

'OK, but even then. Knowledge that you can get to the top of that tree isn't enough. You have to get up there. You'd need a familiarity with the high ropes, you'd need equipment, and you'd also need real ability and confidence,' said Harry.

'You're implying that that restricts the person responsible to staff only, but I'm not so sure. Also, there's nothing to say that it was the killer who tried to dispose of the weapon up there anyway. Could've been an accomplice.'

'Or someone who's trying to fit Lee Parker up, shift the focus on to him,' said Harry, thinking.

'Except, like you said, we might never have found it,' said Nicola. 'Who are our key suspects who could've done it? We have to include Valerie Doyle. Knife missing from her lodge and we know Val's already lied about where she was.'

Harry looked sceptical. 'You think she could get up there?'

'Oi! Don't disrespect the mature woman!' said Nicola. 'She's fit, she's strong, she's been here before – she might know the course, where the tough bits are.'

'I can't see it myself, but that's no shade on her,' said Harry. 'Who else?'

Nicola was looking at the map of the site. 'Lindsey Moorfield. She has access to every system; she could get in anywhere and she knows the site inside out. She was probably here when they installed that section.'

'Is she a climber, though?' wondered Harry aloud.

'That's something to ask her. She has a long history with Winters. I don't believe she's told us the full picture.'

'Can I say a mad thing?' asked Harry.

'You never normally ask permission.'

Harry ignored her. 'D'you think it could've been dropped up there by drone?'

Nicola looked sceptical. 'Can you do that?'

Harry shrugged. 'I'm thinking about all the precision stuff they're doing with drones in wars. Dropping bombs and that. Is it too crazy to think you could stick that knife on there and then fly the drone up that high, and have it drop the knife . . . ?'

'Have to be an expert drone pilot, wouldn't you? You said it was properly embedded in the wood,' said Nicola.

'It was,' said Harry. 'I'm just wondering if that was because it was like dropped or released from higher up, so it landed there with force.'

'That's a super-precise operation,' said Nicola doubtfully. 'What about the risk of missing? And why would you leave it there if you could pilot it out on a drone? Why wouldn't you keep going, away from the whole site and ditch it in a field or a river? Also, that would mean it was our friend Keith and, professional history aside, I'm not even sure he knows how to work that drone properly. When I first met him, he'd just crashed it.'

'I'm not saying it DID happen. I'm just wondering if it could. We can't rule him out, can we?'

'No, we can't,' said Nicola reluctantly, rubbing her face while looking back at the map. 'OK, take it in order.'

'First things first,' said Harry.

Nicola looked askance at him. 'Are you mocking me?'

Harry seemed offended. 'I'm *quoting* you.'

'Oh, OK. Thought you might be taking the piss.'

Harry laughed. 'Why would I do that?'

Nicola backtracked. 'People have done.'

The ghosts of rooms in Liverpool, when she first joined. The team of men mocking and teasing and taking the piss, out of her, and her accent, and her place in the world. It still came to the surface, even now.

She liked how offended Harry was that she'd suggested he was being disrespectful. A different generation. Not just that. A different man.

She looked back at the map of the high ropes. 'Let's talk to Lee Parker.'

51

'Here they come then. What a surprise.'

As Nicola and Harry approached, Lee Parker stopped packing up for the day and stood defiantly in the entrance to the tiny cabin which housed the high-ropes equipment. His posture was planted, his arms folded and he eyeballed them all the way in, clearly wanting them to feel they had strayed on to his territory. Lee Parker clearly saw himself as the last knight defending the castle.

'Hello, Lee,' said Nicola, glancing past him to his fiefdom. There was a small work area built into the wall, with a few pieces of paperwork and folders, along with a tea-making station. Further in the back, a small locker was open with Lee's clothes and belongings visible inside it. The equipment appeared to be organized in a rigorous system.

'I feel like a man about to be screwed over,' he said. He didn't shift from his position, meaning the two detectives were forced to come to a halt in front of him.

'Why?'

Lee stared back at her and Nicola felt herself being weighed up. Not just professionally: looks-wise, style-wise, personality-wise. The way Lee rolled his eyes over her, she felt like he'd carried out a full scan and assessment and mentally ranked her in his own personal filing system. It was an unpleasant feeling. It felt *invasive.*

'Convenient for you lot that you found something up there.'

‘Trust me,’ said Harry. ‘It wasn’t convenient at all.’

‘You go looking on a hunch, and, oh, look, there’s something here! What a surprise!’ said Lee.

‘Not a hunch, a tip-off based on a credible sighting,’ said Harry. ‘Which has now been confirmed.’

‘OK, mate,’ smiled Lee coolly. ‘Whatever you say.’

Nicola was watching Harry and Lee. She had not seen this side of Harry before. He was bristling. Harry did not like Lee at all. Interesting.

‘We located an object that’s been sent for testing. It’s possible it may be connected to the murder of Darren Winters,’ said Nicola.

‘All right. I’m not an idiot. Where you’ve just been, that’s right at the very edges of what’s accessible to any of us. Not many people can get up there. So, what, you leap to thinking, oh, must be the bloke who runs the place!’

‘I’m not interested in assumptions,’ said Nicola. ‘Our job is to discover the facts.’

‘OK,’ said Lee. ‘Then for the avoidance of doubt, the facts are: I have not put anything up there in that area. I have not been up there this week. Do you need me to be any more clear?’

He stood, arms still folded, still defiant.

‘Very helpful,’ said Nicola, not looking away from his gaze.

‘Who else could confidently get up there?’ asked Harry.

Lee looked like he wanted to punch Harry. ‘Anyone who’s working on the team can go up there. Security can, but I’ve never seen them do it during my time. Maintenance, obviously. Anyone who’s worked in this section over the years would know how to get up there.’

‘And have you seen anyone unusual up there, or around that area, or behaving suspiciously in the past couple of days?’

'Yeah. You two,' said Lee.

Nicola felt Harry shift his weight from one foot to the other, as if ready for something to kick off.

Lee continued, 'Other than that, no. This is my manor, and people know not to mess with anything here. And if anyone came around doing anything, I'd know about it.'

Nicola thought that Lee's ego wasn't doing him any favours. He might have thought he was showing them how important he was. In reality, he was putting himself more in the frame.

Harry said witheringly, 'You think someone who's just murdered a man would be worried about the comeback from hiding the murder weapon in *your manor*?'

Suddenly, Lee squared up to Harry. 'What is your problem, mate?'

'Whoa, whoa, whoa!' said Nicola as the two men stood toe to toe, jostling like a couple of boxers at the weigh-in. 'What are you doing? Stand back, Harry.'

She pushed Harry back as Lee said, 'Yeah, come on, Harry, do what Mummy says.'

Now Nicola wanted to punch him. She turned and said, 'Lee, a man you know has been killed. The murder weapon has possibly been found very close to where you spend most of your time. Why the hell are you taking this attitude with us, when we're only trying to find out what happened?'

She could feel Harry behind her, breathing heavily, still wanting to lamp Lee.

'Anyone can see what this is. A stitch-up,' said Lee. 'Or were you two thinking you're cleverer than the rest of us?'

Nicola couldn't figure out Lee's approach – confrontational, defiant. Was that because he had nothing to do with the knife being up there, or did he think aggression was the best way to distract from his guilt?

'Did you put the knife up there, Lee?'

Lee looked Nicola straight in the eye. Almost too direct, she thought, too deliberate. It was like he was enjoying this conflict, this attention. 'I did not,' he said.

She wanted to say to him: I hope my son doesn't grow up like you. And then the thought of that, the image of Ethan from last night, the unresolved anxiety she was desperately trying to keep at bay, to compartmentalize, came smashing back into her brain and body. Her stomach lurched.

Separate it out. You cannot do both these things right now. Stay in this moment.

She heaved herself mentally back into the present, realizing that Lee was still talking.

'You want me to go down this road with you? All right, fine. Let's play your game.'

'It's not a game,' said Harry darkly.

'You think I don't know that?' Lee shot back. 'But you come into my workplace, throwing accusations around, so I'm saying, right, I'll humour you. For the purposes of this discussion, pretend it *was* me.'

Nicola and Harry stared at Lee. He wasn't smiling. His expression was intense, unreadable. Was he toying with them?

'It wasn't. But say it was, I would have to be all kinds of stupid to put a knife I've used to commit a murder at the top of a tree in the section of Parkwood *nearest to where I work*. Why would I put heat on myself? I'd take it out of the park. I'd drive it miles away. Otherwise it's just drawing attention to me. It would be insane.'

'Or arrogant,' said Harry.

Lee fixed Harry with a stare. 'Not arrogant. Insane.'

'Unless it was a double bluff,' Harry retorted.

Nicola watched Lee shift uneasily, like Harry had

penetrated his armour with a jab of something sharp, or said something Lee hadn't imagined the police might consider. 'How'd you mean?'

'Just what I said,' responded Harry levelly. 'In this fictional scenario, you're arrogant enough to think nobody else will see the weapon up there, because no one other than you ever goes that high. And if they do, you can argue that you'd never discard it so close to your main area of work – there's no way you'd do anything that foolish or careless if you were the killer.'

Nicola watched Lee's eyes narrow, and she felt like he was regulating something close to fury. He was not a man who was used to being challenged. 'Seriously, mate? Is this how the police think these days? Double bluff? How am I supposed to win if you think like that?'

'What d'you mean by "win", Lee?' asked Harry, so calm now. 'Why would this be about winning?'

Lee's ire was now raised. 'No, no, no –' he started, more fiery again now, advancing towards Harry. 'I'm not having it – by that thinking, you can go for anyone on anything by saying, "Oh, it's all a double bluff – you're so unlikely to have done that thing, that proves you're a killer, which means you must have done it!" Fuck kind of logic is that? I mean, come on!'

He looked at Nicola as if she were an adjudicator. He was red in the face now. He looked like a toddler on the verge of a tantrum.

Nicola was not going to adjudicate. Harry had managed to get beneath Lee's arranged demeanour. 'Did you kill Darren Winters, Lee?'

Lee looked back at her, furious. 'Why would I? Tell me why!'

Not a denial.

'We'll need a DNA swab from you.'

Lee looked alarmed. 'What? Why?'

'We're getting the knife examined. The DNA swab will help us compare any material found on the knife to your sample. So we can rule you out. Which is obviously in all our interests.'

'Oh, and by the way,' added Harry, 'that plaster on your finger.'

Lee looked at his finger as if seeing it for the first time. 'What about it?'

'Hurt yourself?'

Lee stared at his finger, then looked back up at Harry. 'Cut myself. Got it snagged on a line.' His attitude returned at full power. 'Why, d'you want that as well?'

'Yes,' said Nicola, to Lee's evident surprise. 'And the packet of plasters it came in, please.'

Lee looked bewildered. 'In that first-aid kit over there,' he said as Harry walked over, pulling on a pair of plastic evidence gloves. 'What've plasters got to do with anything?' he asked as Harry opened the first-aid box.

'Got 'em,' said Harry, holding up a box of plasters and placing them into an evidence bag he'd taken out of his pocket.

Lee looked to Nicola. 'How long you gonna keep this area closed?'

Trying to regain control, thought Nicola. 'As long as it takes to search,' she said. 'It's a big area. We'll be looking everywhere. Someone felt it was a good place to hide things. Who knows what else we'll find.'

'You're gonna have a riot on your hands,' Lee replied churlishly. 'You close the pool. You close this place. These are what people come for.'

'You let us worry about that,' said Nicola. 'We'll get someone over with a swab right away. And if you think of anything else we should know, get in touch immediately, will you?'

Lee did not move.

Nicola and Harry left him in the cabin. When Nicola looked back, he was still watching them from the doorway.

On the walk back to the lodge, Nicola told Harry, 'Get that fucker's cell phone sited.'

'With pleasure,' said Harry.

'I've never seen anyone quite rub you up the wrong way like that before,' observed Nicola.

'Dunno what you mean,' replied Harry.

'What is it about him that gets to you?'

Harry was quiet for a moment. Then he said, 'He reminds me of me.'

They walked on in silence, both preoccupied in different ways by what that meant, only interrupted by Nicola's phone buzzing.

It was Lindsey Moorfield. She sounded agitated.

'You need to get down here to the Sports Arena *immediately*. The guests have called a protest meeting.'

52

They were barely through the door of the standing-room-only Sports Arena Bar when someone shouted, 'Here they are!', and all heads turned and the barracking began.

Nicola spotted a myriad of familiar faces – both guests and staff had crammed into the space; word had clearly got round the Parkwood site like a virus – as a particularly vociferous woman with a Yorkshire accent strode forward.

'Right, you lot, we've had it! Not good enough! Half this place is closed, the kids keep hearing people talking about murder, we're being told we can't leave, there'll be no refunds, and nobody's telling us anything, so we don't know whether the killer's coming for the rest of us! You're *ruining* our holiday, and we don't even feel safe. We're paying to be here, you know!'

There was a groundswell of yelled agreement and a smattering of applause.

For a second Nicola felt like she might be on *Question Time*, literally one of her worst nightmares.

We don't have time for this.

She realized that she should have taken the initiative earlier and set up a public meeting for the end of the day, on her terms, in order to update, reassure and placate. But she hadn't because, well, because things had come up and kept coming up, because people (some of whom were in this crowd) had not come forward, or not told the full truth, or misled her and her team.

Right now, though, she could not allow the febrile atmosphere to escalate further.

'All right, thank you!' she called, as she flapped her arms in a downward shushing motion and stepped up to stand on the middle part of a banquette against the long wall of the bar. The cushioned seating beneath her wobbled and Nicola instantly regretted her choice, while simultaneously realizing that backtracking would look like a sign of weakness. She could not look like she didn't know what she was doing.

'I appreciate everyone may be feeling concerned and vulnerable –'

'And bloody trapped!' came a male voice, which was backed up by mutters of agreement.

As Nicola looked out across the bar she saw faces she, Harry and Mel had been discussing, nearly all of whom were up on the walls of Lodge 227. She felt herself mentally mapping them on to their lodges, as per Mel's wall of information. She also noted that some of the people who had cornered her and Harry at the restaurant the previous evening were once again near the front of the crowd, ready to opine and complain. In addition, she noticed a number of staff lurking at the back in the doorways that led to the indoor sports courts: waiting staff, housekeeping staff, security. She saw Lee Parker sidle in.

'I'll keep this brief as I'm mindful of not disrupting your holidays any more than has already been the case. As I think most of you know, an incident in the Splashdome overnight Monday into Tuesday resulted in a man's death. We have now identified that man and located the weapon that caused his death.'

There was a cacophony of questions. Nicola had wanted to drop in the fact that they had found the murder weapon in order to put the killer – if they were in this crowd, or if they had the information reported back to them – on alert. She scanned the room to see if she could locate any of their people of interest. She could see Harry slowly walking round the edge of the room, watching and listening.

'Who was he?'

'What sort of weapon?'

'Have you got 'em or not?'

Questions were being bowled at her as she stood above the crowd. She suddenly felt in a very vulnerable position – the opposite of authoritative, backed against the wall, on an unsteady cushion. She used her deepest, calmest voice to project.

'The victim was not a guest here, and we do not have reason to believe there is any danger to guests.'

'You would say that!' came another disembodied voice, and a low chorus of agreement backed it up.

As more yelled questions piled on top of each other, Nicola held her hand up in a failed attempt to quieten the crowd. She was starting to feel under siege.

'Where are all the police?' came a male voice. 'Why's the place not swarming with you lot?'

'We're mindful of keeping a low profile in order to minimize disruption to your holidays,' lied Nicola. *You should blush, Nicola Bridge.* 'There are extra security patrols during the day and more at night.'

'Why'd you bloody stop our Jack and his mates from helping out? They could've been out there at night keeping us all safe!' shouted a woman.

Before Nicola could get a reply in, a Belfast voice retorted, 'Hey! We don't need youse lot getting up to some vigilante shit on us! I don't need them keeping me safe!'

‘They were trying to *help*!’ squawked back the woman.

‘Please, ladies and gents, not helping!’ said Nicola in as loud and deep a voice as she could muster. The crowd quietened. ‘No unofficial patrols – nobody here is to take matters into their own hands.’

‘We pay your wages! You don’t get to tell us what to do!’ came a voice that Nicola thought sounded as if it was from East Anglia. Norwich? She had to stop playing accent bingo.

She raised herself to her full height on the wonky cushion and looked out over the sea of faces. ‘That’s where you’re wrong. As an experienced detective of some two decades’ standing, and the person in charge on the ground here, right now, I *do* get to tell you what to do. This is a delicate investigation and I need everyone’s cooperation. Anyone who infringes on our work may find themselves charged with obstructing the course of justice.’

She looked across them daring anyone to challenge her.

‘Now. The Splashdome, along with the high ropes, will remain closed at this time while our forensic teams –’

A chorus of groans and outrage drowned out her longer explanation.

One voice floated over the rest: ‘The high ropes too now?!’

Nicola spoke even louder. ‘I understand your concerns, I understand you want your holidays back. We are working rigorously and at speed. Please give us and all the staff here your support and we’ll see everything swiftly resolved. Thank you for your time.’

She stepped down, unimpressed. God forbid anybody’s holiday should be disrupted because a man had been killed. There was a volatile herd mentality already at work, outrage building as people worked each other up and social contagion spread. The atmosphere across the site had shifted quickly from shock to anger to wanting someone to blame. The crowd here felt the need to shame her, and her officers, for not having charged anyone yet.

Nicola stood watching people leave. There was much muttering, hostile glances in her direction. Some people went straight to the bar. Music came back on. She checked around for Harry and located him in conversation with a woman by the bar. She recognized the woman – which dot on Mel's wall was she?

It was then, as the rest of the crowd dispersed, that she saw a young woman curled into a corner tapping away feverishly on her phone.

It was the journalist from the front gate, Imogen Swift.

The one she had forbidden from entering.

53

After he and Nicola entered the Sports Arena bar, Harry deliberately drifted to the edge of the room and began stalking the perimeter. He and Nicola had developed this unspoken arrangement as their partnership developed: if she was at the centre, he would move to the edge. In a room of many people, the multiplicity of perspective usually yielded something.

As the heckling began from the middle of the room, Harry moved round the back. He noticed a number of people he'd interviewed, including Emma Slater. He checked around; she seemed to be here alone, without husband Conor or daughter Bella. Interesting, and possibly useful, thought Harry. He nodded from a distance. Emma smiled back. Harry sensed an opportunity. Here was the wife of one of their prime suspects, alone.

His attention was caught by the crowd barracking Nicola and as she climbed on to a banquette, Harry wondered if he should leap to her assistance, or whether that would make things worse. He decided it was the latter. Nicola would not thank him for making her look like she couldn't stand on a chair without the help of a young male assistant.

He was relieved to see her manage it. As Nicola began talking, Harry drifted back through the crowd, engineering it so that he ended up a few steps away from Emma Slater. She noticed him again and took a handful of steps towards him. Bingo.

'Not loving the vibe,' said Emma.

'No,' said Harry. 'How did this even happen?'

'Someone knocked at our door and said we should come. I think they went round every lodge. Conor didn't fancy it. I thought I'd better. He's taken Bella to the playground.'

'I'm sorry this has affected your holiday,' said Harry. Standard-issue statement for all guests right now.

'It's not about us, is it?' said Emma. 'I'm just thinking about the family and friends of whoever died. They must be in such shock right now.'

Harry nodded non-committally as Nicola was shouted down.

'Getting a bit rowdy,' said Emma quietly from next to him.

'I suppose people are anxious,' said Harry.

'People are fucking idiots,' said Emma under her breath to him.

Harry turned to look at her. She had one eyebrow slightly raised: am I right? Harry resisted a smile. 'I wouldn't say that.'

'You wouldn't, but I very much would.' Emma paused. 'Must be a lot of pressure on you guys.'

Harry wondered what she was digging for. Did she realize Conor was a suspect? 'We'll have it sorted, soon enough.'

Emma looked at him. 'You sound very confident.'

A couple of people turned round to see who was talking, which prevented Harry from having to reply.

'Guess it'll be hard for whoever did it to get away with it, given it's such an enclosed environment,' said Emma. 'With all the security. There's nowhere to go, is there?'

Harry looked at her. What was behind that? As he was about to reply, an older woman nearby turned and shushed them. 'I'm trying to listen!'

Emma held up her hands in apology. Harry thought she

looked uneasy and preoccupied. She also looked like she had more to say.

As the meeting concluded, Harry knew he should go over to Nicola. He had been hoping to speak more with Emma, but he could hear an argument breaking out across the room. He looked over to see Nicola remonstrating with a woman in the corner.

'Out!' Nicola wasn't quite yelling but she wasn't far off. She looked like she might haul the woman to her feet any second, which Harry knew was not a good look. 'Now!'

'Better go and –' he said to Emma, nodding over at Nicola.

'Yeah,' said Emma, not moving as Harry walked away.

He was reminded of the feeling he had once had back in school when he left a party feeling like he was leaving behind a girl who really fancied him but had been too shy to declare it. He did not think Emma Slater fancied him, but he did think she was on the cusp of letting something slip.

'Remember Imogen? She's the journalist we instructed not to come on-site,' said Nicola to Harry as he arrived at where his boss and a woman in her mid-twenties seemed to be having a stand-off.

'I'm allowed to be here!' said Imogen.

'You're absolutely not,' said Nicola. 'You're not a guest, you're not a member of staff, you're not a member of my team, you broke into the site when it was shut down for reasons of evidential security and you are taking notes on a meeting intended only for guests and staff at a private facility. Now me and DC Ward here are going to walk you to the gate, while you tell us how you got in, and we are going to ensure you do not come back until you're allowed. Move.'

Imogen moved and Harry and Nicola flanked her as they exited the bar.

'People have a right to know what's going on,' said the journalist, as Nicola flagged a passing buggy from outside the Sports Arena bar and instructed the staff member to drive them all to the front entrance.

'Who do you work for?' asked Nicola as they bumped along.

'I don't have to tell you that,' Imogen said sullenly. Harry watched her wilt under Nicola's gaze. 'I don't work for anyone. I'm freelance. I thought I could come in and film, sell the story, get someone interested if I had material no one else had got.'

'Get out,' said Nicola, pointing to the security exit. 'Don't come back.'

She nodded to the security guard to raise the gate. Imogen Swift stood there for a moment and then walked towards and under the gate and off down the lane. She looked back poisonously at Nicola. 'You should be ashamed!' she called.

As the gate closed behind her, Nicola turned to Harry. 'I'm going back to the lodge. I need some food and some peace to go through Sarah Welland's stuff.'

Harry thought for a second. 'I'll join you in a bit. There's something I want to do first.'

54

The long days and lack of sleep were catching up with Nicola, but she could not afford to lose focus. She had worked hard not to lose her cool completely in that meeting, but the implication that they were doing nothing and failing to protect people had left her riled. *If only you knew how fast we're actually working.*

And obviously she could not have told the crowd that some of the people at that meeting were key suspects: Lee Parker, who knew Darren Winters of old and who was the suspect most capable of disposing of the murder weapon where it had been found; Lindsey Moorfield, who also had known – and by her own account disliked – Winters for just as long, and whose account wasn't quite adding up. Both of them could've broken into Darren Winters' house after killing him if they were looking for something. And what about Conor Slater, the guest she'd had to stop from leaving, the one who had been involved in a fight at the standing stone, the man whose statement Harry had made clear he did not believe.

Then there was the unexplained disappearance of Sarah Welland echoing down across the years. Sarah's mother, Val, seemed to have kept coming to Parkwood on the forlorn but understandable hope that either she would discover something new or her daughter might walk back into her life. Or at least that's what she had said. Could Val be trusted? Was her grief so potent that she would kill for it? She had motive, opportunity – and the missing knife from her lodge could feasibly be the murder weapon; they had taken a DNA swab from Val before leaving and were having it tested against the knife Harry had retrieved. But could Val really have disposed of the murder weapon up there? She was fit enough: she'd talked about going to the gym every morning while here. But did that mean she could scale those heights?

Was Keith Hammersley really looking for Sarah Welland's body here – or ensuring it stayed undiscovered? Or could he have been so haunted by the case that he'd pursued a vendetta that had led to Winters' death? Nicola had met many Keiths in her time: bluff old-school male detectives. Some had turned out to be exemplars of their profession, some others were the nadir, using the cover of the job to disguise their own involvement in criminal activity. Which was Keith?

For all that they had ruled out a vast number of people through their statement-taking and Mel's growing wall of evidence, many possibilities were still live. And Nicola felt she also couldn't rule out the solution being something else they hadn't yet discovered.

She had taken refuge in her bedroom in Lodge 227. She needed a moment to herself, away from Mel's continuous drone of low-level complaints (a sort of self-generated mood music which seemed to keep him happy as he worked, if happy was ever a word that could be applied to Mel's state). She had wolfed down pasta pesto – six minutes' cooking time, three minutes' eating time, a reminder of when she was first training to join the police and it was all she lived on – and brought a load of the case files from Sarah Welland's disappearance in with her. She'd instructed Mel to work his way through the more data-rich files so he could provide a catalogued summary of anything factually relevant.

Nicola herself had taken the more personal pieces of evidence: Sarah's work calendars, notebooks where she wrote to-do lists and notes to herself about work and life, and her photograph collection.

It was all new information. Was she wasting her time with it? Keith Hammersley had thought so; when she'd asked about it, he'd said he'd read it all a dozen times. 'Just a lot of doodles and scribbling.' Was any of it really likely to be connected to the murder of Darren Winters? She rubbed her temples, her head pounding. She would devote the rest of tonight to assessing these documents. If nothing seemed relevant, then she would not waste any more time. This was not the crime she had been assigned to investigate. This had been Keith Hammersley's case and he had failed to resolve it. No body had ever turned up, so for now, she reminded herself, it was not even a murder case.

She was sitting up on the bed. The sun was starting to slowly set outside, flooding the sky with orange light. She knew if she reclined and put her head on the pillow, she would be asleep in ten minutes, a combination of carbs and exhaustion, so she sat upright and went through the photographs.

Lots of photos of Sarah on her travels – smiling, pretty, having fun. A variety of locations around the world. A *lot* of Japanese temples. A large number of different colleagues and friends. Nicola peered at them, searching for something: did Sarah look worried or scared or sad or withdrawn in these photos? Did her smile reach her eyes? Maybe not, at least in quite a few, but Nicola felt the same about herself in every photo ever taken of her. *Say cheese.* No.

The notebooks offered little, other than a litany of tasks in order of priority, scribbled accounts of phone calls and action points, shopping lists, possible holiday destinations, home furnishing desires, and notes to talk to Tim about stuff. There were costs of IVF, dates, test results, summaries of conversations with doctors. Pages were sometimes festooned with doodles and scribbles and smiley faces and sad faces and angry faces all next to each other. There were customer account numbers and phone helpline numbers, and reminders to pay speeding fines. There were also many, many pages where Nicola could not make head nor tail of the words or references. There were endless, *endless*, grids of noughts and crosses, and half-completed games of hangman. The scribbles of somebody bored on the phone or at work, playing games and asking somebody else to join them.

One page was entirely made up of question marks. Another had the words 'touch the stone touch the stone touch the stone' written in three sets of vertical lines. In another pen, Sarah seemed to have scrawled 'ABSOLUTE BULLSHIT' over those lines. On the next page was a cartoon which seemed to feature two stick people, one man and one woman, with the man next to what Nicola realized with a jolt looked like the Parkwood standing stone. Was it? There was a speech bubble coming from the man's mouth which said, 'It will give you a baby.'

Lindsey had said people projected all their beliefs on to that stone. Were fertility claims among them? Even if they were, and even if that was Parkwood's stone, Sarah seemed to have given it short shrift. Though Nicola also thought back to the underwear she had retrieved from beneath the stone.

How did any or all of these things fit together? Nicola scrunched her eyes closed, trying to see the patterns in her mind.

There was a tentative knock at the door. It could only be Mel. Even his knocking was irritating.

'Go away,' called Nicola.

'It won't take a sec,' said a muffled Mel.

'I'm concentrating,' Nicola said to the door.

There was silence and for a moment Nicola thought Mel might have gone away. Then there was a tiny creak from the floor and his voice came through the door once more.

'I think you might want to know,' it said.

Nicola sighed, got off the bed and opened the door.

'This'd better be good,' she said.

Mel was looking away with his hands over his eyes.

'What're you doing?' asked Nicola, bewildered.

'Are you decent?' asked Mel, his hand still over his eyes.

'Course I'm bloody decent. I'm not sitting around in my knickers; this is a workplace!'

Mel had taken his hands away from his eyes as soon as she said she was decent, but as Nicola used the word 'knickers' he winced.

'I don't know, do I?' said Mel. 'I don't want to be accused of . . .' He struggled to think of the specific charge that might be levelled at him and then just said, 'Well, anything!'

'I'm going through Sarah Welland's notebooks. What's so important?'

'Keith Hammersley had a restraining order against him, preventing him from being in contact with Darren Winters.'

Nicola had to privately concede that this probably was worth knocking on the door to tell her.

'When was this?'

'Two years ago. Darren Winters had it taken out, claiming Hammersley wouldn't leave him alone, was making his life a misery.' He paused to demarcate between fact and opinion. 'It did make me think, if you're ex-job, you know all the ways to plan and cover up a murder. For example, do it in a swimming pool where you know forensics are compromised.'

Nicola couldn't deny that Keith Hammersley was perfectly placed. 'Agreed. But then, why did he bring us the murder weapon?'

'Maybe he thought that if he tipped us off, it would distance him from suspicion. Pretty convenient that he found it, isn't it? I know he has hours of drone footage, but all the same.'

'Thank you, Mel. I'm going to get back to Sarah's notebooks now.'

Mel nodded. 'Let me know if there's anything else I can do.'

Nicola closed the door, and took the handful of steps back to the bed deep in thought. Could Keith Hammersley have lost his moral bearings since leaving the job? Had the case broken him to the extent that he had killed Darren Winters?

She resettled herself on the bed and returned to the pile of Sarah Welland material. As she did, she thought she should change her thinking. This wasn't a case to be solved. This was a person to listen to: another witness who had something to tell them. Nicola's job was not to solve a cold case here. It was to pick up on the information Sarah could give them that might help unlock the truth about Winters' murder.

They might not be able to question Sarah, but that didn't mean she had nothing to say.

Nicola picked up the notebook she'd been looking through before Mel's interruption. She looked back at the stick-person cartoon, and the 'absolute bullshit' page and then flicked back and forth for any other references which might connect to either of those, however tangentially. She found none. The notebooks read like a stream of consciousness.

The only other things that caught Nicola's attention were one page marked (presumably by Keith) with a red dot, where *3k* was scribbled in the top-left corner. And then another, the penultimate in the book, where in the bottom right-hand corner, there was a tiny noughts and crosses grid. Except instead of noughts and crosses, this had words. Nicola had to bring the book close to her face to read the tiny writing. It seemed to be multiples of three words: *Su*, *Hat* and *Jo* in different combinations, on the three-by-three grid. Nicola could make no sense of it. On the rest of the page were the details of the Parkwood stay: the number of their lodge, 49, arrival and departure times.

3k.

She had got three thousand pounds out in cash over a number of weeks.

Was that to pay someone here?

Nicola's head was now swimming. She peered again at the not-noughts-and-crosses grid.

Jo Su Hat
Su Hat Jo
Hat Jo Su

What did those words mean? Anything? Names of friends? Jo, Susan, Hattie? Colleagues? People staying at Parkwood? She would ask Keith and also have Mel cross-reference all these possibilities.

Nicola leaned back on the pillow, trying to solve that particular riddle – if it even *was* a riddle. When it came to Sarah Welland, it seemed like they could barely be sure of anything.

Her mind returned to Val, Sarah's mother, and what any parent would do to protect their child.

Nicola felt a wash of tiredness flood over her and surrendered, just for a second, to the desire to close her eyes.

55

Emma Slater, catching sight of herself in the bedroom mirror of Lodge 141 as she got changed into her running gear, stopped and looked at herself. She wondered about this woman that she was looking at right now.

Who are you, Emma Slater?

She knew who Emma *Masters* was. She had been Emma Masters since birth. Emma Masters was a fun, dynamic go-getter who worked hard, played hard, did well and could always be relied upon to deliver, even when times were tough. Emma Masters had been constant through school, university and then work. Sometimes she had too much of a laugh, partied a bit too hard, but it never affected her ability to do what was needed. People enjoyed being on Emma Masters' team; they had told her so. Emma Masters was cool. Emma Masters was a laugh. Emma Masters got things done. Emma Masters had mastered life.

But this Emma Slater, she thought, looking in the mirror, was more of a conundrum. Emma Slater had only been in existence for eight years.

Emma Masters had always been full of certainty, about herself and about others. Emma Slater had over time become filled with more doubt.

Maybe that was because she got less sleep than Emma Masters used to. A child will do that to you.

Maybe it was because Emma Masters only ever had herself to think of. Emma Slater had a daughter and husband to factor in. That might account for Emma Slater's latent anxiety, or the fracturing of certainty she felt, compared to Emma Masters.

She pulled her mind back. She was just Emma. Just Emma. Same Emma. The surname didn't matter.

Except it did.

She had to be honest with herself now. And honest with others.

Emma stood on the edge of the living space watching Conor, the man she loved, playing with Bella. Bella adored her dad. He could make her fall about laughing in a way that Emma could never manage. For some reason right now, Conor was putting on and removing different-sized saucepans from his head, while making daft whistling noises and pretending he was searching for the perfect-fitting saucepan hat. Bella was the hat assistant to whom he was complaining about the poor fit of the saucepans, and she was falling about giggling. He was supposed to be calming her down for a now much later than normal bath and bedtime; instead he seemed to be getting her more excited.

After a few moments standing there observing, she was spotted by Conor.

'Going for a run?' he asked, noting her outfit.

'Thought I would,' she said. 'Maybe bit of a bike ride too.'

'It's your time,' said Conor.

They had a system for dividing up the hours while they were at Parkwood, so that they both got 'me' time. It was a good system.

So long as nobody broke it.

In front of the house, she took a bike. She would not need to ride far in order to carry out her plan.

She only hoped that the person who was the other part of her plan had picked up her signal.

She located herself on a bench on the corner of the pathway that led down to Lodge 227, with her bike upside down in front of her, looking like its chain had come off.

The chain had not come off. Emma did not feel the need to go full method acting.

It was only seventeen minutes before she saw the young detective walking down the pathway. When he saw her, he raised a hand and she smiled back.

As he arrived, the detective gestured to the bike.

'Problem?'

Emma nodded her head and said, 'No.'

The detective looked understandably confused and so Emma clarified. 'I was hoping I might see you. I wanted to make it look like I was here because I'm hopeless with bikes. Which I'm not. And there's nothing wrong with it anyway. Just if Conor came out here. Which he won't. I don't think.'

She paused and looked closely at the detective. He was good-looking and very much her type. Possibly a bit young for her now, but she had never had much trouble attracting men and thought that if she saw him in a club, she would not regard him as outside her range.

Were she not married.

'Do you want to talk here or would you like to walk?' asked the detective. He had taken the cue.

'I think I'd like to walk,' said Emma, flipping the bike the right way up.

So they did, side by side, with Emma wheeling the not-broken bike. She glanced to her side, sizing up the young detective.

'I can't remember your name,' she said to him.

'DC Ward. You can call me Harry.'

'I'm Emma.'

'Yes,' smiled Harry and she felt like she could trust him. 'How can I help?'

Emma did not immediately say anything. The pathway was leading them deeper into the pine forest, the lodges fading away behind them. She was trying to think how best to approach it all.

After a while she said, 'I love my husband.'

She saw the detective – Harry – look a little surprised and unsure what to say in response.

Eventually he settled on, 'Good.'

Then he left the conversational space open further.

Again, Emma struggled to know how to put things.

'I work for a sofa company, Sofa So Good. I'm their marketing manager.'

'I know the one,' said Harry. 'I've seen your ads on my feeds.'

'Oh, cool!' said Emma. 'Ever clicked through?'

'No,' said Harry. 'Is that bad? In fairness, I'm not yet in the market for a sofa.'

'I'll let you off,' said Emma. She had not come to talk about sofas, but she wanted him to understand her. 'What I'm trying to say is, I'm a successful professional woman, good at her job. I'm in no way an idiot. I'm fucking smart.'

That last phrase came out a bit more emotional, a bit more desperate than she'd intended. But then she was holding a lot of emotion in.

'I understand,' said Harry.

'So when I say I love my husband, I mean it, but the second half of that sentence is that I'm not blind to his faults. Which are many.'

The bike bumped on the mass of pine needles and sticks on the forest floor.

'We've known each other a long time. We'll have been together fifteen years next year. When we met, I was super wary of him. He was a party guy. He liked to enjoy himself; he was the life and soul. That's hugely attractive, right? Especially in your twenties. Then as you get into your thirties, you have to evolve a bit. Certainly your late thirties. And definitely once you're married with a daughter.'

She saw Harry nod sympathetically.

'Which is why I'm so angry with him,' she said.

Harry's expression changed to quizzical. 'Sorry, why's that?'

'Because he's fucking lying to both of us. You and me.'

That spilled out. The world did not rumble. The ground did not swallow her up. The detective's expression did not change.

'OK,' said Harry.

'*Fuck*. I feel like *I'm* betraying *him* here. I just need you to see us not as a couple but as two individuals.'

Emma felt upset. *No, wait. I'm not upset*, she thought. *I'm angry*.

Channel it.

'Because I am *not* his alibi,' said Emma ferociously.

That had been boiling inside her for a while. Her love was being taken for granted.

'Right,' said Harry.

She kept going. 'He is not his best self when he uses.'

She looked to Harry to see if he understood.

'I see,' said Harry.

Emma appreciated the quiet neutrality she was being offered.

'He's only a recreational user, and only sometimes,' said Emma. 'I know why – he's trying to recapture that energy, that party vibe. He won't let go of that person he used to be. He won't join us where we are now.'

'When you say recreational user. Of . . . cocaine?'

Emma nodded. 'He didn't bring any in,' she added hastily. 'I'm sure. First, we agreed he wouldn't. And second, I checked his case. Cos it can be problematic.' She wanted Harry to understand. 'So he must've got it here.'

The detective nodded slowly. 'Any idea where?'

Emma shook her head. 'I don't know where he got it, or how much, or . . . I don't fucking know anything.' She could feel a dam beginning to break. 'I don't know who he was with. I don't know where he went. I don't know when he got back to the lodge. But I know what he told you, when you asked, was not the truth. And he is banking on the fact that my love for him will outweigh the fact that I know he lied to you. And it fucking *won't*, let me tell you.'

She paused. She had more to say but she didn't know whether she should. But then Emma Slater felt Emma Masters grab her by the shoulders and demand to know what she was thinking by holding anything back.

'Also . . .' She started the sentence but worried about completing it. 'Also . . . he can be violent when he uses. Not to me – he's never . . . I wouldn't be with him if he had – but with others he can get physical. And I think that's what was happening at the Solstice thing. I think he'd taken some beforehand. He gets violent and then . . . he also doesn't necessarily remember being that way.' She watched the detective nod.

'When you say that you don't know where he went –'

'Later that night. I sort of don't want to know. While also I do.'

'Have you asked him?'

She shook her head. 'Does that make me a coward? Because I am not a coward.' She knew it did.

'Not at all.'

She was grateful for that. She shared the final thing.

'He put a wash on, you know. When he got back. I found it in the morning. I don't know why he did that.'

She saw the detective's eyes widen by the tiniest of degrees.

'Can you remember the clothes he washed?'

Emma nodded.

'It would be great if you could isolate them for us.'

She suddenly felt unsure. She nodded nevertheless. 'What will you do now?'

'We'll talk to him again,' replied Harry. 'First thing tomorrow, I'd expect.'

After a moment she said, 'You cannot tell him I told you. If you say I did, I'll deny it.'

She glanced at the good looking detective and got on the bike. She suddenly, viscerally did not want to be here.

'I'm going now,' she said and cycled away, over the bumps of pine needles and sticks, deeper into the forest.

She glanced back – the detective was watching her go.

She felt ashamed of her marriage. But more so of her husband's behaviour.

He was a liar and a coke addict, and she did not know where he had gone on the night Darren Winters was murdered.

Well, now he would have to say.

56

Mel Hardiman, as ever installed at his computer screen surrounded by an array of paper, was surprised to hear a knock at the door of Lodge 227.

He looked up and around.

He waited for Nicola Bridge to come and answer it. She did not.

The knock came again.

Mel felt like he was in a stand-off.

'It's not going to be for me!' he said.

Mel often spoke his thoughts aloud. He didn't understand the reluctance of others to do so.

Further knocking. More urgent.

Mel wearily got up and went to the door.

He opened it to the woman from IT who had blue hair and multiple tattoos.

'Can you come out to play?' she asked, and Mel thought perhaps that he'd been working so much that he had begun to hallucinate.

'I refuse to go home tonight until I've cracked this, but I've hit a wall with my skills,' Esther said to Mel as they walked over to her office. 'Like I say, I came from security. Kizu would normally do this, but she's in some spa in Thailand with her new baby and I can't get hold of her. I've basically been banging my head against the desk since you came in. So I'm admitting defeat and calling you back. I'm not going home till I know who had that pass. I wouldn't even sleep. But I need a genius. Which is you. Are you a Melvin? Is that what's it short for? Or Melanie? Or have you always been just Mel?'

Mel found that if he did not really say anything, Esther kept talking. So he just looked ahead and did little more than grunt. She did not seem to mind.

When they got into Esther's office, she offered him her chair at the computer keyboard. 'Make yourself at home, handsome,' she said, flashing him a smile that Mel didn't know what to do with.

He looked round for the other person in the room who Esther was referring to. Then he realized it was just the two of them and now he felt as if he was losing his social bearings completely. Mel wasn't used to people being nice or complimenting him. Certainly not someone like Esther.

'C'mon, you. Only handsome one in this room,' insisted Esther, and Mel felt a sequence of weather events occur on his face. First he felt alarmed, then he blushed, then he felt like he might smile. At the end of this trilogy, Mel knew he was looking incredibly confused.

He shoved himself into the chair behind the desk as if it were a refuge. His eyes became glued to the screen.

Esther came and stood close to him, leaning over. Mel felt an air of slight panic, but thought it best he didn't tell her that was what she was inducing.

'Talk me through it,' he said, determinedly not looking at Esther.

'These are the staff records, these are the pass keys, these are the list of security events from Monday going into Tuesday. What I can't get them to do is match this particular one and I wondered if –'

'OK, thank you, got it,' said Mel, as his fingers began to fly over the keys.

Esther looked surprised to be interrupted and Mel could feel her stare at him, half offended and half delighted. He didn't have time to account for that. She had asked him here to work on something and he was now working furiously.

'And everything here is backed up how frequently?' asked Mel, still not taking his eyes off the screen.

'Every half-hour, I think. Don't break my systems now. I can't get into trouble.'

'If anything, I'm going to make it function far better,' said Mel, with complete confidence and no sense of arrogance.

It was not the answer Esther was expecting, but she seemed to like it.

'You do that, I'll love you for ever,' she said.

'Well,' said Mel, and then could not find any words to follow that one and the room lapsed into silence except for the sound of softly clicking computer keys.

As his work brain carried on working, another part of Mel's brain idly mused that he and Esther were like two different chemical elements at polar ends of the periodic table. Mel wondered whether having two such elements in close proximity to each other was going to cause a meltdown or create an exciting new compound.

'I can realign a number of things in the UI without touching the underlying systems and databases and it should all connect up and become clearer. Are you happy for me to do that?'

'Is anyone else going to notice? Like head office?' asked Esther.

'It depends if they're paying attention or have put any protocols in place to notify of UI changes. Looking at this,

I somehow doubt they have. Anyway, I can put it back afterwards. You can always blame me if there's a problem,' he said.

'Oh, I will, lover, don't you worry about that,' Esther replied.

Mel worked silently for a couple of minutes. Esther paced the room, eyes on Mel.

Then she noticed his key-clicking go quiet – he had stopped and was staring at something on the desk, transfixed.

'Everything all right?' she asked.

'I like your Smurf,' Mel said loudly.

For a moment he worried that it sounded like he'd just used some sort of unacceptable sexual innuendo that he would have to apologize for. Luckily Esther did not respond in that way. Quite the opposite.

'Thanks, babes!' said Esther delightedly. 'You've passed my Smurf test.' She picked up the tiny blue toy figure from her desk.

'I've got quite a few of those at home. My parents used to get them from petrol stations when I was a boy,' remarked Mel.

'Now there's a collection I'd like to see,' said Esther.

Mel could feel his face making an unfamiliar shape that reflected his inner state, which was part happiness and part confusion. 'Here we are,' he said. 'Now we know security employee Mandy Jones, the designated night patrol, checked the pool area as per the rota.'

'Correct,' said Esther.

'But another pass key seems to have also accessed the pool that night. This temporary pass key which you've been trying to trace to an employee.'

'That's the cookie.'

'Well, according to the history, the temporary pass key is

also linked to Mandy Jones. It was issued by her, to herself, on her own ID.'

'No, no, no. I mean, what the *actual*? That doesn't make any sense.'

'It's right here on the system; we can see Mandy Jones accessed the Splashdome multiple times across the night but using two different pass keys. One of them her regular one, the other a temporary one,' Mel insisted. 'Why would she do that?'

'Right. So let's go ask her.'

Mel and his new best buddy Esther found Mandy alone in the security lodge, watching YouTube on an iPad and eating Quavers. The lodge smelled of cheese powder. Mel quite liked it.

Esther got straight to business, taking a stern tone. 'My friend Mel – DC Hardiman to you – needs to talk to you about your pass key,' she said.

'What about it?' asked Mandy.

'How,' said Mel with a flourish, 'do you explain these?' He laid out the printouts.

Mandy looked from Mel to Esther in bewilderment. *Who is this nutter?*

'I don't know what those are,' she said.

'No, but I do, so listen to me for a moment and it'll all become clear,' said Mel in a not entirely unpatronizing manner.

Mandy looked put out at Esther. Esther laid her hand on Mel's shoulder, as if to say, *I'm with him.*

Mel flinched and then carried on. 'This is you, on patrol here, at the usual time you check the pool, correct?' He pointed to the printout.

'Looks right on time, yeah,' said Mandy, peering at the lines of numbers.

'But the key card that's used for that admission is a temporary pass key. Why's that?'

'Shit, yeah,' said Mandy. 'OK, I see what you mean now. I hadn't even thought about it. I'd mislaid my pass key. Couldn't find it before I went on patrol so I made myself a temporary one. I can't pretend I'm that good at doing it, but I managed it. Used that to get in. Then when I came back here later, I found the other key under the desk. I nearly rolled across it with my chair when I got back from finding . . . the body. Must've fallen down the back or something. No idea why I didn't spot it first time round.'

'But when you returned to the pool at five forty-seven in the morning, there's no pass key used –'

'Cos I didn't need to. The door was already jemmied open when I arrived. Stick in the door.'

'Isn't there an alarm for that? If the door stays open?' asked Esther.

Mandy looked at her. 'You know there is, or there should be! But we don't get notifications back here cos of this issue with the system – they had a bollocking about it on the last fire inspection. They were supposed to be repairing it. This was months ago. So they obviously haven't done anything. They'll probably do it the day before the reinspection.'

'So . . .' said Mel, shuffling the papers around, 'here's the problem, Mandy. There's an admission to the pool with your main pass key *after* you've done your close-down check, and *before* you arrive in the morning and find the body in the pool. Can you explain that?'

Mandy looked confused. 'That can't be right.'

'It is.' Mel showed her a piece of paper with more data on it. 'This is *your* key card ID. The one you said you'd lost that day.'

Mandy looked none the wiser. 'Right.'

'It's used to gain access to the pool around eleven thirty p.m.'

Mandy looked outraged. 'You're shitting me.'

'I can assure you I am very much not shitting you,' said Mel.

'But it was lost,' said Mandy, looking from Mel to Esther.

'So you say,' said Mel, and then took pity on Mandy as he realized another possibility. 'Or maybe stolen, and then returned here and made to look as if you'd just mislaid it.'

Mandy whistled. 'Fuck me.'

'Right?' echoed Esther.

'Who would do that?' asked Mandy.

'Can you think of anyone who might have had the opportunity, maybe towards the end of the day?' said Mel.

Mandy sat thinking for quite a long moment, during which Mel started to run the probability of whether all of this was just an elaborate lie by Mandy, who was now drifting into the frame of suspicion. Then he watched her eyes widen, her face redden and her teeth clench, which Mel suspected was fury.

'I can do better than think,' she said purposefully. 'Come back in forty-five minutes.'

'Can't do that,' said Mel. 'Given this business with the cards, you're this close to being a suspect. I need to remain with you so you don't get any ideas about running off or interfering with evidence.'

'You *what*?!' snapped Mandy.

Mel saw Esther's expression change to alarm and realized he might have inadvertently done that thing again. Why did people have to be sensitive and impossible to predict?

Beneath this thought, he could hear Mandy saying to Esther, 'How long have you known me? How long have I worked here? And you're gonna let him accuse me?'

Esther said, 'He's police, mate. Show him he's wrong and we're all good, right?'

'Obviously,' said Mel. He didn't understand why there had to be such a fuss. Hadn't he basically said the same thing?

Oh, maybe he hadn't. Ah well.

Mandy worked at a screen, scrolling through images for a little less than twenty minutes, glowering every so often at Mel like he was public enemy number one. Then she snapped bolt upright.

'Got it,' she said. 'Come look.'

Mel and Esther crowded round the screen she had ready for them.

'The entrance gates are the only areas covered by CCTV, right?' Mandy said. 'But the angle of the cameras means the footage overspills the entrance to this lodge. Nobody knows that unless you work in here. So I've been thinking, whoever got hold of my key card without my knowledge must've done it earlier in the day. They made me think I'd lost it, and then put it back later that day. Or rather in the middle of the night, while I was out on patrol. Look.'

Mandy called up on screen the CCTV footage. It was marked 4.47 a.m. A figure was exiting the security lodge.

'That's me, going out on the early patrol. So at this point I've got my temporary pass key.'

She scrolled forward seven minutes. At 4.54 a.m. a figure appeared at the security lodge door. It tapped a key against the entrance and went in. After thirty seconds inside, the figure darted out again.

'Gets in, using the pass, dumps the pass to make me look like I've dropped it, then gets out.'

'So whoever that is must've been on-site all night,' mused Mel.

'I always knew there was something off about him,' said Mandy bitterly.

'Do you know who it is?' asked Esther.

'Oh yeah. The fucking fucker,' said Mandy eloquently.

She froze the footage. The three of them leaned in close and peered at the screen as she zoomed in on the footage.

Exiting the lodge at 4.55 a.m. on Tuesday morning was Lee Parker.

King of the high ropes.

57

Nicola snapped awake from a dream in which Ethan and Harry were trying to solve a word grid about different types of weed.

She had fallen asleep, fully dressed, lying on the bed reading Sarah Welland's notes.

It was dark outside. She looked at her phone. 1.17 a.m. *Shit.*

She hadn't done that in years. She felt like a kid. The past forty-eight hours had caught up with her and now she was completely discombobulated. Also, her mouth was dry. She got up from the bed and went to get a glass of water from the kitchen.

In the living area, she was surprised to find a fully dressed Harry, lying on the sofa, surrounded by an ocean of paper. He sat up to attention as Nicola came in. He looked exhausted.

'Harry, you should be in bed.'

'That's rich coming from you. I figured you were still up working so I should keep pushing through.'

Shall I tell him I was napping?

Harry stood up and stretched, wincing. 'My only mistake was lying down. For future reference, that sofa is not comfortable. I'll be putting that in my TripAdvisor review.'

Nicola grinned. 'I think Parkwood may have bigger reputational problems right now.'

Harry shrugged. 'I dunno. I'm gonna word it pretty strongly.'

'No Mel?'

'Wasn't here when I got back. His bedroom door's open so he must be out somewhere. How are the Sarah Welland files?'

Nicola exhaled. Maybe it would help to talk it out. 'I don't know how useful it is. I have to keep reminding myself: there's no body, so there's no forensics. I've been through the lists of guests and staff at the time, cross-referenced with our current guests – nothing I can see that stands out. Plenty of statements taken, but you can boil them down to: nobody saw anything happen. Because that's the question: how did she just disappear?

'The other unresolved issue is the money. Three thousand pounds, strategically withdrawn from cashpoints over the previous couple of weeks. She wasn't being physically forced; there's footage from cashpoint security cameras. So what would three thousand pounds get you? Was she planning to elope with someone? If so, why hasn't she turned up? Was she being blackmailed and had to pay someone off? Neither her mum nor her partner knew anything about the withdrawals and didn't think she was in trouble with anyone. Now obviously, Sarah could have been having a secret affair. But there's nothing in her electronic records, emails or texts to suggest that. No unknown or blocked-caller number records, nothing in her email spam. No threats, nothing untoward.

'And her notebooks are full of drawings and scribbles. She was clearly wounded by not being able to conceive. There's a weird doodle that looks like it's the standing stone here. And so many noughts and crosses puzzles. None of it's useful, as far as I can see. What else has been going on?' asked Nicola, deliberately omitting *while I've been napping*.

'After that meeting in the Sports Bar, I had an interesting

chat with Emma Slater, wife of Conor. She sought me out, and she's now blown a hole in her husband's alibi for the evening,' said Harry. 'Conor was not in the lodge at the time he said he was. And she let it slip that he's a recreational cocaine user, and she thinks he'd been on it Monday night.'

'Wife turning on husband, interesting,' said Nicola, exhaling. She rubbed her eyes. She felt exhausted again. She noticed Harry watching her.

'D'you mind me asking,' he ventured cautiously, 'is everything all right with you?'

'Yeah, course,' she said defensively. 'Why wouldn't it be?'

'You were off-site last night, got back really early. If I'm not overstepping the mark, you looked a bit rattled when you came back. Just wanted to check you were OK.'

Oh, Harry. She had spent all this time since they were first partnered teaching him to notice things. And now the thing he'd noticed was her. She felt like she wanted to cry. Instead, she reached for the bottle of wine on a side table. 'Is there any left in this?'

Harry nodded. 'Parkwood supermarket's finest. I thought it was acceptable when working after midnight.'

'I think we can agree that as a guideline,' said Nicola, sitting on the sofa where Harry had been as he went to the cupboard and fetched her a glass. He returned and poured her double the amount she would have poured herself.

Harry realized this as she held it up and stared at it. 'Too much?'

'Absolutely not,' she replied and inhaled a large gulp. It was a bit rough, but it was welcome.

Harry sat on the chair opposite the sofa as Nicola grabbed

a handful of pretzels. She had not had dinner. She ate a couple and took another slug of red wine.

'Ethan got arrested last night. Possession with intent to supply. Ketamine and weed.'

Harry scrunched his face up in a 'whoops' expression. 'Oh shit.'

'Yeah,' said Nicola, sipping the wine once more. 'Got off with a caution, thank God. Not cos I asked for any favours,' she added hastily.

'Didn't think for a second you would.'

'I was so angry with him.'

'I guess you could do without it right now.'

'To say the fucking least.' She realized she was getting sweary.

'Everyone gets in trouble that age. I know I did. You could argue that a bit of a shock now might just set him right.'

Nicola hadn't considered this. Then she remembered something Harry had said earlier.

'What did you mean by Lee Parker reminding you of yourself?'

Harry looked down, away from her gaze. 'Oh. Yeah. I said that out loud, did I?'

'Yep.'

He paused for a long time. 'You just have pathways, don't you, in life? At certain points, you could end up becoming a different person. There was just . . . the people I knew, the things we were doing . . . I just recognize some of that in him.'

'What changed?'

She watched him squirm a little.

'You realize we were talking about you?' he said.

'I thought we were having a conversation.' They were both

avoiding and deflecting, Nicola noted. 'If you don't want to talk about it . . .'

'I don't think I do,' he said. 'If that's OK?'

'Course,' she said, more intrigued than ever.

'Maybe another time. When I'm not so knackered.'

'Totally.'

'But all's OK with Ethan?' he asked.

Oh, we're back on me, are we?

She took another glug of wine. She would go to bed properly in a moment.

'Define OK,' she found herself saying.

'He's not going to have a criminal record for a start,' said Harry.

'True,' she acknowledged. 'Maybe my job actually helped. For once.' She swilled the wine around in the glass. 'I feel so bad for him, Harry.'

'How so?'

She was reluctant to say it out loud. 'He had a life, and friends, in Liverpool. And I just – we just – threw all that up in the air and came back here, middle of nowhere, and expected him to be OK. I mean, if I'm honest, I didn't think about it enough. I was too wrapped up in . . . well, I was just too wrapped up. I didn't factor him in enough and I feel ashamed about that now.'

'I'm sure he'll be fine,' said Harry.

'I'm not,' said Nicola. 'It's all so uncertain for him and his mates. How are we supposed to guide him? Study for your A levels, then what? Go to uni? That's seventy grand of debt – what for? Get an apprenticeship or a training course? What's he going to do that AI isn't going to replace? How do you go, oh, this'll be all right; this'll be a good one for the next forty years?'

'Does he know what he wants to do?'

'He's not going to follow me or his dad, that's for sure. So that's two big useful careers we've managed to completely deter him from.' She found she'd drained the glass. 'Kids, be glad you haven't got 'em yet.'

'I'll bear that in mind,' said Harry.

She instantly felt bad. Who was she to say that to him? She wondered whether he'd discussed kids with the mysterious Audra. 'I don't mean don't have 'em. It's the best thing, truly, but fucking hell they put you through the wringer, right when you don't need it. Like now. And also they lock you in to something that . . . maybe . . .'

She stared past Harry's shoulder, out of the window into the dark of the forest beyond.

'You all right?'

I don't know. Am I?

She felt suddenly all over the place, from having slept, from a fast glass of wine, from the overwhelm of the case, and from Ethan's words in the car the previous night. She kept staring into the trees and the darkness. She felt momentarily hypnotized by it.

'Sarge?' said Harry quietly. Then: 'Nicola?'

He never used her first name.

She looked at him sitting there, concerned for her.

'It just opened up a wound last night. Some of the stuff Ethan said . . . it made me realize . . . something I might feel.'

'About Ethan.'

'No.' There was one particular sturdy tree she was focusing on. She almost didn't realize she was continuing to talk. 'When I was driving back here, I thought . . . look at these people here . . . all trying to make things work, some managing it, some failing . . . I mean, maybe family is just a trap,

Harry. A trap we all fall into. And I thought, what if I've fallen into it, too? Because I'm starting to feel I'm stuck in that trap, constantly having to think about everyone else but not myself.'

She was silent for a second and then confessed the thought at the bottom of it all. 'And then I thought, no. Family's not the trap. It's . . . being married.' She could see the mossy detail on the bark of a tree out there. 'We agreed a fresh start, and Mike is trying so hard, Harry. *So* hard.' And here it was, the nub of it all. 'But I don't know if it'll ever be enough. Or if I even *want* it to work now.'

She pulled her gaze away from the forest and back to Harry.

His expression pulled her up short. Bewilderment, awkwardness, embarrassment? Like he didn't know what to do or say. Like he didn't want to be there with her. It was like she'd snapped out of a trance and realized she'd crossed a line. She felt her cheeks reddening. Why had she shared that with him?

'Shit, sorry, Harry. That's not a conversation for here.'

'No, no, it's fine –'

It wasn't fine. She looked at her empty glass. It had acted on her in just the wrong way.

'It's not –'

'I don't mind,' stuttered Harry.

'No, it's not the thing to be –' She was unable to finish the sentence.

She stood up. He stood up.

Nicola backed off. 'We should get some sleep. Bright and early, we'll hatch a plan.'

She used that line to head to the sink and rinse the wine glass out. She could feel Harry still hovering, unsure what to do. Then she said good night, headed to the bedroom and closed the door behind her as quickly as she could.

Leaning back up against it, she shut her eyes. She felt like she was eighteen again and had talked too much at a cool party.

She cleaned her teeth without looking in the mirror.

When she got into bed, she pulled the duvet up over her head in an act of contrition.

She lay there with the horrified realization that she had confessed something to Harry so personal that she had barely admitted it to herself.

58

Nicola woke with anxiety clutching at her chest.

Why did you say that?

Do you really think that?

She showered, trying to scrub the tension away, and pulled on clean work clothes: a new uniform to cover her personal feelings. She checked her face; she looked fresher than she had any right to or felt. Good, she'd take that.

'Morning!' called Harry, offering her the magic coffee as she walked in. No sense of anything lingering from last night.

She took the coffee awkwardly. 'Good morning, thank you.'

'Tell her then,' said Harry to Mel. He smiled at Nicola. 'He's been on pins waiting for you.'

'Tell me what?'

'Lee Parker,' said Mel, through a mouthful of cornflakes from a white bowl which seemed to contain no milk. (Surely he didn't just eat dry cornflakes?) 'We have CCTV of him entering the security lodge on-site just before five a.m. Tuesday morning, when he said he was at home alone. It also implicates him in the theft of a pass key that accessed the Splashdome Monday night.'

Now here was something to raise her spirits. 'Do we indeed? Good work, Mel.'

'I've got all the documentation,' he said.

'Right, well. That's our first action for the morning. Both him and Conor Slater seem to have a lot of questions to answer. But as a treat, let's arrest Lee Parker first and see how he likes that. Would you like to arrest him, Mel? Given you did the grunt work.'

Mel looked horrified. 'Good God, no. I've got real work to do here.'

Harry nearly choked on his coffee. What, Nicola wondered, did Mel think real police work was if not arresting people?

'Well, thank you for your brilliant work. Get your coat, Harry. I'll call and break it to Lindsey Moorfield on the way.'

Harry did as he was bid.

You are a dynamic, focused, professional boss, thought Nicola. Normal service had been resumed.

She hoped.

Nicola and Harry were waiting for Lee Parker when he arrived at work, limping slightly.

'Go on then. What is it today? It's bad enough your lot are still swarming over this area.'

'It's only going to get worse, I'm afraid,' said Nicola. 'Lee Parker, I am arresting you on suspicion of the murder of Darren Winters. You do not have to say anything, but it may harm your defence if you do not mention when questioned something you later rely on in court. Anything you do say may be given in evidence. The arrest is necessary for a prompt and effective investigation.'

'Are you fucking kidding me?' Lee responded. 'I'm about to start my shift.'

'No, you're not,' said Harry, and Nicola felt that there was a small edge of pleasure to his tone.

59

The drive out of Parkwood and over to the interview suite was silent. Nicola and Harry said nothing, letting Lee sit with his own thoughts and preoccupations. On arrival in Bredy, Lee was given his rights, including a duty solicitor, and booked in.

Inside the interview suite, seats were taken, the recording was started. Harry at Nicola's side. Lee's new solicitor at his.

Nicola began, stony-faced. 'Lee, before we get to specific questions, is there anything you may have thought about on the way over that you'd like to tell us?'

'Like what?' asked Lee, looking from Nicola to Harry and back again.

'Anything you omitted from your previous statements to us, or anything you may have remembered in the time since you first spoke to DC Ward?'

Nicola watched Lee's eyes dart, rat-like, from her to Harry again, trying to read them, looking for a tell.

'No,' said Lee at last, defiant. 'Why?'

Nicola enjoyed a second interview when she felt armed. First interviews were all about the ascertaining: was this person of interest, did they have anything to rule them out or in. At best, a first interview locked the interviewee into a set of claims. Second interviews were about the discoveries made since: the inconsistencies and contradictions, key details previously unmentioned, the facts and forensics that had arisen in the meantime. At best, a second interview exposed any lies and dug into the reasons behind them. The power balance – arguably fifty-fifty in the first interview – shifted for the second. A second interview was much more in the gift of the detective.

Nicola hoped that Lee sensed this, instinctively. He had begun to look worried.

Good. She liked them worried.

She made a show of consulting her notes. She knew that the more she consulted them, the greater the concern in the mind of the person across the table. If it took her *so long* to read through the litany of facts and dates and numbers and statements, it must mean her case was undeniable.

She looked up at Lee before continuing. 'When we spoke previously, you said you were at home all night on the night Darren Winters was killed . . .'

She took a moment to return to the notes, making a show of searching for a phrase. Nicola felt that if she'd had a pair of reading glasses, she would have put them on here and peered more closely at the sheet of paper for effect. Maybe she would need reading glasses in the future and would be able to add this theatrical flourish to her arsenal.

'Doomscrolling,' she said, looking up from the notes.

'That's right,' said Lee.

'Do you want to amend that statement?'

Lee's solicitor, a ruddy-faced man at the end of his career who favoured worn pinstripes, red braces and red socks, harrumphed. 'He's answered your question, Detective Sergeant. Why don't you get to the point?'

Nicola did not look at the solicitor. 'Where were you at four fifty-five on Tuesday morning, Lee?'

'Where I'd been all night. At home.'

Nicola sighed in disappointment and took a piece of

paper from her folder. She placed it in front of Lee. 'This is security footage from the gate lodge at Parkwood.'

Lee all but laughed. 'There is no CCTV at Parkwood,' he said, barely looking at the photo.

'Apart from at the entrance. And unfortunately for you, that entrance camera caught you going in there at four fifty-five in the morning, to replace a pass you'd taken from Mandy, the security guard on duty that night. Didn't it?'

She watched as Lee's inherent cockiness began to drain slowly away. It was remarkable how one fact could change a man's entire disposition. He picked up the photograph and looked at it. His thoughts were clear: *Oh shit.*

Gotcha, thought Nicola. She would enjoy the next few seconds as she waited and watched. Lee glanced at his solicitor, who met his gaze. There was panic in Lee's eyes, Nicola was gratified to see.

Lee's solicitor leaned over and muttered, 'I would advise you to say "no comment" at this stage in proceedings.'

Lee said, 'No comment.'

Nicola nodded. 'We also have you nipping into the security lodge to "borrow" the pass while Mandy was out dealing with another issue.' Lee ran his hands through his hair as Nicola continued. 'You bookend the evening, Lee. Almost like it was planned.'

Another glance at the solicitor. 'No comment.'

Nicola took a moment to look Lee in the eye. A moment of: do we really have to go through this? Lee looked back at the photos, avoiding her gaze.

Nicola made a show of selecting another document. 'We're testing Mandy's pass for your DNA and prints. We will do the same with the murder weapon found near your high-ropes section. Now, until we have those results, you're the only person who knows for sure whether your DNA and fingerprints are on either. But as a gambling woman, I'd put good money that they are definitely on that pass, at the very least.'

'You can put that to my client when you have the results, Detective Sergeant, and not before,' interjected the solicitor.

Quite right, thought Nicola. But she needed to make this stick faster than that. She couldn't allow the slow process of testing to derail the momentum of their investigation.

She brought out a small evidence bag. 'Our forensics team found these in the skimmers at the pool. They're the backing from a plaster. They could only have been discarded in the pool after it had closed overnight Monday, as the skimmers were emptied then. Would you say this is the same brand as the plaster you're currently wearing, Lee?'

She watched Lee look down at the plaster on his hand. He picked up the bag. Looked up at Nicola.

'Loads of people use that brand.'

'Does it match the plaster on your hand? Is it the same size backing as the plaster on your hand?'

'This is a fit-up,' said Lee.

'Yes or no, Lee.'

After a moment, Lee said reluctantly, 'Yes.'

'Thank you. I'm just going to summarize, Lee. We have you on camera around the time a security pass was stolen and returned. We know you lied to us about being given a lift home, and also being at home all night. The murder weapon was found in the area where you work. A backing to a similar plaster you're currently wearing was found in the pool skimmers. You have to understand, Lee, that if you can't now offer up a credible version of events to prove you did not kill Darren Winters, we have to assume you were responsible.

Now, I'm asking you again, were you in the Splashdome that night?'

Lee exhaled. Then he said, 'Yeah.'

The room crackled.

Harry shifted in his seat, sitting further upright.

'Yeah, what, Lee?'

Come on, keep going, Lee. A little further. Tell us all about it.

'Yeah, I took that pass and used it. Yeah, I was in there that night.'

Nicola loved second interviews.

'*Why* were you in there, Lee?'

Lee was looking around the room, as if the answer might be found on the walls.

Eventually he said, 'I offer additional services to guests.'

I'm sorry, what?

A dozen questions flooded Nicola Bridge's mind. 'What sort of services?'

'All kinds of things,' said Lee.

Enough of this.

Nicola leaned forward. 'Do you know what "garrulous" means, Lee?'

Lee looked caught off guard. 'Like, chatty?'

'Talkative,' said Nicola. 'And I need you to be much more garrulous in your responses now. Full and frank answers every time, otherwise my patience is going to snap spectacularly and that's not going to help either of us. Now, *precisely* what sort of "services" do you provide to guests? Because as far as I can see, Parkwood provides a pretty full set of activities, all bookable and payable in advance.'

Lee thought about it for a minute. Then leaned back in his chair expansively.

'When I started out, I got a job at this high-end hotel in

London, part of the concierge team. Junior of the juniors. When I say high end, it was boutique, beautifully designed and for a bit it was *the* place to stay. Everyone wanted a room there. People you can't believe you're seeing in real life, A-list or even triple-A-list celebrities, all of them wanting things, but with discretion. And those concierge guys were *exceptional* at providing them with the thing they wanted. You had it drilled into you: there is no request we will not fulfil for them.'

'Presumably within the law,' said Nicola.

'And a few the other side of the line.'

Lee's solicitor put his hand on Lee's arm to stop him talking further.

Lee understood. 'You learned to do what you needed to do in order to get them what they wanted. Special experiences, special access, special circumstances. Special people. Like after-hours access to galleries or attractions or shutting down the London Eye or a big cocktail bar, whatever. You learned how to do it, how it all worked, who people would do things for, which guests didn't quite have the clout they thought they did. It was a proper education. Exhilarating, exhausting. When you pulled something off, it was such a buzz. And then the guests generally took care of you financially as a thank you. You'd get to know them or their staff, almost on a personal level.'

'Dream job, was it?' said Harry.

Lee shrugged, unsure. 'It demands a lot of you. Big buzz, but also stupidly stressful. The pressure you have to deliver. And it's not a world you want to spend too much time in. It's all great until you burn out.'

'Is that what happened to you?' asked Harry.

Lee shook his head and blew out through his cheeks. 'I

was less discreet than I should have been. Just once. I was so young, still, just a kid. I got talking to this girl in a club, spent the night with her, told her a couple of stories. I hadn't asked her what she did for a living. Turned out she was a journalist, on a tabloid. I still don't know if she targeted me deliberately or if I just got unlucky. She printed the stories and there were details in there that only people right on the inside, basically me, could have known. Two of the people named in the stories twigged who it was and made it clear to my bosses. I was given the bollocking of my life and then fired.

'After that it was like I was toxic, I couldn't get another job in the hospitality industry in London. It's a small world, especially in high end. They all knew each other, knew I couldn't be trusted. So I was out. Quit London, came to live back down here with my parents. Then work came up at Parkwood. And actually, I liked it. Maybe even more than the other place. Being outside, moving all day, much better for my mental health.

'Course, people love the high ropes and zip wires. And like the kids, some of them are terrified when they start, and then by the end of their holiday they think it's the best thing ever, and you can see the confidence boost it's given them. Like they'll have it for the rest of their lives. That's way more of a buzz than getting somebody to close down a cinema near Piccadilly Circus so some American pop star can watch a movie with her boyfriend of the week.'

'What sort of services do you provide, Lee?'

Lee looked back at her. 'Whatever people want.'

There was a darkness to the way he said it that sent a chill down Nicola's spine.

Lee looked out towards the light that was drifting in through the small window. 'It started small. You overhear a lot of conversation as people are waiting, or as they're getting into their harnesses, or people on the ground watching those doing the courses. You hear the chit-chat, what they like here, and what could be improved. And I'd hear people saying what they'd really love would be X, Y or Z, sometimes joking and sometimes serious, and after a time you start to hear the same X, Y and Zs and you think, well, I might be able to sort that or help you with those. That's how it started.'

Nicola looked sceptical. 'What can you do for them that they can't already book?'

'All right, you want to know about the pool, let's take that as an example,' said Lee.

Nicola stayed silent. *Never interrupt your enemy when they're in the middle of making a mistake*, she thought.

'It's one of my specialities. Get an hour, after-hours, in the pool – get it to yourself, you can bring drinks, so long as it's all in plastics. I have a little arrangement that things get left on, a bunce to the pool guys for water flow on the slides and the lazy river and all that, and I make sure it's all off when I go. It's a red-carpet, VIP, golden-ticket thing. Eleven o'clock, sometimes midnight at a push, half an hour only. People have had their dinner, their pre-drinks and it's like clubbing for them. We have to do it relatively quietly, and they know it's not strictly legit, I level with them, so no photos or anything like that, but they love it and they'll pay for it.

'So, yeah, I *was* in there after-hours. I'd promised a group of guests. I did use Mandy's pass key, only cos she wasn't supposed to be on. My normal security guy, we have an understanding.'

'None of the guests have mentioned this in their interviews,' said Harry.

'I should bloody hope not,' said Lee. 'They all know it's

off the books. Everyone is sworn to silence. But . . . yeah, Monday night. It was a birthday . . . I'll give you the lodge number, the name.'

'And management's never discovered what's going on?' asked Nicola, incredulous.

Lee's face clouded. 'They hadn't, no. What you have to understand is that, A, since the new owners came in there are a lot less staff here than there used to be, and B, none of us are on the best wages. Most of these jobs are minimum wage, thirteen quid an hour, some get tips if they're lucky. But the gap between what the guests pay – which keeps going up, man, every year higher and higher, proper premium prices – and what the staff get paid is big. I look after anyone who helps, cut them in. And I'm really careful. I know who's on, and sort it like that.'

'How do the guests even know about it?' asked Harry.

'That's the thing,' says Lee. 'Word of mouth. It's grown over the years. No paper trail. Most of it's a direct recommendation. Honestly, I don't do it loads. Only thing I have is a private Insta account, no posts, people DM me there to get in touch, ask for what they want, and then I say if I can help. Which usually I can.'

'So you're an unofficial concierge service, offering them stuff they can't book via the official channels.'

Lee shrugged. 'If you want to do anything wholesome and outdoorsy, official channels have got you covered. But these days people want more than that if they can get it.'

'What do you mean by more, Lee?'

He stared at Nicola. Then he grinned. 'Whatever you can think of, people ask me for.'

It was an uncomfortable gaze. 'Give us details.'

'What, so you can get your jollies? I don't think so.' He

thought for a moment. 'People want to cut loose. Just cos they're with their mates or their families by day, doesn't mean there aren't people who want weird or dark shit at night. Not exactly news that people have desires, is it? For some people, that's playing away, for others it's introductions, for others it's –'

'I think what you mean is no comment, Mr Parker,' said his solicitor, now looking alarmed.

Lee grinned. He looked back at Nicola. 'People are fucked up and twisted. I got taught that's a business opportunity, a chance to help them enjoy themselves.'

'Even if it causes a man's death?' said Nicola, seriously.

'No. That was not me, or the people I was with, not while I was in there,' said Lee.

'Can you prove that?' asked Nicola.

'Yeah,' said Lee defiantly. 'There were five of them, all women, and me. We were out by eleven forty-five. Four of them went back to their lodge. Number 97.'

'And the other?'

'Karina? I fucked her up against the standing stone. Three times.'

There was silence. Lee did not take his eyes from Nicola.

'I realize a gentleman shouldn't fuck and tell, but you've pushed me into it. I tell them it's got a special energy, the stone, power of the ley lines. Absolute bollocks, but they love it. She certainly did.'

Karina. Nicola had taken her statement.

Lee was gloating now, as if this had been a victory for him.

'That's why I was there all night, and that's why I didn't get to returning the pass until five a.m. I was busy.'

'Did you leave the pool door propped open?'

'No. Why would I have done that? It'd only draw attention.

I've been doing this stuff for a long time and I don't get noticed. That's the whole point.'

'And she'll corroborate it?'

'I don't see why she wouldn't. I presume she's told the rest now. And they can all tell you they were in the pool.'

'Why didn't you tell us all this?' asked Harry.

'Are you kidding me? Cos I knew it would go like this. Cos there are about a dozen sackable offences here. If this shit gets out, it's over here for me. Where do I go then?'

There was a knock at the door. A young uniformed officer asked if Nicola and Harry could step out for a moment. The interview was paused as they got to their feet.

Something had come up.

60

In the interview suite she had found it easy to focus. The instant she stepped out of it, Nicola's mind became a swirling cyclone of multiple questions still to be resolved. A storm of new facts were coming at her. They had to first confirm Lee's story with the occupants of Lodge 97. Nicola thought about the underwear she had retrieved from beneath the stone. Did those belong to this woman, Karina? If she and her friends backed Lee up, where would that leave everything? He had admitted to being in the pool after-hours but had supposedly left before Darren Winters had come to be in there. Did that mean someone else went in after him?

And still, at the back of her mind, were the case files and notes from Sarah Welland's disappearance. Did Lee Parker have anything to do with that? He was happily bragging about going off with female guests. He was working at Parkwood back in 2021. Was he the link?

Reeta, on-site at Parkwood, had requested that Nicola and Harry be pulled from the interview room. Her mobile signal was poor from inside Lee Parker's workspace but just strong enough that Reeta could show them on screen what they'd found there.

Not one item of interest but two.

Nicola's eyes widened.

61

With everyone back in their seats, Nicola restarted the interview. Harry had asked if he could reopen.

'What happened to your leg, Lee? You said you injured it but didn't explain how,' said Harry.

'One of the guests flipped out at me. This was Monday night, when we were taking the girls back to the lodge, before Karina and me –'

'Why would he attack you, though?'

'Ask him. He was really fucking antsy, started kicking and going at me. They all had to grab him off me.'

'What, just out of the blue?' said Harry.

'Yeah.'

'But you'd had nothing to do with him before?'

Lee looked shifty, like he'd inadvertently revealed something he hadn't meant to. 'I dunno. Maybe he'd come on the ropes or something.'

Nicola felt Harry had connected something. 'Have you ever supplied guests with cocaine, Lee? As part of your concierge services?'

Lee looked at Harry with pure hatred. Before he could speak, Lee's solicitor once again placed his hand on his client's arm.

'No comment,' spat Lee.

'Did you ever meet Sarah Welland?' asked Nicola, pivoting the conversation.

'The girl from 2021?' asked Lee.

‘The woman,’ corrected Nicola. ‘Yes.’

‘No.’

‘But you were working at Parkwood at that time?’

‘I was,’ said Lee. ‘Your lot interviewed everyone at the time. What’s this got to do with anything now?’

‘So obviously you knew Darren Winters?’ Nicola asked. She knew where she was going in this interview but first wanted to do what an old boss of hers used to call ‘rolling the pitch’. She thought it was a cricket reference, but she’d never checked. She believed it meant creating the ideal conditions for victory.

‘Course. He was my first boss. This was before the new owners. He interviewed me. He was the one who took me on.’

‘How well did you know him?’

‘I mean, he was the boss; we weren’t having tea together every day. And then when all with what happened, with that girl going missing . . . he was just eased out and Lindsey took over.’

‘When did you last see Darren Winters?’ asked Nicola.

Lee looked at the table in front of him.

Nicola persisted. ‘Not a tricky question, I would’ve thought.’

Lee looked much more tired than when he first came in, she thought. His energy was slowly dissipating, the longer this went on.

Lee said quietly, ‘I saw him during the day Monday.’

This was more like it. ‘Really? Where?’

A hesitation and then: ‘On-site. At Parkwood.’

‘Our understanding is he was barred from Parkwood.’

Lee really was finding the table very interesting now. He sighed in frustration. ‘Yeah. He was really angry about it. I got him into a lodge.’

'How have you got the ability do to that?' asked Nicola.

'There's a lodge that never gets used. It's not on the system; it's there for emergencies if one of the other lodges has problems that aren't quickly fixable, which is rare but not unheard of. I have a key for it.'

Nicola raised an eyebrow.

'It's not difficult. It's hardly in use. Loads of people know about it. Some people use it for . . . the sort of things you think they might use it for. So long as you leave it as you found it, management don't find out . . . Anyway, Winters wanted to be on-site for the Solstice Parade. He was like, it's my baby, my idea, they never let me back . . .'

'He knew you could get him in.'

'Look, he got me this job when I was on my uppers. He understood who I was. And he might've caught me doing a few things when he ran the place, but he was more of the "no harm, no foul" school. So I owed him. We spoke every so often and I told him what was happening. He hated the way it had been left. I checked it was free, made sure it was ready, got him on the system with a fake ID. I've done it before. You speak to the right person on the right day in security, easy. Since he left, since the company got bought, nobody's checking. They don't know how we run; they just care we're making money. Now tell me, how would that make sense if I wanted to kill him?'

Nicola replied quickly and coolly. 'It would make perfect sense. You bring him in, you know where he is, you arrange to meet him later. All the while setting up alibis. Is that what happened?'

She watched Lee's face drop. In justifying his actions, he'd given them even more information which placed him in the frame.

'No,' he said.

'Did you not think it was weird he wanted to do this on the anniversary of Sarah Welland's disappearance?' asked Harry.

'That was part of it. He said he had to be busy. Nothing's ever been proven against him, has it? You should know that better than anyone. I just arranged for him to stay. He was gonna watch the parade from a distance. He probably would've gone the next afternoon, but then –'

'But what?' Nicola felt like the natural end of Lee's sentence was 'but then he got killed'. Or was his instinct to stop himself saying 'but then *I* killed him'?

'Lindsey found us in the lodge together Monday afternoon. There was a massive barney; both of them just – I dunno – lost it? She was saying she'd have him forcibly evicted and he was accusing her of betraying him for years, all sorts of things. It was nasty. She was raging.'

Nicola noted Harry scribbling away. This was information which Lindsey herself had not provided. Why not?

'Did she know you'd got him in?'

Lee shook his head.

'You must've been worried she might find out? Wouldn't that be another sackable offence? Didn't it worry you that he might say something to her?'

Lee looked exhausted. Nicola let the silence sit for a moment.

'Lee, while you've been here, we've had our forensic team going through your workspace at Parkwood.'

Lee looked alarmed. Did he have an inkling of what was to come? She slid a sealed evidence bag on to the table which contained a branded Parkwood glove.

'Does that look familiar?'

Lee leaned forward to look at it and turned the evidence bag over. Shrugged. 'Company glove.'

'Your size?'

'They only have two sizes. Why?'

'We found one matching this in your workspace, hanging up.' She picked up the evidence bag. 'But d'you know where we found the first?'

'You're dying to tell me.'

'At Darren Winters' house. The day after his death. The house had been trashed and this had been left behind.'

'Then it's not mine,' said Lee defiantly.

'We'll have it tested,' said Nicola.

'You do that. I've never been to his house.'

'We found one other item of interest in your work area, Lee. Shoved down behind your locker. Darren Winters' mobile phone.'

'Fuck off,' said Lee, staring at her in disbelief.

'We've been looking for it ever since his death,' said Nicola. 'How d'you think it got there?'

Lee looked both rattled and angry now. 'I didn't put it there. I've never even seen it. Test that one too while you're at it, cos I've never been near his phone. I don't even know what it looks like!'

'Why would it be there, Lee?'

Nicola could see Lee's mind moving fast. 'It's obvious, isn't it? I'm being stitched up. Same person who put the knife in the treetop, now they're putting other stuff connecting me to him where I work. You won't find my DNA on the phone or the knife.'

'Or the glove?' asked Harry.

'We'll hold you a while longer,' said Nicola. 'We're going to need access to your phone to look at your call records, messages, emails and photos in case they tell us anything.'

Lee looked at his solicitor. 'Can they do that?'

His solicitor confirmed it with a nod, to Lee's growing frustration.

As Nicola terminated the interview and she and Harry stood up to leave, Lee threw his own questions at them.

'Tell me this then – what's the motive? Why would I do it? I've told you everything. I liked him. He'd had a hard time. I didn't wish him harm. Why would I kill him? And why there? How does any of that make sense?'

The door closed behind Harry and Nicola.

62

Nicola and Harry drove immediately back to Parkwood. Their next task was to interview Conor Masters, following on from Emma's conversation with Harry the previous evening. Then they would talk to the occupants of Lodge 97 to see if they could corroborate what Lee Parker had just told them. And if they did, that might suggest they should also believe what he'd just told them about Lindsey.

But there was something else preoccupying Nicola as she drove.

'I wanted to apologize for last night,' she said. 'What I said at the end. I was so tired. It was incredibly unprofessional; should've stayed inside my head.'

'Honestly, sarge, it's fine,' said Harry.

Sarge. Hmph.

'It's not. I should have been more boundaried. I'm your senior officer. I can't be saying that sort of thing to you.'

'Honestly, don't worry about it.'

They drove in silence for a bit and Nicola felt Harry was chewing on saying something more. After a while he did.

'I was . . . flattered. That you trusted me enough to share. Or confide or whatever.'

Nicola wrinkled her nose. 'Yeah, I dunno if it was confiding.'

'Oh. OK. No. Sure,' said Harry nervously.

'More like blurting,' said Nicola. 'I was just knackered and burbling and I got really distracted by the trees and how dark it was.'

'Right,' said Harry.

He looked through his phone. Then he showed Nicola an image on the screen. She glanced at it.

It was an image of the police T-shirts from the 2021 stag do.

WHAT HAPPENS AT PARKWOOD STAYS AT PARKWOOD!

It took her a minute to understand what Harry was saying to her. Then she realized he was confirming it would stay between them, that it was OK. At least that's what she took it to mean.

'Thank you,' she said.

'Welcome,' said Harry, nodding. He was quiet for a few moments and Nicola glanced across at him. His lips were pursed and it looked like he was stopping himself from laughing.

'What?!'

'You got distracted by trees,' said Harry, trying to hold in his laughter.

Nicola was speechless. Her DC was taking the piss out of her in a way that nobody really did, and it did not feel wrong.

'I did!' she protested and could not help smiling.

'Sure,' said Harry. 'Happens to all of us, every day.'

Oh my God, he was mocking her!

She laughed in disbelief and gestured outside the window as trees went by. 'They're very distracting, look!'

Harry was looking out of the window. 'What was that? Didn't hear. I was . . . mesmerized by . . . branches.'

They were both laughing now like kids.

'All right, stop! Lack of sleep is making us both giddy.'

'OK. Sorry,' said Harry, putting on his serious face.

'It's bugging me what Lee said as we were leaving.'

'Which bit?'

'Why would he do any of this?' said Nicola. 'That's the key

question. What would his motive be? It's like all the evidence is pointing at him. Except motive.'

'He could be lying about how they got on. We've only his word for it. Their phones might tell us something about that.'

Nicola stared ahead. Her instincts were telling her that Lee's outrage was genuine. 'He looked truly surprised about the glove and the phone.' She looked ahead. 'He's many things but he's not stupid. I can't disagree with him – it's too convenient. He'd have to be an idiot to leave the knife, the phone and a matching glove in the area he works. There are so many places he could dispose of them, across the site or even further afield. It's more like someone's thought how to point the finger at Lee and then executed it.'

She could feel Harry looking across at her. 'But who would that be?'

63

'Why've you been lying to us, Conor?'

Nicola dispensed with the pleasantries in record time once they had sat down in Lodge 141. Harry had called Emma ahead of time and advised her to take Bella to the playground, to which she readily agreed. They all knew that Nicola and Harry were about to detonate the bomb that had been ticking at the heart of Conor and Emma's marriage.

'What do you mean? I haven't lied to you,' said Conor Slater on the opposite sofa. He was very chilled, seemingly very happy to cooperate. More bemused than irritated. Nicola felt it was a considered act.

'We have intel which suggests you are lying to us. You weren't in your lodge at two a.m. or four a.m., were you?'

As Nicola spoke, she noticed Conor's foot begin to tap slowly on the floor. As she got further into her speech, the tapping increased.

Nicola watched as Conor took a huge deep breath in, holding it for at least seven seconds before releasing it slowly, as if meditating. He was very much not meditating. He was breaking. Nicola decided it was time to lay down another card.

'Did you bring cocaine with you?' asked Nicola. 'Or did you get it here on-site?'

There was silence in the room. Conor looked both poised and trapped, a man whose body was somehow locked into position but needing to spring away, fast.

After a moment he whispered, 'Go fuck yourself.'

There were two different ways to approach this, thought Nicola. She chose the softer methodology.

'Conor, you look exhausted. And we all know you don't want to be here.'

'Do we?'

'Yes,' said Nicola. 'The first time you and I saw each other, you were trying to get out of Parkwood, away from whatever's going on here for you.'

Conor said nothing.

Nicola continued. 'All we're interested in right now is trying to solve the murder of Darren Winters. We don't care about drug use if that's worrying you. I'm presuming you got it from Lee Parker, right?'

Conor nodded.

'OK. Now, it's vital for us to understand whether we can rule you out of our investigation or not. We know you weren't in bed that night, so I'm going to ask again and you must answer honestly. Where were you Monday night into Tuesday morning, let's narrow it down to between midnight and six a.m.?'

Conor was silent and still. His cheeks clenched and unclenched. Then he allowed a single word to escape.

'Running.'

Nicola was confused. She felt the word was laden with . . . what? Some strong emotion, but which? Shame?

'What do you mean "running"?' asked Nicola. 'What sort of running? Like sports running? On the routes here?'

Conor shook his head.

'In the gym?'

Conor shook his head again.

Nicola despaired. 'Conor, come on. Give me something, please. Running where?'

'Away.'

'OK, but away *where*?'

'Just *away*!'

The phrase echoed round the room like a shot.

Nicola stayed silent and glanced at Harry in an attempt to ensure he did the same. She felt Conor would quickly become uncomfortable with the silence. She was proven right.

Conor ran his hands through his hair and looked out of the window. 'All along I've been told these are the things I should be aiming for. I told Em I wasn't sure. And she *did not listen*. No, she knew better. She was sure. She was all like, *it'll be fine, trust me*. Well, I did trust her, I did believe her and she was wrong.'

'About what?' asked Nicola.

'Bella. She is not the silver bullet. She is not alchemy; she cannot transform me into the thing everyone wants me to be. Maybe even the thing I would want to be if I could. But I can't. Work I get. I'm good. I can do that. Family, being a parent, no. It's a prison and I cannot get lost there.

'I love my daughter. I love my wife. But I am not built to be in a family. To give myself over, to put them first. I can pretend and I can laugh and I can play and I can almost forget in those moments, but when I lie there in bed my skin is crawling. It scares the shit out of me because I am a fraud and I want to escape, but I know the pain I'll cause them. So what do I choose? Their pain or my pain?' He snatched a gulp of air. 'Or do I just keep medicating it away so I don't have to think about any of it?'

Nicola let all of that land in the room. Then she said, 'Tell us about Monday, tell us about the running.'

'It had been a long day. The driving, being in the car with Bella. She's not a great traveller. We had to keep stopping.' He paused, looking around the room as if hearing his own voice bouncing off the walls. 'By the time we were here, the big queue to get in, you know you think you've arrived, you've passed the sign and then it's like gridlock and I was like, why the fuck can we not just go in . . . ? Anyway. I don't even know how long the journey was, maybe six or seven hours total, and, God love my daughter, but that's a long time for us all to be in a metal box crawling along a lane, right? And I was saying to Emma, possibly we have miscalculated on this, we've been overambitious again . . . but she was like she usually is: it's fine. And I'm just fuming, really.'

Conor looked at Nicola. 'We're different, Emma and me. After we'd unpacked, ditched the car and got back into the lodge, then we were getting ready for this fucking Solstice Parade, and even that . . . getting ready, I could feel myself just getting more wound up and tight and . . .'

Nicola watched Conor distractedly touch the end of his nose without even realizing it.

'We had friends come here last year, and they told me to talk to this guy in the high-ropes section – here's his details while you're there. I didn't tell Em, she doesn't really know that I . . . sometimes need a little help.'

Nicola said, 'I suspect she does, Conor.'

Conor looked alarmed. 'No.' The sentence fell apart as it was leaving his mouth. He looked thrown, as if a high ledge on which he was standing had begun to crumble beneath him.

'I'm in trouble,' said Conor quietly, simply, to the room but mostly to himself.

'Did you get some cocaine from Lee Parker?'

Conor nodded. 'And it got me through the getting ready, the parade, the early evening, but . . . I felt I needed more come the end of the night. But he wasn't answering my messages and I'd had the fight at the parade, and it's all a bit of a blur, but I think I saw him again, but he wasn't helpful, and I was just thinking about how much I hated all of this, this horrific place and all the people and most of all being a parent, it's like being a fucking prisoner, and I'm trying to keep a brave face on it and hold it back from Em, but I'm pent up, so I went out for a run.'

'Tell us about that.'

Conor was seemingly lost in his own thoughts. Then he said, 'It was late. I went back out and I started walking. And then I was jogging. Then running. All round the site. And I just felt like I wanted to . . . that I could . . . keep going. I didn't stop. I couldn't stop, didn't want to. I was wired and I couldn't stop. I had to run. To keep running.'

'To where?'

'You're not paying attention; you're not listening,' snapped Conor. He sounded like a spoilt child who was trying to explain something complex to a stupid adult. 'Not *to*. Away.'

Nicola was staring at him.

His voice dropped once again to a whisper. 'Away from them. Away from my family.'

'You mean off-site, out of Parkwood?'

'On foot. In the dark. No phone, just a little torchlight on a headband. Out the approach road first. Then on to the main road. Then keeping going. Just away. I didn't want to be anywhere near them.'

'How long for?' asked Harry.

Conor looked shocked at the answer. 'Hours. Most of the night. I just kept running.'

'Why?' Nicola could not stop herself from asking.

Conor said, 'I am not the right person. For Em, for Bella. I'm just . . . I can't do it. Not long-term. Not every day for ever. In that moment, before that moment, after that moment, I wanted out. I just want it to be me. It's easier.'

Conor was staring wide-eyed at Nicola and she felt as if she could see the structure of his skull. Like the skin had been stripped back.

'I think my feet started to hurt around three. I sat on a bench. I don't know how long I was there. Or even where I was.'

Sure, thought Nicola, your feet hurting was the thing that did it. Or maybe the cocaine wearing off.

'A minicab driver stopped and asked what I was doing. I said I'd come out for a run and got lost. He gave me a lift back to the top of the approach road. The sun was just coming up.'

'You'd better be telling the truth, Conor,' said Nicola. 'Because we'll check the traffic cameras within a ten-mile radius. We'll know if they caught you near the roadside.'

'They will,' said Conor simply.

Nicola instinctively believed him. This was not the person who killed Darren Winters.

Conor was looking at her plaintively.

'You can't tell Em,' he said.

64

You go on holiday to get away, but you can't get away from yourself.

The phrase could have been invented for Conor Slater, thought Nicola. She and Harry were back in the lodge. They had updated the wall map, ruling further people out, and noting where evidence should be requested, as with the traffic cameras for Conor. Harry was following up, trying to track down the cab driver who Conor claimed had given him a lift some of the way back, as well as chasing the doorbell footage which had been promised by those who lived on the same street as Darren Winters. He reported to Nicola that the latter should be there within the hour. Lee Parker was still in custody: Karina and her friends were not in their lodge and Nicola had left a message on her phone. She needed to speak to them but also retained a nagging thought: even if Karina confirmed what Lee had told them, there was still a small window of opportunity for him after he'd had sex with her to have killed Darren Winters.

Nicola knew who she wanted her next conversation to be with, but she needed more data, more corroboration, more answers, before she put everything in front of them. And answers took time. Time and resources were against them. Forensic work, DNA matches, print matches – all of these took longer than they had. *Tick-tock, Nicola.*

She nagged Mel once more to hustle along the initial reports from Darren Winters' phone. She had been desperate to find that phone, and now that it had been found, she was counting the seconds until she could see what it contained. She was pacing so much that Mel had told her to be patient, and preferably in another room. He stressed, with respect, that she was putting him off.

Nicola exiled herself to the bedroom. Sat back on the bed. Looked at the notes scattered around from yesterday. The detritus of two unresolved cases.

Did Lee Parker kill Darren Winters? The evidence was closing in. He had opportunity – but Nicola still did not understand the motive. And something about the circle of evidence that surrounded Lee felt too convenient. Lee was smarter than to leave those things in his work. Wasn't he?

There was something foggy about the pass keys for the Splashdome, too. But her brain couldn't quite wrap itself round what was bugging her.

Tick-tock, Mel.

Nicola flicked through Sarah Welland's notebooks again. The endless noughts and crosses. This time she noted Sarah's favouring of the diagonal win, like a repeating pattern. The drawings. The *3k*.

And then the tiny grid on the penultimate page. A throw-away doodle, seemingly ignored or dismissed by Keith Hammersley or anyone else looking through the files. But why those words? Why only in this grid? *Su. Hat. Jo.*

The scribblings of a girl, Keith had said. Nicola did not believe that. They were the notes of a woman. However small, their placing was unique. She had taken the time to write it out. Nicola did not think Sarah did that by accident. What could they mean?

Nicola used the time to check back through the files. She cross-referenced with the list of contacts from Sarah's phone and computer. Yes, a Susan and a Joanna. But a Hattie or anything beginning with Hat? No. Nothing. Was it a nickname for someone? A surname? Hatfield? Hattersley? Bit more of a male thing to call people by surnames than first names, but all the same, wasn't it? She tried the lists of guests and staff at Parkwood at the time – nothing. The same with now. She spotted one: Joanna Sunderland was the closest she could get. She had a bleary memory of talking to her. Was that a connection? Were these words definitely names? What else could they be?

It couldn't be a phrase, could it? She tried an online search. *Hat Jo Su* . . . Did you mean: hat jokes hat jobs Hat Ja Tau What was Hat Ja Tau? Oh, a Hindi wedding song. No, not that, but thank you anyway, the internet. Devon Hat Shops No, thank you. Su Hat Jo Showing results for Sun Hat John Lewis Fuck off, internet. Even refining it only gave her hats. She kept going: *Hat Su Jo.* Oh, kill me now.

Fuuuck, none of this made sense. And how would this help solve the death of Darren Winters anyway? Her head was swimming. Too much too much *too much*.

The trick to solving any case was hacking away the information that was irrelevant. Whittling the case, like the kids she'd seen whittling sticks in a woodcraft session as she walked round the site the other day. Whittle away the stuff that didn't apply.

There were only ever a few facts that were important, the facts that actually affected the death of the murder victim. A handful at best. Everything else was nothing to do with the case. But every case was like being handed a big box of different people's lives. Which lives, and which decisions within them, impacted the death of the victim? And which were tangentially connected to the victim but had no effect on the act of murder they were trying to solve?

Whittle the stick, Nicola. Hack away the undergrowth.

Wait. The pattern. The diagonal win pattern Sarah favoured for the noughts and crosses. Diagonal order from top left to bottom right. Nicola searched that final remaining combination from the word grid – Jo Hat Su. She braced herself for a further bombardment of hats.

Did you mean johatsu?

No, I did n–

Holy shit.

65

Johatsu.

It meant evaporation.

A Japanese word which also had another more modern meaning.

Nicola read on.

Johatsu was an underground process in Japan by which people disappeared from their own lives. People who were shamed or unhappy or in debt or lacking any hope. A subculture among Japanese society.

As Nicola read, she felt a jigsaw coming together – the pieces suddenly sliding towards each other, gliding and locking quietly into place.

Calm yourself, Nicola. This is not an answer. But it was a possibility at least.

She kept reading.

There were companies and individuals who provided the service, *yonige-ya*, which translated as 'fly-by-night shops'.

Was the solution to what happened to Sarah Welland right here in her own notebook?

She'd been unhappy with lockdown, worried about getting married . . . Had she found a way to disappear?

Nicola's brain felt alive. From dead ends to possibilities, the two extremes. Something was nagging at her from the files she had read. No, two things. Because, because . . . Sarah Welland had spent time in Japan. Three times, her mum had said. She knew the culture. What if she knew about this possibility?

Wait wait wait wait wait.

She grabbed the printout list of the guests staying at Parkwood when Sarah went missing in 2021.

Nicola's heart began to race.

There it was. A single Japanese name. Hideko Matsuko.

Another single person coming to Parkwood.

Single people rarely came to Parkwood.

Nicola looked up Hideko Matsuko and found a LinkedIn page without a photograph. Nicola panned through the list of companies Matsuko had worked for. She checked on their existence and lines of work. There were contact details for this woman from back in 2021. But nothing before. A five-year gap in her profile.

Nicola flicked back to her online reading. Fees for *johatsu* ranged from the equivalent of £600 to a few thousand pounds. Is that what Sarah Welland had needed cash for? An untraceable payment for a new life?

Parkwood had not been an escape for Sarah Welland. It might, however, have been the gateway to a bigger escape. A voluntary disappearance from her own life.

Nicola was already deducing that this would be impossible to confirm; from what she was reading, that was the whole point of *johatsu*. You were never found. People never knew. It was an emotionally brutal decision and placed unimaginable strain on your friends and family. Nicola did not know much about the culture of Japan: presumably it made sense within that. But for a girl from Darlington with a partner back home, holidaying in West Dorset with her mum, would someone be that strong? That cruel?

She had to tell Harry.

They stood outside the lodge as Harry took in what Nicola was describing. She had already added finding a phone number to Mel's job list, much to his irritation, so she thought it best to give him a wide berth as he worked.

'We've been saying everything here was too scheduled and commercialized,' said Harry. 'But this is another level. A service that will disappear you? I don't understand how it's even legal.'

'I guess if it's with someone's consent,' mused Nicola. 'Nobody did anything wrong in a legal sense. Morally, ethically, emotionally, sure – and the impact on those who knew her, that's different.'

'You really think it's a possibility?'

'I think once the kernel of an idea is there, once you know you could leave, then it can just sit in you and grow. And her mum said she was really changed by lockdown, shamed by her inability to conceive. If you're there, with your thoughts, every day, in a small flat, unhappy with your future, stuck with someone you're not sure about . . .'

You go on holiday to get away – but you can't get away from yourself.

Except what if you could? What if Sarah Welland did?

'Maybe Sarah Welland did find a way to get away from herself. Pay a company in another country to get you away from a life you want to escape from. What if she was prepared to ditch everything? Maybe she saw this week as her opportunity. She'd been locked away and trapped during the pandemic. This was the first time she was away from her fiancé, maybe she knew she was never going back. Parkwood became her gateway to the world or to another life.'

'There's no record of her leaving the country, no sightings.'

'Presumably that's part of what she paid for. New identity, getting her out of the country? It might explain why her body was never found.'

Harry was struggling with the idea. 'She just decided to leave her life? Let people think she was dead, let all her loved ones grieve for her?'

'I doubt she was thinking that far ahead. When we're desperate, our minds actively blank out consequences. We don't run the probabilities we don't like.'

'I feel like I'm getting an unnecessary glimpse into your subconscious, sarge,' said Harry.

'Oh, you have no idea,' said Nicola and really meant it.

'I just find it hard to believe someone could be so desperate that they could do that.'

'Harry, people *do* do that. There's a whole industry built round it. There's a *name* for it!'

'In Japan.'

'And you think we're different?'

'Yes. Cultural differences, differences between countries and the characters of people who live there. We don't have this. How could she not think of all the hurt, all the things that could go wrong?'

'Maybe she did,' said Nicola, 'and decided she could live with it. Maybe she wasn't thinking that far ahead. Maybe she prioritized her own survival. You have to remember we were in the middle of the pandemic. I'm not sure we've even begun to deal with what happened to the world in that period. All of us locked away. Thousands of people dying every day, and everyone else panic-buying toilet rolls. None of us knew how long it would last or if it was going to be the end of the human race entirely.'

'Yeah, but just disappearing like that?'

'Did you not hear Conor Slater earlier? Wanting to run out on his life because he felt imprisoned by it?'

'I still don't see how anyone could do that,' said Harry.

Not for the first time, Nicola thought, *You are so young.* It seemed that life had not yet left many marks on Harry. Maybe it never would.

She didn't say anything for a moment. Then very quietly, shakily almost, she volunteered, 'I do.'

It would be a long time before she forgot Harry's expression. It contained multitudes, far more than simple surprise or shock; confusion, questions and disbelief were in there too. Nicola continued before he could interrogate her. 'The chance to reset. The chance to run. The chance of another chance. I get it. Not to that extreme, but I understand it.'

A silence settled over them. Nicola watched Harry take it in, looking at her. She didn't break his gaze. She didn't want to.

Then he simply said, 'OK.' He nodded.

She felt that 'OK' also contained a multiplicity of thought. As if he was maybe communicating: *I hear you. I see you.* Did she imagine that? Probably. She was tired. She was always fucking tired.

'Well, I hope you don't disappear,' said Harry, bursting the bubble of the moment, as Nicola found herself expelling a short burst of surprised laughter. 'But if you do, I guess I'll know which company to call and check. And I'll get to go to Japan, so every cloud . . .'

'On this salary? I'll only get to Croydon,' said Nicola.

'You can probably disappear very easily in Croydon,' said Harry. 'Nobody would ever know.'

'Or care,' said Nicola.

Harry closed his eyes as if trying to solve a difficult

trigonometry problem. 'If it's possible she's alive . . . what does that mean? Does that rule anyone out of suspicion for Winters?'

'I don't think it can. It doesn't change what people thought, or think.'

Mel stuck his head out of the door. 'This is where you're skulking.'

'We're staying out your way,' said Nicola. 'Given you asked us to stay out of your way.'

'Hmph,' said Mel loquaciously, eyeing them both with suspicion. He handed Nicola a Post-it. 'Number for the Japanese person you wanted.'

'Wow,' said Nicola, impressed. 'That was quick!'

Mel sniffed, already going back inside. 'I'm very good.'

Nicola checked the time difference and dialled Hideko Matsuko.

The call connected and a voice answered quickly.

'Hi?'

'Hello, is this Hideko? I'm calling from England. Do you speak English?'

A pause and then: 'Who is this, please?'

Cagey even to start with, thought Nicola. 'My name is Nicola Bridge, Detective Sergeant Nicola Bridge. I'm with Three Counties Police in the UK.'

Another pause. Then: 'Yes?'

'I'm calling about Sarah Welland. I don't know if you remember her. She disappeared when you were over here staying at the Parkwood resort in West Dorset.'

'What is this about, please?'

'I'm seeking some help with her disappearance?'

'No.' The answer was shocking in its abruptness.

'If I could just ask you a couple of –'

'I gave a statement about my stay. There is nothing else to say.'

'There is a company listed on your LinkedIn which I believe may have connections to another *yonige-ya* company –' Nicola knew her pronunciation would be terrible, but she had to push past her embarrassment – 'a company that helps people disappear, *johatsu*. Did Sarah Welland –'

'Please do not call again.' The voice was quiet, formal and curt.

The call was terminated.

There is nothing else to say.

Nicola felt that Hideko Matsuko had said plenty without saying much. 'I don't think we can rule out *johatsu*, Harry,' said Nicola.

'If Sarah Welland isn't dead, Darren Winters wasn't a killer,' said Harry.

'But whoever murdered him may not have known that.'

But before they could do anything, the door sprang open again, nearly knocking Nicola over.

'Careful!' she said.

'It's a very unreasonable place to stand,' complained Mel. 'I thought you'd want to know straight away. Darren Winters' phone, there's a WhatsApp on there from Lindsey Moorfield from late Monday afternoon, suggesting that they meet in the Splashdome. At midnight.'

66

'I didn't send this message.'

The room was silent, save for the whir of the fan on Lindsey's computer. In the distance outside, squeals and laughter could be heard drifting over from the large Parkwood adventure playground as Nicola and Harry stood in front of Lindsey.

When she realized they weren't going to speak, Lindsey spoke again, more insistently. 'I did not send it! I don't even remember seeing it. Do you have any idea how many WhatsApps I get a day? Each department has a group, let alone the individuals. They just keep whizzing through. Half of it I don't engage with.'

When Harry had asked her earlier that day who might benefit from framing Lee Parker, Nicola's mind had gone to Lindsey.

'Lindsey, you told us you didn't know Darren Winters was on-site before he was killed.'

'Right,' said Lindsey briskly.

'Except you did know. You found him at the out-of-service lodge. You knew Lee Parker had got him in, and you had a big argument with them both.'

Lindsey was silent for a moment. Her jaw moved as if she was chewing on the problem itself.

'Who told you that?'

'Lee Parker. He's still in custody.'

Lindsey nodded, as if to say, *I might have known.*

Nicola tried again: 'Why didn't you tell us?'

'Because I was scared about what would come out,' Lindsey shot back. 'Because I'd only discovered the previous day what Lee had done. And as I started to look into it, I found it was the tip of the iceberg. And I'm compromised with –'

She stopped, reset, carried on. 'If it gets out what has been going on here, you know where the buck will stop? Not with Lee Parker. I am hanging by a thread right now. I have given my career to this place and it can be taken away with a one-line email.'

Nicola saw the steel of a woman who had to run a resort of hundreds of staff and guests, but she remained resolutely unimpressed by the lies Lindsey had told.

'Can you imagine how angry I was when I found out? So yes. I did have a massive argument. Yes, I told Darren Winters to leave.'

'So why didn't he?'

Lindsey looked at Nicola like a drowning woman.

'It's . . . complicated,' she said. Her voice was barely a whisper. The office felt like it had become a confessional.

Compromised. She'd said she was compromised.

'What's complicated, Lindsey?' asked Nicola carefully.

Lindsey looked at her nails. Nicola had noticed the care that had gone into Lindsey's nails. Nicola hated the state of her own nails. Sometimes they made her feel as though she wasn't a sufficiently stylish modern woman. She did not look after them, and so whenever a posh do or a weekend with friends came up, she would require a panicked appointment with whichever nail technician she could find to give her the appropriate nail-related glow-up. She felt like a fraud in the manicure game.

As she watched, Lindsey began to pick at her nails, without

seeming to realize she was doing it. Pick, pick, pick, as if at a scab. Nicola winced inwardly. Lindsey was scraping at the beautiful work, worrying it away.

All the while Nicola's question hung in the air. *What's complicated, Lindsey?*

Lindsey looked up. 'My life,' she whispered simply. Her eyes were reddening.

'I did leave here around nine. I did get home around twenty past. We had some dinner. I was late. Ian was a little . . . irritable. Understandable. I'd said I'd be home at seven, eight latest.' She paused, weighing her words. 'The truth is, I don't always enjoy going home. It's . . . loaded.'

'What do you mean by loaded?' asked Nicola kindly.

'I'm successful, right? I'm paid well, bonuses, nice perks, I get the car as well. He's struggled for work since he got laid off last year. It's a tight economy, companies are closing. I think he feels less . . . validated now we're no longer equivalent.'

'He resents your success?'

'I don't know . . . maybe.' Her face dropped. 'There's something else.' She clearly did not want to say it. 'Something Darren Winters knew. Why he felt he could stay, even when I asked him to leave.'

Lindsey looked like she would burst into tears. She tamped the tears down in full sight of Nicola and Harry, taking a deep breath as if her chest and diaphragm could keep them in.

'Myself and Lee . . .' She trailed off.

Oh no. Oh, Lindsey.

'Just once, last year, end of season, a Sunday night, there were drinks, we were in here, just there, and . . . it was a terrible, awful mistake. If I could erase it, if I could take it back, I would. But . . . Lee told Darren Winters. I don't know when, and I really cannot understand why – bragging, I suppose. So Darren was threatening to tell my husband when we had the argument in the lodge.'

Oof, thought Nicola.

'I told him it would be the end of everything, for all of us. He said he'd lost everything anyway, thanks to me betraying him. Why shouldn't he betray me in return? I told him he'd be betraying all the staff here. I'm not proud of myself.' She looked up at Nicola once more. 'I'm scared. People cannot know. I have to keep my authority. They can't know how weak I am.'

Lindsey had just provided her motive, thought Nicola.

'Did you meet Darren Winters again that night?'

'No!' Lindsey was furious. 'I told you: I was at home with my husband. Check with him, check when I logged in and out, check with whatever traffic cameras are between here and my house. You must be able to see where my phone was. I. Went. Home.'

'But if you didn't send that message, who did and how?'

'I don't know,' said Lindsey, staring at her screen.

She paused, a realization flitting across her face.

'Wait, I have WhatsApp up on here all day. It's permanently on my screen. Anybody could come in here and use it.'

'Do you not have a password?'

'I don't need one. It's my office.'

'Was anyone else in your office that afternoon? Did you have any meetings?'

Lindsey shook her head. 'No. I came back here, composed myself, went back out around the site. I spent a long time talking to Lee.'

'So if someone was in here,' Nicola realized, 'they would

have to have had a pass key enabled? And it would be recorded on the system?'

'Correct,' said Lindsey.

'We have the time of the message,' said Nicola to Harry. 'We can see if anyone else was in here.'

67

'Can't keep away, can you, lover?!'

Mel had been sent to Esther once more, this time with Nicola and Harry at his side. They did not tell Esther the reason for the check, only that it was important to get an answer quickly.

'Come and sit right next to me and we'll make sweet music together,' Esther told Mel, as Nicola raised an eyebrow at Harry. She could see Mel blushing, but he also possibly looked happy.

The two worked together to match the data to a pass key.

Within seven minutes, they had a staff ID.

'Does that answer whatever question you're asking?' queried Esther.

They returned to Lindsey to inform her of who had been in her office that afternoon.

Lindsey did not want to believe it.

Nicola and Harry were waiting as their target exited a lodge.

'Hello,' said Nicola. 'We need you to come with us.'

Alice Smith placed her cleaning equipment down, as Nicola told her she was under arrest.

Alice suddenly looked even younger than her nineteen years.

68

Alice was booked in and a solicitor was appointed for her. As this lengthy bureaucratic process was happening, Nicola and Harry were chivvying Mel to provide them with the full documentation they needed in order to talk to Alice.

On the drive over, with Alice in the car, Nicola had felt the case finally revealing itself to her. She felt she knew what evidence she needed and where they might find it to elicit a confession.

Nicola and Harry headed into the interview room, fully armed, they hoped.

The young woman at the interview-room table was small and wide-eyed. Her shoulders hunched in, as if she wanted to wrap her arms round herself.

'Alice, you understand we have arrested you in connection with the death of Darren Winters?' said Nicola.

'I do, but I don't know why you would,' said Alice.

'We've interviewed you once. Is there anything you've remembered in the meantime, or further information you omitted to tell us?'

Alice stared back, unblinking. 'I don't think so.'

'OK,' said Nicola, nodding. Down to business. 'Have you ever been to Darren Winters' house, Alice?'

'No,' said Alice simply.

Nicola turned a tablet screen round in the middle of the

table to face Alice. A still came up, showing Alice on a street at night.

'This is you, correct?'

Alice peered at it uneasily. 'Don't know.'

Nicola pressed play on the footage. The figure who could be Alice was walking towards a house.

'This is you at four seventeen a.m., a few hours after Darren Winters was killed, captured on a video doorbell from the other side of the street to Darren Winters' house. There you are, making your way up the path, looking around, checking nobody's watching. And nobody was. Apart from this camera.'

Alice said, 'That's not me.'

'Well,' said Nicola and scrolled through the tablet for the next piece of footage. 'Working backwards, this definitely, clearly, IS you, isn't it? Coming out of the woodland trail at Eagleforth, caught by CCTV along that road. About nine minutes prior to being caught on the doorbell camera. Same outfit. Can you confirm that's you, Alice?'

'I don't know,' repeated Alice, less sure now. 'It does look a bit like me.'

'Now, of course, what we know is, if you trace the path from this exit back along the woodland trail – it leads to Parkwood, where there's a gap in the perimeter fence, which seemingly all the staff know about and multiple people use as a shortcut. Have you ever used that path, Alice?'

'Maybe,' said Alice. 'Once or twice. Plenty of us do.'

'So this footage shows you went from Parkwood, around four a.m. on the night Darren Winters was killed, through the perimeter fence, along the trail, out at Eagleforth where you went to Darren Winters' house. Didn't you?'

Alice was silent this time.

Nicola called up another piece of footage.

'Here we have you doing the return journey. Is this you leaving Darren Winters' house twenty-four minutes later and heading back to the woodland trail to Parkwood?'

'I mean, I really don't think so,' said Alice.

Nicola noticed her solicitor look at Alice sympathetically.

'We think it was you, Alice,' said Nicola, 'and we think we have other evidence to prove it.' Nicola moved the tablet back. 'Why were you there, Alice?'

Alice didn't speak.

'At first I was trying to work it out – what you were looking for? And then I realized you weren't looking for anything; you were *leaving* something there, making it look like someone had broken in and left something behind – Lee Parker's glove. You put that in there to draw our focus to him, didn't you?'

'No,' said Alice. 'I didn't.'

Nicola adopted a gentle tone. 'You must have had to work fast across the night. Going off to find one of Lee Parker's gloves – did you know he often left the door to his work-space unlocked? Mandy, the security guard, had to close it on her patrol later that morning, after you'd dropped Darren Winters' phone behind Lee's locker, ready for us to find later. You must've been knackered at work the next day, were you? Knackered and traumatized, surely?'

Nicola took a pause. Alice remained quiet and wide-eyed.

'Do you agree that's what happened, Alice? Or do you want to say anything contrary to this version of events?'

Alice said, 'I'm just listening for now.'

'You took a knife from the lodge occupied by Valerie

Doyle, didn't you? A knife which you yourself later reported missing, very smart. How did you get it up the tree, Alice? Did you think it would never be found up there? Maybe you were thinking, if it ever was found, it'd point to Lee. Was that it? What has Lee Parker ever done to you, Alice?

'We know you sent the message to Darren Winters from Lindsey Moorfield's WhatsApp on her computer. It couldn't have been Lindsey; we have her located elsewhere at the time. You were clever, though. You sent it, saw he'd replied, then deleted the thread on her computer, hoping she wouldn't notice. Which she didn't. Your key card entry puts you in that room at the same time as the message is sent. Why did you send the message, Alice? Was it so you could be on your own with him? What were you planning to do to him?'

Nicola let all that settle. Alice was still looking straight at her. Her expression wasn't a challenge or defiance. It also wasn't defeat. It was more that she seemed to be *waiting*.

'This is just some of the evidence we have so far, Alice. You can see there's quite a lot. You're going to have to answer for it sooner or later. If I'm wrong, tell me why. But if I'm right, there's one thing I'd love to know. One thing I don't yet understand. Which is: why? Why would you want to kill Darren Winters?'

Alice sighed heavily. Then she looked directly back at Nicola with such sadness in her eyes.

'I was only trying to help,' she said plaintively.

69

As she sat there, realizing that there was no way to avoid telling the truth about what had happened, she was struck by the sudden feeling that it was now hard to imagine what would happen tomorrow or the day after. That with every word spoken in this room, everything was being disrupted.

Alice Smith thought about her life and her family and her school and her job and for a moment she felt like an observer on the span of her entire young life.

She wondered if this had always been where she was going. She didn't know what to do with that thought.

There were things that she wanted to tell the police. Things *she* wanted *them* to know. These were not the same as the police questions, which were all about the facts, which didn't feel the most important bit to her. They were not what Alice wanted to get across. The facts were obvious and settled and done. The bits before and between the facts were what she wanted to talk about.

She wanted to talk about Lindsey: the reason she, Alice, was here. The reason so many people at Parkwood were. How Lindsey looked after them, remembered them. Like a mother. Because Lindsey had done so many things for Alice without needing to: little bonuses, extra cash, comp passes, birthday gifts (none of her friends had bosses who remembered their birthdays).

The day Alice lost her parents – not that she had lost them; they were taken – but that day, Lindsey had come to find her, with the police. Afterwards, when the police had gone, Lindsey had waited. Alice had not known what to do, had even thought about finishing her shift. Lindsey had spoken calmly and carefully, telling her to take the time she needed, and that if she ever wanted to talk, Lindsey would be there.

She *had* needed to talk, and Lindsey had absolutely been there.

People often called her young for her age. She didn't know what that meant, or why they would presume to know. She had learned to keep herself to herself: at school, and then at work. Housekeeping was perfect for that.

She knew her parents had worried. Her dad would try to coax her out, saying things like, 'You might need to learn to scrap a bit.' She did not want to scrap, but after he had died, she began to understand what he meant. She had lost her greatest cheerleaders in a second, as they drove a six-mile journey home on dark one-lane B roads, smashed into at a crossroads by a drunk-driving nineteen-year-old who had just passed his test.

Then she was an orphan, just turned seventeen. She went back to the house she had grown up in with them, still shared with them, and was overwhelmed by their instant absence. She did not feel anything other than numb for a very long time. Even now it was still there.

Alice could never have afforded therapy or counselling. But Lindsey had listened as she talked, in her own time, in her own office. Who else would have done that? Nobody that Alice knew. In the three years since joining Parkwood straight out of school, Alice had seen Lindsey be amazing to so many people, and not just because of the work. Lots of staff who were there after Covid said Lindsey had stepped in and sorted things and basically saved the place.

The majority of Alice's life had been spent at two places: school, which she had hated, and Parkwood, which she loved. Because of Lindsey.

The police wanted to talk about the things that had happened.

Alice knew it was time.

'I was in the extra lodge, cleaning. On Monday. Lee Parker had asked and paid me to do it. I was doing the far bathroom and I heard the door go. It was Mr Winters being shown in by Lee. They were chatting but they didn't know I was there. I didn't want them to.'

'Why?' asked Detective Nicola. 'If you were doing something for Lee anyway?'

Alice hesitated. 'I've only seen Mr Winters maybe once. I never heard good things about him. And there was that whole big thing that happened. It's like nobody ever wanted to talk about it or him. That's not normal.'

'Did they see you?'

'No, because Lindsey came in, which they obviously weren't expecting. And she definitely wasn't expecting them. It really kicked off. Straight away she had a go at both of them: how dare they, told Mr Winters he couldn't be here, he was barred, told Lee he'd been warned about using the lodge. She asked him what was he thinking, especially with changeover day and Solstice Parade. I think that's why Lee did it, cos everyone's attention would be somewhere else. I've never seen her that angry. It was really unsettling.

'Then Mr Winters said to her – super nasty – don't talk to me like that cos I can bring your whole fucking life down.

'I remember it exactly. "I can bring your whole fucking life down." He started matter-of-fact but then got nastier.

He said she'd betrayed him, taken his job, but that she was the one in trouble this time because he knew about her and Lee. He said, how would your husband like to know? How would the owners like to know? Would you be so popular then?

'I was worried then. I thought if they find me in there, what's that going to be like? I was sure they must be able to smell the cleaning products, or what if they needed the loo?

'Lindsey sounded really shaken. Said he wouldn't dare. And Winters said nothing'd give him greater satisfaction. I thought it was a horrible word to use. Who thinks like that? Lindsey said if he went to the owners, it'd put the whole site in jeopardy. Everyone's jobs, everything that'd been built. She said he didn't understand how close to the edge it all was these days. That the new owners couldn't be relied on and he should think what it would mean to Eagleforth, to everyone who worked here. Mr Winters was just, why do I care? I've lost everything already. And I heard her say, I want you gone.

'Then I heard the door slam. She had gone. Lee said to Winters, let's all calm down, you wouldn't do that, would you? And Winters said, yeah, without a second's thought. Lee was going, come on, man, no, too far. And Winters said, you're the one who shagged and bragged. It'd be on you.

'Lee said they should get some air, cool it down, and they left. As soon as I knew the coast was clear, I got out.'

'It was like a cloud on me the whole day. How it could all go bad now. There's a lot of us who live near; it's all we have. There's no other jobs, not really.

'It's like I had trouble breathing, worrying about it. I was thinking, I'm the only one who knows about this.'

*

Once, when she was fifteen, she'd been found in the changing rooms at school with a boy. The teacher had assumed they were trying to have sex and suspended them both.

Alice had not been trying, but the boy had. Alice had been fighting to avoid it, a small figure beneath a larger boy.

She had been saved by the teacher's arrival. Saved and punished.

It had taught her that life did not always bend towards justice.

'Then, later, I was cleaning Lindsey's office. She was there and she just looked like she'd been broken. Normally she'll ask how you are, chat a little, but there was nothing.

'She got called away to check on preparations for the parade and I was left there alone. I know she always leaves her computer on cos I have to dust the keyboard and the screen always flicks on. I can't say I've never looked. And there were messages between her and Mr Winters.

'I stood there looking at it. And I just had this idea. I thought, she looks after us, she looks after the guests, but who looks after her?'

One of Alice's reports, the year before she had left school, said she 'had issues anticipating and foreseeing consequences'.

Nicola Bridge watched as Alice took a sip of water. Throughout, Alice had been calm and factual.

'So you planned to kill Darren Winters?'

Alice looked offended, her head jerking back in an 'are you mad?' gesture.

'No. The message said, *Can we meet and sort this out please? I have a busy day.* I knew Lee would be taking guests in the pool

Monday night. He boasts about it and it's always check-in day. He told us how it works, the times he does it. He's always finished by half eleven latest.

'I waited outside. I held back until they left and ran over. I put a stick in the door before it closed, so it was open for when Mr Winters arrived.

'I let him go to the poolside. Lee had left the machine on like an idiot. Mr Winters looked confused when I went over. He asked who I was. I just said to him, you have to go now. You're not welcome.

'He said, what did I think I was doing? He spoke like he was my boss, which he isn't. So I showed him the knife.'

'Why did you take a knife, Alice?' asked Nicola. Her heart was becoming heavy for this girl.

'Precaution,' said Alice. 'Nobody knows whether he killed that woman or not.'

Alice had heard people talk about seeing red. Or the red mist.

Alice had never seen red. She saw pale, icy blue. Almost transparent. That's what she felt going round her veins, surrounding her head. It wasn't intense. It was a removal of intensity. A lessening. Not quite calmness, but close. It felt like certainty.

It wasn't, though. It wasn't to be trusted. But she only remembered that afterwards. When the icy blue lifted, she found herself in trouble.

'He called me small. A small girl. A small girl who didn't have the nerve to use that.

'He was bearing down on me. Looming. I thought, you did it. You're a killer. You killed that woman. And now you're going to do it to me.

'I thought lots of things at the same time. I thought about him killing her. About him coming at me. And I thought, I know you, your type. How you see me, what you'd do to me if you had the chance.

'It went deeper than I thought it would.'

There was silence in the room.

Nicola kept her eyes on Alice. Alice's face was unmoving, as if watching a movie replaying in front of her. Nicola thought she looked both very present and utterly absent.

'He looked surprised. I pushed it in. Then did it again. Didn't expect it to be that easy. It's quite soft, the body, isn't it?

'The blood was coming out. His face changed. Like now he knew I wasn't afraid to do it. He said, help me. It was too late by then. I took the knife out and there was more blood and he screamed and turned, and I thought, I mean, I knew, OK, it's done, better to finish it – and I stabbed him in the back of the . . . and he went down. I rolled him with my feet into the pool. And he was face down and he sort of got caught up in the water . . .

'I stood there for a bit to see if he was moving. Didn't want him coming after me. Needed some time to think, so I went back to the spare lodge. Thought it would be better than going home. Washed myself off in the shower. I went back the next day and cleaned it, as part of my rota.'

'Is that where you found his phone?' asked Nicola.

Alice nodded. 'I sat on the bed for a long time, maybe an hour. Time seemed to go really fast. I thought of a plan. Then I had to be quick. Going to his house, getting rid of the knife.'

'When did you put the knife up in the tree?'

'Had the idea walking back from his house. I could see the

trees. The sun was just starting to come up, and I thought all the attention would be on the pool. No one's ever at the high ropes then. This was only just after five. There's two ways up. Lee showed me not long after I joined. Showing off to all of us new girls. I did the rungs as high as they went. No safety.'

Alice Smith was quiet for a long moment again, before looking up directly at Nicola.

'Will you explain to Lindsey? I was trying to help. I was trying to protect her from him. She helped me. I thought I could help her.

'This place is everything to loads of us. People come here because they need a break from their lives. The getaway they deserve, right? But it's the first place I've ever been happy.

'It's the only place I've ever felt like I really belonged.'

70

When Alice had been charged and there was no more to be done, Nicola and Harry drove back to Parkwood.

The journey was silent. Nicola couldn't stop thinking about Alice being only a year older than Ethan. There was a wild chaos to being nineteen, an age that seemed now to Nicola like a precarious wire walk towards maturity, where one trip could destroy an entire future.

And Alice had fallen.

These last hours had made Nicola recognize, if she hadn't known it already, how much Ethan still needed her. She'd once imagined that parental responsibilities all but expired on the day a child turned eighteen, everything signed off, keys to adulthood handed over. Now she could see how much guidance and reassurance was still needed. Not all the time, in fact, barely any of the time, but when Ethan needed it, he *really* needed it.

Nicola's heart broke for Alice.

Mel packed up the lodge, painstakingly taking down and preserving every bit of detail from the walls and returning the lodge to its former state. As he stood there at the end, box in hand, he said, 'I almost feel like I've had a little holiday.' Nicola stared at him, speechless, unable to keep the smile of disbelief from her face. Mel was a lunatic. But he was *their* lunatic.

Nicola and Harry visited Lindsey in her office. They explained to her that they believed Alice Smith had been responsible for Darren Winters' death. They explained the events and Alice's stated motive.

Lindsey's expression became more glazed the more they spoke.

They also told her that recent evidence pointed to Darren Winters not having any involvement in the disappearance of Sarah Welland.

They agreed it was acceptable to let the guests know that a suspect had been arrested. And that if guests wished to leave, they were now free to do so.

Lindsey said she thought very few would leave. Not now the pool was open again.

In Lodge 141 that evening, Emma Slater joined her husband Conor, who was sat on the floor of their bedroom with his back to the bed he had not slept in on the night of Darren Winters' murder. Bella was asleep in the room next door.

She wondered if he could sense the cold rage flowing off her body.

'You betrayed my trust. You made me an alibi to a pack of lies.'

He looked ahead. 'I want to be better. I need help.'

Emma nodded. She weighed her words before she spoke. And when she did speak, she measured them out slowly.

'Why the fuck would I help you? Why the fuck would I trust you now, Con?'

He looked at her, shocked.

'You think you're worth all this shit? That I, we, will put up with this . . . transgression because you're such an amazing husband, such a brilliant dad?' She spat her next words. 'Fuck that. You're not.'

'What're you saying?'

'I'm saying, I love you, but I cannot live like this. We deserve so much better than this.'

'I know,' said Conor. 'I agree.'

'Life is not without strings. But strings can hold you up, too. So you have to decide: do you want to forever be the child, forever in service of your own ego, your own pursuits? Or do you want to put another person first and surrender to what that's like? Because I can tell you that is the goal. That is the win. And I want you to have that. I want you to feel that. And I promise that the joy will be worth the suffering.'

'I don't know how to be the man I want to be.'

'You start by letting us both, me and Bella, in. Fully. By being present. Because this is all going to go by so fast. My nan used to say about bringing up kids, the days are long but the years are short. You're going to miss them, Con. And you don't get these things back.'

She could have said a lot more. But she did not think it was necessary. He understood. Maybe he was even capable of change.

If he was, she and Bella would be there with him.

When Nicola finally got home from her extended accidental stay at Parkwood – having messaged ahead to warn the men of the house that she would be returning and please could it not look like a pigsty when she returned – she was ushered from her car by a waiting Ethan.

'I've been told to escort you in,' he said in a manner which made it clear that he wanted no part in this but was doing so under duress.

He carried her bag in and manoeuvred her through the (tidy) kitchen, out the back doors and into the sunlit garden, where Mike was barbecuing.

There were salads and drinks and a tablecloth.

'I should be away more often,' Nicola said, performing the role of grateful returnee. She knew what was expected.

They ate and drank and made the smallest of talk. When that subsided, there was just the sound of munching. Nicola felt that Ethan was bursting with discomfort.

She was right. He suddenly said, 'I know I fucked up, all right? But I don't want to have another big meeting or conversation. I know what you both think of me. And I've told you both what I think about all of this. And if you're just staying together for me, I don't want it.' Then he got up and left.

Nicola and Mike looked at each other.

'Where did that come from?' asked Nicola.

'What did you both talk about in thc car home that night?' asked Mike. 'He said it was deep and some home truths and I wouldn't want to hear it.'

Nicola could not cope with that now. 'I was mainly furious with him.'

'He's playing us off against each other to distract from his mess. So for the avoidance of doubt, Nicola, I am here and I am with you because I love you. I messed up and I want to put it right. Because I want to be with you for the rest of my life.'

Nicola took a long gulp from the glass of wine in front of her. Her heart was pounding.

'Same,' she said.

What happens at Parkwood stays at Parkwood.

Right, Harry?

71

On a grey and rainy Saturday morning, some weeks after the events at Parkwood, Nicola and Harry journeyed to a semi-detached house in a Darlington cul-de-sac. They could have done it by Zoom, but they had discussed it, and both felt it was kinder to do it in person. It meant a six-hour drive for what was likely to be a half-hour conversation at best.

It was a quiet journey, the radio gently burbling away, playing hits from the eighties and nineties.

The idea of *johatsu* haunted Nicola. When awake at 3 a.m., she would catch herself fantasizing she could do the same, leave her life right now, but instantly her conscious mind told her, you've tried a reset; *this* is the reset: Dorset, from Liverpool. She wondered how long she had to give it to take full effect. Because the interim results were mixed.

Sometimes she felt a strange kind of twisted admiration for Sarah Welland, if that *was* what she'd done – she'd had the ability to detach. Nicola could never disappear like that. She was not that person.

Because here, now, in a dark front room, was the cost. Those left behind.

Over strong tea and thin rectangular biscuits, Nicola explained calmly and simply to Sarah's mother what they believed about Sarah's actions. That the likelihood was that she had not been murdered but that she had disappeared herself. She explained about the concept of *johatsu*, of the *yonige-ya* companies. Of the daughter who wanted to disappear from her own life.

Val listened to Nicola without interruption. When Nicola had come to a halt, there was a lull. Val gulped tea down while sitting very still.

After a while, the silence was broken.

'Do you have any way we can trace her?' asked Val.

'I can give you information on the companies, but they have stonewalled us,' said Nicola. 'We can't be one hundred per cent sure. This is our best estimation. I'm sorry. I don't know whether it makes it better or worse.'

'Worse,' said Val simply.

Nicola nodded sympathetically. She placed her hand on Val's. Val looked up at her as if to say, *you think that'll help?* Nicola removed her hand.

Val didn't say anything for a while. She was struggling, Nicola could see.

'Do you think it's my fault? Did I go on so much about having a child, telling her it was every woman's purpose, and then when it began to look like she couldn't . . . ? It's like . . . she's murdered herself. Without thinking about anyone left behind and the impact it'd have. That man's death, it comes from what she did. She all but killed him.'

The whole room felt frozen. The faint aroma of stewed tea. Biscuit crumbs on small plates.

Nicola did not have the words to soothe that thought. Val was right. The ripples that had flowed out from Sarah Welland's apparent decision to disappear were still moving through the world, leaving only debris in their wake.

They had one other stop to make.

They met Keith Hammersley in a pub called the King's Head. He bought them the soft drinks they asked for and a pint of bitter for himself. He also provided a packet of salt and vinegar crisps which he proceeded to lay open on the table for all three of them to share, only to eat them all himself as Nicola talked him through what they'd found, just as she had done with Val.

With Keith she went into further detail. A rental vehicle leased to Hideko Matsuko had left Parkwood in the hours before Sarah Welland's disappearance was reported. There was no CCTV footage of anyone else visible in the car as it departed. Had she been told to hide in a back seat? Was she even in there? They would never know for sure. The car had been one of many with no connection to Sarah Welland that had left Parkwood that day and been ruled out of the investigation early on. Mel had tried to trace this Hideko Matsuko further in Japan to no avail. The name was most likely an alias.

Once again, there was a long silence afterwards. Keith took the last salt and vinegar crisp and washed it down quickly by emptying his pint glass.

Eventually, he said, 'So you solved two cases and I solved none.'

'Sarah Welland actively didn't want to be found,' said Nicola. 'She didn't care what that meant for those left behind. She didn't think through what ramifications there might be. Or maybe she did and she just didn't care; she couldn't bear to carry on as she was.'

'I had all the evidence you had. I didn't spot it. If I had done . . .'

The thought hovered in the space between the detectives. Darren Winters' death was the fallout from Sarah Welland's first decision. Nicola knew contradicting Keith or attempting to make him feel any better would be pointless.

'It breaks you, this job,' said Keith, looking mostly at Harry. 'Sooner or later. You don't think it will, but it does.' His gaze shifted back to Nicola. 'You didn't do bad on this. For a woman,' he said, winking at her.

'Go fuck yourself, Keith,' said Nicola.

Keith Hammersley's roar of laughter echoed so loudly through the near-empty pub that a couple sharing a ploughman's craned their heads round the corner.

72

A very long way from the Parkwood site, a figure lay open-eyed on a hard mattress, surveying the ceiling.

Thinking about the piece of news she had read the other day.

It was not much. The news of a death in a place she'd once known.

It was probably nothing.

It was probably not even connected.

The woman who had once been but was no longer known as Sarah Welland had been awake for most of the night, thinking about the life she had left behind.

That she had been evacuated from. Evaporated from.

She wondered what her mum was doing. She could only assume she was alive. The same with her fiancé.

She had weighed up the consequences at the time and decided she had no alternative.

She did not feel any differently now.

The woman formerly known as Sarah saw the light peeking through the blinds. It was time to get up.

She slipped out of bed, into slippers, rolled up the futon and left the small room as tidy as it was every day. She took great pride in it. The simplicity of the routine, delight in small things. Her life here was unencumbered.

She would not change anything.

She knew she would have caused pain, even grief, with her actions five years ago. She also knew that others' pain was nothing compared to the pain she had felt in her own life. Her life had been at stake. Without the actions she had taken, she knew she would not be alive today.

There had been a pathway set in her life. She knew she would not have survived it. The choice had been binary: disappear or die – either slowly or very fast.

She was still alive. More than alive. She was calm and quiet and happy.

She could never have dreamed of being those things back in 2021.

She washed and put on her work clothes before meditating in silence for fifteen minutes. When she finished, she found herself less troubled by thoughts of her past.

She took her breakfast as always, quietly, smiling with the other workers and the large family who owned the property.

After cleaning away, she walked, as she always did, up the path alone, enjoying the journey to the fields where she would work again today, in the shadow of astonishing mountains.

She noted with gratitude that for another day she was alive and she was happy.

She had got away from herself.

The woman kept walking, her tiny figure fading into the slowly evaporating sheet of morning mist which lay softly over the vast fields in the shadow of the mountains.

Acknowledgements

Editors Joel Richardson in the UK and Pamela Dorman in the US.

The brilliant team at Michael Joseph: Phillipa Walker, Maxine Hitchcock, Sriya Varadharajan, Ellie Hughes, Courtney Barclay, Roy McMillan, James Keyte and Beatrix McIntyre.

Jennie Roman for the copy editing and Jill Cole for the proofreading.

At 42: Eugenie Furniss, Cathy King, Emily Macdonald.

At Imaginary Friends: Rebecca Roughan (for all the creative conversation, right from the start) and Emily Grimshaw (whose research was invaluable).

For procedural and technical advice: Graham Bartlett (and team)

And to my family: Aidan, Cal and the incomparable Madeline, for decades of inadvertent holiday research resolutely unlike any of the events in this novel!